To THOMAS,

THEY CONQUER WHO
THEY CAN.   - VIRGIL

THE ADVENTURE BEGINS!

Field of Blackbirds

E.S. Hoover

©2005

For my wife, who never had a doubt.

Fact Sheet

- The Black Hand and the Black Tigers actually exist.

- The artifact in the book is fictional; however, the location where it was "found" is real.

- The facts regarding the French Foreign Legion induction and correlating training locations are accurate.

- SPETSNAZ and Alpha Group are real components of Russian Special Forces.

- Information regarding Notre Dame in Paris, France, is accurate.

- The "Field of Blackbirds" is the location in Kosovo of an epic battle between the Ottoman Empire and the Serbian Army on June 28, 1389. It was a crushing defeat for the Serbs and began over 500 years of Turkish rule. The battlefield is memorialized by a lone monument ascending 164 feet into the air. The inscription thereon is known as "The Kosovo Curse." It reads:

> Whoever is a Serb and of Serb birth
>
> And of Serb blood and heritage
>
> And comes not to fight at Kosovo
>
> May he never have the progeny of his heart desires!
>
> Neither son nor daughter

May nothing grow that his hand sows!

Neither dark wine nor white wheat.

- Historical data should be correct; however, any incorrect or misleading information is the sole responsibility of the author. Nevertheless, he does offer that his is a work of fiction in which certain liberties were taken.

Prologue

Dr. Jean Pierre Fournier leaned back in his seat and breathed a long sigh of relief as the plane's wheels left the ground. Leaving the airport in Pristina, Kosovo, for Paris, France, marked the end of phase one of this dangerous endeavor. It symbolized one of the greatest escapes of modern times as far as he was concerned. Dr. Fournier was a professor of history and anthropology at the prestigious University of Paris, Sorbonne. At 67 years old he was all too aware that this would probably be the last adventure of his distinguished career. He was exhausted to his very bones. Indeed, the last ten days may as well have been ten years, considering how he felt.

The internal argument justifying his actions raged in his mind. *'There should be a better way to do this,'* reason told him.

Sometimes the preservation of history requires unorthodox action,' the other side rationalized.

'But this is theft!' reason declared.

'Research for the sake of history is not stealing!' his conscience countered. He tried to shut his eyes and fight the migraine that slowly crept across his skull. "I'm doing the right thing," he said aloud, drawing a suspicious glance from the woman in the window seat.

He smiled politely, then directed his thoughts to the theory he had formed over his years of intense study of the Balkans. A recent stroke of good fortune and the help of a good friend had offered the opportunity to prove his theory. His attention focused on Serbia's first anointed King, Stefan Nemanja, whose younger brother became the first Serbian-ordained Arch-Bishop. The father of these brothers started their path to supremacy in the region in 1170 when peace, not war, marked the birth of a greater Serbian state. It was this family affair that captured Dr. Fournier's attention and led him to this perilous endeavor. Now, in his briefcase tucked securely under the seat in front of him, was this family's legacy.

Before leaving the airport in Pristina, Dr. Fournier placed a call to his friend, Thierry Garnier, an archivist and professional conservator. He asked him to meet him at his office to help him with an important issue. Garnier pressed the professor for more information, but Fournier said it was too complicated to discuss on the phone. He would tell him everything when they met.

The professor arrived in Paris later than he'd hoped. He wanted some time to examine his find before Thierry's visit. Unfortunately, there would be little time for that, but he was lucky to catch a taxi soon after exiting the airport, and he relaxed a little as he headed for the University. As the taxi expertly wove through the streets of Paris, Jean Pierre's cell phone began to ring. He retrieved it from the inside pocket of his jacket and held it far from his face, struggling to read the display without his reading glasses. He was finally able to make out the familiar number of his friend René, still in Kosovo.

"Hello, René," Jean Pierre answered. Static and intermittent words greeted him from the other end of the line.

"… saw you … pursuing … danger …"

Jean Pierre kept trying to interject. "I can't understand you, René, you're breaking up," he said loudly into the phone.

"… police … hear me? …" were the only words Jean Pierre could make out.

"René, we have a terrible connection, can you try to call me back…"

Jean Pierre looked at his phone that had just gone silent. It was unlit, the display screen blank and dark. He tried the power button; nothing. He gave an exasperated sigh, realizing he hadn't charged his phone for nearly 24 hours. He had forgotten all about it.

He rode in silence for a few minutes trying to make sense of what René' had said. Suddenly, his stomach tightened as it dawned on him what his friend may have been trying to tell him.

"Pull over right there," Jean Pierre said to the driver, pointing to a well-lit store on the corner. The driver swiftly pulled near the entrance.

The professor fumbled for a moment in his briefcase. "Please wait for me," he said to the driver as he got out of the cab. "I will only be a moment."

Dr. Fournier worked quickly inside the corner convenience center and hurried back to the waiting cab.

Chapter 1

High School graduation day is a milestone in every teenager's life. It marks the first serious step toward adulthood and independence. Sebastian Bishop tapped his fingers on the steering wheel to one of his favorite songs playing on the radio. He was heading home after a morning of water skiing on the lake with his friends. The windows of his pickup truck were all the way down to let the warm breeze dry his wet hair. His mind was focused on getting home and getting ready for his much anticipated graduation ceremony later in the evening.

Sebastian was the all-American boy. He came from a close-knit, loving family, which was well established and well respected in these parts. His father had started a commercial construction company over twenty years ago and had a hand in just about everything built within a 100-mile radius of home. His mother had gone from elementary teacher to assistant principal of the middle school where she had been for the last eleven years. As far as Sebastian was concerned, growing up in the small rural town of Camden, South Carolina, couldn't have been better.

Most of his peers, however, thought differently. They found life in the small town stifling, complaining about its limited opportunities. Sebastian chuckled as he thought about his friend, Sam, saying he would probably end up scooping horse manure at the annual Carolina Cup race, an event that contributed to the town's coffers and provided a short period of employment for locals once each year. *'Life is what you make it,'* Sebastian thought. He knew he would have to seek opportunities outside of Camden, but he treasured his small town upbringing because it provided him with the values he knew would serve him well 'out in the big world.' He dreamed of seeing what was out there, meeting new and different people, and trying to do something important and meaningful with his life.

Sebastian Carver Bishop was of average height with sandy blonde hair and blue eyes. He had an athlete's build with natural ability, and he lettered three years in a row in both wrestling and football. He worked part-time and summers for his father, developing skills in everything from sheetrock to shingles. His high school days were coming to an end, and he had enjoyed every minute; but he was now looking forward to the future, ready for his adult life to begin.

A month ago, he received an acceptance letter from Clemson University. As if this wasn't amazing enough, he discovered he had been awarded a small academic scholarship. Although Sebastian was a talented athlete, he knew he wasn't nearly skilled enough or big enough to compete against the level of talent vying for sports scholarships at such a large institution. He worked hard to achieve good grades in school and scored very well on his SAT, so he opted to try for an academic scholarship and got it. It wasn't a full ride or even a large sum of money, but he knew every little bit would help his parents pay for college. It made him feel good to know he was contributing in some way to his own education. It would be up to him to make good grades and good decisions as he launched off on his own. His spirits were soaring as he drove toward home.

He barely heard his cell phone ringing as he sang with the song blaring on the radio. He quickly turned the radio down and flipped open his phone. He recognized the number on the caller ID immediately. It was his sister, Alexa. Sebastian readied himself for a fast food order.

His sister was a sixteen-year-old high school sophomore, already breathtaking by anyone's standards with her light brown hair and eyes the same shade of blue as his. Sebastian had spent most of the last year playfully warning his buddies away from her. She was athletic as well as pretty, and extremely intelligent. Their parents and the school were a bit concerned about her upcoming junior and senior years of high school. She was not being challenged enough academically and had already fulfilled a large percentage of her requirements for the next two years. After meeting with the school board and the local community college, she was granted permission to take entry-level college courses in addition to her few remaining high school credits.

Sebastian and Alexa had a unique sibling relationship; they were actually very good friends. He loved it when she came to him for 'big brother' advice, and he leaned on her heavily as he struggled with decisions concerning his future. Of course, they had their moments, but all in all, he knew he would miss her tremendously when he left for college.

Sebastian knew Alexa was over at the Robinson's house babysitting little Hanna. She had a few more hours to work, so a trip through a drive-thru window would be a likely treat for her and her adorable charge.

"Hey Sis, what's up?" he asked as he answered the phone. He knew immediately that something was wrong. She sounded frantic.

"Sebastian, someone's following me. Little Hanna and I went to the store and some guy there tried to hassle me. He wouldn't let me alone, so we left without getting Mrs. Robinson's groceries."

"OK, calm down. Where's he at now?" Sebastian asked.

"He's parked on the street outside. He followed me straight from the parking lot. He's just sitting there, looking this way."

"Check all the doors and windows. Make sure they're locked."

"I did."

"Where's Little Hanna?"

"In her bedroom. She fell asleep in the car, and I carried her in and laid her on her bed."

"Good. I'm on my way," Sebastian said.

"Oh, dear God," Alexa cried suddenly. "He's right outside the window."

"I'm just around the corner, hang up and call 911. I'll be there before you're finished dialing." Sebastian threw the phone in the passenger seat and slammed his foot down on the accelerator.

Chapter 2

It all started innocently enough. A close friend of Professor Fournier had phoned him, stating that he found something of interest. Reńe Morel was a supervisor in the serious crime unit of the French Police in Paris. The two had been friends since secondary school and kept in constant contact. Morel had been designated to serve in the United Nations Mission in Kosovo (UNMIK) as a civilian police officer. He arrived in Kosovo assigned to lead the Regional Crime Squad in the capital city of Pristina.

Dr. Fournier, renowned for his knowledge, was a revered expert in the history of the Balkans. He had visited twice since his friend had assumed his post, using his time there to explore this archaeologically rich area and its ancient monastery. When they last parted, he off-handedly asked Reńe to keep him posted if he came across anything interesting. His old friend didn't let him down.

Reńe was an avid runner who regularly participated in marathons and half-marathons all over Europe. It was during his regular morning run that he came across the reason for Dr. Fournier's third visit to Kosovo. Although Reńe worked in Pristina, he lived in a small flat in the village of Gracanica, approximately 10 miles outside of the city. His running route was a narrow strip of road linking the Serbian enclaves of Gracanica and Laplje Selo. Fields dominated this entire area, and the road stretched like a long scar through the middle of the plain.

In the bright early morning sun, Reńe noticed a white stone just above the grass on a mound in the center of a recently plowed field about 600 yards north of the roadway. All the fields in this area had patches of wild grass and trees sprinkled intermittently throughout. He had never paid much attention to them, but on this morning a white stone caught the sun just enough to catch his eye. Nearing the end of his run anyway, he took off across the field to get a closer look.

As he approached, he realized that the white stone was, in fact, a grave marker. What he couldn't see from the road was a deep depression in the ground containing three unearthed sarcophagi. Reńe was stunned that these large stone coffins lay exposed and unprotected in the middle of this farmer's field. The graves had been ravaged by the elements, but nonetheless remained remarkably intact. Closer examination of the stones revealed writing in Latin which struck Reńe as strange. He didn't know much about the history of Kosovo, but he did know that the Romans had not occupied this area for centuries. He had a hard time imagining that a Roman gravesite dating back to, or before, medieval times could exist here for decades unobserved by anyone except perhaps a few disinterested farmers.

Reńe stood on the mound and looked out at the horizon. From this vantage point, he could see the area from a totally different perspective. He spied something else that stuck out from the landscape. It was about 400 yards away, back toward the road. "I must have walked right past it," he mused out loud. As he walked toward this topographic inconsistency, a remarkable discovery began to unfold before him. He stood at the edge of what he first thought was just overgrowth and underbrush. But before him was the foundation of an ancient settlement. From where he stood he could just make out another white stone. This one however, was laying flat and marked the threshold to one of the settlement's many rooms. Incredibly, it too was inscribed in Latin. A threshold with writing of this kind was an unusual and unique find that caused Reńe's heart to skip a beat. He took off in a dead run toward his accommodation to get his phone. Jean Pierre had to hear about this.

Chapter 3

Sebastian saw an unfamiliar black car at the curb as he approached. He screeched to a halt in the driveway and saw the front door of the house ajar; the wood near the door latch splintered. Alarm gripped him, propelling him out of the truck. Racing to the house, he heard a stifled scream from Alexa.

Sebastian burst through the door and saw his sister struggling to get up from the sofa, her clothes torn and her face battered. Nearly hysterical, she quickly pointed toward the back of the house.

"That way!" she screamed.

He heard the back door burst open and caught a glimpse of the attacker making his escape. His long brown hair was tied behind his head with a red bandana, and he wore a white muscle shirt and blue jeans. In a split second, Sebastian was on his heels. He dashed through the door that was still in motion. The man's arms were pumping and his long legs were pounding the pavement as he raced down the adjacent side street. Sebastian's jaw tightened as he accelerated toward the man who just attacked his sister.

He was catching up to him with each powerful stride, fueled by rage. As he got within striking distance, he pounced forward. Sebastian's fist was clinched, his truck keys still clasped tightly in his hand.

Feeling the impending interception, the assailant turned just as Sebastian swung. With every ounce of strength, Sebastian struck. The timing was uncanny. Like a major league baseball player connecting perfectly with a fastball, Sebastian's fist slammed into the man's throat.

The force of the impact blasted Alexa's attacker from his feet. As he hit the ground, he immediately clutched his throat. His mouth gulped for air like a fish out of water, but his windpipe was crushed. Within 90 seconds the man was dead.

Bobby Rodgers was loading a fishing pole into the back of his truck in the driveway of the house next door when he noticed the commotion. Hilda Green was watering her flowers in her yard directly across the street from where Sebastian caught up to the man. They would both later testify as to what they saw next.

Sebastian stood over the dying man. The look in his eyes was certainly not one of remorse. He rendered no aid and did not take one step toward finding help. He just stood there watching the man gasp for air. In that moment Sebastian personified unbridled rage. He was a good kid, from a great family, and yet in that moment he was raw, primitive, the reaction to the attack on his sister instinctive.

"Wrong family," Sebastian hissed at the man through clenched teeth. "Hell awaits." Tears of anguish welled in his eyes. In an instant, Sebastian Bishop's life was changed forever. Fate would set him on an unexpected course that would alter his future in ways he could never imagine. He would emerge a man much different than he had ever dreamed possible.

He heard the sirens approaching.

Chapter 4

Sebastian sat alone in the interview room. He had been sitting there a long time. He looked at his watch and realized that in half an hour all his friends would be walking across the stage, receiving their diplomas in front of their friends and family. Their lives were about to begin; it seemed as if his had just ended.

Detective Jake Matthers walked into the room. In his early twenties, Jake was a local boy who had been fortunate enough to secure a promising position in the community. After graduating from the State Police Academy in Columbia, South Carolina, he had joined the force five years ago. A tall, dark-haired young man, Jake was a striking figure in the uniform, and he wore it proudly. He was professional in his duty and a credit to the force. Promoted to Detective only eight months ago, the responsibility to conduct this interrogation fell automatically to him. He closed the door softly behind him and walked to the table, greeting Sebastian with a firm handshake. This wasn't going to be easy. Jake had known Sebastian for as long as he could remember. As assistant coach at Camden High, he had coached him in football, and he was a member of the same church as Sebastian and his family.

"Is Alexa ok?" Sebastian asked before Jake even sat down.

"She's fine," Jake replied. "She was asking if you were ok," he continued, smiling.

There was a pause in the conversation as Jake opened his notebook and gathered his thoughts.

"So what do I call you?" Sebastian asked. Jake looked at him blankly. "Do I call you Coach, Jake, Detective Matthers…?"

"Jake is fine, Sebastian." He took a deep breath, "I've read your statement, and I'm afraid I have some tough questions to ask you."

"Ok. Do you think I should have a lawyer present?" Sebastian asked innocently.

"That is completely up to you, Sebastian. You are considered an adult, you have been advised of your rights, and although you are being detained, you have not been officially charged with a crime. However, as a result of our conversation," he paused, "that may change." It took all Jake had to look this young man in the eye and deliver this news.

"Jake, I understand my rights and how this may turn out unfavorably for me. I'm asking you as my coach, as my Sunday School teacher, for crying out loud, do *you* think I need a lawyer present?"

Before Jake could answer, the interview room door burst open and in walked a distinguished-looking man in a three-piece suit. He carried a large leather briefcase which he plopped soundly on Sebastian's side of the table.

"My name is Gordon Jamison," he announced, his commanding presence undeniable. "I am the attorney representing Mr. Bishop."

Momentarily confused, Sebastian's first thought was *'what is he doing representing my father?'* Then it struck him, somewhat comically, that the lawyer was referring to him.

"I haven't requested a lawyer, sir," Sebastian said upon realization of the fact.

"I am here at your father's request, son. Have you been advised of your rights? Have you said anything to this officer yet?" The attorney wasn't even looking at Sebastian; he was rattling these queries automatically as he situated himself at the table, popping his briefcase open. Sebastian and Jake looked at each other. *'Now what?'* they wondered.

"Sir, with all due respect, I would like to speak with Detective Matthers alone."

The attorney stopped his shuffling and looked at Sebastian in disbelief. "Son, I strongly discourage you from talking with this officer alone. I should be here to…"

Sebastian cut him off. "Mr. Jamison, is it? I appreciate your coming in at my father's request; but I don't want a lawyer. I do not need you to protect me from the truth. Please, if you would, kindly excuse us now."

Jake had always been impressed with Sebastian and his sister. They were sharp kids, both with a positive outlook on life. Jake, however, had never been more impressed with Sebastian than in that moment.

Gordon Jamison shook his head in dismay and reluctantly packed his things back into his briefcase. Clicking it shut, he stood to leave. "I'll inform your father of your decision."

"Thank you, sir."

As soon as the door closed behind the attorney, Jake leaned forward on the table. "Sebastian, I want to tell you exactly where things stand, and then I'm going to ask you questions about the incident. I am not trying to trick or deceive you in any way. I will be straightforward and honest with everything I tell you, and I ask the same courtesy in return."

Sebastian nodded his understanding.

Jake continued, "The state's attorney wants to charge you with second degree murder. Essentially that is defined as homicide that was not premeditated. He wants to say you killed that man in the 'passion of the moment.'

Here's what is going against you: when you entered the house, the assailant had already left the scene; therefore, the immediate threat was gone. You, however, gave chase and fatally struck a man that was running away from you. After striking him, you did not attempt to go for help or render aid. That lends itself to intent to kill rather than just trying to stop him from getting away. And finally, from the moment the guy went down to now, you have expressed no remorse for your actions."

"So what exactly are your questions?" Sebastian inquired.

Jake stopped a moment, realizing he had essentially summarized the state's case. "I told you, no tricks. That's where we stand."

Sebastian sighed thoughtfully. "Ok. But to know I didn't render aid means someone must have seen what happened."

"Two witnesses," Jake interjected.

"Well, apparently they aren't testifying that it was just a fluke punch."

"Both stated that they looked over when they heard the commotion. They will testify that they distinctly saw the man stop running as if he had given up, and you continued full throttle, viciously striking him.

One witness is even saying that the guy was raising his hands in the classic surrender gesture."

"So it obviously looked to them like I caught this guy, turned him around, and struck him intentionally in the throat." Sebastian looked down at the table. *'Is that really what happened?'* he thought to himself. What he remembered was the man turning as if he were going to fight. Regardless, nothing was going in his favor at this point. "Jake, the question on everyone's mind will be: *'how do you hit a man in the throat who is running away from you?'* Could you tell me what, if anything, I have going in my favor?"

"Listen, Sebastian," Jake's voice dropped to a whisper. "You need to say that you're sorry; that you didn't mean to kill the guy; that you panicked; do whatever you need to do to plea this down to involuntary manslaughter or an even lesser offense. You've never been in trouble before so you'll probably get probation...."

"Can't you get in trouble for giving legal advice?" Sebastian interrupted, trying to lighten the mood.

"Sebastian, this is very serious stuff," Jake replied. "The lawyer assigned to this case is pushing to prosecute. He's afraid you're going to become the poster boy for vigilante justice. The case is solid, and unless I can bring something different back to him from this interview..."

All expression dropped from Sebastian's face as he leaned in toward Jake. "You asked me to be straightforward and honest, so here you go: a man attacked my sister; I ran him down and struck out with the same rage you would if someone attacked your family. Although I never imagined it possible, I *wanted* to kill that man. In a one in a million punch, I did just that. He made a decision, and so did I. My sister is alive and well, and that man is dead. For that I am not, nor will I ever be, sorry."

Jake's head spun with the impossible position he was now in. Sebastian Bishop was one of the most solid kids he had ever known. It didn't surprise him that he would rather face prison than be untruthful about the circumstances of this incident or his mindset. *'We would all like to think we'd be so stoic in the face of such odds, but few of us really would,'* Jake thought.

Defeated, and resigned to doing his duty, Jake concluded his interview. "Sebastian Bishop," he swallowed hard, hating his job in this moment. "You are hereby charged with murder in the second degree. A uniformed officer will be in to escort you to your cell. You'll meet with the prosecutor tomorrow. You may want to call Mr. Jamison back in here."

Chapter 5

Dr. Fournier grabbed the first flight available to Kosovo after receiving the call from Reńe. He arrived at the Pristina airport early in the afternoon on the following day, hailed a taxi, and headed to the village of Gracanica. He dropped his travel bag at Reńe's flat and walked to the village center. Having been there before to study the monastery, Fournier knew his way around.

He went straight to his favorite coffee bar, walked in, and greeted the owner. "Dobro dan," he said in Serbian. The owner laughed heartily, shaking Fournier's hand and kissing him on both cheeks in customary greeting.

"Welcome back, Doctor!" the owner said in French. In fact, this was about the extent of the shopkeeper's French.

Fournier knew he would have to sit, have some coffee, and visit, even though he wanted to get straight to work. Everything had its own cultural procedure in places like this. Dr. Fournier had studied the latest games, trades, and rumors surrounding the Serbian soccer team, a most popular topic, for just this moment. He launched into a discussion about the Serbian's last loss and what strategies should have been employed to secure victory. The coffee shop owner listened intently, and they debated strengths and weaknesses, personnel changes, and whether or not the men should take their shirts off after scoring a goal. Before long, they had attracted a small crowd of regular patrons, and the conversations became lively and passionate.

When the appropriate time had passed, and the doctor had consumed about seven cups of coffee, he finally motioned the shop owner aside for a private word.

"Can you call Saso for me?" he asked.

"Da Da Da," he replied, pulling his cell phone from his front shirt pocket. He was proud to help his foreign friend who spoke their language and seemed to somehow understand his people. He placed the call, and about ten minutes later, in through the door walked Saso.

"Doctor!" he yelled from the doorway.

"Saso, my friend!" Fournier responded, standing. The two men embraced.

"Welcome back, Doctor. Are you continuing your studies of our beautiful monastery?"

"Actually, I have something else to investigate this time around. May I hire your services again, Saso?" The professor queried.

"Of course; how may I be of service?" Saso had been Fournier's assistant last time around and they got along very well. Saso not only spoke brilliant French, but he knew the village and its people better than anyone. He could get things done when others would hit a brick wall. Even though Dr. Fournier could speak fluent Serbian, a native was able to work the nuances of a tight-knit village like this in ways that the professor could not.

Saso learned French as a linguist in the Serbian Army. Both of them would slip back and forth seamlessly between the two languages, and their friendship blossomed. With not much demand for French-speaking language assistants in post-conflict Kosovo, Saso scraped by working as an electrician around the village; another army skill. The doctor paid much better than any electrical job, so Saso was eager to help.

Fournier thanked the coffee bar owner profusely and gave him a generous tip with the payment for his coffee. The subtle and strategic placement of a few extra Euros helped to maintain important relationships in this bewildering province.

Saso and the doctor walked outside. "I have heard of a place of interest just outside of town," Fournier explained to Saso. "I would like to get permission to study the site and take notes…without interference." This last stipulation was what he really needed Saso for.

"I understand, Doctor," Saso replied. "What is this site?"

Fournier explained the location of the place and said he wanted to photograph it and attempt to translate the Latin found on the stones. Saso knew immediately the spot the doctor described.

"You will not damage the site?" Saso asked seriously.

"Saso, I am a historian, not an archaeologist. Sketches, photos, and notes, that's all." He hated his deceit, but there was no other way to accomplish his mission.

A short time and 50 Euros later, the doctor was guaranteed uninterrupted access to the site from the farmer who owned the land. Fournier knew a straightforward approach like this would circumvent any problems with the local residents and authorities. He was right, after two days at the site, no one paid him any attention.

By the third day, closely studying the layout of the settlement and comparing it to his years of notes and personal sketches from dozens of sources, Fournier believed he had narrowed down the likely area of what he had come for. He shook his head in amazement that no one had told him anything about this site in previous visits. It showed how tight-lipped this community was. They would not offer any information unless asked directly, and often, not even then. He was glad that the residents had become familiar with him on his previous trips; otherwise, this endeavor wouldn't have been at all possible. He took a long look around; the earth had nearly reclaimed this ancient site. It was very difficult to see because of all the underbrush. Imagining what it must have looked like in its three-dimensional state was even more difficult.

That night, he received a phone call from an attorney friend who lived in Skopje, Macedonia. Skopje was Macedonia's largest city, lying approximately 90 miles south of Pristina, Kosovo. Dr. Fournier's friend had lived there for nearly three years working with EU Proxima on diplomatic and legal affairs. Skopje was much more commercial than the struggling post-war Kosovo, so it made better sense to conduct business there.

The package that Fournier had sent from Paris before he left had arrived. It cost him a lot of money to send equipment from Paris to Macedonia, especially sensitive equipment requiring delicate handling. There was still a big risk in sending anything into Kosovo itself. Things had a mysterious way of disappearing as they cleared customs. An item of such value as what Fournier had shipped was almost guaranteed to come up missing. The next day the professor rented an SUV and made the hour-and-a-half trip south to Skopje.

He arrived at his friend's house at about ten in the morning. They had coffee together and got caught up on life since they had last seen each other. Fournier skirted the issue about what was in the box and what he was doing back in Kosovo simply by chalking it up to more research. Finally, Fournier said his goodbyes and carefully loaded the wooden crate into the SUV, thanking his friend profusely. The crate was roughly the size of a miniature refrigerator, and was nearly as heavy. As he crossed the border back into Kosovo, the Macedonian Border police made him open the box and show the contents, which Fournier had fully anticipated. He showed them his university credentials with his French passport and explained he was doing research. The Macedonian police could not have cared less. They just wanted to make sure he wasn't transporting humans, weapons, or drugs. Other than that he could have had proof of extra-terrestrial life, and they would still have waved him through.

By early evening Fournier was settled back in Rene's accommodation where he carefully unpacked the crate. With great care he began testing what would determine success or failure on this trip; ground-penetrating sonar.

Chapter 6

Sebastian had been up all night reviewing his charge and reading the exact wording of the law. He also went over due process in a ratty old law book that a thousand other cell-block lawyers had perused as they faced the courtroom the following day, week, or for some, month. The right to a speedy trial was at the mercy of the congestion of the docket.

At about three in the morning Sebastian struck up a conversation with one of the midnight shift county jailers. He was an amiable old black fellow whom Sebastian quickly found to be a wealth of knowledge. This guy, who insisted Sebastian call him Sam, knew the law inside and out. He knew the court system as well as, or better than, any attorney did and, above all, he knew the players.

Sam leaned back in his chair against the wall just outside Sebastian's cell. He faced the row of seven cells all under his direct control. For the next three hours the two talked like they'd known each other for years. After explaining exactly what Sebastian could expect from this point forward and elaborating on some of the finer points of the law that Sebastian had not known, he asked the big question: "Who is your presiding judge?"

"I'm not sure that one has been assigned as of yet, but someone mentioned a Judge Bailey," Sebastian replied.

Sam hung his head for a moment.

"Not good?" Sebastian asked, noting his response.

Sam sighed, "It doesn't surprise me that Judge Bailey is trying to get your case." He coughed and cleared his throat before continuing. "Judge Phillip C. Bailey is a Yankee." Sebastian smiled at the southern reference to anything north of Richmond, Virginia. "He's a young guy, married to a real nice lady from down here. He graduated from one of those Yankee law schools and started out as a prosecutor. Then he switched sides for whatever reason. Some say the money his fellow defense attorneys were making from their drug dealing clientele seduced him. After a few years of getting good and soaked in the slime of his profession, word has it his wife missed home, so he decided to jump into the political game of judgeship, vying for a position down here. With his wife's daddy's help he got voted into a magisterial position in some county around the upstate.

His 'charm' took over then, and he maneuvered into a General Sessions appointment judging felony cases in this particular part of South Carolina. He saw quickly that the people responded well to stiff sentences and a no-nonsense approach to the job, so he started taking folks to the cleaners. Everyone knew they were going to do time if they appeared before him. Well, his zeal caught up to him as he came under scrutiny for giving particularly harsh sentences to minorities. The law community conducted a half-hearted investigation and, of course, found his decisions to be within the constitutional standards of sentencing for the state. However, the media painted a very ugly picture of this young man, and he has been fighting for his professional life ever since."

Sam removed his glasses and cleaned the lenses with his uniform tie. "He has been looking for a case like this one, Sebastian. He wants to show he can be just as tough on a white boy as he can any minority. Equal opportunity gallows, I guess. This will help his image and swing the popular vote, securing his future on the bench. He will come after you with all he can, I fear, if you are found guilty."

After a slight pause, Sam continued by explaining what was needed in order to prove Sebastian's guilt; telling him this case was really about the letter of the law, not justice. Sebastian listened intently, absorbing every word. Sam finally wrapped up his law lecture and looked down at the floor, trying to think of anything he forgot. The two men sat silently for a while, serenaded by a chorus of snoring coming from the adjoining cells.

Sam knew Sebastian's story, and he sincerely felt badly for this kid and the hardship he was now facing. The possibility of prison time, coupled with the rigorous legal process, could suck the life right out of a person. He'd seen it many times before. Sam finally broke the silence. "You going to say you're sorry?"

Sebastian sat on the edge of his cot, elbows on his knees, and his head in his hands. He stared at the concrete floor, mulling over everything he had just learned. Sam's question penetrated his thoughts and he snapped back to the reality of his situation, intensely aware of the bars that separated the two of them. He slowly lifted his head and looked at Sam with searching eyes and asked, "Would you?"

Chapter 7

Dr. Fournier's interest in Yugoslavia began as an undergraduate student in the 1960's, majoring in Sociology. He became fascinated with the way President Josip Broz Tito had rebelled against the mainstream Soviet communist ideology and implemented his own brand of National Communism, commonly referred to as Titoism. Somehow, with all the fractioned ethnicities and religious fervor of post World War II Yugoslavia, Tito was able to hold all these peoples together. He formed unlikely alliances with countries like Egypt, India, and Ghana. He pursued a policy of peace, opening his country's borders to foreigners, abolishing visa requirements, and encouraging industrialization. His new version of Socialism was capturing the world's attention, including a young academic named Jean Pierre Fournier.

However, Jean Pierre's true passion dwelt in the Balkans of Antiquity: the times of Roman occupation, the development of trade routes, and the ultimate emergence of an infant Serbian nation. He poured over ancient documents, studied medieval cartography of the area, and interviewed countless academics and religious figures from Belgrade to Rome. He wanted to know why this area was such a hotspot. What brought the ethnicities of Yugoslavia together? What drove them apart? The professor was captivated by these questions.

He came across several interesting facts concerning the chancellor to Pope Alexander III, who became the Vatican's legate to Croatia in the late 12th century. The more the professor examined the facts, the timing, and the subsequent events that unfolded during this historical period, the more he became convinced that the beginning of Serbia had somehow been sanctioned. *'It had to be,'* he thought to himself, *'how else could a country declare itself?'*

After arriving at this conclusion, several fundamental questions came to the forefront of his studies, such as: How is a nation established? Who has the authority to make such a declaration? And once this status is achieved, how do others become convinced to recognize the new nation as a sovereign state?

Dr. Fournier realized that Israel went through this process in modern times, and suffered immeasurable "growing pains" to put it mildly. The collapse of the Soviet Union brought other struggles for national identity among the fractured empire. Czechoslovakia brilliantly unburdened itself from the yoke of communism without bloodshed during the Velvet Revolution. The country then split into Slovakia and the Czech Republic, both parts striving for self-determination. The examples went on and on. However, the late twelfth century did not have the diplomatic framework or international monitoring and assistance of modern times. Dr. Fournier knew that 'nation' status had to be established somehow, and there were no significant wars in the area at the time; so how?

The answer, or at least the beginning of the answer, presented itself in ancient notes of Papal daily affairs in the year 1172. Merely a footnote to the day's business, Serbia took a giant step in nation building by a nod from the Bishop of Rome. Before the General Council was established in the Catholic Church, the Pope was directly responsible for decisions considered of the highest importance. This was the time of Crusades, and the Pope was consumed with planning the fourth campaign. Timing, coincidence, and the boldness of Serbia's first Prince set the course for two centuries of prosperity in the new nation. However, when the mighty Ottoman Empire descended upon the Balkans, their claim of sovereignty had to be hidden, preserved for the time Serbia found herself again. To prove his theory, Dr. Fournier agonizingly put all the pieces together, and found buried among the ruins of that ancient settlement what was as important to the Serbians as the Declaration of Independence is to the Americans. His heart beat like a jackhammer in his chest. '*What have I done?*' he thought as the taxi pulled to its destination.

The professor paid the driver generously and got out with his things, feeling relief at setting foot back on the grounds of his beloved University. He walked briskly toward his office as early evening blanketed the campus.

Four men watched him from their cigarette-smoke filled Mercedes parked nearby. It was time to pay a visit to the French thief.

Chapter 8

The meeting with the prosecutor did not go well. Detective Matthers stood in the back of the interview room while the prosecutor and his assistant sat at the table. Sebastian, relenting to his father's advice in retaining Mr. Jamison as his attorney, sat next to the impeccably dressed gentleman. Sebastian looked relaxed, but his lawyer looked like a coiled spring.

The prosecutor looked at Sebastian over the top of his rimless bifocals, cleared his throat, and began. "I just need to clarify a few points from your statement, Mr. Bishop. Was the victim still in the house with your sister when you arrived?" He lifted his eyes from his notes to measure Sebastian's reply.

Sebastian thought for a moment before answering. "I find it interesting that you refer to that rapist as the victim. Let me state for the record that my sister was the victim."

The prosecutor bristled and straightened in his chair. "No one disputes the fact that your sister was attacked. If her assailant were still alive, he would be sitting where you are right now, and he would be prosecuted under due process of law." Tension hung heavy in the air, and the interview had just begun.

"No," Sebastian said.

"What?" the prosecutor asked, confused.

"In answer to your question, 'no,' the assailant was not in the house when I entered. He had just escaped through the back door."

"Did you stop to call the police?" the prosecutor pressed.

"No, my sister handled that," Sebastian replied.

"Before or after you gave chase?"

"As I was en route to the house, I instructed her over the phone to call the police, but she may have been a little too busy being attacked before she was able to make that connection." Sebastian took a drink of water from the cup in front of him.

"There is no need for sarcasm, Mr. Bishop," the prosecutor grumbled, his bald head reflecting the glare from the overhead lighting. "We are simply trying to establish a timeline for the events as they occurred."

"No, sir, you are trying to establish that I acted unreasonably, that a reasonable person would have stopped and notified the police and rendered aid instead of giving chase to the offender. You are trying to prove that from the minute I entered that house and saw my sister I intended to kill whoever was responsible for her attack." He had learned a lot from his midnight conversation with Sam.

"That's enough, Sebastian," Mr. Jamison counseled.

"Please continue, Mr. Bishop," the prosecutor smirked and folded his arms across his inflated chest. The interview was being recorded by both audio and video.

Sebastian felt himself getting angry. His father had always advised him to slow down, think things through when you find yourself in an adversarial situation. Instead of letting your anger take control, remain calm and approach the conflict from a rational angle. This was good advice that had served him well in the past, but he couldn't seem to let it guide him now. Sebastian was determined not to be goaded into letting someone twist his words.

"Passion, intent, non-remorse: these are the cornerstones of your argument, correct?" Sebastian asked. "Let's not waste each other's time, Counselor. I passionately pursued that man, I wanted to kill him, and I am not sorry that he is dead. From what I understand, you need to prove three things: motive, opportunity, and ability. You can easily explain to the jury that the motive is self evident. I had the opportunity to kill him when I caught up to him, and I had the physical ability to kill him; which I did. Now let's look at it another way." Sebastian ticked off his points on his fingers. "I had no weapon, I've never struck another human being in anger in my life, and I had no idea I was going to be able to catch him as I ran through the house. I didn't think it was even possible to kill someone with a punch. So, technically, my actions worked counter-intuitively with my belief." Sebastian leaned back in his chair, folding his arms across his chest.

The prosecutor responded evenly. "But you did catch him, Mr. Bishop, and you did kill him. The issue here is not what you believed possible or impossible. The facts remain unwavering in the face of speculative conjecture; weapon or no weapon, history of violence or first offense, questioning the odds or absolutely sure, you made it clear both in written and oral statements that your *intent* was to kill this man. Your ability produced the opportunity; you ran him down and caught him. Opportunity handed back to ability, you had the physical strength and focus to strike a deadly blow; and ability completed the act. You punched this man with such force as to end his life.

This flow chart is very easy for a jury to follow. Each step afforded you the chance to make a decision to cease progression toward the next. You made the choice to commit this heinous offense. You made clear decisions that resulted in actions that stemmed from rage. The law sets the elements of the crime, and you've hit every single one. In short, you killed the man you found so reviling." Silence hung heavy as the prosecutor's summary sunk in. He leaned forward on the table toward Sebastian, "So what exactly separates you from him?"

Sebastian felt the weight of the world press squarely on his shoulders. He looked the prosecutor straight in the eye. "This guy was a predator; *his* act was premeditated," Sebastian said, desperation gripping his voice. "Why hasn't anyone talked about *his* intent?" Sebastian's mind revolted as it fought the notion that he was anything like the man who attacked his sister.

Jake looked down at the floor. He admired the stand this young man had taken, but he was just a kid, out of his depth and too immature to let his attorney speak on his behalf. He realized Sebastian's promising young life was going to be shelved in a prison cell somewhere. The prosecutor gathered his papers and packed his briefcase.

He stood from the table, adjusting his tie. "There will be no plea bargaining in this case, Mr. Bishop. You have requested a jury trial and you will have one." As he picked up his briefcase, he added, "in all of your self-righteous misdirection, Mr. Bishop, the bottom line is this: You killed a man, and whether or not he deserved it, is a judgment you are not qualified to make." The prosecutor, his assistant, and Detective Matthers all began to leave the interview room.

"Mr. Prosecutor," Sebastian called out. The Assistant State Attorney stopped and turned around. "God help you to make the right decision if terror visits your family."

Mr. Jamison hurried after the prosecutor as the group exited the room, leaving Sebastian sitting alone at the table. He sat in silence, realizing in that moment that the prosecutor was right. In his zeal to offer a clever and profound defense for his actions he had instead sealed his own fate.

The trial was quick. Mr. Jamison put up an excellent defense and a very convincing argument for reckless homicide at most, but the jury, however sympathetic, couldn't get around what they felt to be the facts of the case. Sebastian pursued and killed a man in the heat of passion in response to an incident that should have been handled by the proper authorities. The deliberation took two-and-a-half hours. Guilty of Second Degree murder was the verdict.

During the sentencing phase, several people stepped up to testify on Sebastian's behalf. They talked about how kind and compassionate he was, and about how he had never been in trouble. Sebastian had already drifted off. His mind seemed to be going through some sort of automatic shutdown sequence. He was completely and utterly defeated. Listening to these people didn't help. It was like being in attendance at his own eulogy. He knew Judge Bailey had already made his decision as soon as he heard the guilty verdict from the jury. Sebastian was sentenced to 10 years; he would serve at least four in prison, with the remaining six on probation. He was 18 years old. His soonest hope of freedom would be at 22. The next few days were a blur. He took a last long look at Camden as he gazed sullenly out the window of the bus rolling out of town, transporting him to his new home for the next four years—the Trenton Correctional Institution in Trenton, South Carolina.

Chapter 9

Dr. Fournier hurried from the cab to his office. He unlocked the door and turned on the light, quickly relocking the door behind him. It was a spacious office with a large conference table in the center. The work order he put in before leaving for the Balkans had been completed. Above the conference table, the university electricians had installed a fixture emitting light at 50 LUX, the recommended exposure level for sensitive documents. The temperature and humidity sensors had also been delivered and installed. He checked them to find his office at 67 degrees Fahrenheit with about 46% humidity, nearly perfect.

There was a knock at the door. The professor glanced at his watch and smiled, thinking Thierry's curiosity had brought him about a few minutes early. Tired as he was, he was eager to confide his incredible discovery to his friend. As he unlocked and opened the door, his excitement quickly gave way to shock as four men shoved their way past him into the office.

"What is the meaning of this?" Jean Pierre demanded.

The four men spread out evenly and surveyed the room. One closed the door and stood in front of it. Two took positions on either side of the room, backs against the wall. The remaining man, obviously the leader, turned his direct attention to Jean Pierre.

The man's features softened as he smiled politely, "Good evening, Professor. We beg your forgiveness for the intrusion." He spoke perfect French with only a hint of a foreign accent. "My name is Damir Tadic. I am Croatian. My associates are from Bosnia and Albania." The professor quickly glanced around the room, trying to discern who was from where. Damir Tadic took a few steps, staring at the floor in thought, hands clasped behind his back. "Professor, you have taken something for which I feel sure you will most surely regret. Its implications transcend the academic realm from which you operate. The passion of your pursuit concerning this item has, no doubt, clouded your judgment and prevented you from taking into consideration the full ramifications of your theft."

"You know nothing of me or my passion! I am not a thief; I am merely trying to preserve history for the world's benefit!" Jean Pierre replied anxiously. It was obvious the men knew all about the artifact, so trying to deny having it seemed useless. "I admit I don't even know exactly what I found, so its full implications remain a mystery to us all." The professor felt his chest tightening. He dismissed it and tried to concentrate on how to deal with this confrontation.

The Croatian continued in his refined French, "Do not try to deceive me, Professor. I know more about you than you think. You teach History and Anthropology here at the University; you have for nearly thirty years. You are an expert on the Balkans, more specifically the Balkans from around 400AD until the takeover by the Ottoman Empire in the 14th century. You have an exceptional understanding of current affairs in the area as well, although you go to great lengths to stay disengaged from the current 'unpleasantness.' In addition to classes on the past, you teach on Yugoslavia's major modern events, including both World Wars, the Cold War, the fall of Tito, the rise of Milosevic, the ethnic divisions, the ethnic wars, and the ethnic cleansing."

Damir looked menacingly at the professor, confirming he had his full attention before continuing. "Yet with all this knowledge, you act as if you can operate inside Kosovo separate from these facts, shrouding yourself in some protective cloak of antiquity; but what you fail to realize is that it is all inextricably connected. One operates in *conjunction* with the other, not separate from it." The professor's chest was slowly being squeezed with a pressure that seemed more than just fear or anxiety.

Damir became more emphatic. "War has, in fact, prohibited significant archaeological work in the area since the 1920s; fortunate for you, yes?" The jab did not escape Jean Pierre. "Did you really think your theft would go unnoticed?" The Croatian's tone became hauntingly serious. "Professor, the world must never see what you have found. We are tired of conflict, and the one thing you fail to grasp is the intensity of Serbian Nationalism. Yes, you have read about it, studied it, analyzed data, but you've never *experienced* it. Even the possibility that another war could erupt is unacceptable, Dr. Fournier. You possess the petrol to fuel a fire that cannot be contained."

Damic stepped within inches of the professor's face, and in a slow deliberate voice, delivered a deadly ultimatum. "We mean you no harm, Doctor, but we are not leaving here without what you now possess. If you live, or die for the sake of retaining the artifact, is a decision you must now make."

The professor was feeling faint. His brain was sounding silent alarms throughout his body. He weighed the cost of his own life versus thousands of lives that would be affected by what he found. Perhaps it should be destroyed, or at least secreted away, hidden from public scrutiny. This was a question that would have to be settled at another time. His strength was waning.

With a shaky hand, he pointed to the oversized titanium briefcase sitting on the floor next to his desk. Damir picked it up and placed it gently on the conference table. Holding his breath in anticipation, he clicked it open and gazed in awe at the ancient stone container inside. The sealed vessel bore the distinctive mark of the Golden Bull and his heart quickened as he thought about the treasure within. Hastily clicking the briefcase shut, he turned to the professor who had turned quite pale, sweating profusely now.

"Thank you, Professor," he nodded graciously. "You should take precautions. It would be unwise to think that we are the only ones with the knowledge of what you took. Good luck, Dr. Fournier." With that the men left the office as briskly as they had entered.

Dr. Fournier fell to his knees in the center of his office. He clutched his chest and felt pain shooting down his right arm. '*My God*,' he thought. '*I'm having a heart attack!*'

Chapter 10

Trenton struck Sebastian as a nothing town in the middle of nowhere. Situated about 20 miles from the Georgia border, Trenton was just a hiccup on the map traveling down I-20. Sebastian spent two weeks being processed into the prison facility.

He was aware that prison is a hard place filled with hard men. Thousands of different studies conducted on prisons (social studies, legal studies, even economic studies) all confirmed the fact that life inside a prison engages a survival instinct that lies dormant in most human beings. It is a primitive instinct and often provokes an extreme response to extreme circumstances. This reality convinced Sebastian that thinking you are hard is one thing, but doing time in prison leaves no doubt.

Sebastian was housed with another white kid named Tony Jenson. For almost two weeks neither Sebastian nor Jenson said a word to each other, both posturing and feeling out the other; neither wanting to show any weakness nor vulnerability. Eventually they began to speak and learn more about each other. Jenson was in for stabbing a guy that 'made a play on his girl,' as he phrased it. He was nineteen years old and was proud of his membership in the Aryan Brotherhood that went back all of four months, shortly after he got on the inside. Although they were speaking to each other, there was the undeniable fact that Sebastian was not yet 'in,' so things were kept superficial at best. Something would have to give sooner or later.

There are rules on the inside, unwritten but legitimate, and enforced as if they were the Magna Carta itself. The most obvious rule from the start, to anyone who is a part of the general population, is the necessity to choose a side. It is impossible to serve your entire sentence without the protection of one particular group or another. By virtue of this reality, some unlikely alliances were formed at Trenton. Predominantly black gangs were friendly toward Latino gangs to demonstrate a united front against the Aryan Brotherhood. A small representation of the Asian gang community typically stayed neutral and remained relatively un-harassed for reasons unknown. Probably because prison folklore made them more mysteriously dangerous than they actually were. Any other ethnicities fell to one side or the other and aligned themselves accordingly.

Anticipation of the 'new guy' event was maddening. Anyone who found themselves doing time behind bars would be 'initiated' in one form or another to their new living environment. The sociology and psychology of institutional living has been studied for many years, and theories on prisoner behavior are as vast and varied as the characters being punished. The brutal reality for those in the system is that this was a predatory environment where the only theory that truly seemed to apply was Darwin's theory of natural selection. The strong preyed on the weak, and the institutional hierarchy was established by brute force. It was plain, simple, and inescapable.

Sebastian knew his turn was coming. The anticipatory fear made his everyday life nearly intolerable. He dreaded walking anywhere alone. His head was on a swivel in the yard during recreation time, and the showers, despite how cliché it seemed, were terrifying. It marked the time of greatest vulnerability to a gang attack.

Somehow Sebastian made it two months without any problems. He was getting exhausted from his diligence in protecting his health and well being. As he faced the beginning of month three, he pulled dishwashing duty in the kitchen, which rotated every month from one prisoner to the next. It was just after the evening meal, and Sebastian was carrying a small stack of damaged trays to the garbage chute at the back of the kitchen. The kitchen was very large and divided by tables, sinks, and various machines, all manufactured in the institutional stainless steel motif. Usually there were prisoners scattered all around performing their respective duties necessary to maintain the large eating facility.

As he walked, he quickly realized that there was hardly anyone in the back area. There should be. The two or three prisoners he saw were white, and they gave him a hard look as he passed. Things were eerily quiet, the only sounds coming from the large machines washing dishes and conducting other automated kitchen functions.

It didn't feel right at all, and Sebastian was just about to turn and walk back to his station near the front. He froze as he saw the door of one of the small closets used to store brooms, mops, and cleaning supplies, drift open just a crack. He was about ten feet away from it and could hear muffled sounds coming from inside. His heart began to race, and he knew that tonight must be his night. Sebastian set his jaw and decided that he was not going to be jumped as he walked past. He hoped the element of surprise would be on his side and he could just take these guys head on. If this was his time, then he was ready. Using the stack of trays as a shield, he approached stealthily and used the toe of his shoe to flip the closet door open. It flung back just in time for him to witness the event that would change his time behind bars from this point forward. That is if he survived the next few minutes.

Chapter 11

Dr. Fournier slowly opened his eyes. He blinked rapidly and squinted against the harsh fluorescent lighting directly above him. Everything seemed flooded in white. An attractive face leaned into his field of vision.

"You are a lucky man," the female voice said to him softly. "You suffered a serious heart attack, Mr. Fournier. Your friend, Mr. Garnier, must have walked in within a couple minutes of your collapse and found you on the floor of your office. He acted quickly. University security has automatic defibrillators, and they brought you back. You are now in the hospital. My name is Stephanie Boulanger; I'm your nurse."

"What time is it?" Dr. Fournier asked hoarsely.

"It's about 3:00 a.m., but you are going to be here a while, Professor. You are scheduled for by-pass surgery tomorrow. The doctor will be in to explain everything to you later this morning."

"Please, I beg you, listen to me." Stephanie looked down at the professor's hand that had weakly grabbed her arm. "There is a package that will be delivered to my residence first thing in the morning. I will pay you if you will be there to retrieve it for me." He looked at her imploringly. "It is of greatest importance!"

Stephanie had been a Registered Nurse in the Intensive Care Unit at *Hospital Pitie-Salpetriere* for nearly eight years. She had shoulder-length brown hair that she kept pulled back in a barette and expressive brown eyes. At 26 years old, she was attractive in a way that was simple, yet undeniable. She was intelligent and worked hard to achieve her position and excellent professional reputation. Stephanie had been promoted recently to 'Senior Nurse,' but the promotion brought her back to midnight shift where she started her nursing career. She didn't mind. Her life was uncomplicated by choice. No serious boyfriend for over two years, a small group of friends, and occasional contact with her mother neatly framed her life outside of work.

She was born and raised in France and had remained there when her widowed mother had remarried and moved to the United States several years ago.

She got off work at 7:00 a.m., and the professor said the package should arrive sometime between eight and ten. She had time to get to his place for the delivery, but was very hesitant about doing favors for patients.

"The professor who came in with the heart attack wants me to go to his apartment and pick up a package for him," Stephanie confided to her close friend, Dyann, just before quitting time. She sat down next to her at the Nurses' Station.

"So why not?" Dyann asked. "He's a distinguished professor who must have great responsibility. Surely there would be no harm in doing a favor for him."

"I know, but it just feels kinda weird," Stephanie replied. "He seems so desperate; almost as if his life depends on it."

"Oh, for goodness sake, Stephanie, live a little, do something nice for an old man," Dyann chided, as she stapled some reports together. "What harm could it do?"

"None, I suppose. It's just that he seemed really serious about it. He looked almost…scared." Stephanie looked over the counter of the station thoughtfully.

"Well in that case, you better be careful, you may get jumped by a gang of unsavory geriatric gangsters holding PhDs," Dyann teased.

Stephanie grimaced, still considering. "I'm sure the professor will rest easier if I retrieve that package," she commented. "He surely doesn't need any more stress on that heart of his."

"Atta girl, Steph," Dyann said, as she stood and patted her on the back. "I'm off to do rounds. Good luck with your mission. Oh, and beware of those elderly academics. They're always on the lookout for a good nurse." They both giggled.

"Yeah, just call me Good Nurse Boulanger," Stephanie joked as she grabbed her satchel and clocked out.

Chapter 12

Josif Jokanovic sat nervously in the coffee bar near the famous monastery in Gracanica, Kosovo. He had been there only ten minutes, but was already on his third cigarette. His visitors would arrive soon. This was a meeting he had hoped would never come. The hustle and bustle of this Serbian enclave seemed quieter today, the streets less crowded. There are no secrets in Gracanica, and today's meeting was the topic of every hushed conversation in every coffee bar and sidewalk kiosk in the village.

The faction of the Serbian military known as the Black Tigers was infamous and dreaded among the people of the Balkans. Their creative and unorthodox style of violence brought paralyzing fear to the few who had witnessed their wrath. The rest of the population knew the stories well, and hesitated to even speak their name. They were brutal and skilled military operatives who believed in their country's quest to take back the land formerly known as Yugoslavia; land they saw as rightfully theirs. Most people targeted by the Tigers simply disappeared never to be seen again. After the war in 1999, the Black Tigers grew legendary. Word of mouth made them larger than life and unseen phantoms all at the same time.

Gracanica is like an island in the sea with the small Serbian population surrounded now by an Albanian majority. Bitter enemies for centuries, the Albanians and Serbians believe that they will never have peace among their peoples, and Kosovo is now, and always will be, the ethnic boiling point. The Serbian residents of Gracanica remain cut off from the rest of the Kosovo province, most afraid to travel outside the town limits.

Plamen Petrovic was making a special trip to Gracanica from Belgrade. This trip carried risk for any Serb, but for a man of Petrovic's status, this was a *very* high-risk journey. The white Mercedes pulled up directly in front of Josif sitting outside at one of the umbrella-covered tables of the restaurant called "The Blue."

Plamen's son, Slavo, got out of the front seat before the vehicle even came to a complete stop. Slavo was impressive, and one of the most frightening men Josif had ever seen. Only 27 years old and standing over six feet tall, Slavo's face looked as though it's features had been chiseled from a block of hatred. He stood a moment and looked at Josif. It was a look that told him Slavo would rather kill him than grant him the privilege of a meeting. He opened the back door of the Mercedes, and his father stepped out. As he watched Plamen and his son walk toward him, Josif's mind could only think of the scriptural verse in Revelations: *"I looked and there before me was a pale horse, its rider was named Death and Hades followed close behind him."*

The commander of the Black Tigers was an enigma. He was actively pursued by no less than half a dozen international organizations, all of whom acknowledged that catching Petrovic was like trying to grab smoke. His son carried the same bounty, and most wanted them both dead rather than alive. They existed below everyone's radar and rarely surfaced. And yet here they sat, having coffee in the center of the lion's den, with a man who was the reluctant leader of this village.

Fear had left these men long ago. They sat without shaking hands or offering any kind of greeting. *'This is not good,'* Josif thought to himself. He lit another cigarette and noticed his hands shaking. *'This is not good.*

Chapter 13

Inside the closet were four men, three white Aryan-types and one older Hispanic guy with elaborate tattoos from his wrists to high on his neck. The Latino gangster also had what looked like a belt around his throat that had been pulled tight and fastened to one of the shelves behind him. His face was bloody and he was struggling to breathe. Two of the Aryans were holding the man's arms, and Sebastian had opened the door just in time to see the third jam a large homemade shank into the man's gut. There was a moment where everyone just stood there. The scene seemed to play itself out in slow motion. The main man stabbed the tattooed victim three more times.

Sebastian saw the Hispanic man slump against the strap on his neck. The two on either side of the stricken man loosened their grip as life faded from their victim. All eyes turned to the unwelcome intruder. The killer, who had a swastika tattooed boldly on his neck just behind and under his left ear, was the last to turn. Sebastian recognized him immediately. He was an 'up-and-comer' in one of the most feared prison gangs, an Aryan off-shoot gang called the Nazi Lowriders. He knew him only by his prison name, "Reaper," and by reputation as an ambitious gang enforcer.

Everything snapped back to real time for Sebastian as he realized Reaper was talking to him. Sebastian missed the first part of what he said, but picked up at "…you understand me kid? Nothin' happened, and you didn't see nothing.' Now help us move this piece of shit back to the garbage chute, and you can consider yourself a part of the brotherhood." Reaper's head stayed low, and he moved slowly as he spoke, like a predator maneuvering on its prey. He could sense the indecision in Sebastian. If the kid went soft, they would have to drag two bodies back to the garbage chute.

Sebastian nodded as if he agreed to the terms, trying to ease the tension in the air. There was another pregnant pause, and Reaper squinted his eyes, trying to get a better read on what this kid was going to do. In a flash, Sebastian hurled the stack of trays at the group, jumped back from the closet, and rammed the door shut. He broke and ran as fast as he could. He could hear them struggling to get the door to the closet open behind him and a loud string of profanities from a very upset Reaper. Sebastian's only hope was to make it to the main part of the cafeteria where a prison guard sat waiting for the men to finish in the kitchen. Ten minutes before kitchen duty was to end, two other guards on rounds would join the lone guard to assist in prisoner escort back to their cells. It should be getting time for them to arrive, and Sebastian hoped these three would be enough to deter his pursuers.

Sebastian had the length of the kitchen and the serving counter to get through before he would be to the guard. Reaper yelled to the other guys who were pretending to work throughout the kitchen. They started coming from different directions trying to intercept Sebastian. A big thug who was missing most of his teeth made it in front of him and gave him a jagged grin. The distance between them closed rapidly. Sebastian's mind returned to his days on the football field, and he barreled into the behemoth with the best tackle he had ever made. They both toppled to the ground with a loud crash.

Sebastian clawed the floor scrambling to get to his feet as his toothless attacker grabbed at the air trying desperately to get hold of him. Sebastian looked behind him just in time to see his three pursuers gaining ground with frightening speed. With one frantic lunge he was back on his feet and charging ahead. He could now see the long serving counter before him and the cafeteria beyond. He could also hear the footsteps closing in behind him.

Like a quarterback sensing an impending sack, Sebastian could practically feel their hands reaching out to bring him down. With nothing to lose, he catapulted head first, barely clearing the serving counter and landed in a very ungraceful roll on the tile floor in the main cafeteria. He slid to a painful stop against the leg of one of the metal tables. He scrambled again to his feet and looked up to see the guard springing from his seat to see what the commotion was all about. Sebastian ran straight at him, full speed. The two other guards had just walked in the door as Sebastian raced forward. Alarmed by the thought that a crazed inmate was launching some kamikaze-style attack on the lone guard, they quickly drew their batons, preparing to take him down.

Sebastian fell to his knees in front of them and put his hands behind his head. "I need help," he yelled. The guards helped him to his feet and drew him a safer distance away to wait for further instructions from McCants, the prison guard. They looked back toward the kitchen and saw the Lowrider boys skid to a stop and retreat back into the kitchen as their leader took a defiant stance.

"That boy is mine, McCants!" Reaper snarled at the cafeteria guard. McCants cringed, realizing that Reaper knew him by name. "You help him out, and you and I will have unfinished business, too. You know I'm a man of my word. Now release him, and you and your friends just step outside and lock the doors. You can come back after I've had a chance to talk with the boy."

McCants stood silently for a moment, staring across the cafeteria at this madman. 'Unfinished business' was prison speak for the guard being targeted for retaliation. No one ever issued direct threats inside. Everything could come back to haunt you, so inference and innuendo became its own language. It was easy to make this translation.

McCants assessed the situation, and the reality of this evil man gave him pause. Reaper was the second highest-ranking member of the Nazi Lowriders in the prison; he knew that he didn't make threats; he made promises. If he helped this kid out of this situation, there was no doubt he would be a marked man. For the rest of the time he worked at Trenton, they would be plotting to send him out in a body bag.

McCants cursed himself for his moment of cowardice. With his eyes locked on Reaper, he backed to where the guards and Sebastian stood waiting. "Call for backup," he said flatly. "Let's get him out of here."

Sebastian was quickly handcuffed and escorted to a small holding cell by one of the patrolling guards. Back in the cafeteria, Reaper and his minions barricaded themselves in the kitchen. Reaper was three years into a six-year sentence for trying to heist an armored truck in Columbia, SC. This was his second felony conviction, and he knew that if Sebastian fingered him as the killer in the kitchen, he would be a three-time loser and never see the light of day again. In a last act of defiance, he was going to go down with a fight and, with any luck, he would stick a guard or two before it was all over.

McCants retreated to just outside the main cafeteria doors and secured them. The men inside had nowhere to go. He was told that the prison Rapid Reaction Force was en route to take over the situation. Within ten minutes, twelve men suited up in raid gear were at his side.

The Rapid Reaction Force (RRF) guys were huge. The smallest one was over six feet tall and weighed at least 220 pounds. A majority of the team members had specialized military backgrounds, and they lived for these moments. Not only were they extremely aggressive individuals by nature, they were highly trained as a cohesive unit to neutralize any threat within the prison walls.

The team leader, a guy known only as Felix, was a Marine Corps Force Recon veteran. His quiet calm was a strange combination of reassurance and intimidation. He asked for a brief from McCants who was embarrassed that he had very little information to give. He didn't know how many men were inside or if they had acquired any weapons. He did, however, know the layout of the cafeteria and kitchen better than any guard on staff.

As soon as Felix heard there was nowhere for the barricaded prisoners to go and that they held no hostages, he relaxed a little and ordered his men to set up a defensive perimeter outside the door and await further orders. His NFL-sized team moved with amazing grace and silence into their position outside the cafeteria doors.

Felix and the guard made their way to Sebastian's holding cell to get more information. As they walked, Felix called for the second RRF team on standby to be activated and respond to the cafeteria.

Sebastian was sitting on the cot in the holding cell; elbows leaning on his knees, staring at the floor. He was just starting to get the shaking of his hands under control when the two men approached.

"On your feet!" McCants barked. Sebastian stood immediately and faced the two men outside his cell door.

"What's your name?" Felix asked quietly.

"Sebastian Bishop."

"What's the story in there, Bishop?"

Sebastian swallowed hard and then told them what he had

witnessed.

"Besides the men in the closet, how many others are there?" Felix asked as he adjusted the volume on his radio.

Sebastian recalled the whole incident again in his mind, trying to remember the details. "I saw at least four other guys in the kitchen," he responded.

"That brings us up to at least seven men and one presumed critically injured individual," Felix thought aloud. "We'll be back to talk to you some more." The two men turned and left. Sebastian sat back down on the cot, realizing that he was a marked man from this minute forward.

Chapter 14

Plamen Petrovic spoke in slow, measured sentences. His words seemed to have their own gravity, and Josif struggled under their weight.

"Belgrade is not pleased," Plamen said flatly. He studied the unlit cigarette he rolled in his fingers. "You allowed an outsider to enter your village, desecrate a sacred site, and just walk off with one of the most important artifacts of our history."

"We don't even know what he left with…"

Slavo lurched forward suddenly, interrupting Josif mid-sentence and causing him to jump back in his seat.

"Ok, ok." Josif stammered. "It was a mistake. I didn't even realize he was in the village until it was too late. I can make some calls, find out where his plane was going…"

Plamen looked at him incredulously. "Do you actually think that we don't know where he went? Where he is at this very moment?"

Josif felt a cold sweat on his brow. There was a pause in the conversation. Plamen looked down the street and surveyed his surroundings. He saw garbage and filth, dogs running loose, and children wearing rags on their backs. "This used to be ours, as far as the eye can see." He squinted toward the horizon. "The countryside was once beautiful and majestic. Now it is a sewer filled with those who don't belong." For the first time he looked directly at Josif, his eyes glazed with fury, and yet he spoke with a quiet calm. "You obviously no longer care about this land or your people." Plamen and his son stood from the table. "If you have given up on your country, Josif," Plamen's cold eyes leveled themselves on his prey, "then perhaps it is time for your country to give up on you." Josif felt lightheaded, the blood draining from his face. He knew exactly what Plamen meant by his last statement.

The men stood to leave. Not knowing what else to do, Josif stood as well.

Slavo stepped close to him as Plamen spoke, "Walk with me, Josif." Josif knew this was not a request. They walked to the rear of the white Mercedes. Plamen again paused a moment for effect. He looked up and squinted at the cloudless sky. "I once commanded some of the most feared soldiers in the world. Make no mistake, Josif," he turned and looked straight in his face, "I still do." Slavo opened the trunk to reveal a bound, gagged, and absolutely terrified Saso.

Chapter 15

The second team was on site when McCants and Felix returned. An old prison guard approached with a blueprint detailing the layout of the kitchen and cafeteria in his hand. Felix rolled the blueprint open and spoke in hushed tones with the second team's leader as they formulated their plan with great precision. The decision made, they quickly turned to reveal it to their teams.

McCants looked at his watch. Almost forty-two minutes had elapsed from the time Bishop dropped to the ground in front of him to the minute the teams stood ready to retake the cafeteria. The teams donned their gas masks in the event that pepper gas was used and checked their weapons. Most carried shotguns loaded with rubber bullets; however, four team members carried M-4 assault rifles in case deadly force was needed.

On Felix's mark, the two teams entered the cafeteria, guns up, fanning out in an impressive display of organized force. They each marched at equal distance from one another across the spans of open cafeteria. The line of men approached the serving counter over which Sebastian had made his desperate dive. There were two open doorways on either end of the counter leading to the kitchen beyond. Silently, the two teams divided equally and stacked themselves just outside the two doorways for their second entry. With hardly any hesitation, Felix gave the signal, and the teams entered the kitchen area as silent as cats on carpet.

After clearing the doorways, both teams slowed their movement, advancing as both individual units and evenly as a large team. Each team moved together in a deadly oval, shoulder- to-shoulder, with each member making methodical 360-degree sweeps of the area around him. Each man had his assigned sector of responsibility, scanning the area, weapon and eyes moving together with the most heightened sense of awareness, ready for anything.

Felix led his team from the front, his shotgun extended before him. They approached the end of a long stainless steel table, and so far they had seen or heard nothing. Suddenly, at the end of the table, Reaper sprang up, grabbing the barrel of Felix's gun with his left hand and rearing back to plunge his homemade shank with his right. Without hesitation, Felix went with the momentum of his rifle barrel, forcing it upward. He jammed the butt-stock forward, smashing into Reaper's groin.

Reaper let out a pained grunt, the impact stopping the path of the shank mid-air. With incredible speed, Felix readjusted his grip on his weapon and tomahawked butt over barrel, reversing the arc from mid-section toward the skull of the hunched over Reaper. The weapon crashed down on Reaper's head with a sickening thud. The move looked to the others like he was swinging an axe. Reaper was unconscious well before he hit the floor. Felix flipped his weapon back around and continued scanning and moving forward as team members further back would secure the unconscious inmate.

After the flash of violence, an eerie silence fell again over the kitchen as the men advanced. The remaining prisoners knew their fearless leader had been subdued with such ease that they didn't stand a chance.

"Ok, we give up! Don't shoot!" came a plea from deeper in the kitchen.

"Show yourselves, hands up," Felix demanded firmly. Slowly, the men stood with their hands high above their heads. The teams secured six men without further incident. The two teams then performed a very thorough search of the remaining kitchen and finally radioed the all clear.

Medical staff came in to examine the Hispanic victim, but he was no doubt dead shortly after the initial attack. Reaper suffered a serious concussion, and his head wound took 37 stitches to close. He spent eight days in the infirmary, but he would otherwise make a full recovery.

Sebastian was transferred to solitary confinement for his own protection. It took nearly four months for the prison legal staff to prepare their case and for Reaper to recover enough to stand trial, but the day inevitably approached when Sebastian found himself back in court. This time he would be a *witness* in a murder case.

Sebastian asked Mr. Jamison to come back and help him through this whole ordeal. The lawyer was able to negotiate a few things on Sebastian's behalf in return for his testimony. First, Sebastian would serve his remaining time in solitary confinement to protect him from the rest of the general population. Second, he was permitted supervised internet access for the purpose of study. This would allow him to work on a college degree online. And lastly, he was permitted a one-hour extended exercise period each day. The legal team quickly agreed to these relatively simple terms to get Reaper put away for good.

The trial was well organized and expertly conducted by the prison legal staff. They were even able to get one of the other members of the attack to roll on Reaper for a reduced sentence. Sebastian recounted the events with great detail and fingered Reaper, whose real name was Michael Goodson, as the one who struck the fatal blow to the Hispanic man in the closet. The two corroborating testimonies sealed Goodson's fate.

The deceased Hispanic gang member was Emanuel Ruez, a middle manager of sorts for the Nuestra Familia. Word came from the Nazi Lowrider hierarchy that Ruez needed to die. Goodson had eagerly volunteered for the job, hoping for a serious jump in rank as a result. The death of Ruez would probably lead to all out war within the walls of Trenton Prison, not to mention some retaliatory strikes on the outside as well. Sebastian was very relieved to know he would be in solitary while this nightmare played itself out.

An assault on a correctional officer is an additional felony charge. Although a lesser offense than the homicide, it revealed the serious threat that inmate Michael Goodson posed. If convicted it would almost certainly assure that Goodson would be separated from the general prison population for his entire period of incarceration. This would not only help to protect the lives of other prisoners and prison staff, it would make it exceedingly more difficult for Goodson to continue the business of his criminal enterprise. Felix was sworn in and gave his testimony regarding Goodson's attempt to stab him as they cleared the kitchen.

Court for prison trials was held at a facility right on the prison grounds. The building was designed to segregate the inmates from the legal staff and other required participants for the duration of the hearing. Sebastian was behind bars in the courtroom reserved for inmates who were either on trial themselves or, as in Sebastian's situation, testifying against another. Felix's testimony was short and straightforward, so Sebastian was allowed to remain in the courtroom as the trial marched toward its conclusion. He was subject to recall at any time for clarification or if questions arose from others' testimony.

Sebastian was very impressed with Felix. He spoke intelligently and held himself in a manner that left no doubt that he was sure of not only his actions, but his specific role in the difficult operation of a large correctional facility. He led an elite team that required him to make life and death decisions in the blink of an eye. It was quite obvious to Sebastian that there was no better man for the job. As Sebastian considered this man's professionalism, his heart sank at the realization that he would be lucky to be a short-order cook by the time he got out of this place. All his hopes of being a professional in anything seemed far out of reach now.

Chapter 16

Belgrade is a city struggling to re-discover itself. In the wake of years of communism followed by a thwarted military campaign, the city is going to great lengths to convince its neighbors that the Former Republic of Yugoslavia is ready to be part of their Union. Belgrade is leading the way in shedding the past, and emerging as a modern city with great promise. Situated at the meeting point of two great European rivers, the Sava and the Danube, Belgrade offers accessibility and flexibility in commerce and even tourism.

The white Mercedes entered the traffic flow heading toward the city center like an injection into a vein. The vehicle made its way toward the rail yard where it entered one of the many warehouse-type buildings. The interior of this building was cavernous and completely empty, with the exception of another Mercedes parked near the center. The two Mercedes were identical except in color, one white, one black.

Three men stood outside the black Mercedes with the driver staying behind the wheel. Of the three, the one in the center was obviously running the show. His suit hung loosely on his aged frame and his wrinkled skin bore the weathering of little peace and hard smoking.

There was no mistake, however; this venerable warrior was at one time a force to be reckoned with. He now exercised his impressive breadth of control from behind Serbia's diplomatic facade. In his youth, he must have been quite tall, but time had bent his back like a warped piece of wood, making him lose a bit of his commanding presence. His name was Svetozar Dimitrijevic, and he was the modern leader of the Serbian Black Hand.

To his right stood a young man, studious in nature, holding a briefcase. To his left was an imposing man whose life had obviously been shaped by conflict. He was a professional soldier who was awarded his post as the old man's personal security officer through what could only be rigorous proof of service.

The white Mercedes eased to a stop near the men, and Plamen and Slavo got out. Slavo and the soldier immediately took each other's measure, subconsciously calculating odds and likely moves of the other. Death to them was a business like any other, and they both had joined the company early in life.

Plamen looked back and nodded to his driver. He immediately jumped out of the vehicle and went to the trunk. He grabbed Saso from inside and threw him to the ground near the feet of the men.

"This is the man that took the professor to the artifact," Plamen said flatly.

The old man glanced apathetically at Saso and then returned his gaze to Plamen. "You should be in Paris, my friend." The old man spoke in a way that instilled a sense of constant foreboding. His very presence conveyed the message that he knew everything, including what one was thinking and about to say. Plamen always thought it was like visiting a spider in his web. He would determine if you left or, if on this visit, he would devour you.

"I sent a team that…" Plamen tried to reply.

Dimitrijevic interrupted, "I know the incompetents you sent to Paris, thus my observation that *you* should be there. The two inept drones you sent were found dead in a dumpster 30 minutes ago."

Plamen had no response. There was an uncomfortable silence. The old man seemed to revel in it.

"The artifact was not recovered?" was all Plamen could think to ask.

"That is correct. Your team found opposition and a couple bullets to the head…but no artifact." Although frail in body, the old man's mind was like a steel trap, waiting for this irresponsible man's ego to further incriminate him. Plamen was assigned the job of recovery and had failed dramatically. Dimitrijevic struggled to conceal his anger. He was mildly impressed, however, when Plamen said no more.

"We are growing increasingly concerned with your decision-making abilities General Petrovic. Perhaps it is time for you to step down."

The tone of the meeting immediately changed, and the tension seemed to suck the air from the warehouse. "Don't threaten me, Dimitrijevic. I have dedicated my life to Serbia!" Plamen said through clenched teeth.

"The Black Hand *is* Serbia," Demetrijevic hissed. "You would be wise not to forget it." The hint of pure fury quickly melted from the old man's face. He turned to get into his Mercedes. "It seems we are back at the beginning, General. Your orders remain the same, find the artifact."

The black Mercedes sped off.

Plamen stood for a moment in the quiet of the mammoth warehouse collecting his thoughts and getting his emotions under control. In one fluid movement, he turned, pulled a Baikal IJ-70 Makarov pistol from his waistband, and shot Saso in the head. Without hesitation, the men loaded back in their vehicle and drove away.

From the back seat, Plamen said evenly, "Step on it. We have work to do."

Chapter 17

Stephanie stepped off the bus about four blocks from the professor's apartment building. She loved the city in the morning. Paris had been her home for her entire life, and it felt good to be part of the life-blood that coursed through its veins. The air was crisp and the sky was clear; she had the next two days off and plenty of time before she needed to be at Dr. Fournier's apartment to receive the package. She decided to stop and enjoy a pastry and some coffee at one of the many coffee shops that dotted Paris' landscape.

Having some down time was just what Stephanie needed right now. The overnight shift had been particularly harrowing, and it came on the heels of ten days with no time off. She was bone tired and weary. As she sipped her second cup of coffee, she thought about Professor Fournier and the close call he had experienced. Stephanie spent most of the night watching over him. It had been touch and go. He was seriously ill, and yet seemed more concerned about the package he asked her to retrieve than he did about his condition.

The blaring sirens of emergency vehicles suddenly interrupted her thoughts as they careened around the corner in front of the café and disappeared down the street in the direction she would soon be walking. *'Another emergency,'* she thought. *'The hospital will be on alert.'* Stephanie clamped the lid on her carryout coffee and rose from her chair. *'I'm so relieved to be off duty for a while,'* she told herself, exiting to the street. She had no way of knowing that this would be the last peace she would know for a very long time.

Chapter 18

Sebastian was finding it more difficult than he anticipated adjusting to his new life in solitary. He was lying on his cot, lost in thought, the night following the conclusion of the trial. His mind seemed incapable of getting around the concept that he had no future, no hope, nothing to look forward to. He tried to picture what his life would be like the day he walked out of this place. He would be a social outcast, never again to be trusted, unable to secure respectable work; an ex-con.

As he wallowed there in self-pity, a shadow cast itself on the floor before him. He looked up to see Felix, the Rapid Reaction Force team leader, standing outside his cell. Sebastian sat up and looked questioningly at him.

After a short pause, Felix spoke, "I just wanted to tell you that you did the right thing. I know that none of this was easy, and I can pretty much guarantee that the worst is yet to come. But when you look back on all this, your conscience should be clear because you had the courage to stand up to a real kind of evil."

Sebastian slowly shook his head. "I'm behind the same bars, sir. What separates me from them?"

Felix took a step closer to the cell door. "Well, that's the real question now, isn't it? Seems to me that's a decision you have to make."

Sebastian remained silent, lowering his eyes to the floor.

"I know why you're here kid," Felix continued. "I know what you did and why you did it. You got a raw deal, and yet even in here you can't help but do what you think is right. You had no allegiances in here, no gang affiliations, nothing really to gain by giving your testimony before your attorney stepped in." Felix paused, his eyes examining Sebastian for any reaction. "I think you would have testified regardless of his negotiations on your behalf.

You could have denied seeing anything in that kitchen, you could have helped them conceal the body, cleaned up, a whole number of things that would have secured your allegiance to the Lowrider bunch and thereby guaranteed your safety. They would have taken care of you for the remainder of your stay. We would never have been able to prove who had stabbed Ruez, and Reaper would have been carrying on business as usual. May not seem like much to you, but that's a big deal in my book."

Sebastian remained quiet.

Felix straightened as he took a deep breath, pulling his uniform shirt tight from the bottom. "Well that's all I wanted to say. Good luck to you, Bishop."

As he turned to leave, Sebastian finally spoke. "What now?" he said, barely above a whisper.

"Pardon me?" Felix asked, turning back to face Sebastian.

"What now?" Sebastian repeated a little louder, lifting his eyes to look directly at him. "I have three more years here, in solitary confinement no less, only to be released into a whole new kind of prison. What am I supposed to do now?" Sebastian enunciated each word of this question.

Felix came back to the door with a determined step. "I think you'll find solitary confinement as torturous as regular prison life, maybe even more so. But, in spite of it all, you've got two options, Bishop," Felix said more harshly than he intended. "You can just give up, spend your prison time submerged in self-pity until you get out where you can continue on a self destructive path. You'll likely end up dead a short time later because you were successful in convincing yourself that you are worthless, destined to fail." Felix grabbed the bars of Sebastian's cell so hard his knuckles were turning white, "OR, you fight. Quit wallowing in despair, and get disciplined. Set goals, both short- and long-term, and find a way to overcome. Be the man you've always wanted to be despite the adversity. You need to look at your situation through different eyes and gain a perspective of hope. Now I don't know how you do that. I have no recipe for success for someone in your situation. But if men can spend years as prisoners of war enduring conditions far worse than your wildest nightmares, and come out to be leaders, men of integrity and inspiration, then I think you can make it through three years in Trenton."

Felix stepped back and rubbed his brow. He didn't know why he was overcome with such emotion with this kid, but he honestly wanted Sebastian to have a chance.

Sebastian swallowed hard; it was good advice. He noticed the Marine Corps insignia tattooed on Felix's forearm. "How long were you in the Marines, sir?" Sebastian inquired after a period of uncomfortable silence.

"Twenty years," he replied, speaking more softly now. "I went in at 18 and got out four years ago."

"Was it worth it?"

"It changed my life," Felix answered without hesitation. "I went in with trepidation and came out a man of purpose."

Their conversation seemed to stop there. Felix prepared to leave, but stopped, having one last bit of advice for the young man. Sebastian looked up at him, and their eyes locked. "Find your purpose, Bishop. You want to make it in this life, then find your purpose. With that the strength will follow." Felix walked away, and he and Sebastian never spoke again, but his words burned into Sebastian's mind and would follow him for the rest of his life.

Chapter 19

Damir Tadic and his crew were nursing beers after a late dinner. They were booked on an early morning flight out of Charles de Gaulle, and they still had plenty of time before departure. His comrades were quietly discussing the soccer match playing on the flat screen television of the sports pub. It was 2:30 in the morning. The bar would close in half an hour and then they would leisurely work their way to the airport. No rush, no stupid moves, just lay low and get out of the country; the nature of the business.

Damir grabbed the briefcase and told his companions he would be back shortly. He walked to the men's room and found an empty stall. He closed the toilet lid and sat down, placing the briefcase across his lap. Curiosity had been eating away at him since they left the university. He was glad they got the jump on the two Serbian thugs who were undoubtedly in Paris for the same prize. They were sloppy, undisciplined, and apparently unaware of the gravity of their situation. Regardless, they were killed cleanly, and their bodies wouldn't be discovered until the next trash collection. Now it was time to see what they came for.

Damir knew he shouldn't mess with the case. He should simply leave everything just as he had retrieved it, and turn it over to his people unmolested; but he couldn't. He had to see this artifact that was driving countries to make moves that hadn't been seen in years. He popped the latches and slowly opened the briefcase. Inside was the stone container that had held a diplomatic document for centuries. It was intricately decorated with the work of a master stone mason. The Latin inscribed on the lid was chiseled with skilled hands and projected the weight of official business. In the center of the lid was a circular gold plate inlaid with the undeniable seal of the most Holy Office, the Golden Bull.

Damir painstakingly pried open the lid of the protective vessel. The inside began to reveal itself under the bathroom's artificial light. Damir's eyes were wide in anticipation, and then his jaw clenched in disbelief. He screamed profanities in Croatian as he slammed the briefcase shut. He stormed from the bathroom still muttering angrily under his breath. He approached his associates who knew immediately something was seriously wrong.

"We're not leaving yet, gentlemen," he announced. "It seems the professor is more clever than we thought." Damir threw plenty of money on the table to cover the bill, and the group left without further discussion.

Chapter 20

Plamen sent his son Slavo and three hardened soldiers to Paris to finish what the others could not. All the men, including Slavo, had extensive elite military training, and they had all taken lives; up close. Slavo was an impatient leader, who would rather handle situations himself than trust them to others. All who knew him feared him. His life was Serbia, his national fervency fueled his existence.

He was maniacal about restoring Serbian greatness. Hatred coursed through his veins for the peoples of Yugoslavia who hid behind Serbia's shield in times of hardship, and then took from his beloved country all they had fought to protect. The civil wars of recent times were not about ethnicity or religious fundamentalism; they were about Serbian ownership, reclaiming what was rightfully theirs. And the Americans' betrayal of his country in 1999 could never be forgiven.

Slavo was getting shrapnel removed from his thigh at a hospital in Belgrade when the air strikes began. He could not believe the Americans and the British had stepped into their war. It had nothing to do with them. His grandfather had fought the Nazis; his family had been the tip of the spear overthrowing their own cowardly government when it made a deal to join Germany. *'We suffered mightily for the Allied cause; and what do we get in return? Smart bombs, support of Serbia's sworn enemies, capitulations, appeasements, and rights non-Serbs have never earned,'* he thought to himself. His stomach turned in disgust at this new world order that worshipped money and replaced honor with tyranny. Slavo now dedicated his life to revenge and restoration; nothing else mattered.

The plane touched down smoothly, and the four men made their way to their waiting rental car. They moved without discussion, each consummate professionals. The car eased into the nearly empty streets of Paris before it yet awoke to a new day.

Chapter 21

Every day in solitary seemed to squeeze Sebastian's sanity just a little harder. He felt like he was in a compartment filling with water, and each day his space to breath was becoming smaller and smaller. Hour upon hour, day after day of solitude was unrelenting on the psyche. He would read aloud to himself, sometimes even talk aloud to himself, anything to break the monotony of isolation. It felt like he was coming unraveled at times.

Sebastian was given a secluded area in the prison factory where he could perform menial tasks for a ridiculous wage. It was a restricted area that offered only more solitude, but at least it made him feel productive to some extent. It was becoming harder and harder to stay focused and to find any kind of motivation to face another day. He could feel depression building within him.

It had been five months since the incident. Sebastian had established a routine of exercise and study that helped him through his days, but he still saw nothing but blank space on the other side of his sentence. He felt hollow on the inside, and going through the motions of productivity was ironically counter-productive.

Everything changed for Sebastian on a day that had been exactly like all the other days before. He was struck by an idea that seemed so far-fetched that it bordered on hilarity, yet it was the closest thing to hope Sebastian had felt in a very long time. It came to him as he studied the French Revolution in one of his online courses.

Sebastian was allowed to meet with the prison librarian twice a week for research in accordance with his studies. The librarian supervised all internet inquiries and was responsible for entering all search subject matter to ensure it fulfilled stipulated criteria. He now sat at the computer beside Sebastian and looked at him for what to enter. Felix's words, *'Find your purpose,'* echoed in Sebastian's mind.

"Type in French Foreign Legion," Sebastian said.

The librarian looked at him blankly. "You're serious?"

"I am."

Sebastian took an armload of computer printouts from the prison library back to his cell. He spent the next two days going over every detail of every page. He then tried to formulate in his mind how best to approach this ambitious endeavor. He settled on correspondence and sat down to compose a compelling letter formally requesting enlistment in the French Foreign Legion. He explained the totality of the circumstances of his case and asked for immediate placement upon release from prison.

Chapter 22

At the *Division Recrutement de la Legion Entrangere* in Paris, France, a letter arrived from America. Local recruiter, Corporal Mathias Kaestner, opened it and read an interesting plea for recruitment. This did not happen very often anymore, so he carried the letter to his Sergeant for consideration. The Sergeant breezed over its contents as he spoke on the phone.

"No," Sergeant Rasmus Laituri replied, as he covered the phone's mouthpiece.

"But you didn't really look at it, Sergeant," Kaestner replied.

The Sergeant furrowed his brow and glared at the Corporal. "You will remember your place, Corporal, or I will have you scooping camel shit in Addis Ababa by noon tomorrow. The man is a criminal. Now get out of my office."

"Like the French Foreign Legion has never recruited criminals before?" Kaestner said derisively under his breath as he turned to leave. He knew he was pushing his luck, but recruitment was down and could use an infusion. *What's the problem with giving this guy a chance? More than likely he wouldn't even make it through the selection process for Legion Entrangere. And what's the worst that could happen; he becomes a Legionnaire?* Kaestner smiled inwardly at the thought.

He knew he had to send the standard refusal letter, but he also had another thought.

Some time later, Sebastian received a letter through the prison post from France. He excitedly tore it open and read its contents:

Dear Mr. Bishop:

Thank you for your interest in the French Foreign Legion. Our organization is a modern military force employing only individuals who meet specific enlistment criteria. Although we have recruited individuals of questionable reputation in the past, we are no longer in such practice. The era of 'no questions asked' recruitment is indeed a thing of the past. Therefore, taking your circumstances into consideration, we are unable to extend to you an offer to attend our selection process for entry into the Legion.

Best of luck to you in your future endeavors,
Corporal Mathias Kaestner
Division Recrutement de la Legion Entrangere

Sebastian's heart sank. He loosened his grip on the letter, feeling completely dejected, ready to let it slip into the trash. He glanced in the envelope as he released it from his hand and realized that there was something else inside. He snatched at the air as the envelope floated down, finally snagging it right before it landed inside the bin.

He pulled from the envelope a yellow sticky note with a handwritten message. *'There may be a chance; please send a photocopy of your case file to the following address:...'* Below that was the name, Adrienne Dubois, and an address in Paris. He had no idea what it meant, but he ran to the prison phone to place a call to his attorney, Gordon Jamison.

"Hello, may I speak to Mr. Jamison, please?" Sebastian asked the female voice that answered the phone. "Yes, this is Sebastian Bishop. I'm a client," he responded when she asked who was calling. In a moment, Gordon Jamison picked up the phone.

"Hello, Sebastian. What can I do for you, son?" Mr. Jamison asked.

"I have an unusual request to ask of you, Mr. Jamison. I need you to send a sealed copy of my complete case file to Paris." Sebastian spent the next ten minutes explaining that it was a personal matter and that he was not prepared to disclose the reason why to his attorney or anyone else. Finally, he was able to give the address for receipt in Paris and reiterate that this needed to be done as soon as possible.

Sebastian concluded this conversation by being perfectly clear about the rules. "Mr. Jamison, you are bound through client/attorney confidentiality laws to keep any information shared between you and me *completely* confidential. I know you and my father are friends, and I know you want to be helpful by keeping him informed of any contact between us. But, sir, I am asking you to remember your oath because prison phones are recorded; therefore, this information is on record. A violation of my faith in you, from what I understand, will result in immediate suspension followed quickly by disbarment from practice in the state of South Carolina and, in fact, anywhere in the continental United States. I appreciate your discretion, and I look forward to speaking with you in the future." Sebastian quickly hung up without waiting for a response.

Mr. Jamison stood in his office looking at his phone incredulously. "This kid is something else." He said out loud, finally hanging up the phone. "I really wish he wouldn't read so much," he added under his breath as he began looking through his files for Sebastian's case.

Chapter 23

Roughly four thousand miles away from Sebastian's prison cell, Corporal Mathias Kaestner left work early and drove his red Peugeot 307 toward the law offices of Legrand and Dubois near the city center. He squeezed his car into a parking space about a block away and hurried into the office building. The receptionist phoned Ms. Dubois who instructed her to send Kaestner straight back.

Kaestner walked toward the office with a little spring in his step, hopeful that she could help. He observed the lettering on the exterior of the door stating simply: *Avocat Adrienne Dubois.* He knocked and walked in.

"Bon jour, Mathias," Adrienne said cheerfully, standing and kissing him on either cheek. She still made him blush, even though he was now 23 years old. Adrienne had been his older sister's best friend since they were very young. Mathias had had a crush on her since he was seven years old. He grew up in the city of Saarbrucken in Germany, and Adrienne was from Forbach, France, directly across the border. Although Kaestner held German citizenship, he spoke French like a native and had as many French friends as German. Adrienne had grown into a beautiful woman and was a feared fair labor law expert. She held a long-time hatred for the Foreign Legion because she felt that France was prostituting herself by letting foreigners take up arms on her behalf. Little did she know that Mathias had run to the Legion as a direct result of this hatred. Adrienne's announcement of her engagement to the heir of one of France's many large wineries had left Mathias distraught. He was just completing secondary school when he heard the news that would break his heart. Realizing he could never have the girl he loved since childhood, he ran to the one place he knew she hated so much. He would show her, he thought, but his foolishness backfired on him. He had eleven months remaining on his contract to the Legion, and although he had made it through his obligation alive, he would never return to this brutal organization. He had long gotten over Adrienne Dubois, but the Legion would scar him forever. He was convinced that she didn't know any of this even to this day. As he stood in her office, he certainly hoped not.

"How are you, soldier boy?" she jabbed.

"I'm doing great, Renny. How's the wine business?" he gave right back.

"Oh my word, even the smell of wine makes me nauseous." They both laughed. "So to what do I owe the pleasure, Corporal?" She wrinkled her nose at him.

"Please, if you call me by my rank, I may snap to attention and sing the national anthem." She giggled, and he continued, "I have a little situation that fell into my lap that you might be interested in. Actually I was hoping you could help me out with it."

"Ok, have a seat and tell me about it," she said, returning to her office chair."

"I received a letter from an American in prison who will finish up his sentence in less than two years. He wants to join the Legion."

"Ok, so what's the problem? You guys take scum from every corner of the earth anyway, don't you? No offense."

"None taken. Well, that's just it; we *used* to take the scum of the earth indiscriminately, but they've really cracked down on all that. However, we can still accept essentially who we want when we want. And once they're in, they are the property of the French government, and we can do just about anything with them. Probably even make them fine wine connoisseurs." Adrienne smiled at this. "Seriously, the guys that come to us seeking a new lease on life usually become some of the best soldiers. And this guy sounds legitimate, but I'm unable to convince my superiors to give him a chance. I think he got a raw deal from the courts in his country on this one."

"So what exactly do you want me to do?" Adrienne asked cautiously.

"Just take a look at his case. If you think it's legitimate, petition the Legion for his acceptance at least into the selection process. There's a real chance he won't make it any further than that, but at least we will have given him the chance to try. Everybody's afraid of you so they probably won't even contest it. They'll just go ahead and take him." Studying her face as he spoke, Kaestner could see she was considering it.

"Why are you so interested in this criminal anyway?" she queried.

"I don't know. He went to prison protecting his sister. When I thought about my sister, I could really relate, and besides sometimes people deserve a second chance in life. In his case I think it's a first chance for any kind of life."

"You'd make a great used car salesman," Adrienne teased. They both laughed.

"So you'll do it?"

"Yes, I'll take a look at it and see what I can do."

"Thanks, Renny. You're the best." Mathias jumped up and kissed her warmly on both cheeks. "I'll talk to you soon," he said as he turned to leave.

"You better. And tell your sister to call me!" she yelled from behind him as he bounded out the door.

Chapter 24

Adrienne Dubois received a very impressive-looking package from an American attorney by the name of Gordon Jamison. Opening it, she found a complete, sealed case file on one Sebastian Bishop. She leaned back in her desk chair, took a sip of Avian water, and began to read.

Sebastian had found new hope. He realized that he had allowed himself to get out of shape as he half-heartedly exercised in the past, so he began a new fitness routine. With sharpening his body he would also double his efforts to sharpen his mind. Now, in addition to his online degree, he would work every day on learning the French language. Twenty-two months remained on his sentence. With 'good-time' he would be out in closer to twenty, barely enough time to get everything arranged. Each day he outlined specific objectives. Even though this endeavor was a complete shot in the dark, he felt a new sense of purpose. Now with defined goals, and a timeline for completion, Sebastian was able to focus like never before in his life.

By two o'clock in the afternoon, Adrienne had completed her review of Sebastian's case. "Unbelievable," she said aloud. She couldn't understand why this guy would want to become a Legionnaire, but if that's what he wanted, he certainly deserved the chance to try. By five in the evening, Adrienne had drafted her first copy of the petition for induction into the French Foreign Legion on Sebastian's behalf. She would go over it again in the morning, make corrections, and have it delivered by messenger service before lunchtime. She had never taken on the Legion, and she wished somehow that her first case with them had been a little more difficult. The Legion's policy was not to accept convicted felons within their ranks. However, according to the Legion's own bizarre by-laws, if a person wanted to essentially 'start life anew,' they could accept an applicant if he enlisted under a "pseudonym" or different name. After one year of service, the candidate could 'legitimize' his enlistment by solidifying his status under his true identity. The enlisted individual could actually apply for French citizenship after serving for three years, or before that, if he qualified by *'Francais par le sang verse,'* (spilled blood in battle). Adrienne thought the entire system was the most ridiculous thing she had ever seen, but she put in the petition, citing the Legion's own rules as the premise for Sebastian's acceptance.

Sebastian composed a letter to Judge Bailey who had presided over his case. In the letter, he explained how he understood that upon release, one of the conditions of his probation would be no travel outside the continental United States for a prescribed period of time. He asked if a concession might be made in his case if the French Government produced a certified letter confirming his employment in the Foreign Legion. The judge, believing this to be the product of delusion due to extended confinement, replied saying that if such documentation was provided, he would personally sign off on his travel waiver. Sebastian placed this letter in a protective plastic document sleeve, and shelved it safely in his cell.

Corporal Kaestner saw a messenger from one of the local courier services breeze through the recruitment station headed straight for the Captain's office. He had gotten an e-mail from Adrienne yesterday saying that she received the package from America. *'Surely she wouldn't have put something together this quickly'* he thought to himself. But just to be on the safe side, he slipped out of the office for an early lunch. The Captain carried the binder of documents, looking very legal in nature, into the Sergeant's office. He immerged a few moments later with a scowl on his face declaring, "I'm headed to lunch." He walked briskly out of the office.

A moment later, the Sergeant appeared in the doorway of his office and yelled at the top of his lungs, "Where is that imbecile, Kaestner!"

Chapter 25

Sebastian knew the days would be long as a Legionnaire, so he developed a routine in prison mirroring the routine he would soon face. His schedule was from 5:00 a.m. to 10:00 p.m. every day. Over the course of three years, eight months, and 14 days, his regimen of physical training and academic study paid off. He had a very firm fundamental grasp of the French language now, his Bachelor's degree was complete, and his body looked as if it were chiseled from stone. He was thankful to have found such focus and direction, at least for the time immediately following his release.

One month out, he sat down to make a difficult phone call. For nearly four years, his family visited him every other week without fail. They were the lifeline that helped him cling to his sanity while in solitary confinement. It was they who encouraged him and gave him strength to carry on. But in addition to this, they helped him cope with what he had done. He loved his family dearly, but for three years he had been drifting on a course that would separate him from them in both literal and metamorphic ways.

He picked up the receiver and called home. Alexa answered. She was now 20 years old and pursuing her law degree at the University of South Carolina. "Hello?"

"Hey, Sis."

"Sebastian! We are so excited! Mom and I have this whole plan on decorating the house. We fixed up your room, and we're thinking about taking a family trip to the beach. You love the water. What do you think?" Sebastian smiled. She was talking a mile a minute.

"Listen, Lex," Sebastian broke in. "I love you guys, and I am so grateful for all the things you are doing for me, but…I have to tell you all something. Can you get Mom and Dad and have them pick up on the line, too?"

As he anticipated, it took a very long time for all the documentation to clear. Nearly eight months after finally receiving a letter of invitation to the Foreign Legion selection process, Sebastian felt he had everything he would need in preparation for his release. The Legion had, at Adrienne's intervention, permitted Sebastian to enlist in his given name. He had applied for and received a passport prior to his arrest in anticipation of a trip to Europe after high school graduation. It had been confiscated upon his initial arrest, but it was now returned to him by court order.

Judge Bailey was true to his word. After receiving not only certified mail from the French Government, but a phone call from a Captain with the Foreign Legion confirming that Sebastian had indeed been recruited, he signed the travel waiver to France. Sebastian had to make arrangements with the U.S. Embassy in Paris for checking in. An American Foreign Affairs Officer would meet him upon arrival, register him with the Embassy, and then personally drive him to the Legion training facility. In essence, one of the Embassy staff would work as his probation officer while he did his military time in the Legion.

One month later, at 9:00 a.m., Sebastian Carver Bishop walked out of the Trenton Correctional Institution a free man. He had hired a driver for $250 to take him to the airport. The driver was in the prison visitor parking lot waiting for him, and within minutes they were pulling away from Sebastian's home of the last three-and-a-half years. He took a long hard look at the prison, seeing it from the outside for the first time since he arrived. He swore he would never go back, no matter what. His driver took him straight to the airport in Charlotte, North Carolina, where he would wait for his 3:30 p.m. flight to Paris, France.

Against his wishes, his family was at the airport waiting on him. They all embraced him and cried, and hugged him some more. His parents took a few minutes to try to talk him out of his decision, but they could see his mind was made up. They spent the time laughing and enjoying a good meal. Alexa pulled him aside and informed him that they had a lot of catching up to do. He promised they would when he returned.

Sebastian had earned $3,650.00 for nearly four years of work in the prison factory. He held on to one thousand dollars and gave the rest to his mother.

"Would you put this in a mutual fund or something?" Sebastian asked, feeling like he was 12 again. His mother was very good with money, and he knew she would invest it wisely. The time passed quickly, and after a very tearful farewell, Sebastian found himself comfortably situated on board the United Airlines flight to Paris. He knew onboard Air Marshals would watch him until Embassy staff in Paris picked him up. Regardless of the somewhat unorthodox circumstances, he also knew at 22 years old he was about to embark on the first adventure of his choosing in his young life.

Prison changes people without a doubt, but for Sebastian it was in ways he never imagined. It was the isolation, and being deprived of normal social interaction at such a crucial time in life that changed him. He could feel it. He emerged determined to implement structure and discipline into his life, transitioning into adulthood with the skills and experience to make him a productive member of society. As he sat in his coach seat, he would have no way of knowing how much he would be changed by this decision. The next time he returned to America, he would be an entirely different man altogether.

Chapter 26

Damir Tadic and his associates took their time to regroup. They all had enough operational experience to realize that when the unexpected occurred, the possibility of making grievous mistakes to try and right the situation existed. All of their equipment was in the trunk of their car where they left it in the airport parking garage. Anytime a job like this occurred, local sympathetic facilitators took care of the details. They made sure that everything was where it ought to be: cars, weapons, phones, walkie-talkies, etc. When the job was complete, the operational team would simply park the car with everything in the hidden compartment in the trunk, and their people would pick it up after they were sure that the car had drawn no attention.

They went over their plan, checked weapons and communications, informed local contacts of the change in plans, and then proceeded cautiously to the hospital. The sky was just beginning to show signs of a new day.

Slavo and his team drove toward the hospital in silence. What they knew so far was that two Serbians were dead, the professor was in the hospital, and the artifact was gone. Obviously, another team was on the ground, and they needed to know who they were dealing with. Slavo told his men earlier that he would talk to the professor, find out as much information as possible, and they would re-assess at that time. Local surveillance teams were already in place watching venues of mass transit; they had been since Plamen received the news of the first team's failure. There was nothing more to be said.

They entered one of the hospital parking garages, and Slavo got out and put a white lab coat on over his clothes. The fake hospital credentials were convincing enough for this short visit. His silenced pistol was nestled comfortably along his rib cage in its shoulder holster. The plan was uncomplicated: go in posing as hospital staff, find the professor, talk to him, and leave. There would be no reason to kill him unless the information he possessed posed some unforeseen threat. The professor could ramble on all he wanted in his academic circles about some artifact he'd found, but if he couldn't produce any proof, no one would pay him any attention.

Killing people is a messy business, and would be avoided unless absolutely necessary. Slavo couldn't control the variables in France like he could in Serbia, so he would tread carefully, get what he came for, and leave. It was necessary to be subtle like a mist, not violent like a tempest. However, his innate sense of impending bloodshed told him that subtlety would not see him through the course he had embarked on. He could feel the storm clouds of violence gathering.

Chapter 27

Sebastian landed at the Charles de Gaulle International Airport just outside of Paris right on schedule. When the plane taxied to a stop, he stood to retrieve his carry-on bag. He took a moment for reflection, realizing that this was it, there was no turning back. He decided in that moment that no matter what was thrown at him, he would not give up and he would not fail. He took a deep breath and exited the plane.

He walked through the airport and was met at the baggage claim by an expressionless young man holding a sign with the word "Bishop" printed in bold letters. The man had a distinct military bearing about him, but was dressed casually and displayed no military affiliation.

Sebastian grabbed his bag and walked over to him. "Bon Jour," he said cheerfully.

"Follow me," the young man replied in English, sounding as if he would rather eat broken glass than speak to Sebastian. They got into a very plain-looking Citroen C4 Picasso and left the airport, headed toward the city. His 'chauffeur' said nothing for the entire journey. They pulled up in front of the American Embassy in France at just before ten in the morning. A U.S. Foreign Service Officer was standing on the sidewalk waiting for Sebastian's arrival.

It took two hours to process into the Embassy and receive the briefing on how he would be monitored for the next five years of his probation and military service. The Embassy personnel knew that once Sebastian was in Legion custody there was nowhere to run. When they finished, they exited the Embassy. Just outside, two French Foreign Legion soldiers dressed in fatigues waited for them, replacing the young man who had picked him up from the airport. Sebastian, the Foreign Service Officer, and the two soldiers got into a small military van and eased into the city traffic. Sebastian knew exactly where they were headed: Fort de Nogent.

Chapter 28

Stephanie found the professor's apartment building and was greeted warmly by the doorman. All of Dr. Fournier's keys had been left behind in his office at the University when the emergency team revived him and rushed him to the hospital. The doorman examined the note the professor had given her for admission into his suite.

"One moment, please, Ms. Boulanger," he said politely. "Let me get someone to show you to his apartment." Stephanie smiled and offered her thanks. Within moments, the Concierge appeared at her side and introduced himself.

"Welcome, Ms. Boulanger. My name is Claude, and I will be happy to escort you to Dr. Fournier's suite. He doesn't spend much time in residence, I'm afraid, as he is quite involved with his work at the University; and speaking engagements take him all over the world. Dr. Fournier has been gone some two weeks now." Stephanie followed him onto the elevator, and he selected the sixth floor from the control panel. They stepped off into a broad, expensively decorated hallway and proceeded to the professor's suite. Claude extended his hand to unlock the door, but it swung slightly open when he touched the doorknob. Startled, he stood back and gave Stephanie a curious look. "Has he given his keys to someone while he is away?" he asked.

"I'm sorry, I really don't know. I'm just here to pick up something for him," Stephanie replied.

"Well, then," he shrugged. "Let's take a look." He knocked twice, then gently swung the door open. "Oh, no!" he exclaimed, as his eyes fell upon the ransacked apartment. "What has happened here!"

Stephanie stepped closer so that she could see through the doorway. Alarm flooded her brain as she gazed upon the mess. Furniture was slashed and overturned, drawers ripped out and cabinets askew; their contents strewn about. A floor-to-ceiling bookcase that covered one entire wall was cleared; all the books tossed into a pile on the plushly carpeted floor. A beautiful executive cherry desk had been stripped of all drawers; and files littered the area around it.

Both Stephanie and Claude stood motionless; silent, neither

knowing quite what to do. They both jumped when the intercom panel mounted just inside the door blared to life with the voice of the doorman in the lobby. "Uh, excuse me. There is a courier at the desk with a package addressed to Dr. Fournier. May I send him on up?" he asked.

Snapping out of their daze, Claude gave Stephanie a questioning look. She hesitated a moment, then stammered, "Tell him I'm on my way down to get it, please."

As she turned and headed for the elevator, she heard Claude repeat her message into the intercom. "And tell management that I need to see someone in Suite 617 immediately," he added.

The courier was waiting when Stephanie stepped into the lobby. She accepted the package and dropped it into her satchel. After thanking the courier and the doorman, she stepped back out into the bright sunlight. She pulled her cell phone out of her bag and dialed the number the professor had given her. She was anxious to let him know she had it and was on her way to deliver it to him. She was debating whether to tell him about his pilfered apartment as the phone started ringing. Someone answered on the other end. It was a male voice, but she was sure it was not Dr. Fournier.

Chapter 29

Damir Tadic walked toward the hospital entrance with his team observing him through binoculars from a safe distance. He purchased a bouquet of flowers from an early morning street vender and walked purposefully through the automatic door; it was 7:24 a.m.

Inside, he approached the receptionist and greeted her with a smile. "Good morning," he said cheerfully. "I am trying to find my friend, Dr. Jean Pierre Fournier? I was just informed this morning that he had a heart attack last night." Damir did a masterful job of looking distraught at this news.

The receptionist clicked her computer keyboard and studied the screen. "He is in Cardiac Intensive Care, room 434," she said. "Visiting hours start at 7:30, but he has a surgical consult at 8:00, so you better hurry."

Damir thanked her, adding a charming wink. He stood silently, holding the flowers and watching the digital numbers marking the elevator's descent to lobby level. He pressed his elbow to his hip feeling the reassuring outline of the pistol in its pancake holster. When the doors slid open, he stepped in and punched the fourth floor button. *'It will be good seeing the professor once again,'* he chuckled to himself.

At 7:30 a.m., Slavo entered the staff entrance to the hospital directly behind an oncoming nurse. He thanked her for holding the door for him, and then cut quickly to a hallway opposite her direction of travel. He made his way to the Cardiac Care nurses' station.

"Good morning," he said, looking at his watch. The busy nurse glanced up at him and returned the greeting. "I have to do a quick consult with a patient this morning, and I completely forgot which room they told me. Haven't had my morning cup of coffee yet," he joked. "Can you tell me which room Fournier is in? First name is Jean?" The nurse clicked the computer mouse quickly.

"434, Doctor," she said and turned to a stack of folders on the counter behind her.

"Merci," Slavo said, as he walked briskly to the professor's room.

Chapter 30

Fort de Nogent is a recruiting station for the Legion located in the eastern part of Paris. At the moment, Nogent was a very busy place as all the potential recruits were given their first barrage of medical exams and other basic screening tests. The first thing Sebastian was required to do was surrender his passport. *'Well, I've given up my freedom before,'* Sebastian thought as he hesitantly handed it over. Sebastian and the others, when they were not being probed and prodded, scrubbed pots, washed floors, picked up trash, and did whatever other menial tasks the staff could think of to keep them all busy for the next three days. There was really no talk among the recruits. They mostly just kept their heads down and stayed focused on the task at hand.

A few had been disqualified for various reasons, mainly medical, but the majority would be proceeding to the next phase. At the end of the third day, all those remaining stepped up to sign their contract. It was only two pages in length, with the first devoted primarily to personal information. Page two was the binding agreement between the French government and the 'contractee.' The line that stuck out the most to Sebastian read, *'...the contractee has equally promised to serve in the ranks of the Foreign Legion everywhere that the government deems it necessary to send him...'* By day four, with a few less men in the bunch, they lined up to get on the bus that would take them where it would all begin in earnest: Aubagne.

Chapter 31

"Um…hello, my name is Stephanie Boulanger. I have a package that I picked up for Dr. Fournier and this was the number he told me to call." Stephanie was really thinking he had given her the wrong number.

There was a moment's pause on the other end of the line. "Where are you, Ms. Boulanger?" the voice finally asked.

"I'm just outside of the professor's apartment building," she replied.

"Listen to me very carefully," the man's voice spoke in French with just a hint of a foreign accent. "Place your back against the wall of the building nearest you."

"What do you…?" Stephanie began.

"Do this now, please, Ms. Boulanger," the voice insisted.

Stephanie stepped to the apartment building and leaned her back against it. "Ok, I am against the…"

The man cut her off again. "Now look around you. Examine everything you see. Do you notice anything out of the ordinary? Is there anyone who is also standing still that you can see? Anything that strikes you as unusual at all?"

Stephanie looked around, her heart began to beat a little faster, "No, everything looks normal, but what is this all about? I am too tired for games and…"

"Ms. Boulanger, I am afraid you may be in danger. I'm not sure why the professor implicated you in this, but you are involved now," he said, as if thinking out loud. "You must come to me, and we'll try to get this figured out."

Danger?! Stephanie's mind resounded. "What do you mean '*I'm in danger'?*" Stephanie demanded. "I just picked up a package for the professor, that's all. And what are you talking about, '*I'm involved now;*' involved in what?" Stephanie was getting terribly frightened. Maybe Dyann was setting her up. If so this was not a very funny joke.

"Ms. Boulanger, I'll explain. Get in a taxi and come to the Institute of Orthodox Theology. My name is Bishop Brenner; I'll be waiting for you."

With that the line went dead.

Chapter 32

The official headquarters of the French Foreign Legion is located in Aubagne, a small village approximately 15 kilometers east of Marseille in southern France. For the next three weeks, it would be the location of the most intrusive and rigorous physical and mental tests Sebastian could ever imagine. Contact with the outside world during this time was completely cut off. Much like prison, this was a total-control environment.

Things were made perfectly clear to Sebastian from the very beginning. When he stepped up to the table his first day and submitted his paperwork from Fort de Nogent, the Corporal-*chef* looked at him with disdain. "We heard about you," he said in French. "Keep your things with you, you'll be going straight back home soon." He scowled and threw Sebastian's paperwork for the next station on the floor.

Sebastian refused to take the bait. He knew a smart comeback would just make things worse. He simply reached down and retrieved the documents, moving without a word to the next table.

Another small percentage of the recruits was lost at Aubagne. Time passed quickly, however, and before he knew it, Sebastian was in line for the bus again. This time, the destination was Castelnaudary.

Located approximately 50 kilometers southeast of Toulouse, France, Castel is where the creation of a Legionnaire begins. Making some of the hardest and most professional soldiers in the world is serious business, and Castelnaudary has been up to the challenge for decades.

Sebastian was issued uniforms and equipment and was placed in a section of thirty men. He was assigned to his living quarters; a room shared with six others, including his *Caporal* whose duty it was to reside with the men as part of the training staff.

As they marched toward their quarters to stow their gear, the entrance door to an adjacent barracks was kicked open. In the doorway stood one of the most frightening men Sebastian had ever seen. Standing six feet four inches tall and filling almost the entire doorway, was a man with a hard, weathered face, and eyes that looked like slits in a piece of leather. He was wearing a uniform that appeared to have been painted on his body. The first thing Sebastian thought was that he looked like some kind of comic book hero.

The corporal ordered the men to halt and walked over to the soldier. The men's respect for the corporal went up dramatically for having the courage to simply stand before this guy who seemed to be extremely angry. His face did not appear to be designed to express any other emotion. Sebastian's corporal stood at rigid attention as the two men exchanged quiet words. The corporal was silently dismissed and walked briskly back to the group. The giant man in the background looked at the small band of frightened recruits like they would make a nice mid-morning snack.

"Caporal Prenom is the senior NCO for your unit," he said by way of explanation. "He consistently graduates the most highly motivated, top achieving Legionnaires in basic training," Sebastian's corporal announced. "You answer to me, and I answer to him. I can tell you he doesn't like the looks of this group already. Someone has stolen Caporal Prenom's pocketknife. It was given to him by his mother."

Those words spoken, the giant soldier turned to walk back inside the barracks. As he did, he swung his fist, attached to his tree-limb sized arm, and punched a hole through the wall beside the door. It took a minute to register. The man just punched a hole through an exterior wall of a building. Granted they were old wooden units probably built around the 1920's, but it was still impressive.

"Holy Shit!" someone voiced the thoughts of the entire group.

"Welcome to hell," another guy piped up.

"Satan was a Legionnaire?" a brave soul uttered, and everyone laughed.

"Shut your fucking mouths, you shit kicking bastards!" the corporal screamed. "If you decide to speak again without being specifically ordered to do so, I will personally beat you until I'm bored and then tell Caporal Prenom *you* stole his pocketknife. Now on your faces, scum buckets!"

As he walked among the men scattered in the 'push-up' position, he loudly declared, "You are nothing but another vertical pile of skin to be strategically placed for the collection of bullets for the good of France!" Mark my words you worthless bastards, you better start impressing me from this minute forward or pain and misery will be your constant companion here. Not only will you regret your decision to join my Legion, you will regret the day you drew your first breath.

Sebastian imagined they could be the most impressive unit in the history of the French Foreign Legion and pain and misery would still be as constant as their shadow for the next 15 weeks.

"DOWN! UP!" the corporal shouted. Doing push-ups with all their gear was not an easy task. Everything up to this point had been primarily administrative. It was amazing how quickly things could be placed in perspective.

Chapter 33

"Anesthesiology," Slavo announced curtly to the lone nurse at her station with a nod. "Fournier?"

"434," she replied promptly. "Chart's in the room."

"Thanks," Slavo said in stride. He smiled inwardly at this little trick of the trade. What got people into trouble working covert operations was trying too hard, providing too much information and not acting 'normal.' This is what drew suspicion. It was important to think how people normally interact. In a hospital, personnel didn't explain their jobs to each other or the purpose of visiting a patient any further than how it fit logically into the scheme of things. He'd played this perfectly, and now knocked softly before entering the professor's room.

He walked in to find a man standing on the far side of the bed, facing the door, holding a bouquet of flowers. Slavo approached the bed with his eyes locked on the man already there; there was something familiar about him.

Damir raised his eyes to see the doctor entering the room. He started to say how he was just visiting when the words caught in his throat. Instinct kicked in, and he went for his pistol. The 'doctor' also drew his side arm; in a fraction of an instant both men stood with weapons pointing at each other over the professor's bed.

Chapter 34

Step one in Legionnaire basic training is a place called 'The Farm.' For one-month recruits learn basic combat skills and begin the process of learning to work as a single unit. They train day and night, regardless of the weather. Sebastian soon discovered that time was precious here, and every minute of the recruit's life was accounted for. He knew he would have to get used to this pace. Little did he realize that this was just the warm up; real training had yet to begin.

Another aspect of Legion life that he would have to adjust to is singing. The Legion incorporates traditional songs into their combat regimen. Once a song is learned, it is incorporated with marching, providing its own unique cadence.

At the end of month one, the recruit must recite the Code of Honour flawlessly and complete a 50 kilometer march before he is awarded his kepi blanc, a white peaked hat that is recognized around the world. It is the symbol of a Legionnaire.

The pace continued relentlessly day in and day out. Along with marching, map reading, combat skills, and equipment maintenance, came weapons training and shooting qualification. Sebastian looked forward to this most of all. He felt very comfortable on the shooting range.

The Legion uses the FAMAS Assault Rifle. A versatile weapon, the FAMAS employs a delayed blowback firing system, and is designed to fire 5.56mm NATO rounds with a magazine capacity of 25 rounds. The FAMAS has been nicknamed "Le Clairon" (the bugle) by French soldiers. The training staff was quick to realize that Sebastian was a natural shooter, and they subtly worked with him on advanced shooting techniques any time they set foot on the range.

Sebastian had fully expected to be singled out and harassed by the training staff because they all knew his background. He had always heard that the French harbored a special hatred for Americans anyway. But he found that this was not the case at all. Typical to any military environment, the training staff displayed equal hatred to all recruits.

The training of Legionnaires is consistent with military training of raw recruits the world over; break the spirit of young men and rebuild them in the specific mold of a professional soldier. Unique to the Legion, however, is the fact that the recruit base is built from men of many different ethnicities, backgrounds, and cultures. Men take up arms on behalf of France from all over the world: Vietnam, Japan, Bosnia, Mongolia, Germany, the UK; they come from everywhere.

The Legion's ability to take these men and turn them into some of the most feared soldiers on the planet is a phenomenon that baffles military experts around the globe. In addition to this, there is literally no time to single anyone out. There is too much information to get through and too little time to do it. The process of basic training, however, is now nearly a science.

After completing basic training, Sebastian moved swiftly to his next block of training: medical corpsman school. He wasn't sure why he was selected for this specialty, but he embraced the training, eager to learn this important and ultimately marketable skill. He had one year to learn the equivalent of what takes four years to learn in America to become a registered nurse. By the time Sebastian finished this year of training, he felt comfortable performing all kinds of life-saving procedures, up to and including some emergency surgeries.

As he worked his way through corpsman school, he also concentrated on his physical fitness. Sebastian's goal was to become a commando, attending the extremely difficult parachute training school in Corsica. It usually took at least two years of service to even be eligible to apply for this training, so Sebastian was very surprised to be approached by his Sergeant shortly after graduating from corpsman school.

"The 2e REP is very short on combat medics," the Sergeant explained. "You have a chance for early entry if you so desire."

Sebastian could not agree quickly enough, and before he knew it, he was wheels up on a short flight to the Island.

The 2e REP – *2e Regiment Etranger de Parachutistes* (2nd Foreign Parachute Regiment) is located in Calvi on the island of Corsica. The island was beautiful, but Sebastian would never see it, except from the air. For the next four weeks, he would do everything on the run. He had to run to eat, run to use the bathroom, and run to his quarters when it was time to sleep. They learned about the science of parachuting, how to pack their chute, what to do in an emergency, and what to do once they hit the ground. They hooked up to a line in a fake fuselage and ran out of the simulated door. They jumped from 80-meter towers, and they hung for hours on end learning how to untangle themselves from a poor parachute release. It was one of the best times of Sebastian's life. He completed six jumps, including a night jump, and was awarded his wings.

After jump school, Sebastian was sent to small arms school, which seemed an obvious choice with his skills on the range. For two months, Sebastian learned about nearly every type of assault rifle used in modern combat. He was certified as an armorer with the FAMAS and with the military 9mm handgun. He was then subsequently certified as a range master and ran all ranges for his regiment.

Next he was assigned to a six-month language submersion school where he chose Russian as his primary language of study. Every school he attended seemed progressively more difficult, but Sebastian was eager to learn. He seemed to revel in the difficult and challenging military environment. He returned to Corsica only to receive orders to attend Commando training. Sebastian had been going nearly nine months non-stop after he received his jump wings. He would have had it no other way.

Chapter 35

Stephanie kept looking behind her as the cab seemed to move at an excruciatingly slow pace. She felt ridiculous. *'I've watched too many American movies,'* she thought to herself. *'I've no idea what's going on, but I'm going to get to this Bishop or Priest or whatever he is, give him this package, and get home to my bed!'* She was a bundle of nerves as she continued looking out the window. Shaking her head in disbelief, she wondered how doing a simple favor for someone could evolve into such a mess. She silently vowed never to let herself get talked into anything like this ever again.

The taxi driver stopped as near as he could to the Institute of Orthodox Theology. Stephanie got out and walked to the nearest building. The place was very quiet and peaceful, and everyone smiled at her as she walked by. She saw a man dressed in a religious looking robe and approached him.

"Hello. I'm looking for Bishop Brenner," she said.

The elderly gentleman she spoke to conducted himself with quiet sophistication. He had a look of peace about him that would lead one to believe he could see things that most of the rest of the world could not. For all of the questions anyone might have, this man seemed to have found the answers.

"I can take you to him," he answered pleasantly.

They walked to one of several church sanctuaries spread across the campus. As they entered, Stephanie saw a man kneeling alone near the front of the sanctuary. The kind old escort simply motioned to the man and turned to leave. Stephanie walked toward the man who was dressed in a long black robe similar to her escort. She felt as though she was awkwardly interrupting something that she couldn't possibly understand.

"Bishop Brenner?" she asked quietly.

The man rose and turned to her. He was much younger than she would have imagined. He had a neatly trimmed beard and kind brown eyes. He smiled warmly.

"You must be Ms. Boulanger," he said softly.

"Please, Stephanie is fine," she replied.

"I'm sorry I was not out front to meet you, but this is without question a time for prayer." He stepped around her and led her back up the aisle toward the back of the sanctuary.

"I don't know what any of this is about, Mr. Brenner, and I really don't want to know. I'm just doing a favor for the professor," she reiterated. "I am here to give you a package and be on my way."

The Bishop nodded and quickened their pace. "Stephanie, we need to find a safe place for this...item. Let's go to my office, please," the Bishop suggested. He grabbed the cross that hung around his neck, and she could see him mouthing a silent prayer.

Stephanie was tired and getting frustrated with this nonsense. She decided to go along with him as a courtesy, but resolved to throw the package on his desk and run out if she had to. She had completed her little task. It was time for her to go home, climb into her bed, and put this harrowing errand out of her mind.

They walked briskly down the beautiful hallways of the institute, the Bishop simply nodding to others as they passed. They came to a large, thick wooden door that looked ancient and heavy. The Bishop pulled a key like none she had ever seen from his robe. He took a quick glance back at the hallway they had just come down, then unlocked the door, and pushed it open.

Chapter 36

Slavo and Damir stood in silence staring at each other down the barrel of their pistols. Damir was fighting to look calm, but he knew his adversary all too well. Even though Damir had his own impressive military resume, Slavo was in another league all together. Finally, he spoke. "Slavo, the Savage," he greeted the man with his earned nickname. "If you're here, who's running Hell?"

"Like you, Damir, I am here on a mission. I am searching for souls to take back with me," Slavo sneered.

Both men spoke calmly and evenly, but inside they were making furious calculations on whether or not to pull the trigger. For Damir, killing this man would make him a national hero, but he would never make it out of France if he did. The artifact would be lost, or worse, end up in the hands of Slavo's people. It was far too risky to kill him here.

Slavo, on the other hand, needed answers. He could not let his progress be slowed by killing Damir and dealing with the aftermath. The hospital had all kinds of cameras that would no doubt record his identity, and he would be recognized if they were examined as a result of a homicide investigation. The airport, trains, cabs, everything would be squeezed, and his ability to maneuver would be greatly compromised.

They both ran through the options and realized killing each other, although incredibly tempting, did not make operational sense. The professor blinked awake and saw two men above his bed pointing guns at each other.

"Where is the document, Professor?" Damir demanded.

Slavo realized, in this one question, that everything remained in play. The document is what they came for, and if Damir did not have it, this was anyone's game. Dr. Founier's heart rate monitor began to signal an alarm, and the men quickly re-holstered. The professor's breath became labored as the sudden shock of the two men hovering over him, one of whom he'd seen before, overwhelmed him. The nurses burst into the room in seconds.

In the commotion, Slavo grabbed the cell phone beside the professor's bed and slipped it into his pocket. The act didn't go unnoticed by Damir. "He's having a relapse!" Slavo told the nurses as they rushed to the professor's bedside to begin emergency procedures. "I'll notify cardiology," he said in an official tone. He slipped out of the room and headed for the elevator. He saw two other nurses approaching the room with the crash cart, always at the ready, for cardiac emergencies. It would be hours, if ever, before the hospital figured out that the doctor in the room was not a doctor at all.

Damir put on his own acting job. "Is he going to be ok, nurse?" he asked anxiously.

"Sir, you are going to have to leave right now," the nurse directed him sternly.

"Yes, yes, of course. God, please tell me he is going to be ok."

"Now, sir," the nurse insisted.

Damir slipped out of the room and dumped the bouquet in the nearest trash bin.

Slavo flipped open the professor's cell phone and quickly navigated to 'recent calls.' He stopped in his tracks as he looked at the first number and correlating name on the display. "You've got to be kidding me," Slavo said out loud.

Damir grabbed his cell phone as soon as he burst through the door marked 'stairs.' He descended the steps two at a time, giving orders as he went. "Get in the car, and get out of the garage right now!" he barked into the phone. He knew his men were acting on his order even as he continued speaking. "And find me the cell number for Dr. Fournier. Pull the records, and give me the calls he made over the last 12 hours. We have company, and if you don't get me this information in the next few minutes, then plan on reporting to your regiment from here, because we are going back to war!"

Chapter 37

Commando training would push Sebastian's physical and mental faculties to their absolute limit, and beyond. Day one started ominously when the giant Caporal Prenom walked in.

"I am your primary instructor for Commando training," he growled. The class seemed to give a collective gulp. "I will teach you how to kill anything with a pulse, survive on thin air, and walk behind enemy lines as though you are invisible." He took a couple steps closer to the class and everyone leaned back without even realizing it. "And if any of you slack bastards try to cut corners or are caught cheating during any section of this course, I will crush not only your skull but any hope you ever had of seeing the outside world. No one shits in my house. Understood?"

"Yes, Sir!" the men screamed in unison.

About two weeks into Commando training, Sebastian began to feel very comfortable with his skills as a soldier. The harder they were pushed, the more he realized he liked it. He was consistently at the front of the pack in every physical training session, and he had shown clear and quick thinking in most of their stressful combat scenarios.

There was never time to really get to know your fellow soldiers because of the relentless regimen. One evening, however, an opportunity presented itself for conversation. They were all sitting around the barracks cleaning weapons before 'lights out'.

"So why did you sign up?" Sebastian casually asked the guy sitting on his footlocker to his right.

The soldier glanced up at him and quickly back down to the assembly of his rifle. "I like to fight," he responded with a heavy Italian accent.

"Hmm," Sebastian thought a minute. "So where you from?"

"Switzerland."

"Really? I thought you guys were neutral."

The dark-skinned man with Italian features stood. "That is why I am in France as a member of the Foreign Legion."

Sebastian smiled at the guy's comeback as he smoothly re-attached the firing mechanism to his rifle. He had just finished assembling his own weapon when a member of the training cadre entered the barracks. The room snapped to attention. "Bishop, Caprani, front and center," the corporal yelled. Sebastian and the Swiss guy he had been speaking to ran to the instructor and stood side-by-side at ridged attention. "Follow me," he said and led the men from the barracks.

In moments the two young soldiers found themselves before the desk of Caporal Prenom. He spoke while looking down at some papers in front of him. "The Russians have extended an invitation for a couple of our guys to attend their SPETSNAZ training in the spring. Do either of you two dumb asses speak Russian?" Prenom asked, knowing the answer.

"Yes, Sir!" Sebastian yelled.

Caprani looked at Sebastian out of the corner of his eye with disdain. "No, Sir," he replied quietly.

"Well get ready to learn, you Italian prick." Caprani HATED being called Italian. He was Swiss through and through; only his native tongue was Italian. "We have two more weeks of school here and then you will be sent to total submersion language school immediately after graduation. Bishop, you are now Caprani's personal tutor. This will be in *addition* to your regular duties, so don't think you're getting a free ticket to leisure town. Your PT sessions will also double, and you'll get some additional range time. You have six months to be ready. I'll be supervising your progress. Now get out of my office, you talking chimps."

That was Caporal Prenom's way of congratulating them for being selected from a group of stiff competition for elite specialized training.

"What the hell was that all about?" Sebastian asked Caprani.

"This training comes around about every other year from what I understand. Russians give a chance for a couple of us to train with them; they send a couple over here in the off years. Pretty cool arrangement really. We must be doing something right; just about every Legionnaire I've ever talked to wants to go through SPETSNAZ. It's like finishing school for the toughest soldiers in Special Forces. Few get invited, even fewer make it through."

Sebastian looked at Caprani in disbelief.

"No shit," Caprani said, reading Sebastian's thoughts. "By the way, my name is Davide Caprani." He extended his hand.

Sebastian shook his hand. "Sebastian Bishop," he replied absently.

"Well grab your knickers, Sebastian Bishop, we're about to swim with the sharks."

"I'm American, not British, Swiss Miss." Now it was Davide's turn to look in disbelief.

"No shit," Sebastian said matter-of-factly.

They walked in silence back to the barracks. Davide was trying to figure out what in the hell an American was doing in a place like this. Sebastian was still trying to figure out what in the world SPETSNAZ was.

Chapter 38

On October 6, 1908, Austria annexed Bosnia and Herzegovina into its growing commonwealth. Two days later, a large group of men met for a meeting at city hall in Belgrade. The topic: how to stop the Austro-Hungarian Empire from completely devouring the Southern Slavic populations of the Balkans. This meeting, attended by men from very diverse walks of life, gave birth to the semi-secret society known as *Narodna Odbrana* (National Defense).

Their goal was to recruit and train supporters of the cause for war against Austria. The group worked tirelessly, and their nationalistic ideology spread like wildfire. *Narodna Odbrana* caused so much resistance and national unity that Austria raised its mighty hand against the government in Belgrade. The Bear, Russia, was not ready to back the banty rooster, Serbia, so the anti-Austrian insurrection was put on simmer.

Even so, Serbia remained a powder keg ready to blow. Many members of the now impotent *Narodna Obdrana* boiled with rage at an Austria that continued to suck the life from their people. On May 9, 1911, ten men met and formed a new group, *Ujedinjenje Ili Smrt* (Union or Death) also known as the Black Hand.

The Black Hand began terrorist actions against the Austrians. The Serbian government was well aware of the activities and intentions of the Black Hand and supported them both financially and ideologically.

The world underestimated the fortitude and drive of the Serbs embodied in the relentless determination of the Black Hand. On June 28, 1914, seven Slavic assassins set their sights on Austrian Arch Duke Franz Ferdinand as he visited Bosnia-Herzegovina. Franz and his pregnant wife, Sophie, were killed in the attack. The fallout would result in the First World War and hundreds of thousands of casualties the world over.

Svetozar Dimitrijevic sat in the waiting area outside the office of the Minister of Economy and Regional Development in Belgrade. He sighed as he reflected on the past. His grandfather, Dragutin, known more readily as Apis, was one of the founding fathers of the Black Hand, and its first real leader. He was executed by firing squad for his role in Franz Ferdinand's assassination.

Svetozar proudly assumed the post bequeathed by his father as helmsman of the Black Hand. He hoped his father and grandfather would be proud that he had stayed the course through all the uncertainty. Undoubtedly, the debacle of the Milosivic years nearly brought Serbia to her knees, but they weathered the storm.

Svetozar was beginning to doubt he would live to see the kingdom of Serbia rise again; but if this artifact was indeed what was claimed, the Serbs would believe again in their heritage. They needed a strong leader to march them into the new era. Svetozar couldn't help but smile; it was all coming together, and their new leader was right behind that office door.

Chapter 39

Davide and Sebastian were quickly becoming friends. They had been paired for all remaining exercises in the Commando course in order to learn to work as a team. It was helpful that they actually liked each other.

Davide Caprani was from the Ticino region of Switzerland in the town of Ligornetto, a small village close to Lugano, situated near the border with Italy. Davide's father was Italian and his mother Spanish. The result of their union was a son with fire in his veins and a restless spirit. Davide was slightly taller than Sebastian with nearly an identical build. He had movie star good looks and a great sense of humor. Together they quickly distanced themselves from the rest of the soldiers.

Near the end of the fourth week of Commando school, Davide and Sebastian came walking back in the camp after a long day of orienteering, immediate action drills, and ambush training. These last few days were spent tying together all the skills they had learned over the course of the training. The routine had been much the same for three days. They marched about five kilometers to a 'hostile' area, regrouped at a small bivouac site, and transitioned to operational status. This meant using camouflage, hand signs, and tactical weapons work to locate and engage the 'target.' They worked in teams of two, four, six, and eight. Targets were situated in the area everywhere. The instructors activated them, and they would flip up from several different angles. The soldiers had to learn to engage targets tactically, preserving ammunition and not shoot each other. Accuracy went a long way, and no one could come close to Davide and Sebastian.

As soon as they approached the camp, they could tell something was wrong. Caporal Prenom walked quickly toward them. "Give me your gear and get to the chow hall and eat. When you're finished, shower and hit the rack, you'll need rest. I'll catch up to you in a minute for a full briefing." The Caporal was talking to them differently. He wasn't talking down to them for the first time ever. He was all business. Something serious was happening.

The chow hall was unusually quiet. With ninety men in training, there was a rotation system in place in case the soldiers were needed for action. Sebastian's thirty-man section was on alert and a second section of thirty was placed on immediate standby. The third section was in reserve and helped with everyone's gear and transport issues.

As the men sat eating quickly and quietly, the chow hall door snapped open. In walked a very solemn Caporal Prenom. "Listen up!" he shouted from the front of the room. "French regulars are in trouble in the Ivory Coast. Intelligence shows a significant force of African rebels mobilizing in Liberia and moving east toward the border. If they come across, a small airfield lightly defended by regulars will be directly in their path. We need to get there before they do. We'll be jumping in on this one. Finish your chow and get your head down. We move out in three hours." With that, he left exactly as he had entered.

Now the room was really quiet. Sebastian and Davide exchanged glances and went back to eating.

The soldiers got cleaned up and bunked in their racks. There was no talking, and no one was about to sleep. Sebastian could hear someone's watch ticking. He tried to concentrate on the sound. It became like a metronome, and he used the rhythm to calm his nerves and focus on what was about to happen.

In no time, the door to the barracks opened. Caporal Prenom stepped in and said calmly, "Ok, gentlemen. It's time to fight." Prenom was a professional soldier in every way. He had been in several battles and was hardened in a way that these young soldiers could not yet relate to. He was acutely aware of what it took to make men fight. He knew when to yell and he knew when to be calm. These Legionnaires would follow him anywhere, a fact that he would never abuse or take advantage of.

The soldiers poured out of their racks and went outside. All their gear and equipment lay perfectly arranged on the ground in front of them. They went to their packs and the reserve soldiers helped them get situated. Even though they trusted the riggers who packed their chutes completely, the soldiers re-examined their parachute rigs intimately; it was simply protocol. Satisfied with their gear, a total of sixty men walked to two military buses and loaded up.

They drove to the airport where they climbed aboard a C-130 transport plane and taxied for take-off. Sebastian tried to relax. The noise inside the fuselage was deafening, so they had all been given ear protection. In the muffled drone of the engines, Sebastian's mind drifted, thinking of home, his family, and his life up to this minute. Four years ago, he would never have imagined he would be sitting on a military aircraft, an airborne commando for a foreign country, preparing to fly to Africa to possibly fight an unknown enemy. *'Life is strange,'* he thought. And with that he was finally able to fall asleep.

Chapter 40

Slavo gave little thought to his Croatian adversary, Damir Tadic. Damir was a coward, more self-absorbed than concerned for his people. Slavo would kill him soon enough, of that he felt sure. His real focus was on the name he discovered on the professor's phone. He still couldn't believe Fournier's contact was Brenner. He scoffed and shook his head. '*Brenner was the name we gave him; what gall he must have,*' Slavo thought to himself. This was getting ridiculous; he would have to protect the Bishop's identity as best he could. Slavo remained lost in thought as he and his men now sped through the city toward the Institute of Orthodox Theology.

Damir Tadic and his men sped away from the hospital not even knowing where they were going yet. His Bosnian comrade was typing furiously on his laptop and talking at the same time on his Bluetooth phone attached to his ear.

Damir had worked for the *Hrvatska Izvjestajna Sluzba* (Croatian Intelligence Service) for 12 years, garnering a comfortable position from his tenure of five years in Army intelligence. In fact, even now, his colleague was on the phone with *Obvestajna Sluzba Hrvatske Vojsk* (OSHV), the intelligence wing of the Croatian military. In the world of ever advancing technology, the OSHV could hold its own.

The Bosnian handed the laptop forward from the backseat to Damir. He scrolled quickly through the information on the screen. "The Institute of Orthodox Theology," Damir directed the driver. "Let's move; they have the jump on us."

Chapter 41

The plane landed with a thud, and Sebastian jerked awake. They were in Morocco for re-fueling and a mission update. The men filed off the plane and straight into a briefing room that had been prepared for them. In front of the room was a large grid map giving a topographical view of their destination. A Legion Sergeant walked in and began talking before he was even at the front of the room. "Things have changed already while you were in the air," he began. "The rebels have accelerated their advance toward the border. We have no idea why they are launching what appears to be an offensive. The airfield situated here," he pointed to the map, "is right where they are headed. This is a relatively insignificant airfield. We can only surmise that the capture of this airfield is to facilitate bringing more troops and supplies in for a full-scale invasion. The regulars on the ground are not well supplied or armed so you are the element that will hold the line and secure the runway."

There was a pause in the briefing. The Sergeant turned his complete attention to the men sitting before him. "Do not be surprised if you are jumping into a fire fight, gentlemen." He turned back to the map. "The enemy force is estimated at three to five hundred men. We have one hundred twenty regular troops on the ground. You will make the total number nearly two hundred. Make no mistake; if this goes to guns, you will be in a shit storm. This is a low altitude jump; you'll be jumping in at 750 meters." *'No time to pull the reserve if anything goes wrong,'* Sebastian thought. "Hit them with everything you've got. Good luck, gentlemen." With nothing more to say, the Sergeant left the room.

Caporal Prenom stood up. "Fifteen minutes from the drop zone, you will lock and load all weapons on my signal. Every other man will be equipped with night vision goggles. We will secure the perimeter of the airfield until the regulars establish air control and fly in their reinforcements. Let's move out." Sebastian remembered the promise he had made to himself on the plane when he first landed in France; he would not give up, and he would not fail. This was the ultimate test of his resolve.

The men filed out and walked back across the tarmac to the plane. Sebastian looked around as best he could, but there wasn't much to see. '*So this is Morocco,*' Sebastian thought. With the longest leg of the flight yet to come, they would be in the combat zone by sunset. They would fly straight to the drop zone and jump.

"I've always wanted to visit Africa," Davide said, thinking aloud.

"Probably not much to see at night through a hail of bullets," Sebastian replied.

They walked for a minute in silence, "How come nobody rides Zebras?" Davide asked in his typical 'off-the-wall' fashion.

"What?" Sebastian asked, not quite getting the question. "Zebras; they are just different colored horses. Why hasn't anybody put a saddle on them and used them for transportation? Really, nearly everyone in Africa could have one for how many are out there in the wild."

Sebastian scratched his head, always amazed at how his pal could come up with this stuff at the weirdest times. "I think people have tried throughout history, but it just never caught on. The animal is not wired for domestication." He wiped the sweat from his brow. "I guess they have a spirit that just can't be broken," Sebastian concluded.

Davide thought on this as they approached the loading ramp of the huge military transport plane. "A spirit that can't be broken; I like that," Davide said with a thoughtful grin.

Davide stopped before they boarded the plane and turned to Sebastian. "Back to back," he said.

"Back to back," Sebastian replied. They clasped hands for just a moment and then turned to climb on board.

Chapter 42

Four men stepped out of the rental car and walked across the campus. They entered the administration building and looked at the faculty listing board.

Slavo ran his finger down the listings until he found 'Brenner.' Brenner was the last name of a missionary from Belgium killed in Kosovo during the war. He was well liked by both sides, or so he'd heard. They stole his information and used it in the relocation of the new 'Brenner.' His real name was Nikolin, and Slavo knew him well.

Slavo stepped inside the administrative office. "Excuse me, I'm sorry for the interruption, can you tell me where I can find Bishop Brenner?" he asked in perfect French.

Another faculty member walked in as Slavo asked his question and replied, "I saw him walking toward his office with a young woman." He stepped to the campus map hanging on the office wall and pointed. "His office is situated right here."

"Thank you very much," Slavo replied graciously.

He returned to his men, and the pleasantness fell from his face, unveiling the same expression that was the last thing ever seen by so many men.

The Bishop began to pace the length of his office back and forth. The room looked like a small library, designed for prayer and meditation. There were old books lining shelves that went from floor to ceiling. The room was not very big, but it felt safe, almost protected. Stephanie was sure this was why the Bishop chose to bring her here.

"Dr. Fournier didn't think this all the way through I'm afraid," the Bishop said, thinking out loud. "I can't believe he actually found it." The Bishop continued pacing, wringing his hands.

"Found what?" Stephanie asked. "Why do you think I'm in danger?" she insisted.

The Bishop turned suddenly to her. "Did the professor mention anything to you about an artifact?" he asked. Stephanie recalled the professor trying feebly to explain things to her, but she thought it was all gibberish from the medication.

"No. He mumbled incoherently through the night. Bits and pieces, something about Serbia; but nothing that made any sense. Then early this morning he awoke at about 3 a.m., seeming quite lucid, and asked me to pick up the package and call this number; *your* number.

The Bishop took a deep breath, "I believe an explanation is in order, Ms. Boulanger." The Bishop offered Stephanie a chair, and she sat down impatiently. She was anxious to hear this explanation.

"My name is not really Brenner. My name is Nikolin. I am Serbian. I began my ministry at the monastery in Gracanica, Kosovo. That is where I was born and raised. I spent more time at the monastery than at my home, so to me, I was called into service from as far back as I can remember. I have dedicated my life to God and to the service of the church." The Bishop spoke as if he was conducting his own funeral, delivering a brief summary of his time here on earth.

He quickly turned back to the relevance of his story. "Dr. Fournier is an expert on the Balkans and knows far more about my land than I do. On one of his trips to Kosovo, we met and became friends. He was there researching an extraordinary theory regarding an ancient document that he claimed was essentially a real estate contract or boundary settlement if you will, endorsed by the Vatican. At one time, the Vatican represented absolute and irrefutable law.

"Wait a minute, wait a minute," Stephanie interjected. "So my life is in jeopardy because I'm carrying some real estate deal made with the Pope?"

The Bishop was totally flustered; this was too much to try to explain quickly. "Did you know that Serbia was once ruled by Kings?" he asked simply.

"No. I know nothing of Serbia. I'm not even sure where it is," she replied.

He knew that he didn't have time to explain the history behind this bizarre situation. He couldn't figure out why the professor had involved an innocent nurse in this volatile state of affairs. Had things become so desperate?

"Ms. Boulanger, were you followed here today?" the Bishop

queried.

"No. I mean I don't think so. My neck is stiff from looking behind me the whole trip. I didn't see anything out of the ordinary." Stephanie was starting to feel afraid, and she wasn't even sure why. None of this made any sense to her. Thinking it best to just leave the mysterious package with the Bishop and head for home, she reached into her satchel to get it.

"Listen, Bishop Brenner. I have been up all night, I am trying to get home, and you are frightening me with your behavior. Now, if you'll excuse me, I really must be going." There was a rattle of the doorknob. Stephanie and the Bishop both froze. "What's going on?" Stephanie's heart began to race.

The Bishop bowed his head as if accepting some kind of predetermined fate. He moved quickly to a heavy wool rug covering a portion of the marble tiled floor. He shoved it aside, revealing a trap door with an iron ring attached to it. The Bishop pulled hard on the ring. Stones grated together, reluctantly releasing their grip on the ancient concealed door. Below was stone stairs that led down into darkness. The Bishop looked forlorn.

"Ms. Boulanger, I am so sorry you were unwittingly drawn into this. You hold all the answers in your hand. I'm sorry there is no time to explain. This passageway will buy you some time." There was the sound of scraping as the men outside worked quickly to pick the door's lock. "You are now in grave danger. You must quickly make your escape."

Stephanie was completely dumbfounded. She tried to think and opened her mouth to speak, but nothing came out. Things were happening too fast.

The Bishop took Stephanie's hand, urging her to the stairway in the floor. "You must get that package to safety," he said with urgency. Terrified, and realizing she had no other options, she descended the stairs. "Godspeed, my child," he said reassuringly as she looked up at him for the last time. Stephanie could hear distinct clicking as the tumblers were being successfully manipulated in the office door. "Now run!" he instructed frantically as he dropped the door closed.

Chapter 43

The sun had just set when the stand-by light came on in the aircraft. Thirty minutes earlier they had all secured their packs and double-checked their parachute rigs. Caporal Prenom stood and gave the signal. All the men inserted a full magazine into their weapons and snapped back the charging lever. They were now battle ready. Ten minutes out, all the men stood and hooked the release strap for their parachutes to the cable that ran the length of the fuselage. Once they jumped, the strap would automatically release their parachute, allowing it to inflate when the soldier had safely cleared the aircraft. Sebastian was second in line to jump, followed by Davide. Caporal Prenom would be the first out the door.

As they approached the drop zone, Sebastian strained to look out the open door. When he was finally able to catch a glimpse down toward the ground, he couldn't believe what he was seeing. The ground looked like some kind of laser light show. Tracer rounds zig-zagged furiously back and forth across the landscape. Sebastian's heart began to race. This was it; they were jumping into full-scale battle.

"Thirty seconds!" Prenom yelled, holding up the corresponding hand signal. No one could hear him, of course, over the roar of the engine and the rushing air from the open door, but everyone knew it was time. Silent prayers went up in a number of languages as Prenom turned to the open door, waiting for the red jump light to turn green.

Sebastian clenched his teeth and tightened his grip on the release strap. Each man had to slide the strap along the cable to the doorway before jumping. Once outside of the aircraft, everything became unpredictable. Sebastian's mind ran through his parachute procedures, landing drills, and what he would do once he hit the ground. The light turned green. No turning back.

Prenom jumped, and Sebastian was right on his heels. In less than ten seconds, everything went from deafening noise to virtual silence, as the parachute inflated and Sebastian began to drift toward the earth. It was a phenomenon that never ceased to amaze him.

He looked down to the ground and watched as the intense firefight raged on. He could now hear the gunfire and was starting to get perspective on the battlefield. The main battle was at the south end of the runway. French regulars were fully engaged and had dedicated all their resources to this area, leaving the long runway stretching behind them unguarded.

Parachuting at night is dangerous business. You never know exactly when you're going to hit the ground, so your body remains tense, anticipating the impact. Sebastian landed well and rolled just as he had been taught. He spun around to his back as his chute began to drag him a little. He realized that he was being dragged across small pieces of gravel. He quickly gained control of his parachute and stomped it flat. He hit the release to separate him from his parachute rig and swung his weapon around to the ready. He dropped to a knee to take a moment to get oriented to his surroundings. In a fraction of a second, he realized he had landed on top of a building with a long flat roof.

"Son of a bitch!" Sebastian heard someone say with a thick Italian accent. He ran toward where the voice had come from, and in the half-moon light, saw a parachute tangled around one of the ventilation chimneys on the roof. Hanging over the side of the building, still attached to his chute, was a very angry Davide.

"Nice landing," Sebastian whispered, looking over the side.

"Pull me up, dammit," Davide hissed, squirming like a worm on a hook.

Sebastian planted his feet against the edge of the roof and pulled hand over hand. Davide was finally able to turn toward the building and climbed his parachute cord to the top.

Once on the roof, and after a very long string of Italian and French profanities, Davide took a knee next to Sebastian. Sebastian was pulling out the night vision goggles from his pack. He turned them on and held them up in an attempt to survey the battle. He needed to see exactly where they fit into it.

"Most of our airborne guys are assembling around that hangar in the middle of the airstrip," he said, pointing. "It's about 300 meters from us. I suggest we get down from here and head to them."

Sebastian was about to put the goggles away, but thought he should make a quick scan of the whole area. As he looked to the far right, toward the northern end of the runway, he thought he saw something move in the trees framing the airport. He refocused the goggles, concentrating on the tree line.

"Take a look," Sebastian said, handing the goggles to Davide. "They're flanking us. Looks like fifty to seventy-five men." Sebastian thought quickly, knowing that their immediate action was the only way to save their fellow soldiers' lives. "Find Prenom and the two heavy machine gunners we brought. Get them to turn and lay down as much fire as they can," he instructed Davide. I'm going to try to identify and take out the ranking officers leading the charge. Hopefully, that will confuse them and slow them down a little."

"I'm on it," Davide responded, taking off at a full run toward the roof's access ladder. Sebastian's FAMAS was not equipped with a scope and he knew the advancing troops were at the very edge of the accuracy range of his weapon. He needed to make a decision.

"Hey!" Sebastian heard Davide shout from beneath him. He quickly looked over the edge. "Seve broke his leg when he landed. It's bad, medics dragged him behind cover and are working on him. Come down here and get his gear." With that Davide ran back into the darkness at full speed.

Seve was the unit sniper. He carried an FR-F1 sniper rifle that Sebastian was very familiar with. He practically slid down the ladder, grabbed the weapon and extra ammunition, and scurried back up. Now it was a different ballgame.

The FR-F1 is a sniper rifle of French design regularly carried by the military. It has a ten round magazine capacity and fires 7.5x54mm cartridges. The rifle is bolt action with an effective accuracy range between 600 and 800 meters. This particular rifle had been outfitted with a night vision scope.

Sebastian got back into position and settled the weapon on top of the one-meter wall surrounding the rooftop. He concentrated on slowing his breathing and began to look for targets through the scope. He saw the men slowly advancing through the tree line. They were being cautious not to draw attention to themselves. They wanted to capitalize on total surprise. Sebastian identified an apparent leader walking in front of the rest of the soldiers. He settled the crosshairs on the man's head and squeezed the trigger.

The rifle bucked and sounded like a cannon to Sebastian's ears. The advancing soldiers stopped in their tracks staring in disbelief at their now headless leader. Sebastian quickly acquired another target and squeezed off another accurate round. The soldiers began to panic, not knowing whether to advance or retreat. Sebastian began to drop enemy troops as fast as he could activate the bolt. Dropping the first magazine, he took a moment to look through the scope toward the Legionnaires on the battlefield, hoping that someone else was about to join his fight. He saw Davide and Prenom running with two heavy machine gun teams toward a strategic firing position. Sebastian slammed the next magazine home and scanned for more targets. The African troops were now completely disorganized and running around chaotically in the woods. Some were returning sporadic fire in his direction, mostly hitting the building below his position. Sebastian squeezed another round. All of a sudden, the two Legion machine guns opened up in full symphony. They left absolute carnage in their wake.

Sebastian finally drew a long breath. He surveyed the battlefield again through the scope and knew it was time to move. He slung the sniper rifle over his shoulder and grabbed his FAMAS as he headed to the ladder. Once on the ground, he ran to the back portion of the frontline. He grabbed ten Legionnaires and told them to come with him. Sebastian knew they needed to secure the far end of this runway. They all headed away from the new frontline to reinforce exhausted French regulars on the south end. Two battlefronts had formed on either end of the runway. Sebastian knew they were lucky with the first wave and didn't have the manpower to handle another flanking maneuver.

They were joined as they ran by Davide and ten more Legionnaires. Davide and Sebastian integrated their men with the stragglers from the regular battalion. Opposite of Prenom engaging the enemy on the north end, Sebastian's group fanned out, setting up a defensive perimeter as best they could. Sebastian was troubled by the gap in between his small band of men and the force fully engaged at the other end. He put his night vision goggles back on and scanned the terrain in front of him. The advance had ceased and he could see the rebels retreating through the trees. He turned to look at the other battle line; he could now see Prenom directing men to fill the gap along the length of the runway. They were all starting to get organized and would soon have a decent perimeter around the runway. Fifteen more men ran down and joined Sebastian's group. Once they were situated, Sebastian moved over to Davide. "Let's go back and help the Caporal," he said.

Davide jumped up and the two of them ran back to offer assistance. Sebastian put the night vision goggles back on as they ran. Prenom was about two hundred and fifty meters away from them, facing the tree line where they fought back the flanking rebels. Sebastian quickly surveyed the tree line again as they ran. To his horror, he saw a group of about ten rebels who had apparently regrouped. In the confusion, they must have crawled through the darkness parallel to the airstrip. They would soon be behind Caporal Prenom and the other Legionnaires holding the line. Legion soldiers were still trying to get situated into a functioning defensive position, and there was still too much space between the men. Sebastian saw the rebels taking positions; stomachs on the ground, bringing their weapons forward to begin acquiring new targets.

"West side!" Sebastian yelled to Davide. "On the ground! Watch my tracers and put lead on target!" The two Legionnaires broke out in a full run; Davide going on Sebastian's direction. They closed the distance quickly. The rebels were just about ready to engage. Sebastian and Davide yelled as they approached to draw attention to themselves. The rebels turned and both soldiers opened up on fully automatic. Prenom instantaneously realized what was happening and turned, engaging the advancing enemy full on. The rebels returned fire, and Sebastian heard several rounds fly past his head like angry supersonic bees. The Legionnaires along that side of the runway now also returned fire.

Sebastian saw Prenom go down and ran straight to him in a crouch. Davide was right behind him and took a knee beside the two men.

Facing the dark field where the crawling enemy had been silenced, he acted as lookout while Sebastion administered aid to Prenom.

"I'm fine," Prenom said. "I just caught a ricochet in the calf." Sebastian pulled out his trauma pack and quickly began wrapping Prenom's leg. "Give me that," he said. "I can wrap my own damn leg; finish setting the perimeter!"

Sebastian and Davide ran from position to position, checking for wounded and redistributing ammunition. The French regulars were getting organized as well during what appeared to be a cessation of fire. Sebastian and Davide grabbed all available Legionnaires and situated them strategically until the entire runway was secure. All of the soldiers hunkered down for the rest of the night. There were bursts of jittery fire throughout the night, but it looked as if the rebel force had, in fact, retreated.

Chapter 44

Just before dawn, they heard the drone of approaching engines. Three large transport airplanes came in, one right after the other. Reinforcements had arrived. The men cheered as the planes taxied to a stop, and the relief soldiers began to file out. An hour later, a full mechanized division with armored vehicles arrived and reinforced the perimeter. They had prevailed, but it had come at a price.

In the light of day, the battlefield came into sharp and horrible focus for its participants. Sebastian and Davide helped load injured and dead soldiers, enemy and friendly alike, onto the transport planes. By lunchtime, Sebastian and Davide were finally able to sit down for a break. They went back up on the rooftop where they initially landed the night before.

"So what do you think of Africa?" Sebastian asked.

"It's a beautiful country," Davide replied as they looked out at the savannah. "The fighting was just a bonus."

No one really likes to fight, Sebastian knew. He also knew that Davide had been just as scared as he was, and his talk was just euphoric bravado in the 'thank-God-I'm-alive' afterglow of terrifying warfare. They both sat quietly, lost in their own thoughts.

Sebastian knew that they fought well last night, and they did their job professionally. They had been baptized by fire, and he knew that the Regiment would now look upon them differently. He felt different.

By early afternoon, it was time to go. Modern warfare was a strange business. Helicopter gunships now zoomed overhead like angry hornets protecting their nest. Amazingly, the uninjured Legionnaires, now forty-four in total, were loaded on a bus from the battlefield and driven to a nearby commercial airport. The traffic at the now fortified airstrip was reserved for supply and fighter aircraft and medical transport. '*What a weird way to leave,*' Sebastian thought. They had entered so dramatically, been engaged in a fierce battle, and now they were loaded on a nice bus as if they were part of an African tour group.

Prenom was at the airport waiting for them when they arrived. "All military aircraft has been reassigned to help in the area. The French government chartered a commercial aircraft for our return," Prenom said flatly.

Sebastian settled into his quiet, comfortable coach seat and looked out the window as the aircraft gained altitude. '*Did all that really happen?*' he asked himself. Soon they would be back in France. Sebastian reflected on his training, his first combat jump, and the battle. He realized two things: first, he had stopped the advance of a potentially devastating flanking element, and second, he and Davide had done what they set out to do for the majority of the battle—fight back to back. Sebastian now knew that becoming a professional soldier was absolutely the right thing to do.

Chapter 45

The doorknob to the Bishop's office turned with the final click of the lock pick. The door swung open slowly and dramatically, and in the doorway was Slavo in all his controlled rage.

"Knock, knock," he said sarcastically.

Now that Stephanie had escaped, the Bishop no longer seemed afraid. He had been afraid for her; not for himself.

"So, Nikolin, it has been a long time," Slavo said, now speaking in Serbian. "Where is the girl?"

"She is no longer here. She knows nothing. I was afraid you might think otherwise, so I sent her away," the Bishop replied.

"Yes, I'm not a very trusting person, unfortunately," Slavo said airily while walking around the study, looking at various books and religious icons. "And even though you are a man of God and it is against you're very nature to tell a lie, I have to err on the side of caution."

"She's just a nurse. She was simply delivering a message to me from Professor Fournier." The Bishop knew he needed to negotiate quickly or Stephanie would be dead by nightfall.

"What was the message?" Slavo asked with mock innocence.

"Exactly what you already know; that he found the artifact." The Bishop and Slavo were delicately dancing with information now. The Bishop didn't even know if Fournier had found the artifact, he was simply using deductive reasoning.

There was a pause as Slavo rubbed his chin and looked up at nothing in particular. "I am growing impatient, Nikolin." The muscles in Slavo's cheek flexed repeatedly as he fought back his anger. "No need for the girl to come in person for that message. I will give you one last chance to tell me who this woman is, and what she knows. Does she have the artifact? Is she working with Tadic? Are you in on this whole treasonous plot, you cowardly worm?" Slavo was nearing his breaking point, stepping closer to the Bishop with each question.

Nikolin tried to think quickly, *'Tadic? Damir? The Croatian? What does he have to do with this?'* his mind raced furiously. "Well, Tadic always was smarter than you," Nikolin finally replied.

Slavo struck the Bishop with an open hand on the side of the head. Nikolin's ear rang, and the pain radiated all the way down his jaw.

Slavo quickly grabbed Nikolin's head in his hands, bringing their faces close. The Bishop saw for just a moment a look of remorse from Slavo for striking him. He leaned in close to Nikolin, and spoke with sincerity, "We allowed you to leave Gracanica five years ago, Nikolin. We helped you with your visa, your identity, with getting on staff in this place." He motioned around him, "And this is how you repay us? You help our enemies steal our heritage and then try to hide behind the robe of God?" Slavo stopped, and took a deep breath, releasing the Bishop from his grasp. "You were spared for the sake of our mother, nothing else." The men of Slavo's team all snapped their heads toward their leader, trying to be sure they heard correctly.

"We are no longer at war, Slavo, no matter what you and Father think," Nikolin replied flatly. "We have no enemies. And the ones we did have were of our own creation. I have walked through the valley of the shadow of death, and the evil I found there was you." Nikolin no longer even recognized the monster his older brother had become. How dare he try to take credit for his relocation to France. How dare he act as though it was his blessing that made his life possible. "Men may fear you, but I fear only God. It is for people like you that Serbia suffers."

Without warning, Slavo slammed into the Bishop with his forearm, knocking him over the desk and onto the floor on the other side. Slavo cursed loudly in Serbian as his brother's words stung, and his anger again flared.

Slavo stood in the middle of the room for a moment as if frozen in that spot. He took a deep breath, regaining his composure. He decided to change the subject before he did something truly regrettable.

"We did not see the woman leave. There is only the exit where we entered the building at the end of the hall." Slavo surveyed the room inquisitively. "How did she get out of this room?"

The Bishop stood, struggling to catch his breath. He walked to the end of one of the bookcases and depressed a hidden lever. He then pushed the bookcase open like an oversized door. Behind it was a well kept and often used passageway. "It leads back to the main sanctuary," the Bishop explained. "All paths lead to God."

Slavo looked less than impressed. "I think it is time for you to return to Kosovo, Nikolin. Your path to God is making an unscheduled detour back to hell."

Damir Tadic and his crew pulled up to the Institute of Orthodox Theology. Damir and one of the Albanians jumped out. Before heading for the campus office, Damir spoke back through the opened door to the Bosnian before closing it. "Run a trace on the last number the Bishop received on his phone. Find out who it belongs to, and try to get a current location on that phone," he instructed.

They jogged to the office and walked in. Damir checked his watch. "Good Morning," he greeted the receptionist cheerfully, "I'm looking for Bishop Brenner please?"

"He's a very busy man today," the receptionist replied. "He usually doesn't see this many visitors in one day."

"Really?" Damir said innocently. "Perhaps it was my colleagues. We scheduled a meeting with the Bishop to talk about donations and needs of the Institute."

The receptionist reacted ever so slightly to the mention of donations. The Institute, like any other academic institution, needed as much funding as they could find. "Oh, is the nurse part of your group, too? She seemed a bit anxious."

Damir tried to roll with this new information, "Yes, she is an integral member of this committee. Her input is invaluable to our efforts." The Albanian standing beside him showed no reaction; a real pro.

"Well, the other gentlemen arrived about twenty minutes ago, your nurse about fifteen minutes before that I would say. I'm sure they are awaiting your arrival." The receptionist pulled a small campus map from behind the counter for reference. "You are here, and you'll need to walk to this building here, and his office is down the left corridor, the third door on the right. His name is on the door."

"Thank you so much for your help," Damir smiled warmly, "Au

revoir et salut."

The men ran to the office and found it empty. They ran back toward the waiting car, Damir on his phone the whole way. "A female, yes, I know." Damir listened a moment, "What do you mean the signal just ends?" he asked impatiently. "That's the name it comes back to? Ok, give me everything you can on this Stephanie Boulanger person. We're back where we started." Damir snapped his phone shut muttering curses in Croatian.

Chapter 46

Stephanie was surrounded by darkness. Complete darkness. She was breathing fast, gripped by fear. Everything was totally out of control, and she still had no idea what was going on. Whatever it was, she wanted no part of it. There was nothing to do but follow the passage to wherever it led.

With her satchel draped across her chest, she held her hands out to the side and felt the cold stone outlining the narrow passageway. She had no light, so she proceeded by taking one cautious step after the other forward. She then remembered her cell phone, extracted it from her satchel, and opened it. There was no signal, of course, due to her depth underground, but the small LCD screen emitted some light. She could now see a few feet ahead of her.

The passageway was only inches wider than her body. She couldn't believe how narrow it was. It continued before her into darkness, and with her new light source, she was able to pick up her pace. She walked through intricately woven cobwebs by the dozens. There was a moist, green fungus under her feet that stained her white hospital shoes. The air seemed to thicken the further she walked. This hidden route had obviously not been used in quite some time. So far, there was no movement behind her. She forged forward, just wanting to get out of this nightmare, call the police, and never make another delivery for the rest of her life.

Chapter 47

Bishop Nikolin Petrovic sat between two thugs in the back of the rental car. Slavo turned from the front seat and spoke, "Give me your cell phone."

Reluctantly, he handed the phone to his older brother, remembering when Slavo was just a happy kid running the streets of Gracanica with their friends and cousins. Now he was something so very different. Hatred had consumed him; he worked tirelessly to share his misery with others, drawing them into his own private purgatory. His father was to blame, fueled by his own hatred that peaked when war claimed the life of their mother. He groomed Slavo in the art of malevolence and warfare.

Nikolin looked out the window and began to think about Kosovo. For centuries Kosovo had represented the "Holy Land" for the Serbs. Nikolin loved his life there, especially at the monastery. And then things went horribly wrong; Milosevic spun out of control, NATO came in and pummeled the province, and finally the Albanians brought a new reign of terror to the land he loved.

Nikolin did not hate the Albanians, who now made up the majority population of Kosovo, but he did hate what they had done to dozens of monasteries and religious sites throughout the land. They destroyed completely and without mercy. Many of the churches demolished dated back to the 14th century and were of inestimable spiritual value to the Serbian people. Most of the churches also contained some of the most beautiful Byzantine frescoes the world had ever seen.

He knew he would be returning to a world that he had long since mentally left behind. The Serbian people still left in Kosovo were depressed and, in many ways, oppressed in their new post-war lives. As a servant of God, he knew that the people needed him, but he was comfortable and productive in his new life in France. The words of Job rang in his head: *'Naked came I out of my mother's womb, and naked shall I return thither; the Lord giveth and the Lord taketh away.'* He felt ashamed for feeling sorry for himself. He prayed for forgiveness of his sins and those of his captors and surrendered himself to God's path for him now.

Chapter 48

Upon their return from the battle, the troops, including Sebastian and Davide, went in for full debrief. The battle was broken down and all the statistical data disseminated as appropriate to the fighting men. Sebastian knew there was much more to the story, but he also knew that grunts were spoon fed information, as the officers would say, for their own good.

After the meeting, Sebastian was pulled aside by the senior executive officer. "Don't think we underestimate the significance of what you did out there," he said. And with that, he walked off, saying no more. Sebastian smiled as the officer walked away, and then hurried to catch up with Davide and the guys.

The men had some down time to recuperate from their experience. They all went to the small recreation facility on base to shoot pool and watch television.

"Hey, turn this up!" one of the soldiers yelled. The TV was tuned to CNN, and they were talking about the Ivory Coast.

"...French forces attacked a small group of African freedom fighters in the Ivory Coast near the border of Liberia yesterday. Many Liberian soldiers were killed, adding to the tension in this volatile area. In other news..."

'Boos' and 'hisses' went up from all over the room. Someone threw a shower shoe at the TV.

"Unbelievable," Sebastian said to Davide.

"I'm surprised they got the continent right," Davide responded, leaning over the pool table for his next shot.

Because of their selection for specialized training, Sebastian and Davide didn't return to their respective units. Instead, they were stationed near main headquarters for language school. Additionally, they were assigned to help with the new recruit classes coming through.

Their days were now divided between six hours of submersion language instruction and six hours of running PT sessions and basic combat training with new recruits. Sebastian's Russian was getting very good, and Davide worked hard to get command of the language. They tried to talk in Russian as much as possible and even found a new recruit from Belarus who helped them with harder pronunciations.

Four times a week, Prenom ran them through a PT session of his own design that was absolutely brutal. Three times a week, they were on the shooting range for the entire second half of their day running weapon drills until they could practically do them in their sleep. Their marksmanship was now measured in millimeters at ridiculous distances. They were allowed only a half-day of rest on Sundays. This pace continued relentlessly for six months.

By the third month, all their instructions and communication had to be in Russian. It was exceedingly difficult. Although Sebastian had a head start with his earlier language training, he was still finding it difficult to think in Russian. They learned all Russian small arms weapon systems and were given an introductory course in their small unit tactics. By now, Sebastian clearly understood what SPETSNAZ was; Russian Special Forces training. In fact, the name itself meant 'Troops of Special Purpose (Spetsialnove Nazranie). They were heading to this training as if they were Russian soldiers. They would be treated the same and be expected to perform on the same level. This nine-month course would be conducted in Balashikha, Russia.

Chapter 49

Stephanie walked for what seemed like ages. Finally, she came to a set of stairs leading up. As she ascended, she could tell that this doorway did not come out through the floor but rather opened like a regular door; at least she hoped it would. She tried to wipe the cobwebs from her face. She spat the webbing from her lips. It felt like sticky hair. She stood on a small landing facing what looked like a wall. She searched the wall for some kind of handle or release lever. She leaned close to the wall searching its surface, finding nothing that looked or felt like a latch. And then, as if on cue, her cell phone went dead.

Again, panic seized Stephanie. She desperately began running her hands all over the flat surface in front of her. '*There has to be something here,*' she rationalized. She pressed herself close to the wall, stretching as high as she could reach, thinking maybe the latch was above her. As she moved to the far right, her foot hit something at the base of the door. She stopped and tapped around with her foot. There was something there. Slowly she lifted her foot and lowered it onto the small object at her feet. It moved slightly. She stepped down harder on it a second time. There was a loud 'click' as the door catch was released. With a deep sigh of relief, she pushed against the door with all her strength. Welcome light flooded the darkness.

Chapter 50

By the time Davide and Sebastian stood in line for the flight to Moscow, Sebastian had been a Legionnaire for just over two years. He had combat experience, advanced combat skills, and had recently been promoted to *Légionnaire première classe.* He had adapted very well to his new life and looked forward to the adventures yet to come.

An attractive woman with her small daughter was in line behind Sebastian and Davide. The little girl was complaining because she had to use the restroom. The woman told her daughter in Russian, "Sweetheart we can use the toilet on the plane. It will just be a few more minutes."

Davide looked at Sebastian and smiled. He turned to the woman, "Excuse me, ma'am, there is a restroom right over there. We will hold your place in line if you'd like to take your daughter."

The woman smiled warmly at Davide, "Thank you, sir." Sebastian was sure he saw her eyelids flutter.

They hurried off toward the restroom, and Davide turned back to Sebastian. "It's amazing what you can do when you're properly motivated," he said with a grin, referring to his still struggling language skills.

"Six months of language training, and you use it to pick up women. You're really something. She's probably married to an ex-KGB commander or something. Someone's going to kill you in your sleep," Sebastian said.

"She's probably a Russian movie star looking for some strong soldier-type to have and to hold. And remarkably, I'm available," Davide replied dreamily.

"Are you crazy?" Sebastian asked.

"Just optimistic, brother. You're always looking at things from the wrong angle. Sometimes life works out just as you'd hoped."

The woman returned and thanked Davide again. They began talking, and Sebastian noticed there was no ring on her finger. Davide turned and winked subtly at Sebastian. Sebastian just shook his head and stepped forward in line.

Chapter 51

In 1163AD, during the reign of Louis VII, construction began on Notre Dame de Paris, one of the largest and most recognized churches in the world. The church has seen the ebb and flow of history from a unique perspective. Soldiers from the crusades knelt in her sanctuary before heading to battle. She was pillaged during the French revolution with everything stolen and melted down, except for her great bells. Napoleon had crowned himself emperor in her majestic halls, and General Charles de Gaulle raced to her altar to give thanks for the liberation of France during World War II. Yet through all the times of war and peace, the epic Cathedral survived.

There is a large plaza in front of the church that, until the mid-1960s, was the site of several buildings dating back to the Middle Ages. The structures were in various stages of disrepair and blocked the view of Notre Dame in all its glory. A decision was made to tear the buildings down. When the site was razed, however, artifacts and remnants of ancient Gallo-Roman life were discovered.

These amazing finds attracted the interest of experts, so an official excavation of the area was launched in 1965 by the *'Direction des Antiquîtes de l'Ile de France.'* In conjunction with this effort, a museum, The Archaeological Crypt of the Parvis of Notre Dame, was constructed by the city of Paris to house these treasures. Built entirely underground, it is the largest structure of this type in the world.

It is in this museum, which is open to the public, that Arval Tristam worked his tradecraft. At eighty-three years of age, Arval was in remarkably good health. Age had not withered his body or his mind. He moved effortlessly and wore glasses only for his work. His sharp blue eyes and full head of silver hair gave him a very distinguished appearance.

Arval had taught medieval history at one of the secondary schools in Paris for forty years. Retired now for nearly nineteen years, Arval devoted himself to his passion: medieval calligraphy. For centuries, the only way to record history or to copy documents of any type, including scriptures, law, and music, was entirely by hand. Medieval calligraphy is an art of the rarest form and is, indeed, practically extinct.

Visitors to the museum could watch Arval work from behind thick plexiglas as he copied and expertly translated several texts onto vellum paper. The church actually used his work as a small source of revenue by selling some of it in the gift shop. In return, twice a week, he was allowed into the inner sanctum of Notre Dame, directly below the main sanctuary. He worked in a tiny library where he had access to literature that was the exclusive property of the church. He studied the writings and emulated the original text of these precious documents. To Arval, this was the highest privilege he could imagine, and he often lost all track of time as his mind drifted over 800 years into the past.

It was at his worktable in this ancient place, under the protective soft glow of the examination light, that the strangest thing happened.

Chapter 52

The plane landed in Moscow, Russia, in a misty rain, feeding the stereotypical view of the ex-Soviet Union as a dismal and depressing place. Davide and Sebastian walked into the main terminal to retrieve their luggage. It took a long time for the conveyor belt at the baggage claim to move, but it finally jerked to life. Fifteen minutes later, they stood, bags in hand, looking for their ride. There was no one that appeared to be looking for them.

"This is not good," Sebastian finally said, breaking the silence as they scoured faces and signs, looking for their contact.

"I knew I should have gotten that girl's number," Davide replied. "At least I would have had a place to stay tonight."

"Yeah, thanks for looking out for me, pal. I'll remember that," Sebastian said.

They stood around for about an hour, getting more anxious with each passing minute.

"Ok, why don't we walk around a bit," Sebastian suggested. "Maybe we're in the wrong place."

"Yeah, *'we'll meet you at the baggage claim'* leaves a lot of room for interpretation," Davide replied sarcastically.

"Well you got any other ideas? Or are you just going to stand there and sass like a little girl?"

"Take it easy, cupcake. I'm just saying we're in Russia. I'm not sure 'wandering around' is such a good idea."

As the two of them bickered with each other, a smartly dressed uniformed soldier approached.

"Legionnaires?" He asked.

"Da," Sebastian replied.

"There has been a transportation problem. You will have to stay in Moscow tonight. There is a room waiting for you at the Izmailovo Gamma-Delta Hotel. Be ready at 0700 tomorrow." His instructions complete, the soldier turned on his heels and marched off.

"…But how do we?…Excuse me…" Sebastian tried to ask, but in

moments, the soldier was gone.

"Nice," Davide said, as they stood holding their bags with the whir of the baggage claim behind them.

The two legionnaires began walking toward the airport exit. "You got any money on you?" Sebastian asked Davide.

"I have about 20 Euro, I guess," Davide replied.

"I have forty, I think," Sebastian said. "We need to find a money exchange and catch a cab."

Just before the exit, they were able to find a small window with Cyrillic writing above it that said 'currency exchange.' Forty Euro got them about 1,360 Rubles. They held the other 20 Euros in reserve in case they needed it later. They walked out of the airport, and jumped in one of the many cabs waiting out front.

"Izmailovo Hotel, please," Sebatian said.

The cab sped off. It was about 3:30 in the afternoon and the weather had cleared up. The two soldiers peered out the windows of the taxi like a couple of tourists. The driver pulled up in front of the hotel like a racecar in for a pit stop. Sebastian handed him the fare while Davide grabbed the bags from the trunk. They had heard of cab drivers pulling off with your luggage after getting paid, so they made sure this was a coordinated effort.

Bags in hand, the two young men entered the hotel. Davide whistled, looking around, "This is a lot nicer than I imagined."

Sebastian was momentarily lost in thought. He turned to Davide, "You don't think this is all a set up do you? You remember how our first days in the Legion were? We ate well, everyone was relatively nice, and then we got to basic training and it was our worst nightmare?"

Davide's shoulders slumped, "You're kinda depressing to be around, you know that?"

Sebastian shrugged, "I just think we better enjoy tonight, because something tells me a storm is brewing." He headed to the counter to check in.

The room had two full-size beds and a clean bathroom. They couldn't have asked for more. Sebastian and Davide dropped their bags and headed out. They were only three minutes away from the tube station, Izmailovski Park. They boarded the subway and were in downtown Moscow in less than 15 minutes. They had an exciting evening, taking in as much of the city as possible in less than eight hours. They made it back to their room just after midnight and both fell fast asleep.

Chapter 53

Peering over his reading glasses, Arval Tristam turned from his calligraphy table and saw a disheveled young woman in a nurse's uniform suddenly appear from the wall of his small study.

"Bon jour," he quietly greeted. Silence hung in the air as the woman stepped hesitantly forward in obvious distress. She began to sob, large tears streaking her dirty face. Arval quickly laid his calligraphy pen down and rose from his chair. He walked over to the woman and patted her gently on the back, "There, there, my dear, are you ok, are you injured?" The woman shook her head. Arval took her by the arm and led her to a soft leather chair near his table. She sat down and tried to regain some composure.

"Thank you, sir. My name is Stephanie Boulanger," she said, suppressing a sniffle, "and I've had a very bad morning." With that, she began to weep again.

"It's ok, Stephanie," Arval said reassuringly as he offered her his handkerchief. "My name is Arval Tristam, and I will help you in any way I can." He tried to grab a few of the floating cobwebs from Stephanie's hair as she cried.

She looked up with red eyes and began wiping her tears away. Drawing a shaky breath she asked, "Could you please tell me where I am?"

"Of course," Arval answered, wondering how in the world she got here in the first place. "You are in the lower level of Notre Dame de Paris."

Stephanie looked at him in disbelief, "Are you saying…you mean just above us is…" Her lips quivered as everything just became too much for her. "I can't believe what has happened to me this morning. It is so bizarre it must be just a bad dream. I don't know what to do.

Arval smiled warmly. "Perhaps you would permit me to help you?"

"I can't do that," Stephanie replied. "It's probably just paranoia on my part, so I won't involve anyone else in this foolishness."

"My dear Stephanie," Arval said, taking her hand in his. "I am already involved. I have known about that passage for a very long time. But, until you stepped through it just now, I had nearly forgotten about it. I know where it leads. Therefore, I believe it was providence that brought you here to me. I am, therefore, obligated to lend my assistance."

Stephanie thought for a moment. It would be so easy to relinquish the package, and all the trouble associated with it, to the kind old gentleman. But Stephanie could not, in good conscience, do it. She needed to go somewhere and think the whole situation through.

"Mr. Tristam...," Stephanie began.

"Please, call me Arval," he insisted.

"Arval, please just show me to the street and let me have a few minutes to collect my thoughts. Perhaps a cup of coffee would help me clear some of these cobwebs away," she joked as she swept her hand through a few straggling webs still clinging to her hair.

Arval looked at Stephanie in her dirty uniform and green-stained shoes. She looked bewildered and tired. "Of course, Stephanie," he smiled warmly. "But, please, dear, take my card," he said, handing her his business card with his contact information printed in beautiful calligraphy. "If you are in trouble, call me, and I will help you. Whatever it is, please don't deal with it alone."

Stephanie smiled, kissed Arval softly on the cheek, and followed him from the depths of the cathedral to the street above.

Chapter 54

At exactly 7:00 a.m., a van pulled up in front of the Izmailovo Hotel. It looked as if it were held together with twine, but Sebastian and Davide climbed in without question. Their driver was a young Russian soldier. He had a hard look about him and was not the least bit sociable. The three men rode in silence as the van extricated itself from the grip of the big city. Once they hit open road, there was very little to look at. Mile after mile looked exactly the same; barren and desolate.

Sebastian used the time riding in this jalopy to reflect on his life to this point. He hadn't thought about prison once since he left America; his mind working hard to block out that period of his life. He realized he had very little input in the decisions thus far in his life. The only personal decision he had made about his life was entering the Legion.

Others controlled his professional life and direction. He had entered the Legion hoping to learn a marketable skill like computers or communications. Instead he had been selected to become a professional soldier, specializing in clandestine combat. He was not angry or bitter about this path; he simply wondered what kind of life lay ahead when his military obligation ended. What skills would he actually have to carry on after this?

His thoughts were interrupted as the van pulled off the highway onto a side road, hitting potholes so severe that Sebastian thought he would be bounced into the seat behind him. Davide swore as his head banged off the window he was looking out of. After a few minutes on this washboard, the van rumbled to a stop outside the gates of what was apparently a military base, but looked more like a concentration camp. Two guards with AK-47s approached the van on either side. These soldiers also looked weathered and much older than they probably were. They spoke in fast Russian to the driver, using a lot of slang. Sebastian could just make out a derogatory remark made by the driver about his passengers. The guards shared a companionable laugh as they looked at Sebastian and Davide with disdain. One of them gave a nod to another soldier who opened the gates. They entered the camp, and the driver pulled in front of a building that looked like every other building and stopped.

"Get out," the driver said without looking back at them. Sebastian and Davide got out with their bags and stood in the brisk morning air. The driver just drove away without saying another word.

"This is going to be fun," Davide said sarcastically under his breath. The door to the building they were in front of burst open. A robust and very jovial soldier bounded out. "Legionnaires?" he yelled.

"Da," Sebastian and Davide said in unison.

"Welcome comrades!" the hefty Russian soldier yelled again, rushing toward them like a charging bull. The two Legionnaires didn't know whether to run or get ready to fight. The soldier grabbed Davide and kissed him soundly on both cheeks, turned quickly to Sebastian and welcomed him in the same way. This guy could not have been any more polar opposite than their driver or the guards outside the gate. He was warm and welcoming with a permanent grin on his face.

"Come," he motioned inside the building he had just come from. "We are very happy you are here. It is always a pleasure to have Legionnaires in our training. How is my friend, Prenom?"

"He took some shrapnel in Africa a while back, but otherwise he's doing fine," Sebastian replied a little puzzled.

"He and I fought side-by-side not long ago." The Russian's mind seemed to drift for a moment to a battlefield that didn't mean much to most, but meant everything to a few. "He is a very good soldier and an even better friend." The smile seemed to fade for a moment from his face as he reflected on things in his past. It then returned full force as he yelled, "Forgive me!" Both Sebastian and Davide jumped. "My name is Ivan Antonovich. I will be your liaison officer, so to speak. I will be monitoring your progress. It is my job to make sure you make it through this training alive." Sebastian noted that this was said much more like a statement of fact than a humorous remark.

Ivan led them into one of the buildings and showed them their bunk as they walked through this skeleton barracks. They had one footlocker to share for stowing all their gear. Ivan went on for a while about the great Russian military, emphasizing their rich history and bravery on countless battlegrounds. He spoke solemnly about Stalingrad, commenting that only the Russians could produce such an impenetrable wall of resistance and fight with such ferocity. It was all actually quite fascinating, and Sebastian appreciated the slow, deliberate Russian Ivan used to speak with them. He was able to understand almost every word.

Suddenly, Ivan became very serious, his introductory speech was now over. He put his arms around Sebastian and Davide and pulled them close in a huddle. He spoke much quieter now and in a manner that demanded the two soldiers' absolute attention. "Gentlemen," he began, "I must tell you that the training you are about to undergo is some of the toughest and most severe in the world. I assure you, you will immerge on the other side of these nine months different men. Stay the course, endure the trials, and know that eventually it will all be over. And the next time we meet, we will be brothers." Sebastian realized that although these words were few, they were powerful, and probably the most important they would receive in this endeavor.

"Ok!" Ivan yelled, releasing them and nearly breaking their eardrums. "Meet in front of the barracks for your first formation at 0930hrs. Goodbye, my friends, and good luck." And with that, Ivan Antonovich disappeared out the front door.

Sebastian and Davide stood alone in the center of the barracks. It was very quiet now. "I had a job once repairing copiers," Davide said, breaking the silence.

"Really? Well, that seems completely relevant to our present situation," Sebastian replied dryly as he leaned his bag against the wall near their rack.

"It was an amazing job," Davide continued, as if Sebastian had said nothing, "every week I entered office buildings full of beautiful women and turned a few screws. I would average at least two phone numbers a day. I had dates every weekend for ten months straight." He grabbed the pillow off the top bunk and shook it. A roach fell off and scurried across the floor. "And now here I am at the Russian Roach Hotel, facing a Soviet-style ass-whipping while sleeping in a room full of scurvy men for nine freaking months. My career advisor must have been smoking crack."

"Your mom was your career advisor, man."

"Hey, don't talk bad about my mother, dude."

"I have complete respect for your mother, buddy. I'm just saying you were an undisciplined hoodlum on the fast track to 'Nowheresville,' and your mother told you to join the military and make something of yourself. When you realized the Swiss Army hadn't fought in a war since 1291 you decided to go where you had a chance to fight. You already spoke French, so the Legion was the obvious choice. So now buck up, dude, and make your mama proud." Sebastian stretched out on his bunk.

"And to think I was going to have you write my biography," Davide said with mock appall. They both chuckled.

The two Legionnaires sat around for 60 anxious minutes. At 0925hrs they walked out of the barracks and stood for formation. By 0935hrs, they remained the only two soldiers present.

Chapter 55

Slavo's team pulled up to the *Hospital Pitie-Salpetriere* and found a place to park.

"Why are we here?" Nikolin inquired with growing anxiety.

"The professor has caused us enough trouble. He has outlived his usefulness. Belgrade wants his knowledge to accompany him to his grave. I am afraid his medical condition is about to become terminal," Slavo said evenly.

"NO!" Nikolin shouted, lunging forward from the backseat. The two thugs responded in a flash, jerking the Bishop back in place.

Stephanie stopped in a mobile phone shop and bought a charger for her phone. She then went to a little café to drink a cup of coffee, and gather her thoughts. She found an outlet near her table and asked the manager if she could charge her phone for a minute. He nodded reluctantly and went back to his morning routine. It was only after the man's disapproving appraisal that she realized how she must look. She was too tired to be embarrassed and went back to her coffee.

She needed to think clearly and try to figure out the next logical move. It seemed the best thing to do would be to call Dr. Fournier in his room and explain everything that had happened. She would take the package back to him and be done with it once and for all. He could call the police or do whatever he felt was necessary. Then she would go home, go to bed, and try to forget any of this ever happened. Satisfied with her plan, she finished her coffee and turned her phone on to place the call.

Slavo looked back at his baby brother as if he were a stranger, "Serbia is for Serbians, brother. We cannot have a foreigner laying claim to one of our greatest artifacts of national identity." The other thugs were nodding in agreement. "These are things a traitor like you just can't understand. Your friend, the professor, will go to his grave for his crime against our country." With that, Slavo turned back in his seat, preparing to get out. The Bishop grabbed the cross around his neck and prayed with newfound intensity.

Slavo's Information Technology (IT) man was tapping furiously on his keyboard, "WAIT!" he exclaimed, "don't go yet. Her cell phone is back on line."

"Find her," Slavo ordered, and turned his attention to his little brother. "Well, the professor gets a small reprieve. Our priority now is to get the girl. I think you'd better start praying for her!" He grinned evilly and gave his brother a wink. Nikolin felt like he was going to be sick.

"I have a signal!" the Bosnian exclaimed from the back seat.

"Where is she?" Damir asked as the driver slowed for directions.

"Stand by one, OHSV is activating the GPS and jamming all outgoing on her cell phone. We should have a location in three minutes."

Chapter 56

By 0950hrs, the two Legionnaires began to get a little nervous. "You think we could find a taxi on that super highway out there?" Davide nodded back toward the cow path they jostled in on.

"We are where they told us to be, and we were right on time, so let's just be patient and see what happens," Sebastian replied.

It was chilly standing there, but it was very quiet as well. Sebastian pointed his face to the sun and closed his eyes. His mind flashed back to his childhood. Autumn in South Carolina with his father chasing him around the yard, threatening to throw him in the pile of leaves they had just raked up together. He remembered his excitement, his energy, and his innocence when he thought life couldn't be better. He remembered how he roared with laughter when his father caught him and they tumbled to the ground, wrestling playfully. And finally, how he laid his head on his dad's chest with his face pointed to the sun and drifted to sleep at the steady rhythm of his father's breathing.

The quiet was broken with the sound of engines in the distance. Slowly they approached and stopped, rumbling loudly just outside the gate.

"And so it begins," Sebastian said under his breath.

The gates swung open, and in came two large troop-carrying trucks the U.S. military refers to as 'deuce-and-a-halfs.' Inside the back of each truck were twelve soldiers. They pulled to a stop almost directly in front of Sebastian and Davide. The men, including the drivers, lumbered out and made a loose formation where the two Legionnaires stood.

Sebastian noticed immediately why they were late. Some of them had blood on their uniforms, and he saw the dark residue of gun powder on the end of their weapons indicating they had recently been fired; a lot.

"These guys just came from a fight," Sebastian whispered to Davide.

"I've got eyes, maybe they're just faking us out," Davide replied. Then his eyes got big as the driver of the second truck got out with a blood-soaked rag tied around his left bicep.

"I don't think so, Sebastian murmured.

As the men stood there, a door opened on another building across the way. Two men in uniform approached. One stood about 5'7" tall and was obviously the ranking officer. Beside him walked a tall, thick officer who was the junior of the two, but looked very intimidating. He stood to the side of the formation, perfectly straight at parade rest as the shorter man walked slowly in front of the group. The commanding officer spoke very clear, proper Russian and, within only a moment of hearing him speak, it was easy to see that this was an intelligent, experienced warrior.

"Good morning, gentlemen," he began, surveying the group. "I am Polkovnik (Colonel) Ivan Lazerev, and I will oversee your training here for the next nine months. For those of you who just arrived, medics will be on hand to address your various injuries. If you are unfit to continue, you will be returned immediately to your respective unit."

This was obviously no place for pity, or mercy. There was a pause as the commander continued to pace, looking thoughtfully at the ground. "Most of you are veterans of some type of combat. You have seen violence and administered violence in return." He stopped now and looked directly at the group. "But be advised, your training here will be unlike anything you have ever experienced, and I assure you there will be times when you will wish you were back ducking bullets instead of being here. At least there, death would more than likely be relatively quick. If you survive this training, you will be tools of warfare. You will remain expendable assets to your respective governments; however, you will possess the skills to carry out missions that few people on earth could even comprehend, let alone undertake. Our job is not only to make you skilled, but to make you hard. You will view death, your own and others, much differently. You will understand fear and limitation more clearly than you ever imagined. We will take you far beyond what you feel is possible and rational. If you succeed, you will walk through life with the knowledge that, all things being equal, you alone could change the course of a battle, and together you could turn the tide of a war."

Sebastian let his eyes rove subtlety over the others, and he could see the effect this man's words were having on the group. He swallowed hard, hoping he could keep up with these men. Most of them looked like they killed there way here.

The commander paced back and forth as he continued, "The most important thing you will learn here is perspective. If you understand what you are capable of and know why your skills are necessary and where they should be employed, then you are a *real* special operator. Although we will train you to successfully operate as an individual that is absolutely the last option. If you demonstrate at any time that you cannot function as part of a team, we will get rid of you. We are in the business of making warriors, and it is a hard business. Make no mistake, we are in charge here, and we know what it takes to become a professional soldier."

The commander now stood in front of the group, his hard weathered face seemed to show one single moment of empathy for what these men were about to go through. He then delivered his closing thoughts. "Brace yourself for pain, because there will be a lot of it. Forget about sleep, because there will be very little of it. And prepare for physical training, because there will be no end to it." Sebastian began to have some serious doubts about being here. His heart was beating fast at the prospect of failure. It was the first time he had ever considered it. Things were about to get worse.

"Allow me to introduce your senior instructor in this training." He motioned with his hand to the tall soldier who had walked forward to join him. The man immediately snapped to attention as all eyes focused on him. There was something about him that frightened Sebastian and probably most of the other soldiers. This man was more intimidating than Prenom, and Sebastian never imagined he would meet an individual that filled that description. "This is Vladimir Rodchenko. His rank is not important as long as you all realize that besides me, he is the most senior officer on this compound. As of this moment, I relinquish operational command of this training to him." The commander took one last long look at the group. "Good luck, gentlemen." With that, he turned on his heels and strode back to his office.

Rodchenko looked at the group with cold, unfeeling eyes. Some of the soldiers shifted their weight uncomfortably under his gaze.

"Gentlemen," he said calmly, with pause for effect, "it's time to fight."

With that, a whole team of instructors burst out from surrounding buildings where they had been waiting. The instructors were yelling at the tops of their lungs. They rushed forward, surrounding the group, stopping suddenly just short of the formation. Composure left the soldiers as they fought panic, wondering what to do.

Chapter 57

For two solid minutes, chaos and confusion reigned. The instructors ran around the small formation of soldiers, pushing them from behind, shouting profanities at them. Then, as suddenly as it began, the instructors fell silent, and the lead instructor spoke, the timing and coordination of all this was like a well rehearsed and long performed play.

"The men behind you are my training staff and your instructors for the next nine months. These men have killed more people than the plague. They have operated in hostile environments that can only be described in apocalyptic terms, which are far beyond your feeble minds to comprehend. As of this minute, you better start earning their respect or you will have a very miserable nine months." The exaggerations and threats were part of a common training technique for specialized units. It is imperative for the students to respect and, in this case, fear their instructors in order to succeed. The trainers' job is to literally break the spirit of these young warriors and build them again from scratch, impressing upon them that they can accomplish any objective, under any circumstances, against any enemy, any time, and anywhere on the planet.

Rodchenko continued. "The instructors will select you by pairs, and you will fight. If you do not fight each other then you will fight one of my instructors. If you fight an instructor you will lose. We frown upon losing in this training."

Sebastian could see some of the other soldiers breathing hard already as fear and adrenaline released throughout their systems. "Fight hard, and fight to win. If I am not pleased with your performance you will be required to fight me. If you fight me the medical staff will see to it that you are cycled back to your respective units once you are released from the hospital."

Davide looked at Sebastian with wild eyes indicating his disbelief at their instructions. Sebastian fought to stay calm.

Rodchenko's final words put a very fine point on his introduction, "This is day one, gentlemen."

With that, the instructors began to grab soldiers and shove them toward each other yelling, "Fight!" The chaos quickly resumed as soldiers began to grapple and throw uncoordinated punches and kicks at each other. One thing was for certain, they were going at it as hard as they possibly could. Several fights were going on simultaneously, and Sebastian tried to gather his wits. Suddenly, he was grabbed from behind and thrust toward a Russian soldier. The Russians were trained in a martial art called 'Sambo' which employs several variations of grabs, throws, and strikes.

Sebastian walked right into a well-directed elbow, which caught him on the browbone of his left eye. The impact caused a wide gash that immediately began to bleed profusely. It also brought him to his knees. He knew there would be a quick follow-up to this well-placed hit, and his vision cleared just in time to see a knee coming straight at him. He threw his left shoulder back and leaned quickly to his right. The knee missed its target, and Sebastian countered with a quick powerful strike to the man's groin. The soldier doubled over in pain, and Sebastian sprang to his feet bringing his own knee up. The impact blasted the soldier's head backward and knocked him out cold.

Reverting back to his commando training with the Legion, Sebastian immediately began looking for other attackers. An instructor yelled at him to stand down and grabbed him, snapping him out of his gladiatorial trance. They physically moved him to a group that was still standing and now assuming the role of reluctant spectators. Medics on standby quickly bandaged Sebastian's eye and stopped the bleeding, at least for now.

Sebastian watched as Davide took on another Russian soldier. Davide was a street fighter with lightening fast hands. He hit his opponent four times in the face before the man could even close the gap between them. The soldier stumbled forward with blood running from his nose. Davide adjusted his footing to step out of the way of this charging bull. The Russian changed his tactic, stopping his forward motion and began to back-peddle. As Davide stepped in to finish him off, the Russian ducked Davide's advancing blows, dropping to one knee. In a blur of movement, the soldier swung his right leg around, sweeping Davide's legs. He went down hard, and the Russian was on him like a cheetah on a gazelle. On the ground, the two men fought furiously for position. Eventually, they were the last ones fighting, and everyone else stood around shouting encouragement to both of them. The fight continued, and Davide would not give up. Davide had managed to turn into a kneeling position with his opponent behind and on top of him with his arms locked around Davide's torso. The Russian was becoming more and more frustrated that he couldn't get the upper hand. As they struggled, Sebastian saw the Russian's hand disappear along the side of his leg. In a sudden burst of brute strength, Davide stood up, lifting his opponent with him.

Out of thin air, Sebastian caught a glint of metal and realized immediately, as did everyone else, that the man had a knife and was raising it against Davide as they separated. There was a collective gasp, because there was no time for anyone to react, least of all Davide. As the Russian soldier swiped downward with the knife, his arm was grabbed in mid-thrust by Rodchenko. In almost undetectable and instantaneous movement, Rodchenko disarmed the man, breaking his wrist. In the same instant, two of the instructors had drawn their side arms and pointed them directly at the young man's head. He had nearly made a fatal mistake. Davide stood panting, wondering what he should do next. Two other instructors grabbed the young Russian soldier under both arms from behind. They dragged him off, and all the new SPETSNAZ recruits, both victorious and defeated, stood for a moment in the morning sun in absolute stunned silence.

"The killer instinct is not a bad thing," Rodchenko said to the group. He quickly handed the knife off to another instructor so it would not be the focal point of his words. "Knowing when to use it and when to refrain separates control from chaos, civilized from barbaric, the soldier from the terrorist." It was impressive how he had turned one man's fit of rage into a very poignant lesson. Sebastian felt that the soldier/terrorist theme would be recurring regularly throughout the next nine months.

"Grab your packs!" one of the instructors yelled. The men all turned to see backpacks already prepared for them. "NOW!" the instructor shouted. The chaos was back. The men all ran to the nearest pack and struggled to get it on. Each pack weighed nearly fifty pounds. It was becoming obvious that this training was going to be relentless and merciless. Sebastian replayed Rochenko's words in his mind, *'This is day one.'* His eye pulsed with pain at the thought.

"This is a timed event!" Rodchenko yelled. "Follow the lead instructors. Move out!"

The instructors at the front of the group carried identical packs, and they took off at an incredible pace. The soldiers scrambled to catch up and keep up, battling the overwhelming fatigue that sets in after a fight.

Indicating this was a timed event added stress to the participants. Again this was on purpose, an exercise that worked to wear down their senses. They had no idea how far they were going, what time was considered passing, or what event would be next. Did they need to conserve energy or was it more important to concentrate on making the time? What about water and medical attention? What happens if you fail? Every variable chipped away at each individual soldier in different ways. Sebastian began to sweat, and it poured into his cut. It stung so badly it started blurring his vision. His wound had begun to clot, but was still seeping blood.

As his body numbed with pain, his mind drifted to the steady rhythm of the running. He remembered reading about the training of the U.S. Navy SEALs. The very beginning of their BUDs training began with 'break out' where the instructors would shock and nearly overwhelm the soldiers by bursting into a quiet classroom unannounced and putting them through extremely demanding physical exercises for undetermined amounts of time. This was the SPETSNAZ version of 'break out' Sebastian rationalized.

His eye was killing him, and the road stretched out before him to the horizon. He heard Davide quietly singing the 'Do Ra Mi' song from *The Sound of Music* behind him and, regardless of how miserable he felt, Sebastian couldn't help but smile.

Chapter 58

Sebastian knew they had been running for well over five miles. He had also carried enough packs to know that the one he was carrying was at least fifty pounds. The straps had cut into his shoulders long ago, and his lower back began to ache from the weight. All of the soldiers had managed to keep up with the instructors, regardless of their fight injuries and the pain of running.

Soon they saw a medical truck on the side of the road with three small tables set up and six medics standing by. The men came to the truck and were ordered to stop. At this point, they were ordered to take their packs off and strip down to their underwear. They all stood in line to be examined. The soldiers would find this routine repeated over and over as the training progressed. The medics could disqualify you at any time at their discretion so everyone tried to look as tough as they could during the examination.

While the soldiers were examined, a water truck pulled up to their location. Everyone began to look on their packs for water canteens to fill. No one was able to find anything to hold water.

Sebastian's eye was cleaned and loosely closed with butterfly stitches. Rodchenko jumped down from the passenger side of the water truck as the last soldier was patched up.

"Line up on me!" he yelled. The soldiers ran over to grab their uniforms and Rodchenko screamed, "I did not tell you to get your uniforms! LINE UP ON ME!" The men ran over to him and lined up in front of the water truck in their briefs and t-shirts. The sweat had evaporated long ago, and most of the men were already shivering in the crisp, cool air.

"Push up position," he ordered. The men fell to the ground in the 'up' position of the push up. The soldiers' shoulders were still burning from the packs. Rodchenko left them like that as he walked over to talk to the medics. They stayed there for ten minutes. Some of the soldiers were shaking from the strain.

Rodchenko finally returned. "Ok, no serious injuries," he announced. He looked at the group and saw some of them shaking under the strain of maintaining the push up position. "Are you kidding me?!" Rodchenko yelled suddenly. "Listen to me very carefully you pieces of shit, we haven't even begun yet. What you have done this far does not even constitute a warm up, so if you are struggling already, you need to stand up, walk to me, and quit. From what I've seen, I would encourage all of you to quit right now." He stood there waiting for someone to stand up. The soldiers all remained in the push up position.

Rodchenko nodded to his instructors. They ran and began to pick up everyone's pack and placed them on the soldiers' backs. The added weight sent spikes of pain through Sebastian's body. His shoulders felt like burning embers as he made subtle compensations for the weight.

Rodchenko walked away again, leaving them in this difficult position. He conferred with his instructors, and then walked back to the front of the group. "Ok, let's do some push up's shall we?" He began putting the men through the paces with push-ups. He would make them go half way down and hold it, and quicken and slow the pace, anything to make the exercise more difficult. The soldiers were starting to struggle now.

He stopped them in the 'up' position. "Let's quit wasting each other's time. I tell you what, if one of you will quit, we can take a break." None of the soldiers moved from their positions. "How about you think about it while we do more push-ups?" Rodchenko made them do more push-ups and yelled the commands loudly. He did this so the men would not hear one of the instructors unraveling a hose from the back of the water truck.

The instructor turned on the hose and began to spray the men with ice-cold water. The water seemed to pierce their skin like a knife, and the sudden inhalation from the shock of the spray made them waste precious air and energy. "This is as easy as this training gets ladies. Come on, you don't need this shit. Just quit. All I need is one." The water continued to cascade over the soldiers. None of the men gave in to the temptation.

"Get up!" Rodchenko screamed, "and don't you dare let those packs hit the ground." It had to be quite comical watching the soldiers trying to get up without letting the packs touch the ground. When they finally made it to their feet, after almost every pack had hit the ground first, Rodchenko paced in front of them. He looked furious. Maybe he had never had a group where no one quit, or maybe he just always looked furious. It was hard to tell. "You have two minutes to get your uniforms on," he spat.

The men sprinted to their uniforms. They were shaking so hard it was very difficult to get dressed. They were still working on buttons, zippers, and lacing boots when one of the instructors yelled, "Packs on! Fall in on me!" and with that he took off running again down the road back toward camp. All the men had a difficult time getting back into stride, but they finally got it together for their return run.

As soon as they entered the camp, more instructors were standing there with AK-47s for issue. "Get your weapon and fall in line," was the only command given to the men as they arrived. They stood in line and the serial numbers of their weapons were recorded by one instructor as another gave further instructions.

"We will now go to the tables situated over there," he pointed to four tables near one of the buildings. "Break the weapons down, making sure they are clear and clean, check them to your satisfaction, oil them, conduct a functions check, and await further instructions. Fall out."

They conducted their weapons check in silence. As they worked on their weapons, they were not allowed to take off their packs. Sebastian and Davide were very grateful for the training Prenom had put them through. Handling the AK-47 was like second nature to them.

Beside the cleaning table was a pile of bottled water. No one dared touch it until ordered to do so, but the thought of drinking it was maddening.

"On me!" one of the instructors yelled as they finished their function checks. "Grab two liters of water and drink up. Finish them before we reach our destination." They took off running again. It was hard to drink on the run, but they managed downing both liters before they had barely cleared the camp. This time they ran to the firing range situated about three-and-a-half kilometers outside the camp. They spent the next several hours qualifying with their newly issued weapons. The sun was setting as they finished. They policed up their brass and fell into formation.

Four new instructors arrived at the range. They had packs and rifles identical to the recruits. "On me!" one of them yelled. They marched away from the range and into the night. A truck drove behind them with its lights on; this was an endurance exercise, not a combat exercise. The truck had to accompany them in case of a medical emergency or if one of the soldiers quit the training. They continued marching for three hours. Finally one of the instructors yelled, "Double time!" and they began to jog as a group. This lasted for another ninety minutes and, miraculously, the soldiers kept up with the instructors.

In the last ten minutes, however, one of the soldiers began to lag behind. Sebastian recognized him as the driver of one of the trucks who had his arm bandaged before any of this even began. Sebastian continued to look back and monitor the soldier as he fell further and further behind. Davide looked at the ground, not wanting to meet Sebastian's eyes when he looked back. Davide knew what was on Sebastian's mind, but he was hurting himself and was wondering how much longer he could keep up this pace. Finally, Davide shook his head and looked up. Sebastian smiled at him, which drove Davide crazy, and nodded his head. Davide reluctantly nodded in return, and the two soldiers peeled away from the pack and ran back to the struggling soldier.

Sebastian grabbed the man's backpack and threw it over his shoulders on top of his own. He then got behind him and began yelling encouragement. Davide grabbed the man's arm and put it over his shoulders. He wrapped his arm around his waist and practically carried the soldier, trying to catch up with the others. The other Russian soldiers looked behind them at what was happening. Soon they all fell back and began to help the soldier, taking turns with the pack and pushing the soldier along.

They made it back to camp at 2:30 a.m. Waiting for them was the medics, tons of water, and a huge hot meal. In the courtyard area, they were given their final orders to eat and drink as much as they could, and have their weapons cleaned before day two began. All Sebastian could think about was food and the fact that day one had finally ended.

Ivan Antonovich smiled from the back seat of the monitoring truck. The Legionnaires were doing very well.

Chapter 59

Stephanie flipped open her phone and dialed the hospital. All she got was a strange sounding busy signal. She tried dialing again with the same result. Thinking it was maybe something with the hospital phone system, she tried her friend Dyann's cell. Same signal. Now she was getting a bit concerned. She got up from her seat and walked out onto the sidewalk, examining the strength of her signal. All bars. *'What's going on here?'* she thought.

"Got her!" the Bosnian stated triumphantly. He gave the address to the driver who pressed down on the accelerator. Damir checked his watch; 10:12 a.m. He hoped they would have the package and be headed back home by early afternoon.

"We're about 13 minutes away from her," Slavo's man announced. The rental car tore out of the hospital parking lot and slid smoothly into mid-morning traffic.

Stephanie went back to the mobile phone shop to see if they could fix her phone. Her frustration level with lack of sleep and this whole ridiculous situation was rising to critical levels. They had better be able to fix her stupid phone or she was going to explode. The young tech behind the counter took her phone and began to expertly examine it. He furrowed his brow as he pushed a series of keys that were supposed to open the inner secrets of the phone. "This is weird," he said more to himself than to Stephanie.

"What is it?" she asked, stifling a tired sigh.

"Well the phone is working fine, but it looks like your signal is being…jammed or something." He scratched his head and looked at Stephanie, perplexed. "I've never seen this particular problem, ma'am. You want me to call the manufacturer troubleshooter guys?"

Stephanie thought for a moment that she would rather just throw it to the floor and stomp on it, but instead reached for it and said, "Um, no thanks. I don't think I have time for that right now. I'm just going to shut it off and see if it will reset later."

The tech powered the little phone down and handed it to her, "Ok, sorry I couldn't help."

"Lost her again," the Bosnian declared as he intensely studied his computer screen.

"What do you mean *'lost her?'*" Damir asked urgently.

"The signal is gone. She must have shut off her phone. The GPS signal should continue to transmit from the cell even if it is off, but it will take a minute for our people to re-configure for it."

"Ok, ok," Damir said, thinking of their next move. "We will go to her last known location. The signal was moving very slowly, so she has to be on foot. Upload her image to each of our cell phones. When we get within a block of where the signal went dead, we will split up, one man for each direction. We'll see if we can get a visual while we wait for the GPS to come back online. Everyone clear?" They all nodded.

"No one moves without talking to me first. Do not draw attention to yourself and absolutely no weapons."

The car now fell silent, each man lost to his own thoughts, as the driver maneuvered through the city traffic.

Chapter 60

Stephanie walked back toward Notre Dame, deep in thought about what to do next. She decided that enough was enough, she would call the police, tell them what little she knew, give them the package, and call it a day. She looked for a pay phone and saw two on the corner directly across the street from the entrance to the famous church. One was out of order, and the other had a person on it with another waiting in line.

Stephanie just shook her head as her rotten luck continued. She walked toward the Church, thinking that surely there would be more phones around this popular tourist attraction. Dozens of people crowded the courtyard in front of the church. Children squealed and ran about, and old folks sat, probably the same as they did every day, talking of current issues and ancient history. Pigeons scattered and took flight as Stephanie briskly walked through the courtyard toward the front entrance. She was looking for more available phones when she saw Arval walking in her general direction. His head was down as if he were deep in thought. Stephanie walked quickly toward him. He lifted his head, saw her, and smiled.

"Ms. Stephanie," he said cheerfully.

"Hello, Arval," Stephanie said a bit sheepishly. "I'm back."

Arval smiled and nodded, "I had a feeling you might be."

They walked in the fresh air, and sat on a nearby bench. This time, Stephanie did not hesitate to share her troubles with Arval. She recalled the events that transpired from the time she received the package at the professor's apartment to this very minute.

"...so I think the best thing to do is turn this over to the authorities and let them handle it." She could tell Arval was formulating several questions in his mind, but before she gave him a chance to speak, she asked, "May I use your phone, please?"

"Yes, of course." Arval patted his pockets, trying to remember where he put it. "Phone trouble?" he asked innocently.

"My cell phone quit working. I took it in to that mobile shop up the street and the tech guy said the phone is fine, but there is some electrical interference with my signal; like it's being jammed or something."

Arval's face became very serious. "Don't you think that's a little odd, Stephanie?" he asked with growing concern.

"Well, yes, but…"

"Jamming a signal is a very sophisticated task to accomplish. It requires technical expertise at a very high level," Arval explained.

"I suppose so, but…" She stopped abruptly as realization dawned on her. They looked straight at each other, then they both began looking frantically around.

Chapter 61

The training continued relentlessly. Time was no longer measured in days or weeks, but by the end of one specialized skill and the beginning of another. Although they started out strong as a group, inevitably men began to fall out, quitting for various reasons. Most were medical, but a few were the result of the severe mental strain of the training.

The first two weeks for the 'volunteers' was brutal simply for the sake of being brutal. It was designed to weed out the weak so that only those with a true desire to succeed remained. By week three, the real training began. Because the soldiers involved in this training were already skilled, their lessons became very technical, like refining the Olympic athlete. The training focused on a variety of skills specific to the Commando soldier, including deep infiltration, sabotage, and survival.

Sebastian, Davide, and four other Russian soldiers were pulled from the rest of the group at the end of month two. They were transferred to Alpha Group, which focused on counter-terrorist Special Forces training. They learned hostage rescue tactics, storming nearly every type of structure or vessel available. They became extremely skilled with explosives, both standard and improvised. They learned advanced techniques for both armed and unarmed close quarter battle, and at least twice a week they fought each other. At the end of every week, they employed the skills they had acquired in a practical military exercise. Every week was a new scenario, requiring the men to use all their newfound skills for successful completion. These exercises became more and more complex every week, but the soldiers could see the practical effects of their training, and it kept them motivated. There was no break or time off, just day after day of pushing the envelope just a little further.

Sebastian felt himself changing. By the third month, he was able to completely ignore the physical pain. The mental pain took a little longer to sort out. Over time, though, he was able to defuse the emotional cluster bombs dropped daily on his psyche. One thing was clear, extreme pressure brought acute focus, and he found his knowledge and ability growing with each passing week. It was undeniable; he was getting good at his tradecraft. He was becoming an instrument of warfare.

In the middle of the sixth month of training, the trainees were assembled in one of the classrooms. It was roughly 0900, and they had already run eight kilometers, marched six kilometers in full gear in a circuitous route to the firing range, and spent ninety minutes working live fire and maneuver drills. It was a relatively easy morning, and they all knew something was up.

The door opened, and Rodchenko entered, barking the command for attention. The soldiers snapped straight up from their seats. The SPETSNAZ Commander entered the room swiftly behind Rodchenko and went straight to the front of the class. The Commander was, as Sebastian remembered, a polished operator. This was a man forged by war who had experienced a lifetime of conflict. However, he seemed more refined than the other commandos Sebastian had seen around the camp. He was obviously well respected, but Sebastian had a feeling that this man's responsibility to his country went far beyond the command of the training camp. In fact, Sebastian thought he may be here as a kind of holiday to decompress from his regular job.

The Commander stopped in front of the class and told the men to be seated. He paused for a moment, formulating his thoughts before he spoke. He began slowly and reassuringly; the soldiers knew this was not a good sign. "Gentlemen," he began. "You have endured several weeks of very difficult training. Your numbers have decreased dramatically from that first day, which is a testament to your skill and tenacity. Unfortunately, your numbers will decline even further before this training is complete." He paused again to let this last statement sink in.

"Having the physical skills to learn and endure advanced combat tactics and the mental toughness to deal with the stress we have placed on you to this point has brought you success. But I am afraid in this line of work it is not enough for what you may be asked to do in the future." The Commander took a moment to survey the class before continuing. "I am here to give you your first and only warning of things to come." Sebastian observed many of his classmates readjusting themselves in their seats, bracing for the news.

The Commander continued. "In the future, at a time known only to me and my training staff, you will be put through what is widely considered the final and most difficult phase of this training. It is what will determine if you join the elite as a Special Operator or return to your respective units simply as a better trained soldier."

Sebastian blinked slowly and looked down at the floor. He was tired. Mentally and physically, he was raw. In five-and-a-half months, he and Davide had hardly spoken to each other. In fact, it was amazing how all the men had come together as a team when they hardly ever spoke to one another. If they did communicate, it was directly related to whatever exercise they were performing. Every minute of their day was accounted for by a training objective. By day's end, all they wanted to do was sleep, so there wasn't any conversation in the barracks. It was a very strange environment, and the lack of simple communication took its toll. There was no outlet for the unrelenting pressure. Some men couldn't handle it and quit on this premise alone. Although the men functioned as a team in every practical facet of the training, in reality they were becoming more isolated internally as individuals. This was actually the objective of the training; to demonstrate that as a team they were impossibly lethal, but the team was never absolutely necessary to complete the mission. The byproduct of this type of training was a commando who would complete any operation down to the last man, regardless of the casualties suffered by the team as a whole. Just imagining that this training would get worse was almost too much to deal with.

The Commander surveyed the faces of the soldiers to be sure he had their undivided attention before proceeding. "You will be required at some point to complete an exercise that will simulate capture behind enemy lines. You will be dropped in an area of operation with specific secret information that you must not disclose under any circumstances. Survival, evasion, and resistance will be closely evaluated. Two things you can be assured of: you will be caught, and your captors will try to break you." The body language of the Russian soldiers in the classroom reflected a closer understanding of what was meant by 'break you' than did Davide and Sebastian. "We have found in our experience that it is counter-productive for us to try to give you false encouragement regarding this exercise." Sebastian interpreted that as meaning it doesn't help to give you some sense of hope that you might evade capture and return to base for the 'Most Clever Soldier' award.

"Gentlemen, I give you advanced information on this exercise for several reasons. First, we give you time to think this over and decide if this lifestyle is for you or not. It is certainly not for everyone, and you may quit this training feeling a great sense of accomplishment in making it this far. Secondly, you must understand, this is an extreme exercise that will bring you so close to reality that your mind may confuse the two. In fairness to you, we want you to have time to prepare yourselves. Pay attention to this because if you make it through, you will use many of these same preparation skills for live operations in the future. And lastly, we want you to pay very close attention to the training you will receive from this point forward, because it will help you be successful with the 'behind enemy lines' exercise." Sebastian thought about quitting. He didn't need this. He could just return to France, finish out his contract with the Legion, and concentrate on starting a new life. This was ridiculous, of course. He had never quit anything in his life, and he knew he wasn't about to start now. He expelled a sigh, which indicated the decision had been made. He would dig his heels in, strengthen his resolve, and brace himself for the worst they had to throw at him.

The Commander concluded, "One last thing, the longer you evade capture and the longer you resist will make your remaining time here with us much easier. Conversely, if you don't give everything you have during this block of training, we will see to it that your military record directly reflects your efforts."

The room was absolutely silent. This last threat seemed to really affect the Russian soldiers. Sebastian knew what he was willing to give and he knew Davide, complaining to the very end, would give the same, and that was everything they had. This was without a doubt the turning point in the training.

Chapter 62

Stephanie's mind reeled. She had never been so tired, so frightened, or so bewildered. She desperately needed to get rid of the damned package still nestled in her satchel. But how? If she went to the authorities, they would take one look at her in her filthy uniform and disheveled hair and think she was a crazy woman. She felt like a crazy woman. Who would believe such a cock-a-mamie story anyway? It was too weird to be real.

"Stephanie," Arval said, snapping her out of her hopeless ruminations, "who did you say asked you to pick up the package?"

Stephanie told him again about how Professor Fournier came in as a patient, asked her to pick up a package for him, his ramblings about Serbia, everything that she could remember. Arval nodded his head, taking it all in.

"Dr. Jean Pierre Fournier from Sorbonne?" Arval tried to clarify.

"I think so," Stephanie responded, trying to remember his chart.

"I know of Dr. Fournier," Arval said reflectively. "I've attended a few of his seminars at the University. He has a theory based on his extensive research of the Balkans that he has never been able to prove. Perhaps he has discovered some tangible evidence…" Arval thought for a moment. "I may have an idea what you have in your possession. If it is what I think, then it would be safe to say that you are going to become quite popular to some very dangerous people." He was trying to convey the gravity of the situation without driving her further into panic. "We need a plan."

"We?" Stephanie asked. "No, Arval, this is my burden to bear. If I am in some kind of danger, I will not bring you into it as well. I'm going to the police."

"That would be perfectly rational under normal circumstances, dear," Arval replied softly, "but let's think for a minute. If the people who are after this package have the capability to block your cell phone, would it not be reasonable to think they have connections within the police department as well?" Stephanie looked at Arval, analyzing his expression.

"Are you serious?" she asked in disbelief. "Arval, I don't know anything for sure. I don't know if my cell phone is just malfunctioning because it spends its life bouncing around in my satchel, or if the Bishop was just a looney priest from the 'Parish of Paranoia,' or if I'm carrying the professor's grades for last semester! What I do know is that everyone is frightening me with all this talk of some mysterious document that has nothing to do with me. I've been up all night, I can't seem to do anything to get rid of this package, and I am not going to run anymore. I'm calling the police."

Stephanie flipped her phone open and turned it back on. Arval didn't respond, he just kept surveying their surroundings. "The stupid phone still isn't working!" she exclaimed in frustration. She was about to put it back in her purse when it rang.

Chapter 63

The eighth month of training began, and the big training exercise they had been warned about still hadn't happened. There was no question, though, that since the warning from the Commander, the training had intensified. And although no one forgot about the inevitable exercise, they had certainly filed it away so they could focus on the training at hand. The training became more technical as they learned to prepare deep infiltration operational plans including GPS coordinates, operational objectives, and encrypted communication with other units, particularly air units. This week was a large-scale simulation exercise for all of the trainees. They were divided into teams and given their objectives.

It is well known that the Russians suffered serious economic problems with the end of the Cold War and the 'experiment of communism.' Their military was in a poor state, underpaid, working with antiquated equipment, etc. However, the SPETSNAZ did not suffer the same fate as the other military units. Every nation needs someone they can count on to perform the impossible, to protect the interest of national security through surgical strikes at the heart of the enemy, to train friendly forces, and to be the legend that people can believe in and ultimately pin their hopes on. SPETSNAZ was Russia's answer to this difficult problem.

Therefore, the Spetsialnove Nazranie received excellent equipment, unlimited operational resources, and better pay. Every soldier wanted to be a commando, but very few ever made it to this level. The selection process alone broke the spirit of most men. In addition to the national backing, SPETSNAZ received additional funds from countries like France who sent their own soldiers through this grueling training.

The outside funding was used strategically by the Russian military command, of course, and not all of the money went to SPETSNAZ. It was, however, usually used for units in support of the Special Forces unit, especially the air units. Fuel for jet aircraft is expensive.

Sebastian witnessed this firsthand toward the conclusion of their exhausting four-day training exercise simulating deep infiltration. The objective was for Sebastian's team to infiltrate deep into enemy territory and "paint" a bridge, meaning laser-illuminate the target for air attack. When they reached their objective, they called it in, lit it up, and waited for the fighters.

They were briefed before the exercise began that the pilots were practicing 'map of the earth' flying using aircraft instruments, primarily for navigational purposes. So this would not be a typical bombing run. They were also staging the attack in daylight for other training objectives specific to the air command. This was going to be a treat, Sebastian thought. It was also a huge morale booster for the soldiers who had just endured four days of shitting in plastic bags, no sleep, and very little food as they executed a stealth approach to their target.

The key to operating deep within enemy territory is to never leave a trace that you were there. That means everything you take in, you must take out. No fires for warmth, no 'cooked' meals, and essentially no conversation. Special Forces are phantoms appearing from nowhere to inflict maximum tactical damage and then disappearing without a trace. In addition to the physical damage they inflict on the enemy, they also inflict a serious degree of psychological damage as well. It is demoralizing to combat troops to be attacked where they feel safest.

It takes a tremendous amount of discipline and training to operate at this level. It also means enduring great discomfort and danger beyond most soldiers' comprehension.

Sebastian and his team stayed perfectly still, camouflaged so well the assessment instructors near the target site could not see them, even with binoculars. They held steady on the target. The target was a very old bridge in a deep valley that must have been used at one point for the miners in this particular area of Russia. It had not been used for years and was, in fact, condemned, with heavy barricades blocking both ends. A replacement bridge had been constructed in this valley about 10 kilometers to the north, and was now the used passage. Regular Russian troops had shut down the new bridge earlier in the day for this exercise.

They didn't even hear them coming. Flying in at nearly super-sonic speed, two Russian SU-37 fighter planes ripped down the valley at practically eye level with Sebastian's team. They released four rockets and immediately went completely vertical. The bridge exploded dramatically, and the pieces crashed to the river bed far below. It was one of the most impressive spectacles Sebastian had ever witnessed.

It did wonders for the men to conduct such an operation, even if it was just a simulated exercise. All of their training came together in this particular case, and the feeling of success was euphoric. The team crept back out of the area much the same as they came in. This was a crucial time. It was easy to get sloppy when you've had a mission success.

Upon returning to camp, all the commandos had stories of their big operations. Davide's team blew up a mock air traffic control tower and then got to shoot a drone aircraft out of the air with a shoulder fired, surface-to-air missile launcher. The plane simulated one that was trying to get away from the airfield.

As the second week of the eight-month drew to a close, the men were in great spirits. This was as much as the soldiers had ever talked to one another, and the instructors eased up a bit while the men ate their evening meal.

They should have known something was up.

Chapter 64

The office door opened and Svetozar Dimitrijevic struggled to get his old body to stand. Deputy Prime Minister Dragan Bradic and his small entourage emerged. They frantically scribbled notes as Bradic gave instructions concerning the day's business. The Deputy Prime Minister stopped in his tracks at the sight of Dimitrijevic. Svetozar smiled warmly, "Good morning, sir," he greeted.

Bradic approached the old man, giving a wary glance at his staff. "Good morning, Mr. Dimitrijevic," he replied, shaking the old man's hand. "This is unexpected."

"Ah, yes. I'm sorry for dropping in unannounced, but a matter of some importance has presented itself." Dimitrijevic measured the response of his young apprentice, making sure he was understanding his cryptic statements.

"Of course. Mariana, cancel my appointments." His secretary nodded, knowing not to question her boss. She hurried off to begin damage control for this unanticipated development.

The two men exited from the rear of the government building and got into a waiting limousine.

Dimitrijevic briefed the Deputy Prime Minister on the situation regarding the artifact. "It should be back to its home here in Serbia by this evening." The Deputy Prime Minister nodded his understanding. His heart rate quickened as he began to realize that what they had talked about for nearly ten years was beginning to unfold. "The Russian General will meet us in Odessa. Most of the groundwork has already been laid; you will just need to put your political seal of approval on the plan. They are ready to support us unconditionally, confirmed in the shipment of 10 Migs to be delivered within the week. That will be the first item of business when we meet."

Deputy Prime Minister Bradic had dreamed of this moment since the Serbians were humiliated on the international stage under the leadership of a weak, and arguably insane, Milosivic. Bradic was now on the threshold of greatness, standing at the helm as his country at long last regained their kingdom, after over 800 years of occupation.

In two months, he would make his bid for president, and his platform would rest on the original document that would prove to the world that the land ripped from their grasp and given to their enemies had been the rightful property of Serbia from its very birth.

Chapter 65

The chow hall was filled with laughter and the theatrics of the men recounting their bravery and skill in their respective 'missions.' The men were always given only thirty minutes to eat, and they were nearing 45 minutes of uninterrupted dining and fellowship. No one noticed the Commander who slipped into the back of the chow hall and situated himself quietly in a corner to observe. An instructor subtly took his place in front of the men. He had in his hand a stack of small envelopes.

"Listen up!" he yelled suddenly. The room fell silent. "Come to the front when your name is called, pick up your envelope, and return to your seat." The soldiers looked around at each other, each with their own suspicions about what the envelopes contained.

The instructor began barking out names, and the men retrieved their envelopes and returned to their seats. After they each held an envelope, the rest of the training team entered and stood over the men like hawks.

"You may now open your envelope." The soldiers tore into them. They all reacted differently, but there was a collective air of dread. All eyes turned to Rodchenko as he entered the room and walked briskly to the front.

"You have 10 minutes to memorize the information on the paper in your hand," he began. "Your final exercise has begun." Sebastian felt his palms moisten as nervous anticipation embraced him. "Two things you need to know. First, a mild sedative was added to the water all of you drank with your evening meal. It will make most of you sleep. Second, there is now no turning back. You will soon be dismissed to the barracks. I encourage you to simply lie down and rest. You will need all your strength."

It was very difficult to concentrate on the information on the card in front of him. Sebastian tried to calm down. He could feel his heart beating like mad in his chest. He imagined everyone felt like that. Although he was extremely anxious, he could also feel his muscles relaxing as the sedative began to take effect. His accelerated heart rate helped pump the chemical quickly though his body.

The paper contained GPS coordinates of artillery placements, the name of a fictitious Commander, and a contrived operational frequency. Sebastian focused to get the information committed to memory.

After ten minutes, the instructors took all the paperwork from them. They put the papers in a metal container and set them on fire. Duplicate information specific to each soldier was locked in the safe in the Commander's office. The interrogators would use it to make sure the information retained was accurate. If it was not, it could be a failing element of the exercise.

Rodchenko again took center stage. As he spoke, a large, military, topographic map was lowered from the ceiling behind him. He turned and focused his attention on it. "This is your area of operation," he said, circling the entire map with an extendable pointer. "It is 100 square kilometers in size consisting of a wide variety of terrains. Your objective is to make it here." He tapped lightly on a darkened square just slightly off center in the southeast quadrant.

Throughout the training up to this point, the men had been given a small indication of what to expect. They were trained specifically for this day, but not given any specifics *about* this day. They knew they could not write anything down; they would enter the field with hardly any equipment, and no food or water. They knew they had to pay attention to landmarks and general direction. Finding their target location would be a matter of natural navigation and dead reckoning.

"10 minutes," Rodchenko said, indicating the length of time they had to study the map.

Sebastian noted the target was on a sharp bend of a river that ran roughly west to east. The structure to be surveyed for intelligence was on the northern bank of the river. There was also a single mountain of considerable elevation in the north-central section of the operational area. He noted quickly that the southwest corner looked like a densely wooded area on undulating ground. Nothing too extreme, just time-consuming to get through. The northwest corner was rocky with some severe terrain. This area looked most susceptible to exposure to enemy patrols. The northeast was mountainous and would be very difficult to navigate through. The southeast was flat and relatively smooth. Sebastian knew they would not put anyone in that area; too easy.

"The 'stand down' phrase is 'Valor and Honor,'" Rodchenko concluded. "This will be repeated three times to signify the exercise is over. Any questions?" There were none. They put the map away and the Commander, who had remained silent since entering the room earlier, rose from his seat and slipped back out.

Rodchenko took a breath as if to say something, and then thought against it. Finally, he simply looked at the men and said, "Good luck."

The soldiers made their way back to the barracks. There was no more laughter, no backslapping, or excited conversation. Each man retreated into his own mind, engaged in full-scale battle with the kind of fear that can only be brought on with the anticipation of severe hardship. Men facing the prospect of going to battle have an acute sense of this kind of fear.

Whatever they gave them to make them sleep was effective. As Sebastian lay in his cot, he wondered for a moment if it was even legal for them to do this to the soldiers. It was the last thought he had as he fell into a very deep sleep.

Chapter 66

Stephanie looked questioningly at Arval as the phone rang.

"Wait a minute, don't answer it yet," Arval said, thinking fast. He pulled out his own cell phone, dialed his house and waited for his answering machine to pick up. "Ok, now," he said, holding his phone close to the earpiece on Stephanie's phone.

"Hello?" Stephanie answered hesitantly.

"Stephanie Boulanger?" the male voice asked on the other end.

"Yes."

"My name is Damir Tadic. I know that you have in your possession a package. You must bring it to me right now. You are in grave danger. I am close to you; tell me exactly where you are, and we will keep you safe."

Stephanie looked at Arval with wide eyes. Arval shook his head insistently. "Why should I trust you?" Stephanie asked.

"You should trust no one, Stephanie, but I am the best option you have right now, both for your immediate safety and for the safekeeping of what you have."

"Are you the one who blocked my phone?" Stephanie asked.

"Your time is quickly running out Stephanie. It's time to make a decision."

Stephanie snapped her phone shut, looking desperately at Arval.

"We have to get away from here, Stephanie. Take the Metro, get off at Place du Chatelet, and I will pick you up there," he instructed.

Stephanie grabbed her satchel and stood up. "And give me your cell phone," Arval ordered, taking it from her hand. "You take mine." She took it, looking at him pitifully. "Don't worry. Just make your way to the street from the train. I'll be there." The old man turned and walked away. Stephanie began to jog toward the big round white sign with a blue "M" in the center.

One of Slavo's boys halted his brisk walk mid-stride. He squinted hard, looking to his left. About a block and a half away he saw a woman in a nurse's uniform jogging toward the Metro. He keyed the throat microphone of his radio and gave a description of what he saw. He broke into a light jog toward the woman.

Damir was on his cell phone asking for updates. The Bosnian told him the cell phone was powered off again, but he had the signal. It was traveling toward the rear of the church of Notre Dame. Damir was about to head that way when he saw a man break into a run across the street from where he stood. He looked ahead of the man, surveying the throng of people before him. Then he saw her; she was heading quickly toward the Metro. "Shit!" he exclaimed as he broke into a dead run.

Chapter 67

Sebastian stirred awake; he was disoriented. It felt as if someone put a blanket over his mind. Slowly he began to come around, and immediately he wished he was back asleep. His hands were bound behind his back, and there was a hood over his head. The noise was deafening and coming from an unmistakable source, the aircraft's engine; he was airborne. His shoulders strained as his bound hands were under a pack on his back. By the feel of it, it was a parachute rig. His heart rate quickened. He had done dozens of jumps, but never blindfolded with his hands tied. As much as they bragged that they could, the prospect of actually doing it was terrifying.

Heavy hands fell on Sebastian and yanked him to his feet. He heard the jump door open and felt the rush of cold air cut through his clothes and the hood. As he was shoved toward the door, Sebastian felt a wave of panic and began to resist. His handlers became extremely aggressive and forced him to the door's edge. Sebastian was yelling, but no one could hear him, including himself. Behind him, they hooked his tandem parachute cord to a wire that ran the length of the fuselage. This would automatically release his chute as soon as he left the aircraft.

At the last possible moment, they pulled off his hood and cut the binding off his wrists. In one motion, they shoved him from the aircraft. In an instant, Sebastian was jerked upward as the parachute inflated with air. He grabbed the straps at the base of the cords to the parachute. He was still yelling and finally started to get control of himself as he settled into the descent. He was only about 1200 feet in the air when they shoved him from the aircraft. He had only a few seconds to look around and try to get his bearings.

It took only an instant to recognize the features around him from the map they had been shown. He could see the mountain in the distance, roughly northeast of his position. He saw the river snaking its way through the terrain. Looking down, he realized that he was coming into the densely wooded portion southwest of the target location.

He crashed into the trees at a dangerous rate of speed. With jumps from this height with these old rigs, one had the tendency to maintain some serious velocity upon touchdown. He prayed he wouldn't break a leg or get impaled on a branch. The limbs slapped at him relentlessly, cutting his face and ripping his clothes in various places. He came down where the limbs of two trees had intertwined and grown together; fortunately far away from the base of either tree. It was good in that the limbs were not as thick here, but they were plentiful. He hit the ground hard. He was relieved he made it through, and he was able to quickly pull his parachute down as well. Assessing his injuries; he found just a few cuts and bruises, but otherwise he was ok. He took a minute to survey his surroundings and recover from the jump. Before setting out, he felt in all the pockets of his standard issue uniform to see what, if anything, they gave him for survival. He was pleased to find a good knife, but there was nothing more.

Sebastian could hear dogs barking in the distance and realized he had no time to waste. Based on what he had seen from the air, he immediately made an arrow out of three twigs pointing in the direction he needed to go. He then set out cutting up his parachute into small strips for bandages and large pieces for warmth. He cut all the parachute cord from its base to where it attached to the parachute itself and wrapped them tightly for future use. Using the parachute rig as a backpack, he stuffed all his supplies inside.

Kicking away the three twigs of his makeshift directional indicator, he was about to set off when he patted his breast pocket again. He had missed something. Inside he found a small packet containing water-purifying tablets. This was like discovering gold. Sebastian was in excellent spirits as he set off. He might make it through this after all.

Chapter 68

Judging from the position of the sun, Sebastian figured it to be early afternoon. His muscles still felt like mush as he moved lethargically through the woods. He knew he needed to hide. They had been taught to travel only at night and rest during the day. Darkness provided excellent cover. Sebastian stopped for a moment and looked at the dense forest before him. He knew it was going to be slow-going getting through these trees; but hard for him meant hard for those pursuing him, too.

Shortly, Sebastian found a large tree that had fallen years ago and was relatively hollow. He began clearing out the inside as completely as he could. It was going to be a tight fit. The insides of the log were like grabbing wet paper, and each handful Sebastian grabbed was full of a variety of bugs. He took care to hide each handful trying to leave no trace of his presence in the area.

Satisfied he had enough room to fit, he tucked in all his clothing and buttoned the top button of his uniform shirt. He took a piece of parachute and wrapped it over his head and around his neck, tucking it into the neck of the shirt. He hoped he left no openings for the bugs to reach his skin. He backed feet first into his hiding place to rest until nightfall. Sebastian then reached out from the end of the log and pulled and pushed until his opening was as flush as possible with the log's stump. In essence he closed the door to his home. He backed further into the log and situated his backpack under his head for a pillow. Pulling his hands inside his sleeves, he was finally tucked into his temporary log home.

Sebastian realized this may not be the best form of concealment, but he figured he had only about four or five hours until darkness, and he wanted to try to rest some and get the sedative completely out of his system. Once he settled in, he discovered that this was not so bad; in fact, it was pretty comfortable. He could no longer hear the dogs and hoped this was a good sign. Within 15 minutes he actually fell asleep.

By the time he woke, the sky was nearly dark. He cautiously stirred from his makeshift cocoon and listened. All he could hear was the sounds of nature chirping in harmony around him. Sebastian took a couple minutes to stretch and rub some life into his muscles. He had subtly laid out a directional indicator near where he had slept. He looked to the stars and then began hiking into the woods.

Sebastian knew he would make about six kilometers a night at his current pace. The woods were thick, and it was very slow going. He used the stars to help navigate a general course. Sebastian knew he simply needed to find the river, and from there he could locate the target objective.

As morning approached, Sebastian found another place to hide for daylight hours. They had been taught to make camouflage rest posts for just such an occasion. He started well before sun up to make sure he was as invisible as possible to the casual, and even the not so casual, observer. Once satisfied with his work, he crawled in and tried to sleep. It took a long time to relax. He continued listening intently to the sounds around him. Finally, as the sun broke over the treetops, he drifted off to sleep.

The next night was the same routine, plowing through thick woods with his senses in hyper-drive. At what he figured to be 2:30 or so in the morning, Sebastian stopped and listened carefully. After just a few seconds, he was convinced he could hear running water. He crouched low, looking and listening intently. If he was near the river, he may be near the objective, and that meant increased enemy patrol. For the next two hours he crept slowly toward the sound of water. It took him four hours to cover only three-quarters of a kilometer. He did not want to be caught this early in the exercise.

As the sun came up, he sat concealed in the foliage on the bank of the river. He really was not sure where he was in relation to the target on the river. He took an educated guess and began to creep along the bank, heading downstream.

Sebastian was getting tired from all the exertion of moving stealthily and being so aware of everything around him. It was mid-morning, and he knew this was not a good time to stop; but he also realized that fatigue led to silly mistakes that could cost him dearly. He found a place where the riverbank hung over the water, stretching several hundred meters. Slowly and deliberately, he took off his uniform and stuffed it in his pack. He would keep his backpack elevated over his head so he would have dry clothes to put back on.

Cautiously, he edged over the bank. He slipped into the frigid water and floated a short distance downstream. He used the water to keep progressing forward with the least amount of effort, to rest his aching muscles, and to throw off the scent of search dogs. Sebastian saw a log jammed against the riverbank and headed straight for it. He wasn't sure exactly what he was going to do, but he thought he could somehow hide near this log to get some much needed rest.

Sebastian realized the river started to curve a bit as he approached the log. Once he neared the log, the river before him seemed to disappear. He grabbed onto the log, and straight before him was the opposite riverbank.

It suddenly dawned on him that this was the sharp bend in the river. His pulse quickened as he realized he was now practically on top of the objective. Sebastian swore under his breath, angry with himself for taking the easy route. He hesitated, wondering what he should do next.

Slowly, he crept up the riverbank above the log. It was extremely slow going as he employed every tactical movement skill he could muster. The bank was slick, making progress not only slow, but frustrating. Finally, he crested the bank and cocked his head to the side peering over with only one eye. Remarkably, the coast was clear. In one smooth, fluid move, Sebastian popped up from the river and darted into the woods. The mud covering his body helped camouflage him in the wood line. With very controlled movements, Sebastian got his clothes back on and warmed quickly; adrenaline still pumping through his body.

He sat still for several minutes, trying to get his breathing under control. As he recovered from the sound of blood pumping in his ears, he realized he had to move. Exercising great skill and caution, he made slow progress downstream for the remainder of the day. He could not believe that he didn't see any patrols or any signs of his objective. Just as he began to question whether or not he was in the right vicinity, he heard voices. Sebastian had now been awake for nearly 22 hours. He cautiously moved into a position of cover as best he could. He wedged himself under a log and pulled as much foliage around him as possible. Finally, he could hold out no longer and gave in to sleep. Just before he made his final descent into slumber he could hear a dog barking alarmingly close to his position.

Chapter 69

Sebastian woke with a start. Nothing had happened, but his mind seemed to turn on like entering a room and flipping the light switch. It was still very dark which made it impossible to determine what time it was. He lay still for what seemed like an eternity. Finally, the sky began to lighten as the sun started to surface.

Sebastian moved slowly, keeping watch ahead as far as the foliage would allow. He stopped his progress and peered through the trees. He could vaguely make out a structure. It was gray and boxy. There were two heavy machine gun emplacements flanking each side of the building. They were covered with camouflaged netting and manned with two soldiers each.

Sebastian moved a little closer and squinted at the soldiers; they were hard to see through the netting. Something wasn't right. At that moment, another soldier with a German Shepherd came from around the corner of the building, stopping to speak with one team of machine gunners. They both laughed at whatever the patrol guard said. When the soldier came into full view, Sebastian's eyes widened and his head snapped down.

He worked to get his breathing under control. He kept reminding himself this was just an exercise. This wasn't real. But something wasn't adding up. There were no aggressive patrols around the secondary perimeter, which would encompass the area where he was currently hiding. He had run into no resistance or signs of search parties on his way here. All signs indicated this was a legitimate installation hidden deep in the woods, conducting normal operation and not expecting enemy activity. '*There is no way,*' Sebastian thought to himself. He was extremely disquieted by the fact that the soldier he saw was wearing a Chechen uniform.

Sebastian finally regained some control. Concentrating on the mission at hand, he began taking inventory of everything he could see concerning the objective. He began to note number of doors and windows, antennae configurations on the rooftop, and the weaponry on site. He was concentrating on these things intently when he saw the guard with the dog grab his radio. Obviously, he was receiving some urgent information. His body tensed, and he began scanning the tree line where Sebastian was hiding. Sebastian froze and concentrated on his breathing and pulse rate. He needed to stay calm so that he could react tactically to whatever was happening.

Suddenly two more guards came from behind the building. They were quickly exchanging information with the first guard and apparently formulating some kind of plan. Yet another guard with another dog came out from inside the building. They all began to run farther down the river away from Sebastian. He couldn't see very far in the direction they ran because of the density of the woods. He readjusted and leaned out as far as he dared. His heart almost stopped; they were running to a narrow footbridge that crossed south, bringing them to Sebastian's side of the river.

Trying to remain calm, Sebastian settled back into his hiding spot, not wanting to do anything out of panic. He decided to move farther back into the woods to find better cover. His heart was now pumping furiously. He tried to remain optimistic, thinking maybe another soldier had been spotted and they were pursuing him. He didn't wish ill will on any of his fellow SPETSNAZ brothers, but his survival instinct was kicking into full gear. Sebastian slowly turned his back to the river. A thousand things ran through his mind; he shouldn't have made his approach so quickly, he should have found something to eat and drink, he should have done better recon, the list went on and on.

He heard the voices getting closer as the soldiers shouted to each other. Sebastian felt the calm evaporating from his body. He stood up almost entirely erect in an attempt to run a short distance deeper into the forest. As soon as he did, two men in full sniper ghillie suits stood straight up just 10 meters in front of him, pointing their weapons and yelling for him to stop. He froze, knowing that he was caught. The other soldiers quickly came crashing into the wood line, screaming at Sebastian in Russian with thick Chechen accents. The dogs barked and snapped their jaws viciously, begging their masters to let them tear into their captive. It was chaotic and extremely frightening. Sebastian looked to the sky, going over his many mistakes in his mind as one of the soldiers approached. The Chechen soldier delivered a ferocious blow to his stomach, sending him straight to the ground.

Chapter 70

Stephanie quickly descended the stairs into Paris' underground subway system called the Metro. She got a ticket from one of dozens of automated machines and headed for the train. An eerie feeling enveloped her as she sensed someone following her. Instinctively, she quickened her pace and walked ahead as if she were going to ascend the stairs on the far side of the platform. The train to Chatalet pulled in as she walked, but she kept heading for the stairs.

Behind her, the Serbian began closing the gap. He was sure this was their mark and imagined the package was tucked in the large satchel secured across her chest. He kept his teammates appraised of the details as he drew closer to their target. He had just radioed that she was going up the far staircase when she darted onto the train at the last minute, and the doors slid shut behind her. He turned to jump on one door down from her.

Damir closed the gap on the Serbian quickly. He could see the clear, spiraled cord of the Serb's earpiece disappearing under his shirt. He knew he was using a throat mic to communicate with Slavo and the others. Damir saw Stephanie headed for the stairs and wondered what her plan was. When she darted onto the train at the last minute, he got it. She knew the Serb was following her, and she was trying, in her clever way, to shake him.

As the Serb turned to jump on the train, the Croatian ran into him, making it look like an accidental collision between pedestrians. In reality, Damir rammed a Kubaton, a small hard plastic device that looks like a miniature baton, into the Serb's ribs with deceiving force. It was a short stroke that only the trained eye could detect, but the blow brought the Serb to his knees struggling for breath. Damir kept walking and peered into the train car as it pulled away.

He stopped when he spotted Stephanie. She stood from her seat and moved to the window as their eyes locked. Damir nodded to her, and then moved to the stairs to exit the train station. Slavo and his two remaining men descended the stairs that Stephanie, the Serb, and Damir originally came down. They jumped the last five steps, pushing people rudely out of the way as they ran to their fallen comrade.

Chapter 71

Sebastian was quickly bound with flex cuffs and yanked off the ground. He was pushed ahead of the soldiers with the dogs still barking maniacally at his heels. They crossed the foot bridge and walked in between the building and one of the machine gun emplacements to the back of the facility.

In the back, several men sat around a smoldering fire with a coffee pot resting over the coals. The man, who was obviously the leader, turned with a large cigar hanging from his mouth. He eyed Sebastian with a look of genuine surprise. This was not a good sign. Either this guy was a great actor, or before him was a real Chechen rebel leader who just had a spectacular prize delivered to him on a silver platter.

Sebastian could not imagine the leaders of their training actually dumping the trainees in an area controlled by real local enemy forces; and without weapons, no less. But then he thought a move like this should not come as a complete surprise from such a hardcore unit. The gravity of the situation weighed heavy on his mind.

"Well, well. What have we here; an unexpected guest? Who are you?" the man asked with a thick Chechen accent.

Sebastian did not reply. He was instantly struck in the kidneys by an unseen fist behind him. It nearly brought him to his knees, but he stood back up straight and defiant.

"Hmm," the leader mused, sticking his unlit cigar back in his mouth. He then flicked his hand as if he was suddenly completely uninterested in the prisoner before him. Immediately, the soldiers grabbed Sebastian and jerked him toward the building.

Once inside the building, he blinked and squinted as he tried to adjust his eyes to the dim interior. They pushed him to a doorway about a quarter of the way down the hallway on the right. One soldier turned the key hanging from the doorknob plate and yanked the door open to reveal a windowless room. It was approximately five feet deep and three feet wide. There was nothing but bare concrete walls; no chair, toilet, bed, or anything. They shoved him inside with his hands still bound. The momentum from the shove carried him off-balance into the far wall. He turned and absorbed the impact with his right shoulder. The door was slammed shut behind him and locked. *'That wasn't so bad,'* Sebastian thought to himself.

He settled in, standing to keep blood flowing to his lower extremities. Time passed slowly, and he began to lose feeling in his hands; his shoulders began to ache. After what he guessed may have been a couple of hours, the door was unlocked and he was yanked out into the hallway. They dragged him down the corridor to another room on the left. Sebastian tried to take in as much of his surroundings as possible, but there was nothing notable so far that he could file away; the walls were dingy and bare. His observations were quickly ended as they crashed him head first through the door into a small office.

Once inside, Sebastian lay for a moment on the floor. He shook his head, trying to shake away the bells that were ringing in his head. He rolled to his butt and stood up in the middle of the room. Before him was a simple table with two chairs, one on either side. Sitting in the chair on the far side of the table was a very clean and sharp looking fellow in an immaculate uniform.

He stood and smiled warmly, "Please, sit down." He motioned to the empty chair. Sebastian didn't move. The man leaned slightly, looking behind Sebastian. "Oh, I'm terribly sorry." He said with sincerity. He called one of the soldiers back in and gave him an order. The soldier pulled a knife from his gear and Sebastian reacted immediately. "No, no, please," the man held his hands up, trying to calm Sebastian. "He is simply going to cut your restraints." Sebastian's shoulders were burning, and he really had no other option. Reluctantly, Sebastian offered his wrists, and the soldier cut the flex cuff in one smooth stroke. Sebastian rubbed his hands as they felt like a thousand needles were being stabbed into them simultaneously.

"Please, sit," the man requested again. Sebastian knew he was in no shape to make any moves, and besides, such bravado would probably only bring on more beatings. He sat slowly, eyeing the man across the table skeptically.

"My name is Artem. What is your name?"

The man spoke very proper Russian, and he spoke with a tempo that made it very easy for Sebastian to understand. Still, he offered no reply.

"Please, sir. We mean you no harm. We simply want to know who you are and how we can help you back to your unit. Perhaps you were separated, yes?" Sebastian knew it was way too early to offer any kind of information. Silence was his only defense right now.

The man smiled and pulled a pack of cigarettes from his pocket. He offered one to Sebastian who sat expressionless. The man shrugged and lit a cigarette. He took a long drag and leaned forward in his chair. "I know you are afraid," the man began. "My soldiers have not treated you very well, I know, but you must understand they were quite alarmed to find you hiding in the woods. Of course, we are going to be tense. It would help if we knew who you are." He leaned back again, looking very relaxed, waiting for Sebastian to reply. When he did not, the man continued, "You are wearing a regular army uniform, with no rank or unit indication. That is quite curious. We would like to think that you are a simple soldier who somehow got separated from his unit during an exercise. That is the optimistic version of your present circumstance. On the other hand, we know that certain other soldiers operate in such a way, and they are our most feared and hated enemy. They have done things to our brothers that are beyond forgiveness." The man's expression changed to one of hatred, "God help you if we find out you are SPETSNAZ."

Chapter 72

There was a heavy silence that seemed to push down on Sebastian's shoulders. The cigarette smoke drifted lazily, illuminated by the light from a single small window high on the far wall.

After a long pause the man spoke, "If you tell us you are regular army and the unit you are with, we will release you as quickly as possible back to your commanding officer. We have no desire to hold you here. Your presence taxes our resources as it is. The sooner we get rid of you, the better."

Sebastian did not like the sound of the last sentence. Was that a Freudian slip?

"I tell you what," the man began, "just tell me your name, and I will give you some food and water. What harm could there possibly be in giving me your name?"

Sebastian thought about this for a moment. With the adrenaline he had been running on for the past several hours, he had not realized how hungry he was. He hadn't eaten for nearly 56 hours. He didn't think he would find the river so quickly. He had planned on another night in the woods and trapping some small game. His accelerated progress had caused him to forego his chance to eat. After careful consideration, Sebastian remained unmoved in his chair, indicating his refusal to answer the man's question.

"Very well then," the man sighed, tapping out his cigarette in a beat up ashtray on the table. He called for the guard who came in aggressively and pulled Sebastian to his feet. He shoved him face first into the far wall and pressed him hard against it. The man interviewing Sebastian whispered something into the guard's ear. Immediately, the guard made Sebastian interlace his fingers behind his head. He then made him stretch his feet out far behind him, supporting his weight with his forehead pressed into the wall.

They had been coached on 'stress positions' during training. There was really nothing one could do to alleviate the pain. You just had to let your mind drift to a place of comfort and relaxation. Sebastian thought about home. He thought of how his mom used to pamper him when he was sick. Boys are often bigger babies than girls when they're sick. He smiled to himself, remembering how she would make him chicken noodle soup and sweet tea. She was the best, and these memories helped him to cope with the pain of the present. The guard took up post in the corner of the office.

After standing like this for a long period of time, his stomach muscles were screaming in pain. When he could hold it no longer, he dropped to his knees. The guard immediately punched him in the shoulder blade. Because of the tension on his upper back from his hands being bound and then laced behind his head, the punch felt like a gunshot.

The guard yanked him back to his feet and forced his head back into the wall. Sebastian's brain was registering pain alarms from all over his body. His muscles began to shake uncontrollably. Finally, the man came back and told Sebastian to sit. Sebastian didn't need to be told twice, and he quickly took the seat.

He had no idea how much time had passed since the last interview, but it was enough time to make Sebastian re-think what he was willing to put himself through before he offered information. His muscles continued to spasm as he sat facing the man who called himself Artem. They sat there staring at each other for a good five minutes. From out of nowhere, it seemed, a bowl of rice and a glass of water were placed before Sebastian. His stomach was aching from lack of food.

"Tell me your name," the man said, this time not nearly as friendly as before.

"Rubble; Barney Rubble," Sebastian replied seriously.

The man nodded to the guard to check out the information. He then motioned for Sebastian to eat. He wolfed down the bowl of rice and drank the water.

The man continued to stare at him as he ate. "You are not Russian," the man observed from Sebastian's accent. "That makes your presence here very intriguing, indeed." The man worked his pack of cigarettes back out from his pocket. "Who do you work for, Mr. Rubble?" Sebastian had just finished eating every kernel of rice from the bowl and started laughing when he heard the man refer to him as 'Mr.

Rubble.' He couldn't stop laughing. The man's face began to flush with anger.

The door to the office burst open, and the guard rushed to the interrogator's side and whispered in his ear. He then took up a position behind Sebastian who had finally stopped laughing. In a flash of sudden violence, Artem sprang forward over the small table and punched Sebastian in the side of the head. Simultaneously, the guard yanked the chair out from under him. Sebastian sprawled across the floor and grabbed his eye. The man's large ring on his right hand had caught him on the orbital bone directly under his left eye and cut it deeply. He would now have matching scars, one above his eye and one beneath. Sebastian saw the blood drip on the floor as he was again yanked to his feet.

"So that is how you want to play this? Think carefully, this is your last chance." Sebastian offered no response. There was nothing funny about this anymore. The man nodded to the guard.

Sebastian was taken back to his cell, facing the far wall. This time the door stayed open and a guard stayed behind him for the entire night, placing him in different stress positions and not allowing him to sleep.

The guards rotated regularly, and each one brought new and inventive ways to torment Sebastian without actually laying their hands on him. They all threw ice cold water on him about twice an hour. His body was now shaking uncontrollably, and he was starting to get delirious from lack of sleep. His muscles were cramping, and he was getting panicky from the pain. After what seemed like an eternity, Sebastian was pulled from his cell and taken back to the office. His interrogator sat in his regular spot, looking exactly as he had the day before.

Sebastian sat shivering in front of the man. "What is your real name?" the man demanded. Sebastian said nothing. "Let me explain what is going to happen next. You are going to have pain redefined for you until you decide to cooperate. It will take me another 24 hours to find out your real identity, so in the meantime, you can go ahead and tell me what I want to know, or you can subject yourself to my wrath.

If you thought that I would tolerate being made to look like a fool, you are sorely mistaken." The man rose to leave. "Twenty-four hours, soldier, and I will make you a shell of a man." He briskly walked out, and Sebastian felt the anticipated hands yank him from the chair.

Chapter 73

Stephanie exited the train station at Place du Chatelet. She ran toward the street, looking around desperately for any sign of Arval. She was really scared now. Someone was after her without a doubt; actually, it appeared several people were after her. '*They are not after me; they are after this damn envelope,*' she reminded herself. A couple of moments passed and still there was no sign of Arval. She was about to move, run, do something other than just stand there when the cell phone Arval gave her rang. "I see you. Look to the right; I'll be pulling up in a second."

Stephanie scanned the roadway, looking for Arval. As scared as she was, she couldn't conceal her amusement when he ripped up to the curb in a BMW Roadster. She jumped in and looked at him with feigned surprise. Arval smiled. "The secondary school retirement system is excellent," he offered by way of explanation. Stephanie knew there was way more to the story than that. She wondered who her new friend really was.

"Arval," she said breathlessly, "people really are after me. A strange man chased me to the train station. As I was boarding, he was intercepted by another man who killed him, I think."

Arval listened gravely. "Stephanie, I've been giving this a great deal of thought. I think it best to get you to a safe place and then decide what to do about this unfortunate situation. Your uniform is now a dead giveaway, pardon the expression. There is no time to go to your apartment. Besides that, it may be staked out by some of those who are pursuing you. We are heading for the airport where you can purchase some new clothes and shoes and clean up a bit while we await your flight. I made some preparations for your escape while you were on the train. Do you have your passport with you?"

"Yes," Stephanie replied, her head spinning. "It's in my satchel. I carry it with me."

"Good." Arval glanced across at his nervous passenger. "I need to tell you about the information I believe you are carrying," he said as they merged into traffic. "But that can wait until we get to the airport. For now, I want you to settle back and rest while we are en route."

Stephanie, stressed almost to the breaking point, drew a deep breath and did exactly as she was told.

Chapter 74

Sebastian's captivity was about to take on a new level of hardship. They fed him a bowl of rice and a glass of water again at nighttime, and allowed him six hours of uninterrupted time in his cell. Sebastian had, of course, lost all track of time and had no idea how long he had been in captivity. He slept on the hard floor, but kept jerking awake, thinking he heard the guards approaching. Finally, his fears were confirmed, and the guards came back. They took him back to the office.

Sebastian's strength was fading, and his ability to concentrate was greatly diminished. He endured another two hours of questioning from his interrogator, and was then left alone in the office. His solitude was soon interrupted by two guards who came in and dragged him back into the hallway.

This time, instead of going back to his cell, they took him further down the hallway. Flush with the floor, and impossible to see until you were practically right on top of it, was a door in the floor. One guard broke his grasp from Sebastian's arm and jerked the door open. Stairs led down to darkness. Sebastian tried to resist, but his strength was all but gone. They shoved him down the stairs into a single room. It was small and bare like everything else in the building. The walls and floor were made of cement. Dirt and cobwebs provided the room's décor, and the only light was a single bulb dangling from the ceiling by an exposed wire. In the center of the room was a chair and nothing else.

The soldiers slammed Sebastian down in the chair and bound his hands again behind his back with another pair of flex cuffs. He was immediately struck with an open hand across the face. The soldiers began to curse at him and make vulgar remarks about his family. They interspersed their comments with various strikes to his face and torso. They concentrated on strikes to the body. It was wearing Sebastian out, and he was now finding it difficult to breathe.

Heavy footsteps announced Artem's presence as he came down the stairs. Moving quickly, he went straight to Sebastian and grabbed him by the face. "What is your name?!" he screamed. Sebastian was struggling to hold on to consciousness. He didn't know what was making him resist, but he had made up his mind that he was not going to break. The interrogator stood and nodded to the larger of the two soldiers. Immediately he brought a heavy fist crashing into Sebastian's face. Everything went black.

When Sebastian regained consciousness he was back in his tiny cell. His eyes were swelling to the point that it was impairing his vision. He touched his nose and winced, it was badly broken.

Outside the cell, Artem and the commander stood in silence, both contemplating their next move. The leader jerked his head toward the office. The two men entered, closing the door behind them. Artem immediately lit up a cigarette.

"He hasn't even given us his name." Artem said, scratching his forehead with the hand that held the cigarette.

A man of few words, the leader nodded thoughtfully and replied, "Have you told him you know who he is?"

"No, but that is my next move."

"Hold off on that a little while longer. I've been working on something for the last 24 hours. I think I have an idea about how to make him tell us everything all at once. I need about 8 more hours."

Artem smiled, "As you wish, sir."

Chapter 75

Unknown to Sebastian, it was afternoon of the fifth day. He was on his eighth day from the time he was shoved from the plane and parachuted into the woods. They had let him be for the longest period of time yet, which was almost as unnerving as being dragged from his cell. They had given him a bucket for relieving himself, and the stench of his own waste made it hard to breathe. His body ached, and his face looked like he had been in a car accident. He knew for sure that his nose was broken, and the cut by his eye was deep enough to require stitches. The inside of his mouth was torn up, but thankfully none of his teeth had been knocked out.

He was laying curled up on the floor with his body wanting to shut down, when he heard feet approaching. He closed his eyes and said a little prayer that this would be over soon, no matter what the outcome.

Sebastian was taken again to the office; however, the audience was slightly different this time. Artem was in his usual seat at the table, and standing beside him was the rebel leader, chewing on his unlit cigar.

"Well, Mr. Rubble," Artem said, chuckling as he looked back at his boss, "I'm afraid you have put us in a position that is most unfortunate…for you, that is." He pulled out a file folder and threw it on the table in front of him. "Go ahead, open it."

After a moment, Sebastian leaned forward and with shaky hands, opened the folder. Directly on top was a picture of his sister. She was walking from a building easily identifiable on the USC campus. Sebastian began to flip through the pictures, instantly feeling a mix of anger and panic overwhelm him. There were more pictures of his sister and several of his mother and father.

Sebastian lunged across the table, grabbing Artem by the neck. The two soldiers standing guard reacted by pouncing on him. He tried to squeeze the life from his interrogator, but the soldiers overpowered him and dragged him to the floor. One of the soldiers had his arm around Sebastian's neck, while the other worked to get flex cuffs back on him. Then they jerked him back to his feet.

Artem stood. "One call, just one call, and those you hold dear will be dead before I even hang up!" Sebastian's mind was free-falling toward oblivion. How did they find out who he was? How did they find his family so quickly? What the hell was going on?

"My name is Sebastian Bishop," he spat. "I am an American."

"We already know that, Mr. Rubble!" Artem said condescendingly, tapping Sebastian on the forehead. "Since you decided to be John Rambo, we needed more information. Who is your commanding officer? Why are you here? Why are you wearing a Russian uniform? Is the American military spying on us, Mr. Rubble?"

"I am in the American military training with the Russians," Sebastian lied. His face was bright red from lack of blood and oxygen to his head.

The rebel leader finally approached Sebastian and said calmly, "Tell us everything you know or I will destroy everyone and everything you've ever cared about."

Sebastian thought about his sister and his parents. How could he have put them in such danger? They could do what they wanted with him, but he couldn't allow them to harm his family. The tension left Sebastian's body. They had won. He was broken.

Sebastian's last holdout was to give them his fictitious information. He wouldn't tell them he was SPETSNAZ until the last possible moment. He stuck to his story about training with the Russian regular army and becoming separated from his recon unit. The soldiers relaxed their grips on Sebastian and, within moments, released him completely. Sebastian stood in the middle of the guards, his hands still behind his back. It seemed Artem had delivered on his promise; he felt like a shell of a man.

His restraints were finally removed as they led him out of the office. Instead of going toward his cell, they shoved him toward the far end of the hall that ended with a door at the back of the building. The group burst through the back door and into the glaring sunlight. Sebastian thought this was it; at least he would die on a pretty day.

Rodchenko stood with his hands on his hips as the guards guided Sebastian toward him. Sebastian's head was like muddy water. Nothing was making sense to him.

"Valor and honor," Rodchenko repeated three times. The exercise was over. Sebastian collapsed as two medics rushed to his side to attend to his injuries.

Chapter 76

Stephanie stirred in her seat as the car slowed on its approach to the airport. Sitting up straight, she glanced across at Arval and quickly refocused on the uncertainty of her situation. "Could you please tell me where I'm going?" she asked, resigned to the fact that this was for real. "I'm supposed to be back on duty at the hospital in two days."

"I'm not sure you should be concerned about work for a while," Arval offered gently.

She sighed, "Of course, what am I thinking. So what do we do next?"

Arval cast a quick glance in her direction. "Well that's the tough part, dear," he began slowly.

Stephanie eyed him warily, "What do you have in mind, Arval? Where exactly am I headed?" she asked, realizing he already had a plan.

Arval took a deep breath as if he needed to get this next part out completely without interruption. "This is all worked out. To keep you as safe as possible, we need to be unpredictable. Getting you out of the country will buy us time. I have some contacts that can help us out with this. A ticket to Montreal, Canada, is waiting for you."

"Montre…" Stephanie started to interject. Arval responded by holding up a hand, stopping her protest.

"Stephanie, this is one of those times when we are ambushed by the unpredictability of life." His voice seemed to trail off to another time, but he was quickly back. "There is nothing to do but adapt to what we're given and overcome all adversity." He looked over at her. She was shaking her head, tears welling up in her eyes, "You can do this, Stephanie. You have the strength to do what's right and the courage to face your fears. This is important, and the package could not be in better hands." He smiled at her reassuringly. She nodded, quickly wiping the tears from her eyes.

Stephanie and Arval pulled up in front of 'Departures' at Charles De Gaulle airport. As they exited the vehicle, a French airport police officer told Arval his car must be moved or it would be towed. Arval thought for a moment. "That would be most helpful," he replied, tossing the officer his keys. The policeman was so surprised by Arval's response that he just stood there looking at the keys as Arval whisked Stephanie inside. Together, they went straight to the Air Canada ticket counter. A one-way e-ticket to Montreal was waiting in Stephanie's name, but the flight would not leave for another four hours. That was fine with Stephanie, as she wanted a little time to gather her thoughts. The last 36 hours had been a whirlwind of life-changing events, and now she just needed a little time to process it all. She was handed her boarding pass and turned back to Arval who was waiting patiently.

As she approached, he intercepted her and redirected her to the airport stores. "You need to change into something a little less conspicuous," he told her, pressing money into her hand. "I'll wait for you in the nearest restaurant while you get yourself some new things and clean up a bit. Then we'll have something to eat while we wait for your flight," he instructed.

Stephanie didn't resist. She purchased an outfit suitable for traveling, undergarments, comfortable shoes, and a fashionable backpack. She picked up some body wash, a toothbrush, toothpaste, and deodorant. She headed to the bathroom with her bags, looking forward to some hot, soapy water. She threw her dirty clothes, shoes, and satchel away. She placed the package upright in the backpack, surrounding it with the rest of her things. Feeling much more organized and mobile, she headed off to join Arval. When she emerged from the restroom, she felt like a new woman; she looked like a new woman.

During their meal, Arval explained the escape plan to her. "When you arrive in Montreal, Captain Luke de Armand with the Royal Canadian Mounted Police will meet you at the baggage claim," he began.

"To help me with all my luggage?" She teased. They both smiled.

"He has agreed to pick you up and take you to the home of a friend of mine. He and a couple of his officers will provide you some protection at the residence. It will take me just a couple of days to arrange everything for your safe return, so try to relax a little.

You'll need to call your work; maybe say a relative suddenly passed or something to cover your time away. Keep everything in your regular life as normal as possible. There is no need to raise any suspicion or make your loved ones worry unnecessarily." Stephanie nodded her understanding.

Arval handed her another card with his new cell phone number and the information for his friend in Montreal handwritten on the back. He pointed at the numbers, "Top one is my new cell number, the bottom is the friend you'll be staying with. He is an older fellow with a dry sense of humor and a keen mind. His wife is one of the sweetest people I've ever met, and the two of them will take good care of you."

He reached into his back pocket and pulled out his wallet. "Here is 500 Euro. Use it to buy clothes, toiletries, food, whatever you need."

"Arval, I can't…" Stephanie began to protest. Arval held up his hand, stopping her mid-sentence.

"Purchase a calling card and call me on my cell phone day after tomorrow. Use a different pay phone each time you place a call. Even though you should only be there a few days, pay attention to your surroundings, and mix up your daily routine. Any time you leave the house, use a different route."

"You seem to know a lot about this kind of stuff, 007."

Arval couldn't help but smile. "I was fourteen when a similar speech was given to me with the French resistance during World War II. I actually got quite good at gathering intelligence. The game has changed, but the fundamental rules remain the same."

She grabbed his hand. "Thank God I found you," Stephanie said sincerely.

Arval felt his face flush. "Providence, my dear, providence. Besides," he added, "I'm a sucker for adventure." The old man winked. "Now I will take care of things on this end. I have no idea how far their hands reach or how aggressively they will try to pursue you. So we will be as cautious as we can until this matter is resolved." They both sat for a moment in silence.

Arval waited a while for Stephanie to process the plan and ask any further questions of him. When he thought enough time had passed and she was resigned to what she needed to do, he broke the silence by suggesting they move from the restaurant to the waiting area for her flight. She grabbed her backpack, and they found comfortable seating in an area where they could talk quietly without being overheard.

When they were settled, Arval took Stephanie's hand in his and spoke. "Stephanie, I promised to tell you about the package you have and its significance to those who are after it. You have quite innocently become the bait in a very dangerous international game of cat and mouse."

Chapter 77

Svetozar Dimitrijevic and Deputy Prime Minister Bradic arrived on the grounds of a private resort north of the city of Odessa, Ukraine. The resort was nestled comfortably on the banks of the Black Sea and had the nicest amenities money could buy. It could easily be mistaken for a private playground for the area's most elite, except for the military security that included heavy mechanized vehicles surrounding the property.

Modern Ukraine was a story of contrasts; vast wealth framed in abject poverty; contemporary police agencies earning the respect of their European counterparts submerged in some of the most sophisticated organized criminal enterprises on earth; new world political objectives struggling to emerge from an old world foundation. Dimitrijevic loved the Ukraine and thought that Serbia could learn a lot from its growth and direction.

The men entered the secure compound and were shown to a luxury conference hall that was the central building of the complex. Inside they found a large circular room with parquet floors, rustic furniture, and a décor reminiscent of a high-priced hunting lodge. The seaside wall consisted almost entirely of windows with a breathtaking view of the water.

Dimitrijevic and Bradic situated themselves around a large table where neat piles of documents, including rolled maps and sealed government files distinguished by priority security markings, were waiting. A smartly dressed staff member brought them coffee and pastries and retreated swiftly from the room, leaving the two men alone in the cavernous atrium. They sipped their coffee in silence, taking in the beautiful view.

About fifteen minutes later, a door flush with the wall on the far side of the room cracked open. It swung wide and a large Russian man, still talking back into the room from which he came, filled the doorway. He concluded his business with whomever he spoke with a dismissive, "Da, da, da." And then he turned his attention to his guests.

"Gentlemen," he greeted with hand extended. The two Serbs rose,

Dimitrijevic slower, of course, than Bradic. The Russian shook hands with Bradic first and then the old man. He sat across the table from his visitors and asked them about their trip, if they had ever been to the Black Sea before, etc.; small talk to relax the mood. The same staff member as before brought their host coffee and a rich pastry and promptly disappeared again.

The room fell silent as the Russian took a bite of pastry and a sip of coffee. He then took a deep breath and began. "Deputy Prime Minister, up to this point our respective staffs have been working on the details of the plan we are about to discuss, with our supervision, of course, but with little direct involvement from you and I. This was of highest importance for the security implications, but now we have reached the final and most critical level. So we must have absolute clarity of intent and purpose, would you agree?"

"I agree completely," Bradic replied.

"So we begin with the basics. We know *of* each other, but we do not really know each other, so let us get to know one another." The Russian smiled his practiced diplomatic smile that remained unnatural for a man of war. "My full name is Aleksey Vasilyevich Chernov; I am the Colonel General over the *Privolzsk-Ural* Military District. You will also hear it referred to as the *Volga-Ural* Military District. I have some of the most professional and battle-hardened troops on the face of the earth under my command." The Colonel General leaned forward toward his guests. "I have watched with great discomfiture, over the last decade, your country tossed to and fro at the whim of foreigners. I understand your plight. My very own blood is Serbian; my mother's family lives in Nic to this day." He paused, pleased at the reaction of surprise from his new political ally. "To be perfectly clear about our position, Prime Minister Bradic, we stand ready to support Serbia as she stands again to her feet."

Bradic swelled with pride at the confirmation of support from the Bear of Russia. "I am humbled and grateful for your support, General. In return, my name is Dragan Bradic. My official title is Deputy Prime Minister of Economy and Regional Development for the people of Serbia. I entered public service in December of 1999 just as NATO began unfairly and unjustly dividing our country. Before I began my political career, I was a ground commander with the Black Tigers. I served under General Petrovic."

"I know him well," the Russian General interjected.

Bradic continued, "I witnessed twenty-four of my men executed by members of the Albanian UCK. We were retreating back to Serbia proper from Kosovo under an agreed, NATO sanctioned cease-fire. My men were ambushed just north of Mitrovica. Only I escaped." Bradic took a moment to close the door on this memory that would haunt him forever. His voice lowered as he continued, "I have played politics for 10 years. Maneuvered for position every day in office. I am now ready to make my bid for President. Early polls show that I am the overwhelming favorite to win. When I do, our plan will immediately go into effect." Bradic swallowed hard, his eyes glossy from the sincerity of his story.

The Russian General nodded solemnly, "We will be ready."

Dimitrijevic smiled as silence filled the immense room. "Well, it seems we are no longer strangers" he said, lightening the mood. "From now on, we talk only to each other; our strategists can now stand down. We have entered the final stage."

Bradic sat up straight in his chair. "General, if it is not too much trouble, will you walk me through your vision of our plan."

The General smiled broadly and rolled a large topographic map open across the table. "It would be my pleasure, Mr. President," he said with a wink.

Chapter 78

"Stephanie," Arval said. "I've been thinking about everything you told me on the bench outside Notre Dame, and I believe the package you are carrying is actually a vital piece of history. When you mentioned that your patient was Dr. Fournier, it all fell into place."

There was a long pause as Arval tried to formulate his thoughts. Finally he began, "As I told you, I've attended some of his seminars and first heard of his theory regarding the Balkans about seven years ago. Dr. Fournier was always regarded as a strange operator within the academic society, kind of a rogue, if you will. However, he is the absolute authority on the Balkans in Europe, actually probably worldwide. He spent a great deal of time there specifically researching the Roman influence on the Balkans from the time they settled there shortly after the time of Christ until they essentially left the area. The last of any recognizable Roman settlements faded around 900AD. There was a turbulent time in this area from roughly 900 until about the late 1100s. By that time Catholicism was well established."

Stephanie had no idea what all this could have to do with her current situation, but she listened intently, trying to follow the ancient history.

Arval continued, "In about 1170 a man by the name of Stefan Nemanja rose to power in the Raska region, striving to solidify a Serbian state. He was very successful, and thus began the Nemanjic Dynasty. His middle son, also named Stefan, who was crowned as the first king of Serbia in 1217 by the sovereign authority of the Pope, succeeded him. Now the youngest son, Sava, the new King's brother, had earlier become a monk, and his zeal to spread Christianity to the region caught the eye of the Vatican, and in conjunction with helping his brother secure the throne, he earned himself the title of Arch Bishop. He was ordained through Papal authority and was the first religious leader for the Serbia his father and brother began to shape. Thus began the golden age for Serbia, which lasted until the Turks amassed their forces against the Serbs in the late 1300s.

Arval was quiet for a moment. He gazed absently at the passing travelers as he concentrated on relaying this complicated bit of history to Stephanie in a way that she would understand.

"On June 28, 1389, history stopped for the Serbian people as the Ottoman Empire dramatically defeated the Serbs, killing thousands on a battlefield situated in the now hotly contested province of Kosovo. This battlefield, forever burned in the minds of all Serbs, is known as the Field of Blackbirds."

Stephanie marveled at Arval's depth of knowledge. He recited this historical timeline with all the major events in a manner that only a learned person with real perspective could do. Stephanie imagined he must have been a very popular instructor. She didn't like history at all in school, but she would have gladly taken a course from this man.

Arval continued, "I cannot stress enough the importance of the Holy Roman Empire and its influence during this time. Keeping that in mind, I must backtrack a bit to get to Dr. Fournier's theory and apparent discovery. There was a man by the name of Alberto Di Morra, a Beneventan from a noble family. He was well educated and became a monk at an early age. He progressed steadily through the 'ranks,' if you will, of the Papal Hierarchy. In 1155 he was appointed Cardinal Deacon, and in 1165 he was appointed Legate to Dalmatia and Hungary. These appointments were made during the reign of Pope Alexander III.

"What is a 'legate'?" Stephanie interrupted.

"A legate is an emissary of the Pope. He represents the Vatican in other countries. Stephan Nemanja, the senior, you'll remember, came into his own around 1170, so the Vatican representative landing on Balkan shores was an opportunity not to be missed. Stephan Senior began developing a relationship with the Legate, seeking in earnest the blessing of God on the rising Serbian state. Serbia had only recently embraced Christianity, but its popularity spread like wildfire throughout the land. To this day, Serbia conducts business by the rule of God, not the rule of man. That principle comes back in this story shortly."

Stephanie realized that Arval had been giving this a great deal of thought since their chance encounter earlier that morning. She was completely engrossed in what he was telling her, but she was still trying to figure out how this could come around to her situation.

"Understand, what happens next," Arval cautioned, "is speculation and conjecture on the part of Dr. Fournier; but in light of recent events, he may very well have been exactly right. Shortly after taking his place as the leader of Serbia, Stephan Senior set out defining the borders of this new country. It took 12 years to survey the land and develop a map of 'Greater Serbia.'

Now here is where things get very interesting. In 1178, Stephan's friend, the Legate, was appointed Chancellor of the Holy Roman Church, and went on to be elected Pope in 1187, taking the name Pope Gregory the VIII. The timing of his rise and the completion of the survey of the land was not coincidence to Stephan; it was divine intervention. He immediately set out for Rome to speak with the new Pope, his old friend."

Stephanie shifted her position on the upholstered two-person seat, leaning closer to the old man. His mind was immersed in unraveling the mystery surrounding this time in history.

Slowly he continued, "During this time, Christianity was almost obliterated in Palestine by the Muslim leader Saladin. Gregory's predecessor, Urban III, was completely distraught by the news of the fall of Jerusalem. Some say he died of a broken heart. Gregory VIII, realizing the severity of the situation, began immediately to plan the fourth crusade to be launched in an attempt to take back Jerusalem. In his preoccupation with this major event, he did not have much time to entertain other matters. However, because Stephan was such a close friend, he was granted audience with the new Pope. He presented the recently completed survey of the land and asked that the boundaries be confirmed as permanent by Papal authority and protected under seal of the Holy See. The request was granted, the details settled by the Papal court, and Stephan was on his way back to the Balkans. Pope Gregory the VIII was only in office for roughly fifty-seven days before he died."

Stephanie looked out the window at the activity on the tarmac, trying to process the story and its significance. Arval glanced at her and realized immediately she wasn't really following.

"Now," he said. "Let me try to bring this story up to date and tell you how it relates to your main question: *'What does this have to do with me?'*" Arval smiled. "During this time the Vatican was the law. It was irrefutable and uncontested. So the new document held by Stephan Senior was equivalent to the official establishment of a country. For instance, when Israel became its own country in 1948 after World War II, they had documentation endorsed by the international community that established their borders, gave them authority of self-government, and granted them permission to establish military forces for her protection. Although not often considered, there is a process for the confirmation and declaration of a new country. This document held by Stephan Senior was a primitive, yet none the less binding, contract of the establishment of the country of Serbia."

"Wow," Stephanie said under her breath.

"This document was passed on to the new King, Stephan Jr. It continued to be passed on from generation to generation until the Ottoman Empire invaded. Then it was lost, and over time everyone simply considered the story a folk tale, the thing of legend that is passed on to one's children. In fact, by modern times the story had barely survived, but the relentless Dr. Fournier dug it up and began to pursue it obsessively. So what you carry Stephanie is his discovery, the establishment of a country."

Stephanie was trying to digest all that Arval was telling her. A few things still didn't make sense to her. "Wait a minute," she said, "surely there have been other documents or treaties drawn with regard to Serbia since the 1300s."

"Of course," Arval agreed. "The Ottomans ruled the area until the beginning of the twentieth century, and then there was Yugoslavia which was established after World War II, and most recently, the Dayton Peace Accords governing the separation of the different Balkan states; but this is the point: separation.

Remember, history has been suspended for the Serbs since 1389. From that time forward, Serbia has simply changed hands from one tyrant to another as far as they are concerned. The greater portion of what we consider the modern day Balkans is still, in the mind of the

Serbians, rightfully theirs. They, of course, conducted the futile military campaign in the 1990s, trying to regain control by force, but the country was not unified. A great deal of the country thought Milosovic was crazy, as did the rest of the world. Don't get me wrong, the Serbs still want back what they believe is theirs, but they also know that there is a certain way to get it. What they need is overt support by someone with muscle like Russia or China, strong Serbian leadership, and hope. If this document falls into the wrong hands, they may get all three."

Stephanie thought about the package tucked inside her backpack as waves of realization crashed on her mind. Arval continued, "Remember, it was Serb Nationalism that ignited World War I. These people believe in their heritage, and their hatred and animosity for those that stand in their way runs deeper than you and I will ever understand. They will use that document you have as the flag that they can rally around as a nation, and probably declare war on the other indigenous peoples of what we once knew as Yugoslavia. They are skilled and fearless warriors and the countries who, under normal circumstances, would intervene, are entrenched in wars in the Middle East. The Balkans could become a free-fire zone overnight."

Stephanie closed her eyes and rubbed her temples. "So, to sum it all up, I am the key to this whole mess."

Arval paused, thinking about that statement. "The document, if that is what is in that package, is the verification and confirmation of the establishment of Serbia. It authenticates an ancient tale and is of the highest importance to a very intelligent and motivated group of people." He paused for a moment, glancing at his wristwatch to check the time. "So yes, I think it's fair to say that to the several million people who make up the Former Republic of Yugoslavia, you just became Public Enemy Number One."

Stephanie put her head in her hands, trying to keep it together. This day had just gone from really bad to a whole lot worse.

Chapter 79

Sebastian was driven a short distance from the torture house, as he came to think of it, to a clearing. Waiting on the ground were two medical helicopters with full crew. An air medic continued work on Sebastian, starting an IV in his arm, trying to get him rapidly re-hydrated. He was numb; they could have done about anything to him and he wouldn't have cared.

The helicopter was being loaded with a few other soldiers who looked to be in similar shape as Sebastian. They lifted off, and Sebastian stared at the wall of the aircraft for the entire trip back.

Once they touched down, the men were transferred to a hospital facility for treatment. Sebastian had no idea where he was; nor did he care. They reset his nose and cleaned the cut near his eye. He received eight stitches to close the gash. He had a hairline fracture on two ribs, bruises and abrasions, and a sprained left wrist. Otherwise, he was all right, at least physically.

Sebastian was having a hard time coming to grips with two things; first and foremost, the thought of putting his family in danger. Even though this was a training exercise, it showed that they were vulnerable to his chosen profession. He hated that feeling. Second, he felt as though he had failed the exercise. He was unable to resist, and hadn't even attempted to escape. In his mind, he thought himself weak, and from his approach to target, to his ultimate disclosure of information, he had failed the last portion of his training.

On his second day of recovery Caporal Rodchenko came to his bedside. The morning sun beamed brightly through a nearby window, illuminating the foot of Sebastian's bed.

"How are you feeling?" he asked.

"Fine, thank you, Sir," Sebastian replied.

"Do you feel up for your debrief?"

"Yes, Sir."

"Ok, today at 1500hrs someone will be in to get you. I'll see you this afternoon." With that, Rodchenko turned and left the sick bay.

Sebastian was restless for the next several hours, waiting for his inevitable debrief. He went over and over in his mind the things he had done wrong. The time finally came, and a regular Russian army soldier of low rank came and told Sebastian it was time for his meeting.

He slowly swung around to the edge of his bed, and the movement caused all of his wounds to ignite. His head hurt so badly it made him woozy, and he thought for a minute he may blackout.

After sitting still and taking deep breaths for a few minutes he was able to stand. The soldier didn't know whether to help him or let him maneuver for himself. Sebastian noticed that the young man was observing him with a look that can only be described as awe. Apparently, he had been informed that the man he was escorting was SPETSNAZ. Sebastian sighed as he stood in his less than flattering hospital gown, feeling like a train wreck, and certainly not feeling worthy of anyone's admiration.

He shuffled along, holding the rail that ran the length of the hallway. His escort motioned to the door he was to enter and knocked on Sebastian's behalf.

"Enter," came the reply from inside the room.

The soldier opened the door for Sebastian, who entered with great effort. Inside were five men: Rodchenko; the SPETSNAZ Commanding Officer, Ivan Lazerev; the robust and friendly man he had met when he first arrived, Ivan Antonovich; the man who played the Chechen Rebel leader; and his interrogator known as Artem. They all sat behind a long table. In the center of the room was a single chair. Sebastian, trying to mask his pain, walked toward the chair and stood beside it. He stood at attention, as best he could and said loudly, "Bishop, Sebastian, reporting as ordered, Sir!" The effort to forcefully say the proper introduction made his ribs feel as if they just snapped in half. His legs began to shake from the pain.

"Sit down, son," the Commanding Officer said with a fatherly tone.

Sebastian sat and tried to focus his eyes that were involuntarily watering from the pain of even the slightest movement.

The men across from him gave him a moment. They could all relate to Sebastian's condition.

The Commanding Officer began. "Tell us how you think you did."

Sebastian had hoped they wouldn't start this way, but he tried to answer truthfully. "I did not do an appropriate job recon-ing the target. My approach was too fast, and I had not taken the right measures to get adequate food or water before committing to the mission. Once in captivity, my desire to get food and water caused me to make another mistake by offering a fictitious name which got me the food, but cost me dearly as a result. I should have been more prepared for this contingency through better prior planning. I resisted as well as I could, but broke too quickly and never once attempted escape."

The men sat in silence, each considering Sebastian's summary. Rodchenko was the first to speak. "Your approach to the target was unimpeded. There were no enemy patrols or booby-traps to contend with. This perhaps gave you a false sense of security and caused you to charge forward without as much caution as was actually prudent. As you can imagine, this is the lesson we want our soldiers to learn. Each step must be taken as if you were walking into the heart of an ambush." Sebastian nodded his head in understanding of the critique.

"You must always take care to find water and nourishment in such circumstances. You had plenty of time, and we even gave you purifying tablets so you could drink from local water sources," chimed in Ivan Antonovich. Again Sebastian nodded his understanding.

Rodchenko started again. "Once you were within the target area, you were going to get caught. We had eyes on you for much longer than you know, I'm sure. You did nothing wrong there, in fact, your method of concealment was quite adequate." He paused for a moment and added, "Tell us what you saw."

Sebastian recalled a full inventory of intelligence from the building. The men furiously scribbled notes as they listened. When he was finished, he thought he saw a subtle smile on Ivan Antonovich's face, but he quickly looked back down.

"Let's talk about when you were interrogated," the Commanding Officer said. The men all turned to the man called Artem.

Somehow, he looked different to Sebastian. He was more relaxed, and his real Russian Army uniform seemed to suit him much better than that of a Chechen. He smiled at Sebastian and began. "First of all, let me introduce myself; my name is Dimitri Shiztokov. I am a

Lieutenant Colonel with the psychological warfare division of Special Operations. I have conducted this type of training for many years. I will begin by saying you did much better than you probably think. You did not even offer us your name after you had been subjected to some very brutal treatment. Some men break immediately; but some, like you, require extraordinary measures to break. However, you must understand something, Bishop; they all break."

This was a small consolation for what Sebastian had endured.

The man that Sebastian knew only as the rebel leader now spoke. "You are probably wondering how we got the recent pictures of your family." Sebastian sat up a little straighter now, anxious to hear this explanation. "First, let me tell you that we have not had to employ such drastic measures to get someone to talk for several years."

He looked down for a moment, realizing he owed a little bit of explanation to the soldier before him. "We are allowed by military law ten days from the time this exercise begins until we must bring the soldiers in, and of course, we are not allowed to use chemical means to extract information. Soldiers who do not find the target or take too long to reach the target are immediately disqualified. If you break within the first 24 hours of being taken captive, you are disqualified.

You lasted a full eight days under severe conditions. Just about all we could legally throw at you. For that, you should be proud. Let me explain how we got your family's pictures. Your information, including your home address back in the United States, was pulled from public records on the internet. You must always assume that the enemy knows or will quickly establish your real identity. If you are going to continue in this business, there are ways to have this information removed, and you need to talk with your technology people about that when you return to your unit. Anyway, by good fortune for us, we had two SPETSNAZ operators cross training at Fort Bragg in North Carolina. It was merely a matter of a phone call, a digital camera, and a rental car, and they had the photos sent to us via e-mail within 32 hours."

Sebastian looked down, slightly shaking his head. He could hardly imagine what would have happened to them if this had been a real operation. Enough said. Sebastian knew his mistakes and how to improve on them. He also knew that overall he did well, and they were very pleased with his performance.

The Commanding Officer stood, and the men at the table stood immediately at his lead. Sebastian also stood as quickly as he could manage.

"You did an excellent job, young man. Hopefully, you have a better understanding of your limitations, and a better grasp on operational procedures under these dire circumstances. I pray that you never find yourself in such a situation." With that said, there was a pause, and at some hidden command, all the men at the table snapped to attention. Sebastian followed suit and reflexively saluted the men before him.

"On behalf of the Spetsialnove Nazranie, welcome to the brotherhood of the greatest warriors of our great Russia." They all snapped a salute to Sebastian and then, one by one they filed around the table and shook his hand. All except for Ivan Antonovich who gave Sebastian a big bear hug.

"Son of a...!" Sebastian yelled in pain. Ivan released his grip, but held Sebastian up as he grabbed the back of the chair he had been sitting in. There was a pause, and then Sebastian chuckled painfully. At that, all the men began to laugh heartily. He had made it; he was now SPETSNAZ.

Chapter 80

At last, it was time for Stephanie to board. She squeezed Arval's hand that she had continued to hold. "Thank you, Arval, for everything," she said trying not to tear up.

"Stephanie, my dear, you have turned out to be a very exciting woman to be around. You have breathed new life into these old bones. Now remember everything I told you, and pay attention to everything and everyone around you." They stood together a moment longer, Arval not wanting to let her out of his sight, and Stephanie wishing he was boarding with her. Time was fleeting, Arval knew, and he had much to do to secure her safe return. He gave her a reassuring hug and kissed the young frightened girl on both cheeks. "You will be fine, my dear," he said, holding her cheeks in his hands and looking straight into her eyes. "Now go."

Stephanie took a deep breath and walked forward to join the boarding line. She folded her arms across her chest and gave one last glance back at the exit doors and the life she was about to leave behind; the line crept slowly forward.

Chapter 81

One week later, Sebastian found himself back in the barracks at the SPETSNAZ training facility. The place was quieter than ever. Only 13 men remained from the original 22 who began the last phase. As Sebastian adjusted his gear near his rack, the door to the barracks swung open. Davide came strolling in as if he had been on holiday for the last two weeks. He had a nasty cut under his right eye that had been roughly sutured with about 14 stitches. Other than that, he looked none the less for wear.

"Hey, man," Sebastian said clasping, his friend's hand.

"How are you, brother?" Davide asked, bringing his other hand up and closing around his friend's hand like a sandwich.

There was a pause, "I'm ok," he answered. "You?"

"They're a bunch of pussies," Davide answered.

"When did you break?"

"Day four," Davide answered with much bravado. The two soldiers laughed heartily.

They had only three weeks left. The training cadre took it relatively easy on them, easing them back into PT and doing a lot of classroom work on covert ops. They spent the last two weeks on small fire team drills and refresher work on building entries. They did a lot of shooting, and spent two days working explosives for entries and a few small sabotage drills. They were slowly building the soldiers' confidence again by working scenarios designed for success.

By the last week, the Russian soldiers were brought in for closed-door sessions preparing them for the teams they would soon be assigned to. Sebastian and Davide had a lot of down time and began to prepare their gear for departure back to France. They didn't speak a word about their experiences in the last phase. They both made it, and that was enough.

Sebastian lay in his rack, struggling to read through a book in Russian that he had purchased in Moscow. It was one thing to speak the language, it was totally another to read or write it. By now Sebastian and Davide's Russian was pretty good. They were

comfortable with the language they had been submerged in for nearly
a year now. Sebastian wanted to make sure he was comfortable
reading it as well. You never knew when you might have to come back
and 'blend in.'

Only two days were left until graduation and their trip back to
Legion Headquarters in France. The door suddenly burst open, and
Davide entered with a serious look on his face. "Grab your gear, man,"
he said in French. Sebastian knew Davide spoke French only when he
was geared up about something serious.

"What's up?" Sebastian asked, spinning out of his bunk.

"We have a live op."

"Yeah, right. Just a reminder, brother, we don't fight for the
Russian Army." Sebastian began to lie back down.

Davide stopped collecting his gear and looked intently at Sebastian,
"Listen, Sebastian, as far as they are concerned, we *are* Russian Army,
and the top of the military food chain at that." Davide continued to
gear up.

"Are you serious?" Sebastian asked.

"Chechen rebels attacked a church in the middle of the service.
They have an unknown number of hostages, and we are the closest and
most capable unit available to handle the situation."

"This is unbelievable," Sebastian said. "Why should we do this,
man? This isn't our fight." Sebastian stood slowly.

Davide stepped toward him suddenly and grabbed him roughly by
the arm, "Because we're the only ones who can, Bishop. There are no
choosing battles when it comes to doing the right thing. We fight for
good no matter on whose soil we stand. We're Special Ops, brother;
this is what we do. Now snap out of it, stop feeling sorry for yourself,
and get geared up."

Davide pushed away from Sebastian and marched out the door with
his rifle in one hand and tightening the straps of his flak jacket with the
other.

Sebastian stood alone in the barracks for a moment. It was time to
make a decision. Davide was right, either make the choice to embrace
this lifestyle or call it quits and crawl back in the rack. Sebastian took

a deep breath, closed his eyes, and exhaled slowly. He opened his eyes and started putting on his gear.

Chapter 82

Arval made his way back to the city. His mind was racing, running through a checklist of things that would need to be done. First, however, he wanted to put an end to the mystery. He drove to *Hospital Pitie-Salpetriere* to meet with Professor Fournier.

After speaking with the information receptionist, he took the elevator and headed to room 434 in the cardiac care unit. A nurse intercepted him in the corridor and asked who he was there to see. When he informed her that he needed to speak to Dr. Fournier, she cautioned him not to tire the professor because he needed his strength to undergo heart surgery the following morning. He assured her that he just wanted to sit with Dr. Fournier and keep him company for a while. She nodded her consent, and he proceeded to the professor's room. He knocked gently on the door and entered slowly. Dr. Fournier lay in the hospital bed with various tubes and monitors running from his pale body. Arval pursed his lips in sympathy for the man lying helplessly in front of him.

He walked to the far side of the bed and sat in the available chair. He waited patiently as the professor slept, not wanting to startle him. A half hour passed, and finally the professor stirred and blinked awake. A nurse appeared almost magically, checking the condition of her patient. She smiled and spoke to him softly. She helped him get a drink of water, and the professor weakly cleared his throat, "Thank you," he said hoarsely.

"You have a visitor, Professor." The nurse nodded to Arval sitting on the far side of his bed. He turned his head, seeing Arval for the first time.

A little wary now of strangers, the professor only nodded feebly.

"Bonjour, Professor. I have news for you," Arval responded kindly.

Chapter 83

Sebastian, Davide, and twelve other commandos jumped into a helicopter that was in full revolution, ready to pop off the tarmac as soon as the last man loaded. Sebastian was a little surprised to see Rodchenko already on board and taking command of the operation. He took a head count and said something to the pilots via his headset. Less than eight minutes had elapsed from call out to airborne. This is what they trained for.

It took twenty-five minutes to get on station. The soldiers unloaded and rallied at a command post established by the local police. The police commander quickly brought Rodchenko up to speed on the situation. Ten hostages had been released: a few old people, women, and children. The clergy was still being held hostage, and the terrorists were demanding a TV crew to broadcast their demands. The police commander stated that he didn't think they actually had any demands at all; they simply wanted to execute the Church officials on live television.

The police commander also added that after interviewing the hostages they determined there were at least seven terrorists and fourteen people remaining inside the Church. They couldn't confirm if they had any explosives, but considering the past exploits of these ruthless terrorists, explosives were almost a given.

Rodchenko had a brief huddle with his soldiers. "They have come here expecting to die, and we are going to fulfill their expectations." Rodchenko was in his element. He began deploying the men to various positions, with the main force going to the front of the church. The plan was the same as they had trained a hundred times before. They would attack hard and fast and kill every last one of the terrorists.

Sebastian was surprised at the ease with which he accepted the mission. He crouched behind a few vehicles and worked his way, with one other soldier, to cover the rear of the church. A few of the local townspeople bulked up their courage, but still stood at a safe distance, with video cameras and camera phones. Sebastian glanced at them and suddenly remembered he had not lowered his balaclava to cover his face and conceal his identity before he started moving. He pulled it down with a hasty jerk and readied himself for the final sprint.

A cement wall, standing about two meters high, surrounded the back of the church. It framed a small courtyard that was overgrown and generally unkempt. Sebastian ran in a crouch across the narrow street to the wall, slamming his shoulder into it and pressing his back flat to check for his partner. His brother commando was right on his heels. Sebastian knew that Rodchenko was not about to sit around and negotiate. He was going to get set up and hit hard and fast, using the element of surprise and violence of action to overwhelm the enemy.

Sebastian quickly found a foothold in the dilapidated wall, slung his rifle over his shoulder, drew his pistol, and started over. Progress was swift at the front of the church.

There was no sufficient cover or concealment in the area directly in front of the entrance to the church. Undeterred, Rodchenko moved his team into attack position. They moved impressively with their guns up on target. As the SPETSNAZ soldiers moved into position, the terrorists saw them coming and began to panic. They had anticipated a much longer siege and all the drama it brought; in fact, that was the cornerstone of their entire mission. They were surprised and unprepared for the arrival of SPETSNAZ soldiers. Rodchenko didn't miss a stride; he charged the front entrance with his entire team right behind him.

A Russian commando built like an NFL linebacker flew in front of Rodchenko with a Stazi 12-gauge shotgun. It was loaded with the special 'lock-buster' ammunition. The commando shot the vulnerable parts of the door, the hinges, in rapid succession. Rodchenko crashed through the door full force. The team spread expertly in full attack formation. The dynamic entry had been so sudden that some of the terrorists were caught trying to chamber rounds; others were simply starting to run.

Just as Sebastian's two feet landed on the ground, the back door of the church burst open. Emerging was a Chechen with his arm wrapped around the throat of a Priest. He immediately started screaming at

Sebastian to drop his weapon.

"Ok, ok, I'm dropping my weapon!" Sebastian screamed in reply. He lowered his pistol very slowly, with both arms fully stretched. Sebastian couldn't figure out why the terrorist didn't just shoot him, but he realized a principle they had learned in training. In life and death situations, especially when a subject had to divide his attention, the survival instinct always won out. In this case, the terrorist was focused on the Priest whom he saw as a shield, and the protection appealed to his primitive instincts. His vital organs were protected and he was making forward progress. This was all his mind could process.

Sebastian continued to scream his compliance trying to fuel the confusion. He had a very small target window of the terrorist's head. He would have a fraction of a second to find his front sight as he lowered his weapon and take the shot. That's why he controlled the descent of his pistol. Just as the weapon came level with his face he picked up the front sight and squeezed the trigger. The shot struck the terrorist directly in the forehead.

As the man fell to the ground, two more figures appeared in the doorway. Sebastian readjusted his grip on his pistol, bringing his other hand up for stability and acquired his targets. He fired his pistol like a machine, the rounds ripping by in extremely close proximity to the Priest. Terrified, the Priest dropped to the ground and covered his ears with his hands to muffle the sound of the reports from the weapons.

As the first rounds from Sebastian's pistol impacted the first assailant, a deafening volley of shots came from just over his head as his partner lit into the terrorists with deadly accurate 7.62mm fire from his AK-47. The escaping enemy didn't even have time to raise their weapons.

While this was happening, gunfire was reporting nonstop from inside the church. In ninety seconds, the entire incident was over. Rodchenko and Davide announced loudly they were coming through the back. Sebastian and his partner lowered their weapons in the 'ready' position. Davide was limping severely, trying to conceal his pain. Rodchenko glanced at the dead Chechens, the terrified priest, and then Sebastian.

"Clear!" Rodchenko yelled, ending the operation.

"Clear!" Sebastian responded. He then re-holstered and asked his partner if he had any injuries. His partner had none and together they grabbed the Priest who was getting close to going into shock. They escorted him back out the front to waiting medical personnel. None of the remaining hostages were injured, except one who caught a ricochet in the thigh. It was a relatively minor injury, and he was able to leave the church under his own power.

All the terrorists were dead. Rodchenko was huddled with the police commander when one of the soldiers yelled out, "Media!"

Rodchenko quickly shook the officer's hand and yelled for his troops to fall in on him. They loaded into a police transport vehicle and headed back to their waiting helicopter.

"Good work, men," was all Rodchenko said.

Chapter 84

Two days after the crisis at the church, the men assembled for a small graduation ceremony in the makeshift parade ground of the training compound. Davide was not in attendance because his ankle had actually been broken during the skirmish with the Chechens. He had been pampered ever since by beautiful Russian nurses and was loving every minute of it. Ivan had even arranged a first class seat for Davide back to Paris. Sebastian could only laugh at his friend who acted like a Roman emperor feigning hardship with every move.

The ceremony was structured, yet short, and before they knew it, it was all over. There was something a little anti-climactic about it all with Davide not there. Ivan Antonovich was standing by after the ceremony with an unusually serious look on his face. He was dressed in civilian clothes and had about three days' worth of unshaven growth on his face. Sebastian barely recognized him.

After Sebastian finished saying good-bye to his new Russian brothers, he grabbed his military bag to meet up with Ivan who was taking him to the airport. Sebastian then saw Rodchenko approaching him with his usual intensity. He immediately dropped the bag and stood at attention, saluting.

Rodchenko quickly returned the salute and held out his hand. Sebastian grasped it, and Rodchenko pulled him close and spoke quietly, "You are one of us now. That means anytime, anywhere." He stepped back and looked intently in Sebastian's eyes. Sebastian nodded his acknowledgment, and with that Rodchenko turned and left. He wondered if he would ever see the robust Russian again.

Sebastian was allowed to change back into civilian clothes for his return to Paris. He and Ivan got into a civilian car that looked like it had been purchased in a back alley about 15 minutes earlier. On the way to the airport, Ivan hardly said a word. He was uncharacteristically silent, and the whole trip was very uncomfortable. As they pulled up to the departure terminal, Ivan got out to go into the airport. Sebastian started to get out as well, but Ivan leaned back in the door and said, "Stay in the car. I'll be right back." Sebastian was sure now that something was up. He was hoping that Ivan was playing a joke on him and making him fret for no reason. After a few minutes, Ivan came back to the car and sat down again in the driver's seat. He leaned back and looked straight out the windshield, saying nothing. This was very unlike him, and Sebastian's brow furrowed at his odd behavior.

"What is it, sir?" Sebastian inquired.

At a loss for words, the large Russian looked around blankly, not answering right away. He cleared his throat and placed his arm on Sebastian's shoulder. "My brother, you are getting on a plane, but not back to Paris. I am afraid you will be staying with us a little longer."

The statement took Sebastian completely by surprise. He was not in the mood for surprises; it had been a long nine months. "Sir?" Sebastian responded, seeking clarification.

"You are a very good soldier, Sebastian; very good. Your military has agreed to send you to advanced training at our request. Highly classified training, Sebastian."

Sebastian was dumbfounded; he couldn't believe his ears. What kind of specialized training did he not already have? What could possibly be left?

Sebastian couldn't dismiss the trepidation he was experiencing as he observed Ivan's uneasy demeanor. He suspected he knew a lot more about what was to come than he was saying.

In a much more businesslike tone, Ivan continued, "I will walk you inside where we will meet two men. When I introduce you, hand me this money." He handed Sebastian a handful of Rubles. "It will simply look like you are paying your driver. Happens here all the time. The men you meet will be very friendly, and they will treat you like a paying tourist. You will be escorted to a helicopter of a local tourist company. Speak to the men in English as if you are here for the first time. That is all I can tell you for now. Stay sharp my friend, and the next time you and I drive to the airport, I promise, it will be for a flight home."

Sebastian sighed and looked out the window for a moment; this did not sound good at all. Finally, he reached for the door handle, knowing it was pointless to try and press Ivan for further information. Ivan reached over and grabbed his arm before he could open the door. He looked intently at Sebastian and spoke sincerely, "The next steps of your journey will be trying and difficult. As much as things around you change, remember who you are. The skills you learn do not define you as a person. The true heart of a warrior is reflected in his character, not his ability."

Sebastian felt a pang of anxiety in the pit of his stomach. *'What am I getting into now?'* he wondered.

Chapter 85

Damir got back in the car with his men. "The girl is gone," he said flatly, giving no indication of his involvement in her narrow escape.

"What now?" the driver asked.

"Signal?" Damir asked the Bosnian.

"Floating merrily down the River Seine," he replied.

Damir looked back at his IT man who shrugged. "She must have thrown it on a tour boat, or gave it to someone who got on…I don't know."

"Time to head home." Damir leaned back in his seat, hoping this girl knew what she was doing.

Slavo and his men stepped out of the metro station and back into the daylight. Slavo was sullen and brooding. His men knew to just keep walking. When they reached their car, they got in and sat in glum silence.

Slavo's IT man opened his laptop, tapped a few keys, and studied the screen. Slowly he closed the laptop again, invoking the silent signal that the woman was 'off grid.'

"Anyone have any ideas?" Slavo asked in a rare moment of inclusion.

The men sat silently for a moment, not wanting to say something stupid. Finally, the IT man spoke. "She may try to make a run for it. Take a train or plane somewhere out of here."

Slavo nodded thoughtfully, "Ok, call Belgrade and have them monitor departures from the airport, train stations, etc. Hopefully, we can at least find out where she's going and make adjustments then."

Slavo sat looking out the front windshield. He was just delaying the inevitable. After some time, he finally opened his door. "I have to call my father," he said stepping out onto the sidewalk.

Chapter 86

Ivan and Sebastian walked through the doors of the airport. They proceeded briskly among the crowds who paid them no attention. At last, they reached two men who wore jackets with Moscow Tourist Company plastered in bright yellow across their backs. They greeted Sebastian warmly, welcoming him to Moscow in broken English. He smiled broadly, keeping up the charade that he was a bumbling American here to burn up his parents' college fund in search of adventure and self-discovery. Sebastian turned to Ivan and handed him the money. Ivan thanked him profusely and made his way back out of the terminal.

They walked through the airport to a small doorway that led directly out to the tarmac. Along the way, the men continued to talk to him in staccato English, shoving tourist maps and hotel brochures in his face as they walked. Outside the doorway, he saw a large Sikorsky helicopter waiting with faded paint reading 'Moscow Tourist Company' in English and Cyrillic. The blades were just beginning to turn, and about eight more people, all looking very 'touristy,' waited to climb onboard.

Once inside, Sebastian realized this was nothing more than a military transport helicopter complete with webbed seats and leaking hydraulic fluid. Sebastian found an empty slot and plopped down. He was given headphones to help muffle the roaring noise of the engines as they cranked up in full throttle for take-off. His escorts shed their jackets and fake personas and reassumed their real identities of professional military air crewmen. He saw them talking with the pilots, looking out opposite windows to make sure they were clear for lift off.

The other 'passengers' removed their outer costume to reveal either flight suits or military fatigues. Sebastian read on one guy's shoulder patch "Russian Special Operations Air Command" in Cyrillic. He sighed and looked out the window at the ground now moving vertically away from him.

The trip to their destination took an hour and seventeen minutes. The helicopter softly touched down and everyone inside unbuckled, preparing to exit. Sebastian followed suit, having no idea what else to do. The aircraft's blades were winding down with a dramatic whine as he exited. The helicopter's occupants all went their separate ways and Sebastian stood for a moment, wondering what his next move would be. In the fading daylight, he saw that he was now at a military airfield. Several Migs were tied down on the tarmac, and just in front of him, a couple of nondescript hangars had *military* written all over them in non-visible blandness.

After a couple minutes, a military vehicle pulled up in front of him, and the driver jumped out. "Bishop?" he asked with a smile.

"Yes, sir," Sebastian responded to the man, about his own age, wearing a military uniform that displayed no rank.

"I'll be taking you where you need to go. Jump in." The soldier grabbed Sebastian's bag and threw it in the backseat.

They drove for about forty minutes and talked almost the entire trip. The conversation was dominated by the driver's relentless questions about America. Sebastian tried to be cordial, answering in vague terms, but wondered if this was somehow another test.

They turned off the main road and continued for another fifteen minutes on a secondary road that was in poor condition. Finally, they turned onto a dirt road that looked like it was used primarily by tractors to get from one field to the next. After five minutes of holding on for dear life, they pulled to a stop in front of an old farmhouse.

Chapter 87

Sebastian got out and entered the house with his driver in the lead. The inside of the house was poorly lit, and it took a moment for Sebastian's eyes to adjust. The foyer was large and flanked on either side by two large rooms. Ahead was a long hallway with a steep staircase rising along its right wall. The hallway led to what appeared to be the kitchen. The driver ushered Sebastian into the dining room where six men were seated around a large formal dinner. The driver introduced Sebastian then excused himself from the room. One of the older men stood as Sebastian entered, holding his hands up warmly. "Ah, our final guest has arrived," he said in formal Russian. "Please, come and sit with us. I believe dinner is almost ready."

Sebastian smiled and nodded politely, walking to the table. All the other men stood and shook his hand in turn. He sat down in the only remaining chair and situated himself at the table.

Within minutes, the food began to arrive from the kitchen, and with it, the conversation came, too. They all talked like old friends about topics that Sebastian realized were safe; sports, women, and stories of bravado that had them all laughing well into the night. It was a very nice evening of good food and good conversation. There was plenty of Vodka to go around, but Sebastian tried to stick with bottled water. The last drink of the evening was unavoidable, however, and Sebastian held up his glass as the man, who was apparently their host, made a toast, "To the qualities we share that bind us as brothers. May we never turn our backs to the enemy."

"Here, here!" the men answered heartily.

As the evening drew to a close, Sebastian was shown to his room by the same old woman who brought them their meal, and prepared it, he was sure. She led the way, struggling up each step of the rickety stairs. His room was small, but private, and the bed was incredibly soft. He was still very confused about what was going on, but his companions made him feel welcome and relaxed. *'Maybe this won't be so bad after all,'* Sebastian thought to himself as he quickly drifted off to sleep.

At precisely 6:00 the next morning, a soft buzz sounded throughout the upstairs, indicating it was time for the men to wake up. Sebastian stirred a little, disoriented and plenty surprised at how hard he had slept. He turned the light on in his small room and threw on his pants and a t-shirt. He decided to take a quick look out in the hallway to see what the other men were doing. When he pulled the door open, he found just outside a washbasin with water still steaming, a towel and washcloth, and a pile of neatly folded clothes. Sebastian brought the items back in his room and washed down his body with the washcloth and donned his new clothes. He assumed he looked exactly like they wanted him to look: like a poor Russian farmhand.

He walked downstairs to find the same group from the night before sitting down to a full breakfast. There was a little less chatter this morning, and the 'host' was engrossed in the morning paper, paying little attention to anything else.

When the men were all finished with breakfast, the host looked up, folded the paper, and set it aside. He took a moment, then stood. The men, as if sensing a hidden command, rose to their feet, as well.

"Shall we?" the man said, gesturing toward the hallway.

They followed him to a small door that led down a set of wooden steps to the basement. As Sebastian reached the bottom of the stairs, he was taken aback by what he saw. In the compact room before him, there were several laptop computers running real time intelligence on a number of sensitive targets. There was a glass projection board where numerous computer images could be displayed and details written directly on the surface. There were several modern cell phones, portable GPS units, and radios charging in their respective trays. The entire set up gave the feeling that information and deception carried equal importance here.

Sebastian recognized his driver from the night before working on a laptop, concentrating on what appeared to be a complex encryption problem. Three other computer technicians were busy working a variety of technological puzzles.

The group walked through this area to a small conference room situated in the rear. It had glass walls, a dry-erase board, and a modern podium with corresponding built-in computer components. The Power Point projector hung inconspicuously from the ceiling, blending tastefully with the décor. The modern, functional conference table, with matching chairs, completed the room like an exclamation point. The men sat down and the 'host,' who had yet to give them his name, walked to the podium.

"Good morning, gentlemen. Welcome to our training facility. My name is…" he paused and smiled, "…not important. You can simply refer to me as Ares." Sebastian remembered Ares as the Greek god of war from his studies and couldn't help but smile. "I am the chief instructor in this training and will be accompanied by my two invaluable assistants whom you may refer to as Alex," he pointed at the shorter of the two men who had risen from the table, "and Oleg." Each of the men nodded as their 'names' were called. With the instructors identified, Sebastian realized there were only four students, including himself.

Ares clasped his hands together behind his back and began to pace thoughtfully. "The fact that you are here at all indicates a screening process so thorough that it boggles the mind. You have been watched for a very long time and evaluated on levels that would be considered intrusive to say the least, and yet you never knew it was being conducted. We know what kind of men you are. We know your physical and psychological makeup, and we know that you represent a percentage of warriors so infinitesimally small as to be almost nonexistent. You are about to enter into a world that seems to be perpetually out of focus; where the objectives are clear, but the orders are not. You will become what every government needs, but unequivocally condemns: *ubeytsa*." Sebastian now realized with clarity brought by un-retractable revelation, like being informed you are terminally ill, what he was here for; what he was here to become. 'Ubeytsa' was Russian for assassin.

Ares stopped pacing and leaned forward on the table, looking at the four young men. "Having said that, let me be clear about the ground rules." In a hushed and ominous tone, he warned. "You will never acknowledge the existence of this facility, you will never return here once you leave, and most importantly, you will speak to no one about what you learn here." Ares resumed pacing. "In return, you will be asked to use your skills only when absolutely necessary and only if all other options have been exhausted or failed." Finished with what must have been his obligatory opening, Ares turned the projector on with a small remote control and waited for the image to come up on the screen. "Now that the disclaimer is out of the way, it is time to start." The image on the screen now came into focus.

Chapter 88

The picture on the projection screen was nothing really spectacular. It looked like a police photo of a skier lying contorted in a ravine; obviously it was a fatal skiing accident.

Ares explained, "The person shown is Sergey Yarov. He was tapped to be the next Chairman of the Council for the Federation Council of Russia. He was a puppet figure for the mafia and an unscrupulous minion. We assisted him to the next world just a little over two weeks ago as he vacationed at Kamchatka Resort."

Ares turned to the men. "This is what we do, gentlemen. History has shown us that bad people occasionally slip through the net, they rise to power, and they make a mockery of everything we believe in and fight for. We do our work to keep our brothers from facing much greater threats in the future. Often, paradoxically, we represent both the first and last line of defense. So this comes down to perspective, gentlemen; you can either see your work as noble or sinister, but the bottom line is this…it is absolutely necessary."

Alex stood and handed out a plain-looking three-ring binder to each of the SPETSNAZ Commandos. Ares continued, "in front of you now is a study manual of sorts. It outlines each of your upcoming operational protocols and the procedures you will be expected to perform. The notebook never leaves this house."

Ares sat down and folded his hands in front of him, "Ok, let me give you an idea what to expect on a day-to-day basis. Each morning, you will be up at 6:00 a.m., you will run six miles and have 30 minutes of weight training before breakfast, regular military physical training stuff. After breakfast, you will all work the fields until lunch. After all, this is an operational farm and we must maintain that illusion. After lunch, you will have classroom and practical training until 6:00 p.m. After our evening meal, you will be dismissed to your quarters where every night you will have, on average, three hours of homework and research. You will be tested every third day on the skills you have learned. We will treat you as peers here more than students, however what will be expected of you will rival the toughest training you have had thus far. We know you are all SPETSNAZ, we know that you are combat veterans and otherwise accomplished soldiers; but this is a totally different arena, gentlemen. This is the science of stealth, deception, and death. When you leave here, you will be among the most feared and phantom-like soldiers on the planet. Your training will last four-and-a-half months and culminate with a practical exercise. Are there any questions?" There were none. "Ok, then. Let's take a walk out to the barn."

Chapter 89

"My name is Arval Tristam. I am a friend of your nurse, Stephanie Boulanger." Arval began.

The professor's eyes widened at the mention of her name. "Don't worry, Professor. She retrieved the package and has it in her possession, but there have been complications." Arval took his time walking the professor through the entire ordeal up to this minute.

The professor closed his eyes. "My God, how could I put that young girl in such danger," he said, his shame projecting clearly on his face.

Arval placed a hand reassuringly on the professor's arm. "I'm not sure anyone could have known how rapidly this would unfold, Dr. Fournier."

"I should have known, Mr. Tristam. *I* should have known." His anguish was unabashed. "I struggled with this entire endeavor from the beginning. In the end, I was blinded by my self-aggrandizing accolades; thinking only of standing out among my peers in the universe of academia; a lust to establish my own prestige for posterity. I am a fool." Suddenly a look of concern swept over his face. He weakly grabbed Arval's arm, "What if she is killed, Mr. Tristam? What if she dies for my discovery? She is completely innocent! She only did this for me out of the kindness of her heart!"

Arval patted the professor's hand, trying to reassure him. "Listen to me, Professor," Arval said sternly. "She is a strong woman, and I have taken steps to protect her. She is out of the country and under police protection now, and I have plans to get her a military escort back to France when it is safe. She will be fine." The professor relaxed a little.

"Thank you, Mr. Tristam. Thank you for helping her; for helping me."

Arval acknowledged with a nod. "Dr. Fournier, it would be of great help if you can answer a few questions for me."

"Of course," the professor replied.

"I have my own ideas, but I guess the obvious question is: what exactly is in the package?"

The professor took a deep breath, "I guess it's my turn to start from the beginning."

Dr. Fournier talked Arval through his research and through the chance discovery of his friend. He spoke slowly, pausing often to rest before continuing. Arval listened patiently, intently, asking questions only when needed for clarification.

"But if this document is over 800 years old," Arval remarked," it must be in extremely fragile condition. Surely you didn't just throw it in a DHL envelope for safekeeping."

The professor smiled shrewdly. "That was certainly a problem." Dr. Fournier went on to explain that after he unearthed the stone container, he took it straight back to his friend's flat. Without compromising the integrity of the container, he carefully cleaned it; wiping away centuries of debris. Upon examination, once the container was completely free of dirt and grime, he found that the box was sealed with pitch. Taking a straight edge razor blade, he cautiously sliced through the pitch at the very top of the lid all around the container. The incision was practically invisible, but it allowed him to ease the lid off.

"I was afraid that the document would be in pieces, crumbling away over such an extended time, exposed to the dampness of the earth. But to my surprise, the document inside was in remarkably good shape, folded twice upon itself."

Arval leaned a little closer as the professor's voice was weakening.

"I had my white gloves on and gently removed the parchment, bringing it to light for the first time in centuries." The professor looked to the ceiling, his eyes unfocused as his mind relived this triumphant moment in his life. After a short time, he continued. "Knowing that oxygen would accelerate the deterioration of the vellum fiber, I placed the document in a rigid archival plastic document sleeve. And then," he stopped a minute trying to think how to describe this to Arval, "have you ever seen the commercials for the plastic bags that you can suck the air out of, and they vacuum seal your goods?"

"Yes, yes, I've seen those. They sell them at the market," Arval answered.

"And at the airport," the professor added. "They even have their own little handheld vacuum device." Arval raised his eyebrows at the marvels of modern products. "I picked up some of these bags before I left Paris, thinking they might be handy for just such an occurrence. I 'vacu-sealed' the document for its protection and placed it back in the stone case."

Arval shook his head, impressed with the professor's ingenuity. "When I arrived back in Paris," the professor continued, "I received a broken call from my friend in Kosovo. It sounded urgent, but I couldn't understand what he was trying to tell me. The more I thought about it, the more I felt the need to err on the side of caution. I had the taxi driver drop me off at a convenience store that also deals in package delivery and mailed the document to myself, just in case I ran into some unforeseen trouble. It was just a precaution, but thank God I did."

A nurse entered the room quietly to check the professor's vital signs. After recording the information into a mini-computer, she asked the patient how he was feeling. "You're not becoming overtired are you, sir?" she asked softly.

"Not at all, the professor replied. In fact, I am feeling quite better just having the chance to visit with my friend here."

"Well, that's fine," she said, smiling. "But please don't overdo it. It will soon be time for your medication. Your visitor may stay until then. Alright?" The professor nodded, and Arval thanked her for her kindness as she turned to leave.

To conclude his story, Dr. Fournier told Arval about the Croatian who came to his office, how he suffered a heart attack, and how the Croatian and another man showed up in his hospital room. Arval took everything in, his mind considering every option. The two men talked for a short while longer, and then Arval bid farewell, promising the professor to keep him informed.

As he exited the hospital, he started making the first of several phone calls.

Chapter 90

The seven men walked out to the large barn situated behind the house. It looked old and weathered by generations of use. Like most everything Sebastian had seen thus far, it was an illusion. The interior was inset approximately twenty feet, concealing a hidden operational command center. To complete the deception, a couple of old tractors were backed into their respective slots along with plowing and seeding attachments. Various other farm-related items that looked to be well utilized were also placed strategically throughout the perimeter. Floor to ceiling bales of hay seemed to fill the center. This well staged area remained quite consistent with the outside.

Ares approached one of three hidden entrances. He moved aside a rack of hay situated on rollers and triggered a remote that he pulled from his pocket. A narrow door popped open with a puff of dust and chaff, and the real facility unfolded before them.

The secondary interior of the barn was quite new. There was a large open room in the center, about the size of a half-court gymnasium in America. It had mats on the floor, striking dummies, and anatomical mannequins showing both muscular and skeletal structures of human beings. Two separate staircases led to the loft where there was a small weight room complete with an assortment of free weights, resistance and cardio machines, and a water cooler.

The upstairs also had a small classroom and a locker room with two shower stalls. To Sebastian's surprise, there was even a sauna. *'Typical Russian,'* he thought. The weight room and classroom had large glass walls looking down on the gymnasium. It was actually quite impressive, and Sebastian had to work to suppress his amazement.

"This is where you will spend a large portion of your time," Ares explained. They took a quick tour of the entire facility. On the ground floor, situated to the right of the large central room, was a simple-looking door. After touring the rest of their training area, they came back to this door. Ares opened it and inside was a shooting range 25 meters long with an electronic targeting system. There were two shooting stalls and a caged and locked rack holding an incredible selection of weaponry, mostly silenced, close-range weapons.

With the tour complete, the men were escorted to the classroom in the loft where Oleg took over. Oleg, Sebastian came to find out, was an accomplished physician who still kept part- time hours at a clinic in the small town forty minutes away. He had gone through his SPETSNAZ training years before in the same class as Ares. From there, the government groomed them into specialists who, between them, had carried out countless top-secret missions the world over.

Sebastian soon fell into a comfortable routine at the farmhouse. He actually looked forward to plowing fields, applying fertilizer, and maintaining the equipment. They were sure to work on the tractors out in the open just in case a digital eye orbiting the earth happened to be looking. It was highly unlikely that the facility was being monitored or was under any suspicion at all. The facility had only been in operation for 20 months after moving from a prior location, wherever that was.

Chapter 91

Aside from the farm work, the academics of termination were in full swing. Each day they worked like medical students on various anatomical problems; however, their goal was not to heal, but to harm. They would practice close-quarter hits, working as teams and as individuals in the gymnasium. They learned about poisons, electricity, blunt force trauma, chemicals, lasers, and a number of other things that could be used to terminate a target. It was extremely demanding work, much more mentally than physically. They learned the use of disguise, camouflage, and environment to conceal themselves, their weapons, and the hit itself. By the time four-and-a-half months had passed, they had become artists of death; a concept that Sebastian did not like to think about.

During the final ten days of training, they were presented with their graduation exercise. They assembled in the gymnasium and huddled around Ares. The job was simple and straightforward, but as always required a great deal of planning. It was not a hit, but a snatch and grab: a controlled kidnapping. The target was a police lieutenant, of all things, suspected of paving the way for human traffickers of primarily young girls to be smuggled out of Russia to various parts of the world. Ares made it clear that this was typically not the type of situation they would be involved in unless they were pressured politically to do so. Even if that were the case, they would just eliminate the suspect and be done with it. However, this would be a real time scenario for the purpose of training, so they couldn't actually kill the participants, now could they?

The intelligence and parameters of the exercise were laid out. "Human trafficking is very lucrative, so we have to assume the players are well-armed and well-connected," Ares cautioned. "This means that our primary target probably maintains a shadow protection team that mirrors his movements and keeps an eye out for trouble. The 'grab' will go down on a Wednesday afternoon near a market area where the target always has lunch. Obviously, this means lots of people, lots of interference, and lots to potentially go wrong. The target is cautious, and valuable to the organization, so grabbing him under these circumstances is actually safer for us. It will be unexpected and very quick. We are not concerned with the crowds. By the time they realize what is happening, we will be racing down the street in an untraceable van to the rendezvous location.

We, as instructors, will be observing your efforts from various locations. I will be driving the escape van, and Alex will be one of the handlers in the van. Oleg will be evaluating your approach and the takedown from the market area. We will maintain radio contact at all times, and only an instructor can make the decision to abort the mission. You will all be carrying silenced pistols loaded with simunition."

Simunition is ammunition that actually fires from pistols, allowing them to function as normal, but are far from lethal on impact. Getting hit by a simunition round is similar to getting stung by a bee, but nothing more.

"There should be no reason to fire weapons on this exercise, gentlemen."

"We will now leave you to plan this mission," Ares concluded. "You will find detailed aerial photos of your target location in the briefing folder in the classroom, along with details regarding the target, and criteria regarding your extraction. The secure computer in the classroom is equipped with three-dimensional imaging software to give you an extremely accurate view of your operational area. We will be available to answer any questions. You have eight days to prepare, and you must present your operational plan at 9:00 a.m. on the ninth day. If your plan is acceptable, it will be executed the following afternoon. Good luck to you."

The four men filed up to the classroom and went to work.

Chapter 92

Sebastian and his teammates took the mission one step at a time and talked through potential problems and subsequent solutions. There was no room for attitude or self-promotion in this type of atmosphere. As each day passed, they inched their way nearer to a viable operational plan for the mission. Finally, on the ninth day, one of the team members, selected by the rest of the group, stood to present their strategy.

The plan called for an even balance of caution and aggression. Essentially, there would be three team members in the market area arriving at different times by different means, but all within thirty minutes of each other. The fourth would be grabbing the target with Alex waiting to receive him in the van. They wanted to have at least thirty minutes of eyes on the target to assess and identify any potential players or problems unforeseen in the planning stage. Conversely, they wanted to minimize their own exposure prior to the event.

The target's vehicle always parked in the same spot on the street with his driver remaining in the car. The takedown would occur as he walked back to the car after his meal. The details were outlined in a thorough and methodical fashion, exactly how it would be presented on a real mission, should the occasion arise.

Upon the conclusion of their presentation, the men were dismissed so the instructors could deliberate and evaluate their proposed mission. This was a critical moment, as the instructors could determine the plan to be weak and ill advised, thereby causing them to re-work it from the beginning. This would delay their advancement and keep them on the farm for an indeterminate amount of time. If the instructors felt the operatives were really far off the mark, they had the option to scratch the whole exercise and put them through remedial training until they demonstrated the wherewithal to get the job right.

Sebastian was hoping they did well. He was ready to go back to France. He wanted to fall back in with his regiment and have a little down time from this whole business. After about forty minutes of deliberation, the instructors called them all back to the classroom for the verdict.

Once they had all taken their seats, Ares stood at the head of the table. "Well done, gentlemen," he said. "You are hereby cleared to proceed with your mission. We will assemble here at 9:00 a.m. tomorrow for departure. The rest of the day is yours."

Sebastian breathed a sigh of relief and went back to his room for some rest. He packed his bag, not that he had unpacked very much since his arrival, hoping that he could leave quickly after the next day's job. He laid in bed and read for a while; waiting to be called to lunch. The meal table was unusually quiet, as it seemed the men had run out of things to talk about. No one mentioned the next day or discussed anything that had to do with the job at hand.

After lunch, Sebastian returned to his room and laid back down for a nap. He slept restlessly, waking about an hour later wondering what to do next. He decided to head to the weight room where he hit the weights for about an hour-and-a-half. Afterward, he camped out in the sauna, letting the steam work on the anxiety in his muscles. Before heading back to his room, Sebastian ended the afternoon with 40 minutes of shooting drills.

Although Sebastian and his teammates got along well and gelled as a unit, they were all similar in the sense that they had no desire to be friendly outside of their responsibilities. They recognized it to be pointless; they would not see each other again after they left, and none of them felt the need for social reassurance or comforting. Sebastian reasoned that this characteristic, as far as he was concerned, was a direct result of his time in prison. He was his own best company.

After supper, Sebastian went out for an hour-long evening run. The wind was crisp and helped clear his mind as he went over every detail of the next day's operation in his mind. He returned from his run and marched straight to the shower. As he entered the gymnasium, he looked up and saw the light on in the classroom. He could hear conversation coming from the room, and thought it sounded like some sort of conference call.

Sebastian crested the stairs closest to the locker room. He had to walk by the classroom to get to the locker room at the end of the hall.

Moving forward, he heard Alex say, "That is your problem! All I can tell you is that team had better be on standby and ready in case we call!"

Sebastian passed by the glass wall of the classroom as nonchalantly as he could manage. He reflexively glanced inside and noticed the slightest expression of surprise on the face of Ares, who saw him first. Recovering immediately, and imperceptive to the untrained eye, Ares smiled and waved at him. Sebastian smiled and waved back as he noticed Oleg subtly press the mute button on the phone console. The entire episode took about 15 seconds, but it left a dramatic impression as Sebastian suddenly felt a sense of uncertainty regarding the next day's operation.

By the time he finished his shower and headed back to his room, the barn was empty and quiet. Sebastian wondered if he wasn't being overly sensitive about what was probably nothing more than the instructors solidifying the final stages of their training. There had to be a thousand details to work out with this kind of training. Sebastian tried to shake it off; he needed a good night's sleep. Now was not the time to start working a conspiracy theory.

Chapter 93

"My biggest concern is the Americans," Deputy Prime Minister Bradic said plainly.

"I understand your concern," General Chernov replied, "but I assure you, the Americans will want no part of what we're about to unleash. They have dedicated their resources to the Middle East. Fighting two wars has spread them impossibly thin. The American people cannot stomach another war; especially one that was so distasteful the first time around," he said, referring to America's last visit to Bosnia and Kosovo. "As for the rest of the Europeans on the ground, they would rather not be there in the first place. All they need is a gentle nudge and the means to get home, and off they'll go. We'll supply both.

"Let me show you how this will unfold." He weighted down the four corners of the large, military-style topographic map. "The Americans have two installations: Camp Monteith, here," he pointed to the map near Gjilan, Kosovo. "It is the smaller of the two; and Camp Bondsteel, here." Again, he pointed to the map in an area approximately 45 kilometers south of the capital city of Pristina. "Neither of these encampments are the least bit battle ready. Bondsteel houses a dozen or so Apache Helicopters that will be rendered inconsequential within the first phases of our attack."

General Chernov leaned back in his chair, continuing, "The groundwork has already been laid for the logistics of the operation. As you know, we established a large bus repair facility about an hour away from the two border crossings. We will use it for the invasion. Buses have been housed there by scores for the past four months; they are serviced and stored for the city lines of both Belgrade and Nic. Even the respective city governments believe it to be simply a central facility for logistical control. In reality, we will transport entire battalions across the border the night of the incursion. Buses will draw attention; this is an inevitability of the entire endeavor, but not nearly as obvious as tanks and APCs (Armored Personnel Carriers). By the time satellites start disseminating photos of long lines of buses pouring into Kosovo, it will be too late."

General Chernov then pulled out two satellite photos of both Camp Monteith and Bondsteel and set them facing the Deputy Prime Minister. He used his pen to point as he spoke, "We will overwhelm the gate security; which, incidentally, is manned at both installations by non-military personnel. Once past the gates, we will flood the camps swiftly and silently with Serbian regular infantry by the busload. By daylight, we will be using the camps for our own military use."

"What of the personnel on the bases?" Bradic inquired.

"The goal is to take the camps without firing a shot. Gate personnel will be taken out by non-lethal means. To give the appearance of normalcy to the outside world, we will secure communications posts with our own people. We will round up the sleeping soldiers and send the Americans to the safety of neighboring Macedonia in the buses we arrived in. I have spoken through deep security channels to my contact in Macedonia. They are in agreement, especially since they will look like the heroes of the region to the international community for providing safe harbor for the Americans."

Bradic studied the photos, mulling over the plan thus far. Dimitrijevic simply sat back smiling, knowing all the details already. The General cleared his throat for his final summation. "While the American camps are being overrun, we will hit KFOR (pronounced "K" FOR) Hill simultaneously. KFOR is mainly occupied by European military and functions as more of a NATO administrative hub than an active military base. We will capture all personnel and transport them to the Pristina airport a short distance away. No commercial aircraft is permitted to fly in Kosovo in the night hours, so the five airlines that begin their regular business day with departing flights at 6:20 a.m. will be commandeered and used to fly the European military personnel out of Kosovo. Within 12 hours, we will have secured all primary objectives by surprise and overwhelming numbers. When the international personnel are removed from the country, we will flood the borders with Serbian ground forces and equipment while I fly in my troops with corresponding air assets."

Deputy Prime Minister Bradic leaned back from the table, heaving a sigh at the magnitude of the plan. The General added in conclusion, "we will then begin pushing Albanians back to Albania, sealing all other borders. There will be saber rattling, threats, and warnings from dozens of nations, but they will soon acknowledge their impotence and settle into little more than frowning at us. The world will collectively clear its conscience of this surprising escort from the land by reminding each other: *'it's not our war.'* But the irrefutable fact will remain the same: the heart of Serbia beats again."

Dimitrijevic closed his eyes, savoring the thought.

Chapter 94

Sebastian and his colleagues assembled quietly at 9:00 a.m. Ares addressed the group as they began checking their weapons, communication equipment, and watches. "Gentlemen, we will be using live ammunition rather than simmunition as planned."

Again, Sebastian had the strange feeling that there was more to this exercise than a pass or fail grade for the training course.

Ares continued. "This has become a real time mission that carries risk. Check your weapons carefully now, and be prepared to shoot to kill."

Everyone was on point and proceeded to load into the SUV that would take them to the airfield. It was cloudy and cool, but it looked like the precipitation would hold off until they had completed their job.

At the airstrip, they loaded on a helicopter that would take them to their destination. They were airborne for approximately 95 minutes and then landed in a nondescript field in the middle of nowhere. The van that would be used for the mission was sitting, with no one around it, near where the helicopter touched down. They unloaded without delay and the helicopter peeled off and out of the area within minutes.

In the back of the van was a small motorbike that Sebastian would use to get into town. One of the other team members would use it to leave town after the job. The others would ride to the outskirts of town in the van and then take a taxi or the bus to the market area.

They all worked silently and organized quickly. Sebastian got on the bike and checked his watch against the others. Once they were synchronized, he fired up the motorcycle and headed toward town. The van turned in the opposite direction to take a more circuitous route to get the men where they needed to be.

The motorcycle came with an antique pair of riding goggles, which Sebastian now pulled down over his eyes. He could only imagine how silly he looked, but at least he could see. The wind was cool against him, but not unbearable. Without the goggles, however, he was sure his eyes would water incessantly, making it nearly impossible to ride.

It took him only fifteen minutes to make it to the outskirts of town. He wove through the streets with ease, recognizing streets and other features from the hours they had spent studying the layout. The 'town' was actually a medium-sized city with a population of approximately 250,000 people. It was just big enough to pull off a job like this with eyewitness anonymity. This meant that so many people would be available to witness the event that its reconstruction would be impossibly inaccurate, yet few enough people to allow for an unhindered escape.

Sebastian approached the market area and parked the bike in the predetermined location. He dismounted and took a cursory look around. Everything looked like a regular Wednesday afternoon, and he left the bike, a little sad to part with his goofy goggles. He entered the raging current of normalcy within the boundaries of the marketplace. He purchased an apple and a newspaper from a sidewalk kiosk and continued to walk, now reading his paper and munching on the apple.

As he approached the restaurant, their target location, he felt his heart rate accelerate just a little. This was the epicenter of the entire exercise. Sebastian found a bench occupied by an old man who looked to be catching his breath before walking the next fifty feet. His hands rested on top of his cane positioned between his legs. Sebastian gave the old man a nod and sat, taking another bite of his apple.

The other team members seemed to appear from nowhere and were hard to spot among the regular marketplace crowd. Sebastian picked them up as he subtly scanned his surroundings for potential threats. He thought if he could pick them out, then others who were trained on what to look for could, too. Sebastian identified five possible close protection operators in the immediate vicinity. They were mixed in with the crowd, but something about them made Sebastian mark them with a mental red flag. They may just be regular guys, but he decided to err on the side of caution.

The marketplace was a long stretch of extra-wide sidewalk. Well-established stores ran along each side, and vendors and sidewalk carts made up the long center row. The restaurant was at the end of marketplace row and took up the entire corner building; two floors of fine dining with a lively atmosphere. There was also a large outdoor eating area that held a few patrons braving the cool spring air. Just beyond the restaurant was a busy street where the target's vehicle sat, illegally parked, with the driver behind the steering wheel smoking a cigarette. Sebastian figured there was about 150 feet from the restaurant to the car, and that represented their window of opportunity.

Ares conducted a communications check over Sebastian's earpiece that he acknowledged with a "copy" on his voice activated throat mic. It was loud enough for Ares to receive, but not loud enough for passers-by to notice. All the men had deep-set earpieces and transparent throat mics under their clothing for communications. For the most part, they maintained radio silence. They had arranged for Oleg to make the call when the target began to move, using code as he faked talking on his cell phone.

After a few minutes, they heard *"I'm sorry I dialed the wrong number"* come across the net. That was the code that their target was preparing to leave. Sebastian stood and stretched and then offered his paper to the old man. He accepted it with a grunt, and Sebastian slowly started to close the gap between him and the street. More code came across indicating the target was moving. Sebastian's stomach tightened like a fighter entering the ring.

Chapter 95

The target exited the restaurant laughing loudly, calling back through the door that there were less cats in the neighborhood now and that the owner should confess what his lunch special was really made of. There was riotous laughter from inside the restaurant as the door closed behind its most loyal and popular customer.

Sebastian, who was now approximately thirty feet behind the target, felt a stutter of anxiety in his step as he realized the man was leaving with a two-man protection detail. This was an overt sign of caution, and if the others that Sebastian noticed earlier were part of the team, that made seven against four. In light of this new development, Sebastian felt sure that someone would recognize this as an unforeseen operational development and call for a stand down, but no such call came.

The objective was a blitzkrieg-style grab of the target, forcing him into the van, leaving no opportunity for anyone to react. If the target was alone, the four team members would have been able to manage it with ease and speed, but now the odds were completely against them. They were facing a fortified target of sorts, with a support element ready to react. Sebastian's mind raced with a thousand scenarios all going horribly wrong as he quickened his pace.

The target began to approach his vehicle, stopping for a moment to light a cigarette. Sebastian heard the tires of the van squeal as it rounded the corner at a high rate of speed about a block away. It was barreling straight up the street toward them. The men all looked toward the noise, and Sebastian could see the close protection boys realizing something was wrong. He broke into a full sprint toward the target, not really sure what he was going to do when he got there.

As the distance closed between them, the two bodyguards turned toward Sebastian, grabbing for their holstered weapons. In a flash, the two men collapsed, both with holes in the side of their heads. The target began to cower, putting his hands over his head and stumbling awkwardly toward the roadway. Sebastian could hear a commotion behind him, but he stayed focused on the target.

The van skidded to a stop with the side door wide open practically simultaneously with Sebastian's impact with the target. Not knowing what else to do, Sebastian simply lowered his shoulder and hit the target with such force that it lifted him, shoulder bag and all, from his feet and propelled him through the air into the waiting van.

Sebastian crashed through the door on top of the target and instinctively turned onto his back. He could now see that his other team members had dropped four more bodyguards. One, however, had been sitting in the outside eating area and had gone unnoticed until he stood, flipping the table he was seated at, revealing an H&K G-36 assault rifle. He struggled to bring the weapon to bear on the van, and in an instant Sebastian had acquired him with his front sight. He fired between his knees as the van accelerated into traffic. Sebastian fired only twice, but both shots struck the man in the torso. He fell back, squeezing off a volley of automatic gunfire as he fell.

The captive's driver, a plump and generally unobservant man, realized something was wrong as soon as he heard the van screech to a stop behind him. However, his brain took several moments to process the incident, and he had only now begun to extricate himself from behind the steering wheel to try and do something. The van was accelerating, and Alex saw the driver struggling to pull a pistol from a shoulder holster that looked brand new. Alex shoved the passenger side door open with malice; the door impacted the driver viciously as the van now passed, snapping it back shut and dropping the poor, untrained slob into the street.

Suddenly, over the communications equipment, Sebastian heard one of the other team members who had been with him in the market, state an urgent warning. "Be advised, be advised, at least one additional peripheral team has mobilized en route to your location. Four 'bravos.'" 'Bravos' was code for 'bad guys.' The team member was talking very clearly and evenly, but there was no mistaking the anxiety in his voice as he was now shifting his focus to self-preservation and escape.

Before the side door could be shut, Sebastian saw to his horror a black Mercedes running perpendicular to their van on a side street, coming at them full throttle. It was just a flash as the van sped past the street, but Sebastian saw enough to know they were coming to join the fight. The Mercedes looked heavy, suggesting it was up-armored, and without a doubt its occupants were not amateurs.

Sebastian slid the van door shut and had just turned to give warning of the approaching threat when the van was struck violently from the opposite side. The impact slammed him against the van wall. He was glad he had flipped the safety on his pistol just a moment before. The Mercedes that rammed them was attempting to pin them against a line of parked cars on the roadway. The collision was meant only to disable the van as the attackers were concerned for the welfare of their employer inside. However, the impact had just enough recoil to give Ares room to maneuver as he ricocheted off a parked car. He slammed the accelerator to the floor as the two Mercedes now fell in behind the van in hot pursuit.

Alex and Sebastian handcuffed, blindfolded, and gagged the captured target. With his eyes wide, Sebastian subconsciously changed magazines in his pistol. This was far more than an exercise, and this man was not some corrupt cop. Sebastian began to wonder if he would ever make it out of Russia alive now.

Chapter 96

Slavo's father was furious. He held the phone away from his ear as his dad creatively cursed him for his incompetence. After several minutes, the General of the Black Tigers regained his composure and lowered his voice. "I want you and that team of imbeciles with you to stay right there in Paris. Do not make a move until I call you. You disappoint me, Slavo. Now I have to clean up your mess."

Slavo looked to the sky, realizing there was no better time than the present to drop the other bombshell. "There is one more thing, Father," Slavo said.

"What else could there possibly be?" the elder Petrovic asked impatiently.

"We have Nikolin."

The line fell dead silent.

Stephanie slept soundly the entire trip across the Atlantic Ocean. She missed the onboard meal and snacks and only woke for the warm cloth given at the end of the flight for freshening up before landing. She rubbed her eyes and face with the cloth and then stood to stretch from her cramped seat. She had a deep kink in her neck from sleeping awkwardly in the coach seat for so long.

A short time later, the plane taxied to a stop and the crowded, chaotic shuffle of disembarking the aircraft began. Stephanie was very happy to extract herself from the stale air and variety of odors that accompany a trans-Atlantic flight. She walked briskly to the baggage claim area and immediately spotted a clean cut, official-looking man standing alone, surveying the crowd. His eyes locked on her right after she had noticed him, and he approached her with purpose in his step. "Ms. Stephanie Boulanger?" he asked in French.

Still shaky from the day's events, Stephanie responded cautiously. "Who are you?" she asked politely, but firmly.

"I am Captain de Armand." He pulled his sports jacket back to retrieve his credentials and Stephanie could see his badge and holstered side arm. He handed her his identification and she examined it closely.

"Thank you," she said, handing it back to him. "I have had quite a day, and I've become very distrustful over the last 24 hours."

Captain de Armand smiled understandingly. "No apologies needed. Arval said you had it pretty rough, and I am under direct orders to take good care of you." They walked out the automated exit doors to an unmarked police car sitting in the 'No Parking' zone. "Are you hungry?" he asked.

Stephanie felt the low grumble of her stomach. "Actually, yes. I slept right through the onboard meal."

"Alright then, I know a nice little out-of-the-way place to grab some food, and then I will take you straight to your accommodation."

They maneuvered out of the traffic web surrounding the Montreal Airport as Captain de Armand became Stephanie's Canadian tour guide by default. He was charming and funny, and Stephanie began to finally feel as though she might be safe after all.

Damir's mind began to drift as they sat in the lobby area at Charles de Gaulle awaiting their flight back to Zagreb, Croatia. He knew there would be no time to rest when he arrived home. They would go in for debrief and then start combing every electronic source available to find the girl. They would find her, of that he felt sure, but his heart sank because he knew that the Serbs would get to her first.

As much as he had hoped to avoid it, Damir knew it was time to change tactics. The time had come to make the call for help. He had actually laid eyes on Slavo, who hadn't been seen for nearly six years. And where Junior was, Daddy was close behind. Damir made up his mind to call INTERPOL.

Chapter 97

Sebastian felt numb as the van sped through the city streets. He overheard Ares and Alex talking agitatedly in the front. "They're not shooting yet," Ares said.

"They will," Alex replied, now situated in the passenger seat. "They are simply waiting for the order that tells them our cargo is better dead than in our hands."

Sebastian popped his head up, taking a quick look behind them out one of the small backdoor windows. The two Mercedes were right behind them. The van didn't stand a chance at outrunning them. He wondered what 'Plan B' was.

"Can we make it to the open road?" Alex asked Ares evenly.

"It depends on when they start shooting. At this rate, we should be able to clear the city limits." Alex nodded in thought. Ares shot him a quick glance. "You better go ahead and make the call."

Alex hit speed dial on his cell phone.

They raced through the streets with reckless abandon, and things took on an eerie silence for a few minutes. Suddenly, the unmistakable sound of burst fire from an AK-47 filled the air. "Sounds like they just got the go ahead," Ares announced. "Brace yourselves for incoming fire."

Before he even finished the sentence, metallic 'tings' started assaulting the van. Sebastian lay as flat as he could on the deck of the van, and glass shards fell on him from one of the rear windows. The van was lightly armored, but it was no match for the heavy 7.62mm rounds now thundering all around.

The van extracted itself from the city, hitting open highway at top speed. With less traffic, Ares began weaving back and forth to make for a tougher target. The men in the Mercedes focused their fire toward the wheels. Sebastian could hear ricochets hitting the undercarriage and knew that time was running short.

One of the tires was struck, and the van took an immediate list toward the right rear. The van was equipped with 'run-flat' tires, which allowed them to keep moving, but forced them to slow their speed.

Sebastian positioned himself where he could see what was happening behind them through the rear windows of the van. He saw one of the men in the back seat of the Mercedes preparing the tube for a rocket-propelled grenade (RPG). He quickly relayed what he saw to Ares.

"We're running out of time. Where is he?" Ares demanded of Alex, swerving to avoid an unsuspecting motorist on the roadway.

Alex was squinting ahead, studying the horizon. Suddenly he pointed. "There he is!" he exclaimed triumphantly.

Sebastian crouched down behind the driver's bucket seat and peered around to catch a glimpse of what Alex was talking about. He spotted it on the horizon, a dark object rising like a predator from the deep. It was coming at them quickly, and Sebastian thought it looked like some sort of science fiction, mutant insect. In fact, it was a Russian-made Ka-50 'Black Shark' attack helicopter.

The man who operated the RPG was starting to lean out his window, trying to maneuver into a sitting position on the window ledge. The other backseat passenger prepared to hand him the weapon that would make short work of the van if it took a direct hit. The shooter was reaching back to receive the RPG when he saw the Black Shark making its approach. He jumped back in the vehicle, pointing to the sky, shouting at his comrades.

Sebastian breathed a sigh of relief as it looked like the assistance of a little air support was working. The helicopter ripped over their heads only feet above the vehicles. It was very intimidating, and Sebastian was sure glad they were on their side. In the momentary cease-fire, Sebastian glanced out the back to see what he hoped to be two retreating protection teams.

"You've got to be kidding me," Sebastian said aloud. "Ares, they are not backing down. Alex, can you get a look at vehicle number two?"

Alex' head snapped around quickly, and he leaned closer to try and confirm what he was seeing.

In the second vehicle, the backseat passengers were preparing a different type of tubular weapon. In fact, Sebastian had only seen this particular weapon in training photographs.

"They have an 18," Alex said to Ares as he hurriedly activated the speed dial on his cell phone again.

"Give me a straight channel," Alex ordered into the phone. After a brief pause, he spoke directly to the Black Shark's pilot. "Be advised, be advised, vehicle two has a Grouse; repeat, vehicle two has a Grouse."

Sebastian saw the helicopter tip up on its side, banking hard to get back on target. A 'Grouse' was NATO's term for the Russian SA-18 shoulder-fired, anti-aircraft weapon that seemed impossible for these men to possess. The rear vehicle had a sunroof and one of the men popped out the top to establish a shooting platform.

"It's a race now to see who will lock on first," Alex said as he watched behind him.

The Black Shark came around with startling speed. The pilot was clearly unafraid and plenty pissed off at this development. The shooter in the Mercedes was struggling to get the weapon up on target. The pilot wasn't waiting for his own missiles to lock; he opened up with his 2A42 quick-firing 30mm cannons that let loose a volley of explosive incendiary rounds. Chunks of the roadway, and then the vehicle, were blown away in an instant, soon leaving just the vehicle's frame, which veered off into the ditch. Practically simultaneously, the pilot had acquired a lock on the lead vehicle. He released a laser guided Vikhr, supersonic, anti-tank missile and peeled off. The impact nearly disintegrated the remaining Mercedes. Sebastian turned his head at the flash of the explosion. By the time he turned back, the helicopter was nowhere to be found, and they were no longer being pursued by anyone.

Ares cursed loudly in Russian. "Get a clean-up team here, now!" he yelled. Alex was already on the phone making arrangements.

Chapter 98

The heavily damaged van limped into its destination. Just off the highway was a valley that served as the actual rendezvous for this particular operation. As they sunk into the valley, Sebastian could see a military transport helicopter with its blades in full revolution, awaiting their arrival. They pulled in close, and Alex snatched their captive roughly from the van. He shoved him into the aircraft and jumped in beside him. The helicopter lifted off and ripped through the valley, low to the ground, only gaining altitude at the very last minute to crest the far bordering hill.

Ares and Sebastian were left with the dilapidated van. "Let's go," Ares said in the now quiet air. "We need to work fast."

The two men climbed back in and were back on the highway in no time. Ares flipped open his cell phone and began making quick arrangements. Sebastian had no doubt that these men had limitless resources, and that they had contingencies in place for everything, but he was equally sure that they had not had an incident like this in a very long time; if ever.

Within minutes, they made it to a police station in a very small village. Ares drove the van to the rear and parked. The police chief walked out the back door and handed Ares the keys to his own personal car, an unmarked Fiat that had certainly seen better days. Ares handed the man some cash, and he and Sebastian were right back on the road again.

They drove for several minutes without speaking, "So who was he?" Sebastian asked, breaking the silence.

"Police Chief," Ares answered absently.

"No, no, the guy we grabbed," Sebastian clarified.

"Here," Ares said, ignoring the question and handing Sebastian a handful of money and documents. "This is a Russian passport, travel visa, and enough money to see you through. You will be taking a very indirect route back to France. I hope you're up for it."

Sebastian took what was handed to him. He had a thousand questions, but it was useless to ask.

As Ares drove, he alternated between looking straight ahead and checking his mirrors. Sebastian felt as if everything was completely out of control. He was freefalling and could only hope that someone would pull the release cord soon.

Sebastian could see the familiar perimeter fence of a military installation ahead. There must have been hundreds of these small camps all over Russia. Remnants of a more controlling era, he imagined. Sebastian felt a bit of relief on approach to the gate as he could hear aircraft engines behind the walls. He couldn't help but wish he were on a flight to anywhere but here as soon as possible. He should have known to be cautious about what he wished for.

Chapter 99

They pulled to the gate of the airfield in the dirty old Fiat and were greeted with caution. Two Russian gate guards brought their AK-47s level with the windshield. Ares presented his credentials through the open window. A very stern and wary soldier took them. "Keep your hands on the steering wheel, and you!" he shouted toward Sebastian, "put your hands on the dash in front of you. If either of you move, it will be considered an act of aggression, and we will respond accordingly!" Ares and Sebastian complied without comment.

The soldier examined the documents carefully while his partner kept the vehicle's occupants in his sights. The lead soldier said something to the other that Sebastian didn't quite catch, but the result was the man dropped his weapon to his side and snapped to rigid attention.

"We apologize for the inconvenience, sir," the lead soldier stated to Ares as he handed back his documents.

"No problem at all, Sergeant. Sorry to have arrived unannounced," Ares replied.

The soldier snapped a smart salute from his position of attention, not exactly sure how to respond to a ranking officer's consideration. He opted for silence as the car pulled through the now open gate.

Once inside, the Fiat moved swiftly to the runway near several closed hangars. A MiG-31 Foxhound was warming up on the tarmac. Sebastian observed a crew of air techs fussing about the aircraft, making last minute checks of everything. Inside the cockpit, the pilot was making his pre-flight checks. Sebastian could see the oxygen mask portion of his helmet flopping loosely as he checked gauges and talked with the tower.

Ares put the car in park and turned to Sebastian, "There will be someone to escort you at least part of your journey home. There is no time to do more than that." He paused and ran his hand through his coarse hair. He apparently thought Sebastian had earned at least a cursory explanation.

"This was not supposed to be an overt military operation. It is truly unfortunate that we had to employ such firepower, but it was unavoidable. We have to work very quickly now to clean up this mess with as little fallout as possible. With that said, you should consider yourself at great risk from this point forward. You have to assume that you were identified at the marketplace. People would have noticed you running like a charging bull at our target. Again unavoidable; you had to adapt to the operational environment. He still had his laptop and cell phone on him when you blasted him into the van. We were incredibly fortunate, and you did an excellent job. We will make sure your superiors know that you performed valiantly here today.

For now, you must focus on getting back to your people. We will give you some assistance for sure, but we are limited in what we can produce on such short notice. Depend on your training, trust your instincts, but trust nothing else." Ares spoke sincerely, and Sebastian knew his future would be uncertain. "I am sure you want to know about the man we captured…" Ares looked out the windshield choosing his next words carefully, "…let me just say that today we have delivered a serious blow to the infrastructure of the enemy of both our countries." Sebastian gave him an intense look, seeking further clarification, but none was forthcoming. "Now go quickly, your ride awaits." He nodded toward the MiG.

Chapter 100

As soon as Sebastian stepped out of the vehicle, a gangly airman ran up to him, helmet in hand. "Here you are, sir," he said, handing him the helmet. "Captain Akimova will be your pilot today, sir. You will be ready to taxi for takeoff as soon as you are strapped in."

The two men jogged over to the MiG, and Sebastian climbed the ladder to get to his seat. The MiG-31 Foxhound, a two-seat, supersonic interceptor aircraft, contains advanced digital avionics and has a multi-target engagement capability. It was an impressive aircraft, and Sebastian couldn't believe this was his ride out of Russia.

The pilot welcomed Sebastian aboard with a quick handshake. The airman expertly strapped him down, and in no time, the aircraft began to move as the cockpit canopy hydraulically closed.

The MiG tore down the runway at an incredible rate of speed. It seemed as soon as the wheels left the ground, the aircraft went nearly vertical, rocketing the interceptor toward its cruising altitude at tremendous velocity. Sebastian's stomach was in his boots, and he moaned loudly as he struggled with the g-forces now gripping his body. They soon leveled out, and Sebastian slumped a little in his seat, panting against the experience that eclipsed even the most monstrous roller coaster ride.

Once the blood flow was restored to his brain, Sebastian looked out his window at the earth far below. He had made dozens of parachute jumps and had experienced many unique things in his young life, but none quite compared to this.

The pilot must have sensed Sebastian's awe or was simply checking to see if he was conscious. "First time in one of these?" he asked over Sebastian's built-in headphones.

Sebastian's voice cracked as he replied, "Da."

"Sorry about that take off, I didn't realize you'd never flown in a fighter aircraft before. They just told me to get you where you're going in a hurry."

"No problem," Sebastian lied. His Russian was now excellent and completely fluent. He wondered how his French would be after being away for over a year.

"You up for some maneuvers?" the pilot asked, obviously proud of his aircraft's capabilities.

Sebastian swallowed hard. Not wanting to sound like a coward, he replied, "Sure." The palms of his hands were instantly moist with anticipation and his stomach involuntarily tightened so hard it hurt. Again the pilot was conscious of Sebastian's concern. "Relax," he said reassuringly. "We're just going to have some fun, nothing crazy, ok?"

Sebastian nodded, "Ok, let's do it."

The pilot's eyes wrinkled with a big mischievous grin under his oxygen mask as he readjusted his grip on the control stick. In a sudden jerk that made Sebastian catch a scream in his throat, the interceptor turned on its side, peeling abruptly away from its original flight path. They descended at an alarming rate of speed, and Sebastian could no longer tell if they were upside down, right side up, or inside out. The pilot leveled off and laughed heartily. "Are you a paratrooper?" he asked as his laughter subsided. All Sebastian could do was nod. "Thought so," the pilot remarked, "you kept grabbing at your chest, trying to pull the ripcord!"

"How could you see…?" Sebastian began, and then he saw the small rear view mirror mounted directly in front of the pilot. Although it looked funny and out of place, Sebastian remembered reading about Israeli fighter pilots who came up with the idea because it made it much easier to see aircraft approaching from behind. Without it, he imagined it would be quite difficult for a pilot to jerk his helmeted head around to see aircraft zipping by with only a flash of metal. The mirror solved this problem. They both started laughing. At least Sebastian thought he was laughing, he might have been crying.

The pilot returned to his cruising altitude and settled in for the duration. After approximately eighty minutes of flight, the pilot seemed to take on a different demeanor. He straightened up in his seat and started checking his instruments and navigational equipment.

"Ok," the pilot said in a serious tone. "We are approaching our destination. When we get on the ground, you will need to disembark as quickly as you can. I put your bag in my storage compartment. I'll pop the hatch on it as you dismount. Once you have your bag, walk straight into the hangar door that I point out to you. A guy in a red jacket named 'Vim' will be waiting for you. He'll take you on the next leg of your journey."

The cockpit was quiet again as they continued their steady descent. The pilot glanced back at Sebastian. "I don't know who you are, or where you're going, and frankly, I don't care, but I think you should know that you are going into an unfriendly area." The pilot was now talking soldier to soldier. "I imagine you will be traveling by ground from this point forward. You need to stay alert, trust no one, and essentially consider yourself OTR."

OTR was military speak for 'on the run.' This was his second warning, and he tried to fight back the anxiety that was so draining. Sebastian nodded his understanding. "Thanks for the heads up." He looked out the window at the terrain below. It looked desolate and uninviting. He turned back. "And thanks for the ride," he added.

Chapter 101

Arval lay in his bed at his small flat near downtown Paris, wide awake. One of the benefits of his service to his country as a teenager was the flat he had now lived in for over 60 years. When the French rebuilt their decimated city in the wake of the war, many loyalists were given first dibs on the new accommodations.

For many, the city represented a hurt so deep that they could no longer stay, and they moved to more quaint living quarters in the country. Arval's grandfather had chosen this route, and through the inevitable passing of time, Arval inherited his country estate, as well. So in essence, he had a city flat and a country estate, both of which he owned outright.

In its most superficial sense, Arval was considered a wealthy man, but truth be told, Arval was an excellent steward of his earnings. He had made very wise financial decisions over the years and lived modestly; well within his means. Now in his twilight years, he lived his life pretty much however he wanted.

Arval had been married for 49 years to the love of his life. Their story was one for the ages, but it was a private romance that Arval kept locked in the most well-guarded room of his memory castle. She had passed on over ten years ago, but each day of Arval's life, it seemed like only yesterday. Occasionally, he could smell her essence in the little flat, and his mind would be swept away in a tidal wave of moments and images that seemed to make his very bones ache in her absence. As he lay in their bed, listening to the tick of the clock, he had such a moment. He felt the heat of tears rushing to his eyes as his stomach still tightened against the pain.

He flung off his covers, and walked to the kitchen to put on a pot of coffee. He had work to do; this was no time for self-pity or rummaging through the events of yesteryear. He sat at his small kitchen table as the coffee brewed and began to focus his thoughts on the present situation.

He tried to summarize it all in his mind. Professor Fournier's discovery in Kosovo had touched off organized efforts by various factions to take possession of what he found. Arval thought about what the professor said of the two men in his room. He knew that the Serbians had to be involved and were probably quite displeased. He wondered whom the other man represented. Regardless, he knew all of them were after Stephanie. More than likely they simply wanted the document she possessed, but there was the chance that they thought she was actually involved and knew more than she, in fact, did. That would make things very dangerous for her, and he needed to act quickly. He had more favors to redeem in the morning to arrange for her safe return.

Arval tried to get a bigger picture in his mind of this situation. If the item discovered by the professor was authentic, then the significance of the ancient document to the Serbians could be compared to the Declaration of Independence to the Americans, or the Balfour Declaration to the Israelis, or even France's own Declaration of the Rights of Man and of the Citizen. This meant the circumstances carried the potential for full-scale revolution in the Balkans.

Arval considered this for a moment; the NATO presence in the Balkan region was the lowest since they first arrived to stabilize the area. The resources to repel such a revolt were simply unavailable as the American and NATO commitments to the Middle East were vast and exhaustive. At a time when the International Community was seriously considering granting independence to Kosovo, this situation had the direst of consequences. It made perfect sense for the Serbs to be so relentless in their pursuit. This could very well be their last bid to regain control of Kosovo and solidify their dominance of the region.

Arval rose, and poured himself a cup of coffee. He pushed a button on his answering machine and replayed the message he had recorded from Stephanie's cell phone as they sat on the bench outside Notre Dame. The man's voice and what he said gave him no clue as to his identity or who he represented. Perhaps he was one of the men the professor had seen in his office or in his hospital room. There was no way to find out, but he knew for sure these were desperate and dangerous men.

Arval slowly shook his head and glanced at the digital clock on the stove, which read 3:24 a.m. His mind flashed to the horrors of war witnessed in his youth. If there were any way to help in avoiding a war among any peoples, he would not rest until he had done his part. He sat again, removed his eyeglasses, and bowed his head.

Chapter 102

The MiG rolled rapidly upon touching down; sights flashing by like images in a kaleidoscope. Sebastian looked closely for any clue to his location. At last, the plane slowed enough that he could make out Cyrillic lettering on the side of the main terminal building in the distance; he had just landed in Kazakhstan. They taxied far away from the main terminal, pulling up to a dilapidated hangar situated near the end of a row of other dilapidated hangars. It looked as if this were once a military airport, but it was operating now as a full-fledged public airport.

Sebastian unbuckled as they began rolling to a stop and climbed out as the cockpit canopy opened for him. He grabbed his bag and thanked the pilot once more before descending the built-in foot holds in the fuselage and jumping the rest of the way to the ground.

As directed, he hurried into the hangar looking for his new contact. At the far end of the hangar, which was filled with junk instead of airplanes, Sebastian could see a figure standing near the exit door. The light shining through the door's dirty window silhouetted the man as he nervously sucked on a cigarette. Sebastian approached cautiously and nodded to the figure.

"Vim?" he asked.

"Follow me," the figure said, snatching open the door, and with a quick look side to side, exited the hangar.

It was an overcast day, and the air was just cool enough to be uncomfortable. They got into a car that looked stolen and pulled away from the airport.

"You got papers?" the man called Vim asked curtly. In the daylight, Sebastian could see that the 'man' was really not more than a boy of eighteen or nineteen. He was roughly the same height as Sebastian, but skinny as a rail, with greasy hair and a pale complexion. This looked like a kid from the school of hard knocks, and Sebastian was immediately distrusting of him.

"Yeah, I got papers," Sebastian replied.

"You got money?" Vim asked.

"I got papers," Sebastian repeated firmly.

"Take it easy, friend. I'm just saying it's going to take money to get out of this place, that's all." Vim was a pro, but Sebastian detected the derision in his concern.

Vim decided to quickly move on, "We're going to head to the docks where I will introduce you to my uncle. He has a fishing trawler that will take you across the Caspian Sea. You will need to pay him 131,000 Tenge." One hundred thirty one Kazakhstan Tenge was nearly $1,000 U.S. dollars.

"I have only Rubles," Sebastian lied. He had about $4,000 worth of various currencies to see him through.

"That's fine," Vim replied without hesitation. It will cost 29,000 Rubles."

Sebastian could have kicked himself because, instead of acting completely appalled by the amount Vim quoted, he had conceded by his response that he was carrying that kind of cash. This kid was good, and Sebastian knew better. He needed to get switched on quick, or this may be his final trip anywhere.

They sped toward the docks, and Sebastian saw flocks of seafaring birds hovering about, looking for easy meals. They pulled into a parking space near the large port. Men of the sea were wrapping up their day's work, which regardless of the specific job, was generally some stage of the continuous cycle of either unloading their cargo or preparing for launch. Their activities, however, left little doubt the day was drawing to a close.

Sebastian and his teenage escort settled into a small coffee house that looked out at the docks. Vim ordered both of them some sort of coffee-type substance that tasted to Sebastian like hardening tar.

"We have to wait here for just a short time for my uncle. He is trying to finish the preparations for tonight's departure. His boat is sturdy, but his crew is small, and it takes a lot of time to make the ship ready."

They sat in silence for several minutes. Sebastian tried to take in his surroundings without looking panicked. He was trying to clear his head from the series of events that had led him to this very minute.

Sebastian needed a moment to assess his situation and measure alternatives and contingencies.

He looked directly at his arranged escort and said, "I'm going to take a little walk; stretch my legs a bit." Just as he expected, there was the unmistakable flash of anxiety in the face of young Vim.

"I'll go with you," he replied, starting to rise.

"No, that's ok," Sebastian stated firmly. "I'm just going to walk up the shoreline a ways. I'll be back shortly."

This was a delicate game, each trying to instill or maintain an air of trust in an arena where, of course, there was none. They were mutual means to individual ends. Sebastian stood and walked away, noting the distinct discomfort on Vim's face. He walked up the shoreline and surveyed the many different shops catering to the needs of men returning from the sea.

The crisp air brought newfound clarity to Sebastian's thoughts, and he was soon able to start working contingencies. The first thing he needed to take care of was his hunger. He was starving from the day's exertion, and needed to find something to fill the void. Besides, there was no telling when he would get food again. His training had taught him to always get food and rest whenever possible. He would never accept food from his escort or anyone associated with him for obvious reasons.

Sebastian exchanged some Rubles for local currency and headed to a narrow food shop whose front, along with dozens of others, faced the docks. Sebastian listened carefully as the man in front of him ordered *besbarmak* and *lepeshka*. Sebastian stepped up to the counter and nonchalantly ordered the same thing. It wouldn't be until much later that Sebastian would find out that besbarmak is actually boiled horsemeat with bits of dough. Lepeshka is the name for bread, the staple of almost every meal for the locals.

Whatever it was, it tasted fantastic to Sebastian, and he ate it all enthusiastically. As he sipped on a liter of bottled water, he looked farther down the shoreline. The cook eyed him suspiciously, as hardly anyone ever stayed to eat.

Sebastian noticed something interesting in the distance. He squinted as he tried to make out a relatively large ship surrounded by a steady commotion.

"Is that the ferry?" Sebastian asked the cook who remained busy with his work.

"Yes, it is," he replied flatly.

"That's the one going to…" Sebastian started, hoping the cook would finish.

"Baku," the cook said, uninterested in tutoring a foreigner on local ship traffic.

"Baku…?" Sebastian prodded again.

The cook heaved an exasperated sigh, "Azerbaijan." He had dealt with these adventuresome, back-packer types before.

Sebastian nodded, squinting harder as he began working a contingency plan in his head. Without looking back, Sebastian began to ask, "and how much…"

The cook tossed his dishtowel onto the counter in front of him; taking a long breath, he went on to explain the ferry cost roughly 50 Euros one way, it would leave tonight around 11:00 p.m., the trip took roughly 18 hours, and you could not take animals onboard.

Sebastian smiled to himself as he continued to look out the dirty storefront window. After a moment, he turned to the cook. "How late are you open?" he asked.

The cook glanced at the back of the shop, which was blocked by a large blanket draped over a strand of fishing rope like a theatre curtain. It dawned on Sebastian that the cook also owned the shop and lived in the back of it. He felt dumb for asking such a question.

"I lock the front door at 10:00 p.m.," the man answered, tiring of this foreigner's company.

Sebastian stepped a little closer to the cook. "If I purchase a ticket would you hold on to it for me until I return? I'll pay you twice the price of the ticket for your trouble."

The man's eyes lit up suddenly, very eager to talk with this young man. That would be more than he would make in two or three months. "Yes I would agree to those terms," he replied coolly as if he could take it or leave it.

"Excellent, then it's a deal. I'll be right back," Sebastian said, shaking the shop owner's hand. He bolted out the door, sprinted up the shoreline, and purchased a ticket for the ferry. He ran back to the shop and handed the owner the ticket and 100 Euros.

"You're lucky, you know," the man said.

"And why's that?" Sebastian asked.

"That ferry only comes in about once a week. It looks like you picked a good night to leave my beloved country." He gave Sebastian a nearly toothless grin.

"We'll see," Sebastian said under his breath as he headed out the door.

Chapter 103

It was a little after 7:00 p.m., and Sebastian knew he had to return to Vim so as not to raise alarm and have every half-wit thug on the docks looking for him. He knew his best bet was to let things play out and make a run for it at the last minute; only if necessary. Sebastian returned to the coffee shop to find his impatient escort still in his seat bouncing his knee nervously like a criminal waiting for the verdict. Sebastian approached calmly, and Vim jumped up as soon as he saw him. "My uncle is waiting for us; let's go," he ordered impatiently.

Sebastian just nodded and fell in behind the now overtly nervous young man. "Where are we going?" he inquired nonchalantly.

"Just up the way here is one of my uncle's favorite restaurants. We'll meet him there."

Sebastian didn't reply, and now began the methodical process of switching his senses into high gear. They entered another seaside shop, this one only marginally wider than the small shop where he made his deal with the cook. The layout was simple enough; the interior was like a rectangle absent of any frills whatsoever. To the left, was a counter behind which meals were prepared. Two cooks worked feverishly preparing meat over a hot open fire. Two grubby sailors were sitting at the counter engaged in conversation, seemingly oblivious to Sebastian's entrance. To the right were two small round tables; one occupied by a roughneck nursing a beer. At the back was a barrel-chested, bearded man who looked so stereotypically like a character from the sea that Sebastian found it comical. He surmised a couple of things immediately: first, the uncle was a pro, he was dirty without a doubt, and he was the obvious mentor of young Vim. Next, the men in the restaurant were not there by chance; Sebastian felt sure they were part of the uncle's crew, and this meeting was designed for intimidation and unopposed conquest. The question was simply what they would want from him.

Sebastian followed Vim to the back table. The uncle stood with a broad smile and outstretched hands welcoming Sebastian warmly. The man's voice filled the room, "Ah, welcome to Kazakhstan, my young Russian friend, and the glorious docks of Aqtau!" Sebastian offered his hand cautiously in return.

The 'uncle,' who never did offer his name, dug into his meal after Sebastian had politely declined joining him. He spoke intermittently about life as a career fisherman and the cruelty of the sea. He also spoke fondly of his ship, claiming no sturdier vessel on the Caspian. The ship had been in his family since his grandfather purchased it for a song from a desperate Russian captain. Apparently the captain had fallen on hard times from a combination of too much drink and gambling and needed money fast. Sebastian found it all mildly interesting, but kept his mind sharp for this congenial meeting to quickly change at a moment's notice. Finally, as the uncle sipped his dark, sludge-like coffee and lit his after dinner cigarette, the meeting got serious.

"Well, we must get you across this sea of ours, eh, my friend?" the uncle began.

"Yes," Sebastian replied. "I suppose we must talk of these arrangements."

The uncle took a long drag from his cigarette, studying Sebastian. "It will cost 1,500 Euro for the trip." Smoke spewed from his mouth with each word. The fact that the price had gone up nearly 600 dollars from Vim's original quote did not escape Sebastian.

He sat silently, letting the weight of the figure compound the tension in the air, "And why would I be inclined to pay such an extraordinary amount?" he finally asked in an almost pleasant tone.

The uncle feigned mock surprise at such a question. "My friend, I offer what no one else can; getting you to Baku quickly and safely is a given with our arrangement; however, once you get to Baku…" he smiled as he leaned back in his chair and took another long drag from his cigarette.

Sebastian cocked his head, anxious to hear the rest. The uncle looked perplexed that he needed to explain any further. "We will get you into Azerbaijan without incident. No one will be aware of your entrance into the country, and you can travel without interference from the Secret Police." The uncle smiled again, satisfied that he had just sealed the deal with his explanation.

"Hmm," Sebastian mused, "I need to think about this proposition." He scooted his chair back, preparing to stand.

He could see the smile drop from the uncle's face with his response. "There is nothing to think about, my friend," he said with an undercurrent of threat in his voice.

Sebastian straightened as a woman came near them, wiping the tables clean, humming softly to herself. She was the perfect distraction, keeping everyone's emotions in check. They continued the charade that this was just a friendly conversation over dinner, and Sebastian stepped back from the table. "I'll return in 15 minutes with my answer."

Sebastian quickly surveyed the scene between himself and the exit door. The three men who seemed to be in the restaurant by coincidence had turned their full attention to him now, just as he had expected. He was sure to keep the proper reactionary gap between himself and the men. He needed time to react if anyone tried to get aggressive.

The cleaning woman was practically right beside him, diligently wiping down an old wooden chair, as he turned his back to the uncle and started toward the door. Everyone remained seated as Sebastian began to walk. He had played that well he thought to himself; he had caught them off guard with his response and bought himself a little time while they tried to figure out what to do next. He thought for sure the uncle would call him back to sit down and re-negotiate the deal.

Sebastian had taken about three steps when he felt a sharp blow to his head, just behind the ear. The world around him began to spin as he felt his consciousness slipping away. He tried to figure out what in the world had just happened. His jaw went slack and he half spun in slow motion to the ground, grasping blindly for something to break his fall. An instant before his world went completely dark, he saw the cleaning woman standing over him, holding a sap. She had struck him perfectly, and now he was in a world of trouble.

Chapter 104

Stephanie arrived at the small quaint cottage in the Canadian countryside outside of Montreal. Her host and hostess met her in the driveway as Captain de Armand pulled in. The elderly couple looked to be in the same age bracket as Arval, and they stood arm-in-arm, waiting to greet their guest.

Stephanie got out of the car and walked toward them with the familiar anxiety of meeting people for the first time. "Bonjour," she said timidly.

The wife, whom Stephanie would come to know as Sarah, broke from her husband and swiftly pulled Stephanie into a warm embrace. "Bonjour, my dear," she said in a grandmotherly tone. "Welcome to Canada. We promise to take very good care of you."

The husband approached now. "Bonjour, Stephanie," he said with a smile, taking both her hands in his. "My name is Etienne. We are happy you are here." He kissed her gently on either cheek.

Stephanie instantly liked her new guardians, and the fear of her situation began to subside even further. Captain de Armand stepped to the little group. "I will have officers checking on you regularly, Stephanie. If you decide to go to town or anything, let us know if you would. I am sworn to keep you safe. Arval will have my head if you get so much as a splinter," he said with a smile.

"Thank you for everything, Captain," Stephanie said, giving him a quick embrace.

"Au Revoir," the Captain nodded chivalrously, tipped his cap, and left the three to get acquainted.

The first evening, Sarah and Etienne left Stephanie to get situated and settled. The next morning, she sat down to an amazing breakfast prepared by Sarah's skilled hands. As they sipped their second cup of coffee after the breakfast plates had been cleared, Etienne broke the silence. "Do you know anything about our dear Arval, Stephanie?"

"No. I mean not much really," she answered. "I do know that he has saved my life. Of that, I'm sure."

Etienne looked into his coffee cup. "Yes, he has a habit of doing that, I'm afraid," he said, smiling and reminiscing of a time that changed so many lives and the face of France herself.

For the next three hours, they sat around the small kitchen table, and Etienne told stories of a young Arval and the last time the world was at war. Stephanie was captivated from the first sentence. She barely dared to breathe as Etienne recounted stories of danger and bravery that she could hardly comprehend. Arval's adventures were the stuff of legend, and now it made perfect sense that he was able to pull resources together that few others could. His words came back to her from the recesses of her mind, *"providence, my dear, providence."* She smiled knowingly.

Chapter 105

Sebastian woke to the taste of blood in his mouth. He knew not to make any quick movements, especially since he could hear talking around him. Things began to come into focus for him slowly. He was face down in an alleyway of some sort, stripped of nearly everything except his pants and undershirt. Blood had run from behind his ear down his cheek and into his mouth. He laid still and listened to the men around him talk.

"The Russians will never believe that story." He recognized the nervous voice of Vim. Sebastian moved his head ever so slightly and could now see the uncle, his three goons, and Vim standing about 10 feet away. One of the men was counting the last of the bills from Sebastian's package of documents.

The uncle finally responded to Vim who was sucking down a cigarette at an incredible rate. "You're right, Vim, the Russians will not believe you were attacked in transit unless we convince them." One of the men struck Vim with a vicious blow to the face. All of the men then jumped in, delivering blow after blow. The fury lasted only a few seconds, but it was certainly effective. The uncle pulled Vim up from the ground and hugged him, laughing maniacally, "NOW you look like you were attacked. The Russians will believe you for sure!" He continued to laugh as he helped his nephew out of the alley toward a waiting vehicle.

"What about him?" One of the thugs asked, thumbing back toward Sebastian.

"We can have nothing to do with his demise. A couple of acquaintances are on their way to finish this. Come, let's get some whiskey and women and go celebrate on the…" Sebastian tried to translate in his foggy mind what the last words were that the uncle said. He flipped through the Russian dictionary in his head and found the word. The uncle had said the name of his boat, which roughly translated to *Sea Scavenger*. He doubted he would remember the name later, so for easy reference, Sebastian decided to call it the Sea Buzzard.

After the vehicle had sped away, he slowly rose from the ground. He spat the blood from his mouth and rested for a while on one knee as the pain nearly made him pass out again. Pain radiated all the way down his jaw and jabbed like nails into his brain all around his head. Finally, he was able to stand, taking several deep breaths to stabilize.

He knew he had to get off the 'X,' meaning he had to get away from the epicenter of danger. His enemy would be arriving shortly; there was precious little time to act. He stumbled forward into the shadows only a few feet away. The pain was making him nauseous, and he had to really focus on what he needed to do in order to stay alive. As he looked around for immediate cover, he heard a car approaching.

Sebastian ran toward the end of the alleyway, directly toward where the car, just out of view, was rolling to a stop. He imagined they were looking to find him laying in the alley, set up for an easy hit. He noticed a depression in the bordering walls near the street opening of the alley where the men would enter. It was a side door to a store that fronted on the street. He slipped into the doorway, which had no exterior illumination, and stood absolutely still. He had just gotten into place when two men entered the alleyway and walked straight past him. *'Thank God they are amateurs,'* Sebastian thought to himself.

They had silenced pistols in their hands, hanging to their sides, and they walked with the cocky strut of cowards not expecting a fight. Sebastian sprung from the doorway just as they passed, grabbing the arm of the man closest to him. Taken completely by surprise, Sebastian muscled the man's shooting arm toward his partner, depressing the trigger in rapid succession. The shots hit the man in the chest as he turned toward the attack in alarm. He fell where he stood, and Sebastian used the confusion to bring a knee to the midsection of the last man standing. The man doubled over and struggled to fight back, but Sebastian deftly folded the man's pistol into his abdomen and squeezed off several more shots. The man crumpled to the ground, wheezing out his final breath.

Sebastian turned and vomited violently as the exertion brought a fresh wave of blinding pain to his head. He spit as he finally finished heaving against the wall. When he regained his equilibrium, he looked down at the two men and slowly shook his head. He hated that it had come to this, but often people make decisions that produce unfortunate results. Bending down with effort, he searched the two men, taking only boots that were two sizes too big, a watch, and the car keys. He cautiously made his way to their car and drove away, trying to find his way back to the docks.

Aqtau was a relatively modern city, not so much in a figurative sense, as a literal one. It was actually built in 1963 as a Soviet 'model city.' Its design was to be the blueprint for cities of the future. It boasted straight, wide streets and sandy beaches, along with all the amenities expected in a city of such size. Aqtau was originally called Shevchenko after the famous Ukrainian poet who was exiled there as a political prisoner in the late 1800's. The city's name was later changed to Aqtau, which means 'white mountain' in the Kazakh language.

With the city's simple layout, Sebastian found the docks with ease, and parked a safe distance away. He looked at his newly acquired watch to find it was only 8:15 p.m. The events that felt like a lifetime to him had actually transpired in less than an hour. He leaned back in the seat to take some time to rest his aching head. By 9:00, his head had leveled out, and he was ready to move. "It's time to find the buzzard," he said out loud as he opened the driver's door.

Chapter 106

Standing only in pants and an undershirt, the cool night air brought a chill that bit deep. He was completely focused on the task at hand, and his concentration pushed any discomfort from his mind. He stayed to the shadows as he cautiously approached the seashore to find the 'Buzzard.' It took nearly forty minutes of casing the shoreline from the shadows before he found what he was looking for.

The ship was moored with the bow facing the sea, ready for the next deployment. Written in big letters across the stern in Cyrillic was *Sea Scavenger,* and Sebastian could hear laughter and music coming from her deck. He was still a good distance away and began to wonder how he would get onboard without being noticed. He crept closer and closer, using every shadow and object of concealment to his advantage. Soon he was only one slip away. He could see the wooden decking of the dock that ran to her starboard and two of her crew walking up each, carrying a crate of alcohol. The crewmen were laughing and shouting to the others who were having quite a party at Sebastian's expense.

The *Sea Buzzard,* as Sebastian called it, was a wooden hulled fishing trawler with an overall length of nearly 60 feet. It had a large deck forward of the bridge for the work of commercial fishing. It was being used now for dancing and fondling of several 'ladies of the night.' Sebastian had to squint hard through the poor lighting to find his avenue of approach. He saw several tires hanging from ropes draped over the ship's side. They were buffers for anything the ship may come abreast of, whether it be another ship or the dock itself. One hung near the aft section of the trawler on the port side, and Sebastian decided this would be his ticket onboard. The catch was he would have to get in the water to get there.

Keeping a close eye on the vessel, he entered the water from the nearby empty slip. The water was so cold that it took Sebastian's breath away. He sat in the water for a moment clenching his teeth together to keep them from chattering. The only upside was the cold felt very good on his aching head, and the water cleaned his wound as he slowly swam toward the *Buzzard*.

The water was black in the moonless night, and Sebastian made an easy and unnoticed approach to the rear of the trawler. He lunged up from the water and grabbed the tire hanging about a meter above the water line. He hung for an anxious moment hoping his effort had gone unnoticed. His fingers found it hard to grip the tire, and it took all of his strength to lift himself out of the water. Using only arm strength, he slowly pulled himself from the water's intense cold, and gripped the rope attached to the tire. His arms burned and his head pounded, but through sheer determination, Sebastian made his way hand-over-hand to the railing. He ascended the railing and came up just behind the bridge. He stood still in the shadows, willing his body to calm as he tried to control his shivering.

He cautiously began to move quickly, finding the companionway to the inboard portion of the ship. He descended the stairs as a surge of laughter erupted from the party on deck. The inside of the ship was empty, and Sebastian worked rapidly. He found the mess and the men's sleeping quarters within minutes. In the quarters, he found a locked footlocker under one of the built-in racks. He picked the simple lock easily with a hook he found on the floor and inside found what he had come for.

With the 'working women' on board, the men knew better than to have their money anywhere around, so they had stowed everything in the chest. It looked like a rush job as everything was just stuffed inside. Sebastian found his papers, his cash, his clothes, and even more money belonging to the men on board. All together, he actually came out about 600 Euros ahead of what was taken from him. He also found the men's identification documents, which he took without hesitation. He would turn them over to the Russians with word of the double cross when he reached home.

He found a plastic bag in the mess and stuffed everything inside. He was about to take his leave when he had an idea. He found the hatch that led down into the engine room and entered. The engines were quiet, and looked to be in generally poor condition. Sebastian wondered if this pile of junk could have even made it across the sea.

He surveyed the small room and quickly formulated his plan. The ceiling caught his attention as it was cracked and split near the joints from years of rough waters twisting it to and fro. He looked around and found a flat pan full of diesel fuel with greasy wrenches soaking inside. He crept back upstairs and grabbed a cigarette from a pack lying around and a few wooden matches. He pulled a strand of hemp from a piece of rope hanging in the engine room, and tied three matches to the cigarette, with the heads sticking just above the filter.

Sebastian then took the diesel fuel and poured it carefully down the wall. He found a rag lying near the engine, and soaked it in the fuel. He wedged the rag in the ceiling in one of the many gaps at the top of the fuel line he had made along the wall. With a small pool on the floor at the bottom of the fuel trail, the job was complete, and Sebastian lit the cigarette. Laying the cigarette on the edge of the small pool of fuel on the floor, he had essentially created a timed fuse. When the cigarette reached the matches they would catch, igniting the fuel, which in theory should follow the fuel up the wall to the rag in the ceiling. Once ignited, it would be the catalyst to a raging inferno.

Sebastian grabbed the plastic bag and headed back toward the deck. He cautiously emerged from the depths of the ship to find the party kicking into high gear. They were completely unaware of Sebastian's visit to their beloved ship.

He slipped back into the frigid water and cautiously retreated from the *Sea Buzzard*. He got out of the water and worked the shadows again to a safe location. Shedding his wet clothes, he quickly pulled his dry ones from the plastic bag. He dressed, donning a newly acquired wool coat, arranged all his documents, and headed to find the shop owner holding his ferry ticket.

Sebastian knocked on the man's door as quietly as he could. He must have been waiting anxiously because he responded almost immediately, and let him in. Sebastian stepped inside and welcomed the warmth of the small shop. The man walked to the back where he slept and came right back holding Sebastian's ticket.

"Thank you," Sebastian said with a huge sigh of relief. "And in return for keeping your word…" Sebastian handed him the extra 600

Euro he had picked up from the ship. The cook's eyes were wide as he held the cash in his hand. He looked at Sebastian, not knowing what to say. "You are an honorable man, my friend," Sebastian said, placing a hand on the shop owner's shoulder. "You have helped me more than you know, and this is just a small token of my gratitude." The man's mouth moved but no sounds came out. "It's time for me to go. I wish you good health, and again, thank you." Sebastian opened the front door and walked back into the night.

"God speed, my friend," the astonished man murmured at last, peering into the shadows long after the young man had disappeared from sight.

Chapter 107

Sebastian leaned on the railing of the ferry, sipping warm tea he had purchased from the onboard concession stand. He imagined that Kazakhstan would be a fascinating place to visit under different circumstances. He held the glass of tea with both hands and watched the flames from the fully enveloped fishing trawler lick the black sky in the distance. Other passengers gathered beside him, chatting curiously about the fire. The silhouettes of several men could be seen running chaotically about, illuminated by the floating inferno, and their panicked shouts could be heard even over the engines of the ship. The ferry slipped out of the harbor and into the night. Sebastian was now on his way to Azerbiajan.

Sebastian wandered aimlessly about the ferry. He tried to stand near anyone having a conversation to pick up any information that may be useful for his arrival in Baku. He found it impossible to concentrate; however, because the cold seemed to follow him everywhere he went. His little evening swim had chilled him through and through, and the cold felt as if it were settling in his bones. Finally, he ventured deeper into the ship, hoping to insulate himself against the outside. He walked the passageways from one end of the ship to the other, then descended to the next deck below. He paced, lost in thought, trying to warm up and pass time. He had just stepped from the ladder onto the third deck down from where he began when he heard laughter coming from ahead on the left. He approached slowly and could hear quite a commotion coming from behind the entryway door.

He pushed the door open and found inside a large, smoke-filled common room, packed with rough looking dock hands surrounding some sort of card game in the center. Sebastian looked like he fit right in with the clothes he had taken from the Sea Buzzard. He squeezed into the room and quickly recognized they were all speaking Russian. He greeted a couple of roughnecks closest to him who brought him up to speed on the game and the stakes waged. Apparently, one of the men at the card table had been caught with the other's sister. So the stakes were: if Romeo won he could keep on seeing the sister; if he lost it would cost him a month's wages, a punch in the nose, and he could never see the sister again. Someone said the sister looked like she lost a few bets herself, and everyone cracked up laughing, except for the brother who was concentrating intently on the game, determined to salvage his sister's honor.

As the evening progressed, Sebastian gained valuable information through casual conversation. He learned that Baku had a very large petroleum-manufacturing factory on the shore, and that they employed just about anyone willing to work. Most of these men had saved their money for anywhere from two to six years to afford the trip over, plus living costs until they could get on full-time with the factory. Then they could send money home regularly to their families, and maybe one day afford to bring them over, as well.

Sebastian sipped at his hot drink, which was some concoction of cheap tea and even cheaper vodka. His glass never seemed to get empty as he enjoyed the company of these men until the wee hours of the morning. Finally, Sebastian was able to extract himself from the smoke filled room, closing the door on another robust version of the Russian national anthem. He worked his way back up toward the main deck where he found a chair in another enclosed common room. He could have paid nearly double his ticket price and gotten a private sleeping room, but he was very glad he didn't. He had gained information that he otherwise never would have. The sitting room he had found was quiet with very few people, and Sebastian nestled in as best he could to try to get some shut-eye.

Chapter 108

Stephanie walked out the backdoor of the small cottage into the crisp early afternoon air. She breathed deeply the rich smells of the countryside and surveyed the landscape. A small pond sat picturesquely about half a kilometer away, nestled in the field of wheat. She bounced cheerfully down the back steps and set out for the still water.

She found a comfortable place to sit beside the tarn, and allowed the sun to embrace her. It didn't take long for her to stretch out on her back, soaking in the sunshine like an old cat. She closed her eyes and reflected on the stories of Arval, her own story thus far, and that loathsome package still in her possession. Her mind would not rest, as much as she willed it to do so. Her story was not over yet, and she wondered what might lie ahead.

After basking in the sun for nearly an hour, Stephanie decided that she needed to get some things done. She had made a mental checklist while reminiscing, and remembered Arval's instructions to purchase a phone card and give him a call. She needed to go into town.

Her mind settled on what errands she needed to run, she got to her feet and headed back to the house. Sarah was in the kitchen gathering the ingredients to bake a pie and Etienne was napping in his easy chair in the cozy livingroom. A mid-afternoon snack of cheese, crackers, and apple slices was waiting for her on the kitchen table. The food was presented as if it had been ripped from a page of a country-living magazine. Stephanie smiled, and poured herself a glass of milk from the refrigerator. She thanked Sarah for her thoughtfulness and gave her a quick hug. They chatted amiably while Stephanie ate, grateful for the refreshment.

After sharing her plans with Sarah, Stephanie dialed Captain de Armand's number, and he happily agreed to come out and pick her up first thing in the morning for a trip to the city. Stephanie smiled as she hung up; she was quickly becoming quite fond of Canada.

Chapter 109

Slavo had known for nearly 24 hours that Ms. Stephanie Boulanger and his package had escaped to Montreal, Canada. He had already sent two of his men home, escorting his brother back to Kosovo. He still couldn't tell if his father was extremely angry or quite happy about the development with his youngest son. Slavo knew his father missed Nikolin desperately because he saw so much of their mother in him. Something had died with his mother in his father's soul. Nikolin seemed to bring flickers of light in the darkness, like striking flint in a cave.

He fidgeted around his hotel room in downtown Paris waiting for updates. His people were having a very difficult time finding where the girl had gone after her plane touched down. She seemed to have vanished after Canadian passport control.

Slavo scoffed at the thought of how the world, following the example of the sanctimonious Americans, had become the proverbial 'melting pot.' He fervently believed in the ethnic purity of countries, particularly his own. However, this time it was actually working to his advantage.

His father had called upon two Serbs, who were actually police officers for the Royal Canadian Mounted Police, to handle the job in Montreal. They were working all available angles on their end, as well. Sooner or later, this little girl's luck would run out, and they could put an end to this ridiculous goose chase.

Damir sat listening patiently to the information being disseminated over his cell phone. Soon after they left the Institute for Orthodox Theology, Damir called his intelligence technicians to start checking into this Bishop Brenner. He wanted to know why this woman had gone there with the package. What he was learning now made him shake his head with incredulity. "His little brother; that is unbelievable," Damir sighed deeply. "Ok, look for passport hits, phone or credit card usage, the usual stuff, and see if we can get him back on radar. Yes, thanks for your help." Damir clicked the phone shut. He knew Nikolin when he was a boy; he was a sharp, gentle kid with a likeable disposition. Made sense he became a Bishop. Damir was thinking of the innocence of youth when a thought hit him like a ton of bricks. He flipped his phone back open, speed-dialing his people in Zagreb. "Yes, it's Damir. I need you to get a team together. I want eyes on the monastery in Gracanica, Kosovo. Forward surveillance units, photos of Nikolin Petrovic and his father, Plamen Petrovic."

Chapter 110

The ferry maneuvered expertly to its berth in the busy Baku Harbor. Sebastian could see cranes, derricks, and smoke congesting the shoreline about a mile north of where they were pulling into port. The oil derricks, he had learned from his late night conversations, were built by the Russians and remained in use to this day. This looked like an ideal location for Sebastian to lay low for a couple of days and make sure he was not being followed before moving on.

Sebastian walked the gangplank from the ferry to solid ground and made sure to fall in behind one of the Russian laborers as they approached the passport control area. He double-checked his documents to make sure he had everything and rehearsed his cover story in his head. He listened carefully as the man in front of him produced his papers and explained his intentions to find work at the petroleum factory. The passport control officer looked as if he had heard this story a million times as he grabbed the papers and thumbed through them. He entered some information on the antiquated computer in front of him, stamped the passport, and yelled "Next!" as he handed the papers back to the elated dockhand.

Sebastian stepped forward and repeated almost the identical story as he handed over his documents. The officer rolled his head on his neck and took a long drag from a cigarette that simmered in a makeshift ashtray made out of the bottom of a Coke can. Sebastian stood silently, hoping to duplicate the smooth transaction of the guy before him. Again the man entered some information on his computer and then thumbed through Sebastian's Russian passport to find a place to stamp. He slammed the entry stamp down and handed the paperwork back. Sebastian felt a huge relief as he reached out to retrieve his documents.

Turning from the counter, Sebastian took about three steps when the officer said, "Sir, excuse me, sir!" Sebastian's heart froze; he turned back to the officer quickly, trying not to look suspicious.

"Yes?" Sebastian replied quizzically.

Still looking at his computer screen, the man asked, "Was your last name Krinov or Kruglov?"

With incomprehensible speed, Sebastian's mind raced back to the farmhouse and his lethal training. *"The easiest question in the world will be the one that gets you killed!"* he heard Ares lecturing during their 'cover' phase. Trying to work, act, and think like someone else is very difficult business. The amount of information you must retain in order to work an effective cover story is nearly impossible to comprehend at first. This is exactly the principle Ares was referring to; you will work so hard to memorize finite details that the glaringly obvious ones get squeezed out of the mind's recall room.

Panic momentarily seized Sebastian, causing him to draw a blank. He smiled and took a couple steps back toward the officer, trying to buy time to think. It finally hit him. "Krinov, sir," he replied calmly. "Oleg Krinov. Would you like to see my papers again?" Sebastian asked, reaching for his inside pocket.

"No, no, that is not necessary. Thank you," the man responded, hitting the computer keyboard harder with each word. "Stupid computers…" he muttered under his breath and then yelled, "Next!"

Chapter 111

Sebastian turned again and walked toward the exit of passport control. His heart was pounding furiously in his chest, but on the outside he looked as if he were as calm as if he just had coffee with his best friend.

He headed off into the city to have a look around. He really just wanted to walk because it was his first feeling of control for quite some time. Free to develop a plan of his own accord, he walked for over an hour, subtly watching for any sign of monitoring by local authorities or otherwise. Sebastian was convinced that he was in the clear; at least for now. He sat and had a coffee and read a local newspaper. Everything appeared normal, so Sebastian began to dial down his 'awareness' just a notch or two.

After the break for coffee, he found a trendy styling salon and walked in. All eyes were upon him as he looked like he had just gotten off the boat from a month at sea. The receptionist informed Sebastian, snobbishly, that a shave and a haircut at this particular establishment was 40 Euro, sure that this would send the peasant on his way. He pulled 100 Euro from his pocket and smiled at the girl. "Shall we?" Sebastian gestured, looking at several empty seats in the salon's main styling room. She snatched the money from his hand, stood with a huff, and reluctantly escorted him inside.

Sebastian glanced at himself in the mirror as he was directed to his seat. He almost laughed out loud. His hair was the longest it had been in his life, he had the workings of a full beard and, amongst the pleasant odor of the salon, he smelled like a rooting pig. The stylist, who seemed to have been the one to draw the shortest straw, approached Sebastian like he had a serious communicable disease. She took him back to the little sinks and washed his hair. The combination of the warm water and her massaging touch nearly put him to sleep. She started cutting his hair slowly as if wondering where to begin, but before long it seemed like she had taken this haircut as a direct challenge to her abilities. She started to explain how she was going to style it, and how he wouldn't be able to recognize himself when she was finished. Before long they were chatting like old friends. Somehow they began talking about America. Sebastian said that he had visited there once several years earlier. This thrilled the young lady immensely; her life's dream was to cut hair in America.

She had finished with his hair, but would not reveal her finest work until she had given him a proper shave. She pulled out a straight razor and lathered his face with warm shaving cream. She continued talking of her dreams, and Sebastian again drifted on the soothing sound of her voice and the methodical strokes removing his beard.

Finally, she stepped back and gave her work one last appraisal. She then spun the chair around so Sebastian could see himself in the mirror. She was right, he hardly recognized himself. Clean-shaven, and with a styled haircut, Sebastian felt as if he were someone else. It helped him to adapt to his new persona as Oleg Krinov. He thanked her profusely, and tipped her twenty Euros. She hardly knew what to say.

"Now that you have transformed me," Sebastian said gratefully, "I have one last favor to ask of you…" He went on to explain that he was going to surprise his friends with his new look. They were supposed to meet him across the street at a little café, but he wanted to sneak up on them and see if they recognized him. His stylist was thrilled to play such a role in his little conspiracy, and showed him out the employee's entrance, which opened to the alley behind the salon.

Once alone in the alley, he shed a majority of his clothing and threw it in the dumpster; anything that would resemble what he entered the salon with. Behind the dumpster, he changed into different clothes from his bag. Then he strolled out of the alley and into the pedestrian traffic flow quite seamlessly. Sebastian knew one could never be too cautious. Not far away was a men's clothing shop. He ducked in and purchased two suits and some casual clothes. They made small alterations while he waited, and soon he was back on his way to his final stop of the day. He found a nice, moderately-priced hotel near downtown and checked in. He was amused at how differently people treated him now that he looked like a modern businessman.

Following a small meal in the hotel's restaurant, Sebastian retired to his room where he took a very relaxing shower, watched a few minutes of local television, and fell fast asleep.

He slept long and hard overnight. Awaking at about 9:00 a.m. with a start, it took him a few seconds to remember where he was and what was going on. He chastised himself inwardly for sleeping so soundly because it made him vulnerable. He stretched and glanced out the window to the street below. Again everything looked normal. He took another quick shower and headed out.

The only thing Sebastian had to accomplish today was finding the train schedule from Baku to Tbilisi, Georgia. The key to escape, in this case returning to France, was avoiding panic. *'Don't move too fast,'* meaning don't run for the easiest way out. This would only draw attention and send alarms sounding where otherwise there would be none. He needed to find a simple path of progression toward safety, employ caution, and reasonable pacing. Other than that, he was going to enjoy the sights of the city and work counter-surveillance to ensure he was indeed traveling unhindered.

Baku is an antediluvian and amazing city. Sebastian made his way to the ancient historical core of Baku, also known as the walled city. He spent the day exploring the Palace of the Shirvanshahs and the Maiden Tower. For a few hours, Sebastian was able to forget that he was a highly trained Special Forces operative on the run, and let history embrace him.

The sun was setting as Sebastian wandered back to his hotel. He had completely forgotten about finding a train schedule, but his problem was easily solved by the front desk staff who produced an entire brochure on the trains, including travel times and fares. Sebastian went to sleep feeling more relaxed than he had in years. He could still not fully enjoy the experience as he had to remain vigilant in surveying his surroundings at all times, but all in all, it was a very good day.

Sebastian decided to leave Baku the following evening even though he wanted to spend at least one more day in the friendly and vibrant city. His desire to get back to France, however, compelled him to move on. By 8:30 p.m. the next day, he donned his European business attire and boarded the train to Tbilisi, Georgia.

Chapter 112

The trip to Tbilisi was uneventful, and provided nothing to see because the entire journey was made at night. Sebastian was in a two-bed sleeper cabin that he shared with an old man who wasn't keen on conversation. That suited Sebastian fine, and he read a copy of the Georgian Times until he felt tired enough to sleep. He laid down and quickly fell asleep, lulled by the gentle rock of the train. By 6:00 a.m. the next morning, Sebastian was gathering his travel bag to depart the train.

He made his way through the terminal. A nearby café was serving breakfast that smelled inviting. This was as good a place as any to get some breakfast and a hot cup of coffee, Sebastian reasoned, as the ducked in the door. Using the time to take in his surroundings and make note of anything out of the ordinary, he was surprised at how busy things were at such an early hour in and around the terminal.

Even though he had nowhere in particular to be, Sebastian knew he needed to project the image of a businessman on the go, so to avoid suspicion, he walked with determination. He needed to find a hotel where he could stow his gear while he canvassed the area to plan for his next move. Hailing a cab, he instructed the driver to take him to the closest lodging. There was a hotel only a few blocks away that would be fine for his short stay. He paid the driver and checked in. After he freshened up, he decided to walk a few blocks to familiarize himself with his immediate surroundings, then get a cab, and explore the city.

Once in the city, he spent some time trying to plan his next move; hopefully the last leg of his journey back to France. Toward mid-day, he came upon an inviting café, and feeling pangs of hunger, stepped inside for some nourishment and a chance to observe the local culture. The café was doing a brisk business, and the food was very good. After a while, Sebastian checked his watch and shook his head slightly as if he were running behind schedule. He stepped out from the café and started off quickly down the sidewalk.

Turning the corner, he saw a police car parked against the curb and two officers trying to talk with a very agitated man accompanied by presumably his teenage son. The man was getting very loud and animated. Sebastian quickly recognized he was speaking English; American English. He smiled inwardly as he realized he now saw Americans in much the same light as Europeans: loud, pushy, and inconsiderate. *'But that's just until you get to know us,'* Sebastian thought humorously. *'After that, we're just as nice as the next guy.'*

He slowed his pace; needing to make a decision. Because he spoke both English and Russian, he understood that the man and his son had lost their bag that contained their passports. The cops were trying to tell them they had found the bag and needed them to come with them to the station to retrieve it and fill out the paperwork. The man wasn't about to get into their police car and so on and so on. This was a very easy situation to fix, but Sebastian knew that it may compromise his cover if he was the Good Samaritan here.

Taking a deep breath, he approached the parties involved. "Perhaps I can be of assistance," he said first to the American man in English, then to the police in Russian. Sebastian quickly explained to the American that the police had found his bag and both their passports, but they would be required to come to the police station and fill out the proper paperwork, just as they would if they were back in the U.S. The man was elated to hear they had found their passports and began to thank the police and apologize to them at the same time for his behavior. Sebastian quickly translated everything, and in no time everyone was happy.

"You're an American, sir?" one of the police officers asked innocently enough.

"No, no," Sebastian replied, "I am Russian."

As soon as the words were out of his mouth, the smiles disappeared from the faces of the two police officers.

"May we see your passport," the other officer said, stepping forward.

"Of course," Sebastian quickly produced his passport from the inside pocket of his suit coat. He realized that something had changed, and his mind raced to figure out what it was. As his mind flipped through a rolodex of information, a news story that he read on the second page of the Georgian Times while on the train jumped out with vivid clarity: *'Relations Remain Strained with Moscow.'* He admonished himself for his sloppy fieldwork. The article had said that Georgia was not even accepting mail from Russia anymore. There was no turning back now, however, so he had to work damage control quickly.

"I work for an American Company," he offered. "I spend more time in New York than Moscow," he laughed weakly. "I am actually here to look at expanding our interests and possibly bringing many jobs to Tbilisi." This seemed to take the edge off a bit, but tension still hung heavy in the air.

After an uncomfortable pause, the older of the two officers handed back his passport and spoke. "Very well, sir. You can be on your way."

Sebastian smiled and turned to leave. He wished the father and son well and tried to walk away at a normal pace. He did not notice the glance that the police officers gave each other as he turned to leave, or one of them pulling out his cell phone as he sat in the car.

Sebastian was very angry with himself. He had compromised his safety to resolve a trivial matter. *Stupid, Sloppy, Unacceptable.* He continued to chastise himself as he walked. He needed to get out of the area immediately. He decided to hail a cab and take a little tour of the city so he could see if he had picked up a tail before returning to the hotel for the evening. He waved down a taxi that looked like the driver had to power it with his own feet. It was a 'Yugo;' probably one of the first off the production line, gauging from how old it appeared. Its taxi markings were so faded that the driver actually placed a magnetized 'taxi' sign on the roof so Sebastian would know he was, in fact, a cab. Sebastian thought about waving this one on and waiting for another, but then went ahead and stepped forward and opened the back door, hoping it wouldn't fall off in his hand. He sat down, and a plump fellow with a pleasant face turned to him and asked, "Where to?"

Sebastian stated he was in the city on business and this was his first visit. He asked if the driver would mind giving him a quick tour of the city before he went to his hotel. The man's face lit up as if he had been asked to talk of his own children. "I will give you the best tour you have ever had, my friend!" the man answered enthusiastically as he situated himself behind the wheel and shifted into drive.

"I will, of course, pay you for as long as we are driving," Sebastian assured him.

"Sir, we will speak no more of money as that will take care of itself. It is my duty and my honor to say to you, Welcome to Tbilisi!"

Sebastian smiled and settled into his seat. He couldn't help but like this driver immediately. This was going to be an interesting ride.

Chapter 113

As they pulled away, the police officers from the earlier incident were in their vehicle stopped at the intersection waiting for Sebastian's taxi to pass. He nodded to the officers who looked back at him with a curious expression that made him uneasy. They both nodded back, but it was not in the least bit friendly.

"Pull over here a moment, please," Sebastian said after they had gone a few blocks past. "I just need to use the phone a moment."

"Yes, of course," the driver replied as he pulled to the curb.

Sebastian got on the public phone and dialed a series of numbers from memory. A female voice answered the line. "T & M Construction Supply, can I help you?"

"Yes, I need to place a rush order, please," Sebastian said, as he looked around carefully.

"Hold, please." Soft music played in his ear as he waited, then a male voice came on the line.

"Yes, sir, how can I help you?" Sebastian again repeated the need for a rush order. The man then went through a series of questions, which included account number, business phone number, name on the account, etc. It all sounded legitimate, in case anyone was listening, but in fact, it was all a complex messaging system built primarily on numbers. The first onslaught of questions were all security questions to confirm the legitimacy of the caller, next was the actual message itself.

"Ok, sir, go ahead with your order," the man said.

"Is it ok if I just use the numbered product identification codes from your catalog?" Sebastian asked, holding up a just-one-more-minute finger to his driver.

"That would make it easier for us, yes, sir," the man on the phone replied.

At this point Sebastian went through a list of numbers, completed his order, and hung up.

He jumped back in the cab and apologized to the driver for the delay. "Let's go see this beautiful city of yours," Sebastian said with enthusiasm.

The driver rubbed his hands together as he grinned from ear to ear. They blurred into the endless stream of traffic, and the driver began his sightseeing tour.

Chapter 114

Damir and his crew finished their debrief in Zagreb and boarded a train for Split. The train eased its way out of the station and began to pick up speed. From his window seat, Damir gazed at the beautiful countryside of his beloved Croatia. Separated by utility poles at regular intervals, the landscape flickered by like watching an old silent movie. He looked down at the file in his lap. The intelligence bureau compiled an exhaustive file on Stephanie Boulanger at his request, and now he just couldn't bring himself to look at it. He wasn't sure why, but he supposed it had something to do with him getting soft.

Damir rubbed his eyes and shook his head. He wasn't getting soft; he was regaining his humanity after a lifetime of separating his emotions from the mission. He realized however, that if he opened that file, he would establish a connection with this unfortunate girl. Right now, he could see her as an inconvenience, a target, an object; but if he opened the dossier and began to read, she would take shape, gain dimension, become a person. He wasn't ready yet. He leaned back in his seat and let the train rock him to sleep.

The train groaned to a stop at *Obala Kneza Domagoja 11* station, and passengers bled onto the platform in a steady stream of humanity. Damir and his three teammates emerged sleepily, in no hurry to get to their operation center. A quick cab ride and two cigarettes apiece later, they pulled in front of their *'center of operations.'* The thought of this made Damir smile inwardly. The real world of espionage was so far removed from what the typical layperson envisioned that he imagined they would be utterly distraught if they knew. The only Bond associated with them may have been "vagabond" as they walked into the decrepit two-story building on the outskirts of the city. This crumbling structure was, in fact, their center of operations.

There was really nothing left to do but wait. The Bosnian and the two Albanians quickly dispersed to their respective sleeping quarters within the non-descript building. Situated on the crest of a hill, the building fronted on a busy highway that ran along a cliff face overlooking the Adriatic Sea. There was a small gaggle of houses on this hill serviced by a single restaurant, a tiny grocery store, and a coffee shop. Damir walked the short distance to the coffee shop and the waiter prepared his coffee without him even having to ask. He settled himself at an outside table, waited on his macchiato, and fired up another cigarette.

He supposed it could no longer be avoided, so he smoothed out the file in front of him, took a deep breath, and opened it. Staring back at him was a college graduation photo of a smiling Stephanie Boulanger; a woman whose life was now forever changed, and may end entirely too prematurely.

Chapter 115

The communications officer walked briskly down the hall holding a folded piece of paper. He found the office he was looking for and knocked twice sharply.

"Enter," Came the voice from inside.

"Sir, this communication just came in under the highest classification codes."

Ares reached for the paper with one hand and adjusted his reading glasses on his nose with the other. He read the contents, and the muscles of his jaw tensed reflexively under the stress of his clenched teeth.

"I need a full staff meeting in fifteen minutes," Ares said, as he re-folded the paper and placed it in his breast pocket.

"Sir, there are nine different priority tasking orders running concurrently that the staff is…"

The sentence was cut short by the intensity of the look Ares directed at him. "I assign the tasking orders in this facility, Lieutenant. I know where everyone is and what they are doing." Ares spoke very calmly, but did not even blink as he addressed the Lieutenant. "Now, I want a *full* staff meeting in fifteen minutes."

The lieutenant snapped to attention, realizing the gravity of his orders.

"Yes, sir," he answered sharply, and turned on his heel to spread the word.

Ares walked into the large conference room exactly fifteen minutes later pleased to see his full staff assembled. Since the latest job, in which Sebastian was instrumental in the successful capture of the target, the farmhouse team had been moved to a state-of-the-art facility so classified that hardly anyone knew of its existence. Ares' team was also beefed up with enough technical wizards, intelligence experts, and communications specialists to make James Bond jealous.

Ares decided to waste no time in getting to the heart of the matter. "One of our operatives is on the run," he began. "It is imperative to this operation and to me personally that this individual reaches safety quickly, and in one piece."

Ares felt responsible for essentially throwing Sebastian to the wolves, as he was so focused on their latest catch and the information he held. They had, in fact, extracted more valuable information from this one individual than any three they had captured in the past. That was the reason his team was so busy now following up on leads and assigning teams to eliminate players they had heretofore not known existed.

"I need the GPS chip imbedded in his passport activated immediately." One of the techno-geeks jumped to his feet and slipped from the room to carry out this order. "Secondly, I want a team in Kazakhstan in twelve hours; I want them to take out every person on this list with extreme prejudice." Ares tossed a piece of paper into the middle of the table. A Special Forces Sergeant Major assigned to the unit grabbed the paper a little too enthusiastically. "I want every fish-gut-smelling piece of shit in that sewer to know who they are dealing with, do you understand me?" Ares looked hard at the Sergeant Major. The Sergeant Major stood with perfect military form and presence.

"Sir!" was all he replied with a sharp salute as he turned and walked purposefully out of the room. Ares knew this man would handle the task with expedient dispatch, and that is exactly what he wanted.

Ares stopped and drew a deep breath; news of the double cross in Kazakhstan had stirred an anger in him that he had not felt in years. It was humiliating to him professionally, for such a thing to occur, and he wished he was there personally to find the men responsible. "I want three teams of four to constantly monitor the GPS information, and anything happening in the surrounding geographic area, once the data starts coming in."

At that moment, the technician that had left earlier, returned carrying a laptop. "Do we have anything?" Ares asked.

"Yes sir, the chip is active. He is currently in Tbilisi, Georgia."

Chapter 116

"Damn it," Ares said, as he looked down at the table and ran his hand through his hair. Mumbles came from around the table as everyone shared their opinion of this latest development.

"Ok, everyone, we all know that under regular circumstances this would be a bad situation, but let me tell you why this is a double-decker shit sandwich. The operative's real name is Sebastian Bishop, he is a French Foreign Legion Commando seconded to us for specialized training. He is a graduate of our Omega Program and was the one who actually shoved our guest into the van. All the progress we have made over the last few days is a direct result of his efforts." Many eyebrows rose at this latest information. "But that's not the worst of it," Ares continued. "He's an American." The room was completely still. "So if he is captured, it is hard to even imagine the fallout that may result."

Everyone in the room now became very uncomfortable. This situation seemed to have no favorable outcome, no matter how you looked at it. Ares tried to stay on task. "He is traveling on a Russian passport so we have to assume, at the very least, the local scumbag secret police are going to look for an opportunity to tune him up a little. I personally trained this kid, and he is a shrewd operator, but if they hem him in, they will pay dearly for it. If he does get cornered, and he demonstrates his skill, they will bring all they have after him, and he will be hard pressed to get out of the country. We have to assume worst case scenario here and work backwards."

The room emptied as everyone filed out to tackle their respective tasks. Within minutes Ares, Oleg, and Alex were the only ones left at the large conference table. The old friends had been through many things together. They sat companionably in the silence. Ares began drumming his fingers on the table and finally spoke. "I never should have allowed this to happen. That kid delivered for us; this guy he handed to us on a silver platter is what…in the top ten of terrorist-related international fugitives? It will take us months to follow up on all the information we will extract from him. It will lead to dozens of further arrests, probably save countless lives, and what do we do in return? Give the kid a handful of money and shove him out the door." Ares massaged his forehead and sighed heavily.

Oleg felt the need to interject. "It is important to remember that this 'kid' you keep referring to is a highly trained, elite soldier. He couldn't be more prepared for this kind of situation. This operation didn't go exactly as planned, but they rarely do. You need to stop acting like a mother hen, and give this a little time to play out."

"I really don't think we need to do anything to help him," Alex chimed in.

"What do you mean?" Ares snapped, his head whipping around.

"He is *not* Russian; he will begin making progress when he stops acting like he is." Alex laid this out, hoping his comrade would figure it out for himself.

"He'll go to the French Embassy!" Ares blurted in his moment of discovery as if he had solved a great mystery.

"Exactly," Alex replied. "Now if I were you, I would get on the phone with Legion Special Forces Command and start explaining how their boy is on his way home and that he is nearly Achilles himself. Tell them that you believe he has officer potential written all over him, that you would take this kid into battle any day, etc."

"He is an outstanding soldier," Ares said, thinking aloud.

"This operation was a good one, for the good guys, for once. Give credit where credit is due. That is how we can help this young man now," Oleg said in conclusion.

Ares gave a nod of understanding. "I'm getting too old for this field work, my friends," he said, standing from his seat.

"We all are," Alex agreed with a grin.

"This may be the one to go out on," Ares said, raising his eyebrows. The men laughed and filed out of the office. Much work remained.

Chapter 117

Sebastian's mind raced as they drove around the streets of Tbilisi. The cab driver was a wealth of information on the city's history. He spoke of the Narikla Fortress established in the fourth century and how it was greatly expanded in the seventh century by King David, the Builder. He explained that Tbilisi had been ruled by Mongols and was fought over by Ottomans and Persians, and how the country finally joined the Russian Empire in 1801. Under normal circumstances, Sebastian would have been engrossed in the mobile lecture. Today, however, he could not shake the look of the two police officers.

They turned onto a side road with little traffic where the driver was making a comment about ancient architecture when he suddenly stopped talking. Sebastian's thoughts were interrupted by the silence, and he looked to see why the driver had stopped his monologue. Directly ahead of them was a police checkpoint made up of two police cars and two officers stopping traffic. Sebastian's heart began to race. "Is this normal?" he asked, as nonchalantly as he could manage.

"There are many checkpoints around the city," the man replied, not really answering the question. Sebastian noticed the driver looking intently at two men, in plain clothes, standing on the sidewalk beside one of the patrol cars. Realizing that this was a very quickly organized checkpoint, Sebastian was trying not to be excessively paranoid; but, it didn't take a rocket scientist to know these cops were looking for something specific. *'More like **someone** specific,'* he thought.

They were too close to the checkpoint to even consider turning around. Sebastian handed the cab driver fifty Euro. "If for some reason I am asked to get out of the car," Sebastian said quietly, "will you please pull around the corner and park?" The cab driver looked at the money, looked out at the officers, and then back at the money. Times were tough in Georgia. "Yes, sir. I can do that," he answered, taking the money and knowing not to ask any questions.

Two uniformed police officers approached the vehicle and Sebastian slid back in his seat, consciously working to slow his breathing and control his nerves. He tried to take in as much of his surroundings as possible as the officers began speaking to the driver. They asked for his documents which he had readily available, of course, as this was his livelihood and he was very familiar with the routine. They asked him some standard questions before turning their attention to Sebastian. One of the plain clothed men on the sidewalk was on the cell phone, the other sucked on a cigarette, taking inventory of everything around them. Sebastian took a final, calming deep breath as he prepared for the inevitable.

"Sir, may we see your passport, please?" one of the officers asked.

"Of course," Sebastian said, handing his passport through the driver's side window.

"Would you mind stepping out of the vehicle, sir?" the officer more ordered than asked.

"Certainly," Sebastian continued with his innocent businessman act. This was the time for compliance and cooperation. He had to get a better feel for what was behind all this. He stepped out of the vehicle. "Is there a problem, officer?" Sebastian inquired.

"There seems to be some sort of discrepancy with your passport, sir. These gentlemen are from the Border Authority." The two plain-clothes guys now approached with friendly smiles on their faces.

"Would you walk with us a moment, sir?" the younger of the two asked. "We just have a few routine questions concerning your documents. We should have this cleared up in no time."

"You're free to go," the uniformed officer said to the cab driver. Sebastian saw him swallow hard as he pulled away.

Chapter 118

The younger of Sebastian's escorts was smooth and refined, the older couldn't maintain the required polite demeanor, and his underlying intent was beginning to shine through. He scrutinized their surroundings to make sure no one was watching as they turned to walk. They went only a few feet and took a narrow alleyway off the sidewalk. As soon as they turned, they each grabbed an arm and dragged Sebastian further into the cut. The older one punched Sebastian savagely in the stomach, and they both threw him hard against the wall.

"Who are you?" the younger asked in a calm, almost quiet, voice.

"My name is Oleg Krinov. I am a businessman from Moscow. Why are you doing this to me?" Sebastian tried to sound terrified.

They punched him again, this time more in the ribs. Sebastian realized that he would have to react soon or they would take enough out of him so he couldn't.

"We know this lie already, you piece of shit," the younger replied with a mocking, sing-song voice. "Now you need to think real hard about you're next answer." The older man snapped open a knife, waving it menacingly, to accentuate the statement.

Sebastian looked at the knife with wide eyes and began to pretend that he was shaking in fear. "I'm telling you the truth!" Sebastian whimpered. "I don't know who you think I am or what you want. I am just here for business." Sebastian cowered against the wall trying to look as pitiful as possible.

There was a pause as the two men surveyed their prey, "Look at him, he is about to piss his pants," the older man said with contempt in his voice. "He is a nobody."

The younger grabbed Sebastian by the hair and yanked his head back. He brought his face near enough for Sebastian to smell his putrid nicotine breath and body odor. "Is that true, little worm? Are you a nobody? Why do you speak such good English? How stupid are you to come to my country broadcasting you are Russian?" He shoved Sebastian's head forward violently.

"You're right, no one could be this stupid and pose a threat to us."
There was a pause as the younger man smoothed his hair and reached
for his cigarettes inside his jacket. "Gut him. We've wasted enough of
our time." He pulled a cigarette from the pack with his teeth. The older
man's eyes glistened with bloodlust as he lunged forward with the
knife.

Sebastian rose from his cowering position with startling speed,
turning sideways to avoid the thrust of the blade. He grabbed the
man's arm with two hands as it passed, and using his attacker's own
momentum, redirected the blade into the pelvis of the younger man.
He screamed in pain as the blade entered to the hilt in the soft area
directly beside his genitals. Sebastian forced the knife down, ripping
through the man's femoral artery. He would bleed out within minutes.

Sebastian quickly repositioned his grip on the man's arm still
holding the knife and broke it at the elbow. He felt the man's knees go
weak with pain. Sebastian tore the knife from the man's hand and
cleanly sliced his carotid artery as he spun away. The two attackers
had terrorized their last victim.

Sebastian burst from the alleyway back to the street. The cops had
disappeared, knowing what the others had planned. He bolted around
the corner where the taxi was waiting. He was thankful the man stayed
true to his word. "I'm ready to go to my motel now," Sebastian told
the driver.

"Yes, ok, no problem," the driver stammered. He took a very direct
route back toward the downtown area.

"This will be fine," Sebastian said, instructing the driver to stop
about a block away from the hotel. He paid him generously and
thanked him for the tour and the ride. He got out, and his friendly taxi
driver sped away before the door even shut.

Sebastian made a cautious approach to the hotel, taking in every
available detail of his surroundings. Satisfied that things appeared
normal, he entered the hotel and went directly to his room. He
examined the door for signs of tampering and found none. He walked
in, ready for anything he may face. His room was silent and still, his
things right where he had left them.

Changing into the clothes he had picked up earlier at the men's store, he now took on the appearance of the typical European adventurer who took indeterminate amounts of time to backpack across regions 'off the beaten path.' He messed up his hair, grabbed a stick of chewing gum, gathered all his personal belongings, and headed out. He emerged from his hotel room with a completely different look, checked out of the motel without incident, and made his way on foot toward downtown.

Chapter 119

The waiter refilled the cup of coffee on the table, and Damir reached for it absently as he read. Ms. Boulanger was 26 years old, born an only child to Gustave and Camille Boulanger in the sleepy little town of Marmande, France. Stephanie's parents were academics; her father, the director of Library Services for the southwest region of France and her mother, a pharmacist.

Stephanie had a good upbringing and excelled, unsurprisingly, in her studies. She was also athletic, competing in the winter months in skiing and cycling in the summer. He studied a newspaper article, photocopied in the stack of paperwork, showing Stephanie winning a local cycling race. She looked about 18 when the article was written. Damir stared at her, standing next to her bicycle smiling, being presented with a modest trophy.

His mind drifted. He could see his eight-year-old niece in his mind's eye, riding and laughing as he chased her down the road. He had found a discarded bicycle a few weeks before her birthday. He and his brother worked on it tirelessly, having to drive to several locations to find parts. They assembled the bike as if they were performing surgery. He couldn't help but smile at the memory. The last thing they did was paint it a bright pink with white accents. The look on her face when they presented it to her was worth a hundred times the amount of work they put into it.

His mind then flashed forward to just a few short months after that time of such joy; cresting the hill with his small band of men in ragged battle fatigues after weeks of fighting. They were all from the area. The smoke hung thick around his village, buildings and houses were gutted; the smell of death lingered in the air. He remembered entering the village, making his way to his brother's house. In the road was the pink bike, crushed by tank treads. He fell to his knees and sobbed unashamedly.

Damir squeezed his eyes shut, shook his head and wiped the beads of cold sweat from his forehead. He closed the file. Stephanie was truly innocent; his stomach tightened at the thought of another such casualty to deadly conflict. He finished his coffee in a couple of quick gulps and started walking back to his men.

Chapter 120

Sebastian's eyes and ears missed nothing; all his senses were alert. Sometimes anticipatory fear is the worst fear of all. He was concerned, based on the ills that had befallen him so far, that something serious would happen to him before he reached his destination. But without so much as a stumble over a crack in the sidewalk, Sebastian walked up to the soldiers standing by the most welcoming sign he had seen in ages: French Embassy.

Approaching the guards with an anxious look on his face that he hoped was convincing, he gave them a story about how he had been backpacking across the region and someone must have stolen his French passport. Apparently, this was not an uncommon occurrence as the reaction of the guards indicated. One of them took his backpack, searched it, patted him down, and then escorted him through the front door. He was handed off to another armed guard and placed in a holding area, much like a jail cell. After some time, he was escorted again by armed guard to meet with a Foreign Service Officer.

Once alone in the room with the officer, Sebastian explained he was a Legionnaire, gave his commanding officer's name and contact information, and told another story about how his colleagues left him stranded as a joke while they were there on leave. Tbilisi's very relaxed policy in regard to hiring intimate companionship lured a lot of young soldiers to fly in to satisfy their urges with the plentiful and beautiful Georgian women.

The officer rolled his eyes at the folly of youth, but apparently bought the story; hook, line, and sinker.

By that evening, Sebastian was on a commercial flight to Paris under armed military escort and hand-delivered to Corporal Prenom, who was now Sergeant Prenom. The Sergeant acted like he was extremely pissed off with his ignorant soldier until the escorts were out of sight. "Heard you had a little adventure," Prenom said with a mischievous grin.

"Yeah, I guess you could say that," Sebastian replied, too tired to go into any kind of detail. Besides, he would have to lie anyway. His four-and-a-half months after SPETNAZ would remain highly classified for the rest of his life.

"Well, you must have screwed up whatever it was in the highest degree," Prenom continued, still smiling.

"What do you mean?" Sebastian asked.

"You have a meeting with The Man at 0800hrs tomorrow morning."

'The Man' was the foot soldiers' moniker for the highest-ranking officer in the French Foreign Legion, Brigadier General Philippe Rion.

"You've gotta be kidding me," Sebastian said in disbelief.

Prenom laughed the whole way out of the airport.

Chapter 121

Sebastian couldn't believe he had roughly eight hours to be ready for a face-to-face meeting with the Legion's highest-ranking officer. After all he had been through, he just wanted a hot meal, a hot shower, and a warm bed that he could sleep in for about four days straight. Instead, he spent over three hours meticulously ironing his dress uniform and trying to remember all the pomp and circumstance involved in a formal meeting with a superior officer. He finally crawled into bed at just after 1:00 a.m. He could have sworn he just closed his eyes when his alarm clock started blasting. It was time to crawl back out of bed and ready himself for what lay ahead.

Sebastian went over formal greetings, saying them out loud, and tried to remember all the etiquette if offered refreshment, etc. He couldn't really remember any of the crap they dumped on him during basic training. He was a little pre-occupied trying to stay alive during those days. Nothing much had changed, come to think of it.

He shook his head, trying to get focused on the task at hand. Donning his dress uniform, he noted it was empty of any achievement badges, medals, or anything else. *'Oh well,'* he thought, hopefully his record would speak more highly than his attire.

Sebastian headed out to a waiting transport vehicle driven by a pimply-faced recruit just out of basic training. He remembered getting servile jobs, like driving people around, and mused at the thought of being chauffeured for a change.

They drove in silence to the impressive administrative office complex where the Brigadier General was housed. Sebastian got out without saying anything to his driver; not out of rudeness or arrogance; he was just so focused on his meeting that he forgot. His anxiety meter was red-lining as he walked up the steps and entered the building.

Sebastian found his way to the General's office and was greeted by his secretary. He introduced himself, and she directed him to a comfortable chair to wait. It was 7:45 a.m. At exactly 8:00 a.m. the General emerged from his office. Sebastian, reading an article about polar bears in one of the tasteful magazines displayed near him, glanced up at the office door. Expecting a junior officer to retrieve him and take him back for the meeting, he jumped up and snapped to attention when he realized it was the General himself. The magazine that lay across his lap catapulted nearly to the secretary's desk.

The General laughed as he walked up; Sebastian saluted smartly. "General, Caporal Sebastian Bishop reporting as ordered, Sir."

General Rion bent down and scooped the magazine off the floor, settling it back on the side table. Sebastian closed his eyes for a quick moment as his face flushed with embarrassment.

"At ease, young man," the General said, extending his hand. Sebastian was unsure of what to do. Throwing caution to the wind, he reached out and shook the General's hand firmly. "Come on in," he said, motioning to his office. "We are very glad you made it back to us safely."

Sebastian walked into the General's office, still off balance from the casual behavior of his boss. Everyone's boss. *The* boss. Sebastian felt his palms begin to sweat.

Chapter 122

The General closed the door behind them and told Sebastian to have
a seat. He sat in a beautiful and comfortable leather chair, one of two,
facing the General's chair on the other side of the desk. Genera Rion
took his seat, placing his forearms on the desk in front of him, and
folded his hands. "Would you like some coffee or anything?" the
General asked.

"No thank you, Sir," Sebastian replied, perched on the edge of his
seat, sitting so erect it looked like his spine had been replaced with a
steel pole.

"Well now," the General began. "First things first, Son, you have
got to relax." He said the last part with a little laugh. "I am your
commanding officer, and this is simply Legion Headquarters; I am not
Zeus, and this is not Mount Olympus." Sebastian smiled and allowed
himself to sit back in his chair. "Good," the General said with a smile.
"Now, I have received a call from some very high-ranking and highly
classified individuals in Russia." Sebastian swallowed hard, his mind
racing. *'They didn't blame me for the market incident, did they?'* he
thought apprehensively. The General continued seriously, "You should
know that individuals of this caliber, when speaking of my personnel,
report to me and me alone." Sebastian's heart was about to explode out
of his chest. All he could think of was whether or not France still
employed the guillotine.

The General pulled out his reading glasses and perused his notes
regarding this report. "The Russians told me that you are one of the
most impressive and capable soldiers they have ever had come through
their program. Your skill, adaptability, and guile made them envious
that you were in our service and not theirs." Sebastian cocked his head
to make sure he understood what was being said. "They also added
their…" he read directly from the report, "highest recommendation
that you be considered for officer candidacy, post haste."

Sebastian sat for a moment, head spinning, trying to put together
what exactly the General was trying to say. Brigadier General Rion sat

back in his chair, studying Sebastian while chewing on the earpiece of his glasses.

The General sighed the kind of sigh that denoted careful consideration of serious decisions. He leaned forward again with more information. "So, while I consider what exactly to do with you, we have a few more things to discuss. I am fully aware of what you are now capable of. The Russians produce some of the finest Special Operators of any military organization in the world. I also fully understand that your new skills may be called on beyond your obligatory service to the Legion. I will be the one who will personally sign off on any operational assignment beyond direct French military involvement."

He looked intently at Sebastian, making sure that he was processing. Sebastian nodded, somehow relieved that his commander would be actively involved in that decision process. "Ok, enough on that; next, you are now eligible for French citizenship." He slid a stack of forms across his desk. "A benefit you are well aware of with our organization. You're chance to wipe your slate completely clean. You will, in essence, be a new person, going a new direction, with a new country. We are your family now."

Sebastian looked at the stacks of forms and pulled them closer. He straightened up the pile and then let them lay, looking back at the General. General Rion knew the young man would have to think long and hard about this step. "And finally," the General continued, "here are some things we owe you." He slid across the desk a shallow cardboard box. Inside were numerous decorations for his embarrassingly bare uniform. He had a combat ribbon, meritorious service ribbon, Foreign Service ribbon, and several other ribbons for service. He also received a medal designating valor and bravery under fire for his actions in the Ivory Coast. He would also be allowed to wear his SPETSNAZ pin for formal ceremonies. Sebastian smiled, feeling the warm elixir of accomplishment coating his internal emotions. But there was something else in the bottom of the box. Sebastian scooted the ribbons aside and pulled out the final item in the box. He held it up and looked at the General. "That's right, son, you are hereby promoted to the rank of Sergeant." The General rose from his seat and Sebastian immediately snapped to attention. He came from behind his desk and pinned the new rank on Sebastian's uniform. "Congratulations, Sergeant." Sebastian saluted smartly. "Thank you, Sir!" he responded.

The General returned his salute. "Well, that's all I have for you now, Sergeant, but somehow I imagine it's enough." He smiled and Sebastian thought he just made the understatement of the year. "Oh, one last thing, you are cleared for three weeks of rest and relaxation. I've talked to the American Embassy already. You will have to call them with your travel plans." Sebastian had nearly forgotten about the Embassy representative who was supposed to keep tabs on him. "They have been advised of your admirable service with us. I had the feeling they had kind of forgotten about you when I spoke with them. Anyway, just stay on point with them so they don't interfere with your time with us." Sebastian nodded absently. "You are dismissed, Sergeant."

Snapping back to the present, Sebastian saluted quickly. "Thank you, Sir!" he barked in reply. He turned sharply on his heels and marched out of the office.

Once outside the building, Sebastian felt his knees go weak. *Promotion, citizenship, Officer candidacy, R&R?* Good grief, it was information overload. Sebastian's pimply-faced chauffeur appeared from nowhere, zipping up to the curb like a racecar to a pit stop. Sebastian got in without thinking; he was on autopilot. He looked down at his little box of awards, shaking his head. Getting his emotions under control, he regained his senses and thanked the young man for his escort. As he settled back in his seat, he started contemplating where to go for his long awaited R&R.

Shortly after the newly appointed Sergeant Bishop left his office, General Philippe Rion's phone rang, "Bonjour?"

The General's face brightened with a warm smile as he heard his friend and mentor on the other end of the line, "Mr. Arval Tristam, how can the French Foreign Legion be of service to you, sir?"

Chapter 123

Jeff Kendle was the CIA Section Chief in Tbilisi, Georgia. He landed at Reagan National Airport in Washington, D.C. ten hours before walking through the web of security at Langley for the meeting with his boss. He had been poring over his reports, trying to organize his notes, photos, and thoughts. Now he sat outside Deputy Director John Hoyt's office ready to lay out his findings.

He had butterflies the size of bats, but it felt satisfying to have some good intelligence, like he was still a productive member of the team. This is what he signed on for, but all the focus in the Middle East made it seem like he would be a forgotten asset, lost in the labyrinth of the lair of an expired enemy.

The door opened and the Deputy Director grunted at him. He entered with his briefcase of information and closed the door behind him. "Ok, Kendle," Hoyt said. "You flew a long way on the government's dime to have my undivided attention. You have 15 minutes."

John Hoyt had all the charm of a constipated crocodile, but Jeff didn't care. He had his ear, and he would make the most of it. The Deputy Director's office was spacious, with its own small conference table and presentation equipment. Jeff popped open his briefcase, handed the director a file of notes, and pulled out a jump drive. He stuck it into the USB port of the laptop waiting for him on the edge of the table. The presentation screen was lowered remotely by the Deputy Director who was now situated comfortably back in his desk chair.

Jeff began to speak as everything dropped down, warmed up, and did whatever else needed for him to present. "Ok, the big things first: there have been significant rumblings that General Chernov, commander of the *Privolzsk-Ural* Military District has been in meetings with the Serbians. We are trying to confirm this information, as we speak. What we do know is that in the last eight weeks General Chernov has made some unusual troop movements, apparently consolidating different battalions. It looks as if they are mobilizing, but not urgently so. It may be a training exercise, personnel inventory, any number of things, but the movement and the timing of the meeting with the Serbs raises a red flag."

The projector was now broadcasting in HD quality the PowerPoint presentation Jeff had prepared. "The Presidential elections in Serbia are just months away and Deputy Prime Minister Dragan Bradic is the heavy favorite to win." A clear photo of Bradic appeared on the screen. "The information we received was that Bradic is the Serbian General that Chernov is in talks with."

"The Russians have always been friendly toward the Serbs, Kendle," Hoyt interrupted. "What exactly is your point?" The Deputy Director was thus far unimpressed.

"I've been doing some digging. I spoke with our assets in Belgrade, and there are whisperings of reserve Serbian Army personnel being placed on standby. I think the elections are the trigger-switch. Bradic was a commander of the Serbian Black Tigers during the war in Bosnia and Kosovo. He is a die-hard nationalist and a shrewd politician. If he wins the presidency, I think his first item of business will be to re-take Kosovo. And I think he has the support and backing of the Russians. Or at least General Chernov, who packs a mean punch."

Hoyt sat forward in his chair, waves of realization crashing over him, "What kind of military assets do we have in the region?" he asked.

"We have skeleton crews of military personnel still on station from the war in the 90's at Camp Bondsteel and Camp Monteith. The entire NATO force in-country is not nearly significant enough to repel a full-scale invasion."

"And we are spread so thin because of our concentration on the Middle East that we would be militarily impotent if the attack did occur," the Deputy Director thought aloud.

"That's exactly right, sir."

"This is a ballsy and dangerous theory you are proposing, Kendle. What kind of hard evidence do you have?" The Deputy Director was now thinking of his responsibility to report this higher up the food chain. He was going to be damn sure he had *all* the facts before he started sounding the alarm.

"Sir, that's the problem. Right now this is primarily educated guesses and deductive reasoning. I have no hard evidence that clearly indicates the *intent* of the players involved."

"You know, as well as I do, that I cannot take this forward without substantiating evidence. Your theory is very compelling though, Kendle. I will give you as many resources as can be spared in the region to dig deeper on this." The Deputy Director continued to look over the notes Jeff had given him. There was an uncomfortable pause, and Hoyt looked up from his notes. "Is there something else, Kendle?" he asked.

"Yes, sir," Jeff replied hesitantly. "This is unrelated, but none the less interesting; I'm not sure what, if any, implications it may have but…"

Chapter 124

"Alright, out with it," Director Hoyt interrupted impatiently.

"Yes, sir. A few months back there was a hostage incident in the small town of Saransk, Russia. By the time we knew what was going on, Russian Special Forces had stormed the place and killed all the terrorists."

"Chechens?" Director Hoyt asked.

"Yes. Then, about six months later, there was a shoot out and kidnapping in Perm, Russia. It looked like a mafia job. They are constantly making power moves over there and this sort of thing is not exactly uncommon." Jeff clicked his remote bringing up on the screen a slightly out of focus image of a SPETSNAZ Special Operator. "This is Saransk, with the Chechens." He clicked the remote again bringing up another even more out of focus shot of a man laying on his back, weapon in hand, pointing out of an open door on a van. "This was taken by a teenager with his cell phone, if you can believe that. Technology is such a part of today's youth that they do things reflexively that would take you and I minutes to process."

"Video game reflexes with the motivation of 'YouTube.' Instant fame makes for a dangerous combination," Director Hoyt confirmed.

"Precisely. Anyway, we run face recognition software on all incidents such as these. It's like tagging animals in the wild; you want to keep up with the players and their activities. So after running our standard analysis, nothing fancy, here's what we discovered." He flipped back and forth from the SPETSNAZ soldier to the guy in the van a couple of times. "This...is the same guy."

"Mr. Kendle, I think our technology is just as impressive as the next guy's," he looked at his watch dramatically, "but you have about four minutes left."

"One last thing, two Secret Police officers were killed in an alleyway in Tbilisi about three weeks ago. These guys were nothing more than thugs, extortionists, and killers. It looks like they pressed the wrong guy. Clean kills, real professional grade counter-attack, took 'em out with their own knife.

"Let me guess…same guy?" Director Hoyt asked, pointing at the image on the screen.

Jeff nodded, "We think so."

"Fascinating stuff, Mr. Kendle, but why exactly am I interested in the happenings of some Russian bad ass?" Hoyt asked, sighing.

Jeff smiled slyly, "Because he's not Russian; he's American."

The silence hung heavy for a moment. Director Hoyt leaned forward engulfing his forehead with one large hand. "So we have an American boy in the Russian military?"

"Not exactly," Jeff replied.

The Deputy Director raised his hands in exasperation. "Can you *please* tell me exactly who the hell he is then, Kendle?"

"His name is Sebastian Bishop. He is a convicted felon in America, second degree murder."

"How did he get in the Russian Army?" The Deputy Director's patience was wearing.

"He didn't," Jeff responded, shutting down the laptop.

"Well then who the f…?!" the Director boomed.

"He's French Foreign Legion," Kendle interjected before the question finished.

Deputy Director Hoyt had to admit, Mr. Kendle had really done his homework on this. He was very impressed with the quality of intelligence he offered, but couldn't figure out what they could do with all of this information other than just monitor the situations. It seemed they did a lot of that, and then would get caught with their pants down when these unpredictable variables lined up to form some chaotic or apocalyptic equation.

"You've talked to the Legion?" Director Hoyt asked.

"Not yet," Jeff answered, "but I imagine they will slam that door right in my face. The Legion protects its own more tenaciously than any other organization I'm aware of."

Hoyt rubbed his chin in thought. "Do you think you can find this kid? Appeal to his patriotic nature or something? I'd like to talk to him; see if we could bring him home to serve *his* country."

"We can try," Jeff said thoughtfully, "but if he is a cross-trained

Special Operator, he could be quite difficult to get a hold of."

The Director nodded his understanding. "See what you can do. Report directly to me if you can put some legs under this thing."

"Yes, sir." Jeff snapped his briefcase shut, preparing to leave.

"And Jeff,"

"Yes, sir?"

"Good work."

Jeff nodded his thanks and walked out of the office.

Chapter 125

Sebastian had decided on a course of action. He was going to spend two days in Paris and then fly home to see his family. He owed them that. He smiled inwardly as he rode the train toward the heart of Paris, France. He had spent a great deal of time in France, but had never seen the city that represented her identity.

His plan was to float down the Seine, see the Eiffel Tower and Notre Dame on day one. Day two would be spent at the *Musee du Louvre*, the world famous museum housing everything from the *Mona Lisa* to *Venus de Milo*. He would leave from the museum and head straight to the airport for an evening flight to America.

Day one was perfect. The day was bright and clear, and Sebastian took in the city at a leisurely pace. He even treated himself to a massage at his upscale hotel before retiring for a sound night's rest.

It occurred to him as he tried to decompress that since his release from prison he had been going non-stop for nearly four years. As a result, his bank account had grown since he had no reason to spend any money. It was a good feeling, and he now knew he would never have that hopeless feeling that consumed him in prison ever again.

The Legion is a hard place, for hard men, but SPETSNAZ and the Omega Program were the icing on the proverbial cake. As he interacted with people, just normal day-to-day people, it became glaringly evident that he was very different. His body, and more importantly, his mind, were as honed as the beam of a laser. He was trained at a level that made him constantly alert, constantly aware on a higher plain than those around him.

Sebastian now understood what his large Russian friend Ivan Antonovich meant when he said, "*As much as things around you change, remember who you are. The skills you learn do not define you as a person. The true heart of a warrior is reflected in his character, not his ability.*" This break was crucial for Sebastian's mind more so than physical rest. It took effort, real effort to relax. He didn't want to return to his loving family with his brain stuck in operational mode.

Day two began much like day one, beautiful weather, no rush, no orders, no weapons. Sebastian walked from his hotel to the Louvre, stopping for a light breakfast and a cup of coffee. By mid-morning, he walked though the entrance of the famous museum. The richness of art and culture enveloped him as he began his tour. Languages and ethnicities from around the globe provided a fitting atmosphere for his trek through history. He walked slowly, examining each exhibit closely. There was no way he would make it through this entire museum in a day, so he wouldn't even try. He'd just get what he could, savoring every step.

He walked up to *Bathsheba at her Bath*, an oil painting laid to canvas in 1654 by the Dutch painter, Rembrandt Harmenszoon van Rijn. Another man stood before the same painting admiring the vivid and elaborate detail.

"From the roof he saw a woman bathing – a very beautiful woman. So David sent someone to inquire about her, and he reported, 'This is Bathsheba, daughter of Elium and wife of Uriah the Hittite,'" the man said in English.

"Second Samuel?" Sebastian asked the man.

He turned to Sebastian as if broken from a trance. "That's right," he said in a friendly tone with a subtle, but unmistakable, accent that can only be from the American south. "You're an American?"

"I am," Sebastian replied, offering his hand. The man took it warmly. "I'm from South Carolina."

"Alabama," the man said.

"Vacationing?" Sebastian asked.

"Not exactly. I'm the Curator for the Berman Museum of World History in Anniston. I come to Paris once a year to attend a conference for us curator types."

Sebastian smiled, "Wow, I bet that is a fascinating job."

"History is my life. It seems to be quite rare for people to make a living doing what they love, but for me..." he shook his head reflectively, "every day is an adventure."

'I can relate,' Sebastian thought.

"Dan McCallister," the man said, offering his card.

"Steve Holland," Sebastian lied, accepting it.

"I'm just starting my tour, have you ever been here before?" Dan asked.

"No, first time," Sebastian replied, grateful the man hadn't asked about his background.

"Well, I've been here dozens of times. I can show you around if you want."

Sebastian's eyes brightened. "That would be fantastic," he said enthusiastically.

The two men spent the day wandering around together. Sebastian listened to Dan's lessons on each display they approached. He absorbed the mini-lectures like a sponge. It was an incredible and fulfilling day.

The time passed quickly, but inevitably Sebastian needed to start for the airport. He thanked his new friend profusely for his companionship and sharing his knowledge of history.

"It was my pleasure, Steve," the man said in that warm, southern drawl. "If you ever make it to Alabama, stop in and say hello."

"Absolutely," Sebastian said.

They shook hands and parted company. *'What a great couple of days,'* Sebastian thought as he caught a train for Charles de Gaulle airport. He was on his way home.

Chapter 126

Sebastian arrived at Charles de Gaulle and went through the routine of security screening to get to the waiting area for boarding. He looked around some of the duty-free shops and finally settled into a seat looking out the window at arriving and departing aircraft.

His thoughts drifted to the reunion with his family. He was excited, but also very nervous for some reason. He wondered if they would treat him differently. It would be awkward the first couple of days, but hopefully they would adjust to each other.

Sebastian's thoughts were interrupted as he caught the reflection in the window glass of a man in Legion uniform approaching him from behind. He recognized the man's rank as a Commandant-Major, and Sebastian rose and turned to meet him. He wasn't sure if he should salute or what since he was in civilian clothes. It must be urgent if the Commandant tracked him down here. "Sergeant Bishop," the man started, obviously knowing exactly who Sebastian was.

"Sir," Sebastian replied.

"I'm sorry to be the bearer of bad news, but your R&R has been cancelled. You have new orders from the Brigadier General himself." He handed Sebastian a sealed envelope. "Your boarding pass is inside. You have about 40 minutes to get to your gate."

'But I just met with the General two days ago,' Sebastian thought. *'He's the one who cleared my leave.'* The Commandant turned and walked away without further explanation. *'Typical Legion communication pattern,'* Sebastian thought. *'Fire and forget.'*

Sebastian tore the envelope open and examined its contents. A boarding pass for an Air Canada flight was on top of the stack. He looked over his new orders: fly to Montreal, Canada, and provide escort for a French citizen, Ms. Stephanie Boulanger, back to Paris. A Second Legionnaire would meet Sebastian in Montreal according to the orders, and they would deploy from there. Side arms, rental car, and all appropriate clearance and return material would be on station. The address of the pickup was at the bottom of the page.

Sebastian sighed, picked up his backpack, and headed for the Air Canada gate. *'So much for vacation,'* he thought.

Chapter 127

Stephanie was thoroughly enjoying her trip to the city with Captain de Armand. He was charming and a little flirtatious, making her feel like a silly schoolgirl more than once over the course of the day. He was patient and made her laugh as she shopped for clothes and tried on several outfits. Stephanie didn't want the day to end, but by late afternoon, she checked her watch and knew it was time to check in with Arval. She was looking forward to talking to him, and hoping he could give her an update on his progress. Eager as she was, however, to get her life back, she knew she would miss this place, her chivalrous escort, and her dear hosts. She knew she could never repay the gracious hospitality of these wonderful people.

Stephanie purchased a calling card and found a pay phone. Arval was in a very serious mood on the other end. He told her about meeting with the professor and informed her that two military commandos were en route to bring her safely back to France.

The phone call put a damper on an otherwise cheery day. "I guess I need to get back to the house," Stephanie informed the Captain. "Two soldiers are supposed to pick me up this evening and take me back to France."

De Armand tried not to look dejected. "Well, that's good news." He nodded a little too dramatically, trying to be positive. "I suppose I'd better get you back then. I'll stay with you until they arrive and make sure you get to the airport safely."

"Thank you, Captain." The weight of reality pressed down upon the two of them, and they traveled back to the house in silence.

Chapter 128

Sebastian landed in Montreal in poor spirits. He was more than a little put off that his R&R, for which he was long overdue, was put on hold for a babysitting job. Even the in-flight movie was awful. His brooding was pleasantly interrupted as he walked up to the designated rendezvous point to find his friend Davide waiting for him.

"Leave it to the Legion to send a girl to do man's job," Davide said teasingly.

"I see your PMS is getting worse," Sebastian gave right back. The two warriors gave each other a quick hug.

"So what's this crap all about?" Sebastian asked.

"No idea," Davide replied. "Picking up some chick sounds like work for mere mortals, not we gods of war."

Sebastian smiled; his friend hadn't changed a bit. "Well let's get this silliness over with. I'm due for R&R."

"I was on the beach in Morocco when this bullshit assignment was handed down. If it wasn't from the very top, I would have put up a protest," retorted Davide.

"Yeah, that always works with the Legion; just say no." They both laughed.

They found their rental car and piled inside, Sebastian driving. "Hey, where did you go after that job in Russia?" Davide asked innocently.

Sebastian was caught off guard and had to think fast, "They asked me to stay on for a while to work with their paratroopers. It was easy stuff and pretty fun." Sebastian hated lying to his friend, who was more like his brother, but he was under oath to never breathe a word of his time at the 'farmhouse.'

"Cool," Davide replied. He then broke into a dissertation of recent sexual conquests, listed chronologically from Russia to the present that left Sebastian shaking his head in disbelief.

Chapter 129

Stephanie and Captain de Armand pulled up the long driveway to the cottage on the hill. Stephanie was saddened by the fact that she would have to leave this haven and the care of her new Canadian friends.

They got out of the car and walked to the front door. Stephanie turned the knob and entered with a sigh. Inside, the hallway led straight to the kitchen at the back of the house. Stephanie eyes fell with horror upon the bodies of her two elderly hosts sprawled awkwardly on the kitchen floor, her perspective framed by the doorway at the end of the hall.

"NO!" she screamed, beginning to run toward them.

Captain de Armand reached for the gun in the concealed holster on his hip. Stephanie only heard the metallic action of the semi-automatic pistol chambering another round. The shot itself was silenced. Captain de Armand's lifeless body fell behind her. Her mind was barely processing the scene as it unfolded. A scream caught in her throat as arms of steel clamped around her and a black hood was snapped over her head. There was a prick like a bee sting in her neck, and the terror of the past few seconds was replaced by her world fading to black.

Sebastian and Davide zipped away from the city, and the conversation of catching up made the time pass quickly. Before they knew it, they were within range of the address on their orders. Sebastian pulled the car to a stop, out of sight of the house. They would make a tactical approach and stick to their training, even if this seemed like a cut and dried assignment.

They got quietly out of the car and started walking. Davide glanced back at the car. "You left the lights on there, genius."

"Thanks, Nancy," Sebastian replied, as he turned and jogged back to the car. They were about 150 meters north of the little house with Davide in the lead and Sebastian jogging to catch up, when it happened.

There was a blinding light followed immediately by a concussion wave of heat. The ripple of explosive discharge seemed to rip the very fabric of the air. The blast knocked both Legionnaires to the ground, but Davide got the worst of it, being closer to the explosion. The house had nearly disintegrated from the force of the detonation.

Sebastian popped up on one knee, his firearm materializing in his hand. Training and instinct immediately took over. He saw a black, windowless van emerge from the west behind the smoldering house. It was headed east at a high rate of speed. He took aim, leading the van as it accelerated in escape. He fired two shots, both impacting the side of the van now about 300 meters away. There was nothing more he could do to stop the disappearing vehicle.

Sebastian hurried to his friend's side. Davide was beginning to move with signs of regaining consciousness. "You alright?" Sebastian asked urgently, making a cursory exam of his body for injuries.

Davide suddenly jumped to his feet. He screamed a string of profanities in Italian, French, and Russian. Blood trickled from his ear. He paced like a caged animal, eyes wild, his rage escalating. "Looks like you've busted an ear drum," Sebastian said matter-of-factly, pointing at the blood. Davide didn't hear him and didn't care anyway.

They both looked at what was left of the house. "Let's go," Sebastian said.

Davide turned and began to walk toward the car, "I am going to find out who did this and kill every last one of them."

Sebastian knew Davide meant every word he just said.

Chapter 130

Stephanie had been injected with a narcotic cocktail consisting of Fentanyl and Morphine. She was nearly comatose. The van pulled off into a wooded area and she was moved from the black van to a modern gurney and strapped in. She was transferred to an ambulance, which would help sell the illusion of the next phase of her journey. Stephanie's two Serbian captors pulled off their overalls, revealing paramedic uniforms underneath. Timing and good acting were all that remained.

The ambulance drove straight to the airport. The 'paramedics' wheeled Stephanie in through a special medical entrance to the terminal. They met with airline personnel specializing in medical transports and handed over a stack of forms, all filled out perfectly with accompanying stamps of clearance for their 'patient'.

The story was straightforward enough: she had suffered a severe head injury in a skiing accident, while on holiday. She had been stabilized and was now being transported to a medical facility in her native country of France. The unseen wizards of document forgery, prostituting themselves to anyone who could pay their price, had produced Stephanie's new passport.

The whole process was very smooth, and the unsuspecting participants were very professional in their respective jobs. Stephanie was situated on the special section of the commercial airliner and strapped in for her trip. An air nurse, working for the airline, would monitor Stephanie's vital signs and overall condition for the duration of the trip. She would also supervise the transfer to waiting medical personnel for ground transport.

The Serbs drove away to stash the ambulance, quite relieved that their part of the plan was now completed. They were confident that the drugs in the girl's system would keep her unconscious for the duration of the trip. Slavo and the others would be waiting for the plane in Paris.

The Serbs could not understand why they couldn't just kill the girl in Canada in the house with the old couple and the cop. It was a lot of trouble to get her back to Paris. Slavo told them to shut their mouths and just do what he ordered. He was so tired of everyone questioning orders.

Slavo's reasons were simple, and his own. He paid approximately 9,000 Euro to facilitate this return trip; he had already negotiated a deal to sell her to his trafficking connections in the underworld for five times that amount. There was no reason for this woman to die if he could profit from her instead. Not to mention her life would be one of never-ending suffering once caught in the web of human trafficking. *'Serves her right,'* he thought.

Slavo stood looking in the mirror, adjusting his cheap clip on tie that was part of his paramedic uniform. Satisfied with his appearance, he donned an overcoat and left the hotel to join his two men who had remained with him in Paris. They drove to the airport in an ambulance to pick up their 'patient.' From the airport, they would take her by train to Vienna, Austria, and then fly straight into Kosovo. It was all working according to plan. The document, a healthy profit, and the return of his father's respect; the future was finally starting to look up.

Chapter 131

Sebastian drove as Davide sat quietly looking out his window at the landscape whipping past. He hadn't even attempted to clean the blood from his ear. Sebastian spoke on a secure cell phone to a Lieutenant Colonel working directly for the Brigadier General.

The Lieutenant Colonel was directing his own staff, talking with Sebastian, and trying to brief the General on another line, all at the same time. This little assignment had just turned into a full-fledged operation, and Sebastian and Davide were one hundred percent committed now.

The Lieutenant Colonel was contacting Canada's military intelligence to start finding answers. Their first priority would be to find the black van that Sebastian had marked with two bullet holes. He did know that local law enforcement and fire personnel were on the scene at the house. As soon as it was safe, the forensic team would get to work. The Lieutenant Colonel told Sebastian that this matter was now of the highest priority and very personal to the General.

Sebastian didn't envy the Lieutenant Colonel's job of informing the General when the remains of this poor girl were found amongst the rubble of the house. It was a hit, masked as a gas line explosion; he felt sure. The question was: what were their orders from this point forward?

Sebastian drove to the house of a doctor on retainer with the Canadian military. He was of French descent and gave immediate attention to Davide when they appeared at his door. Davide still hadn't said a word. People react differently when faced with their own mortality. Some shrivel up with fear, others suffer irreparable psychological damage, but Davide reacted with anger and focus. He was already planning on what he would do when he found those responsible.

The doctor was polite, but all business. A tall, lean man with a hooked nose, Sebastian thought he looked like Ebenezer Scrooge. He took Davide into a small room set up like a regular examination room in a clinic; bed and all. Davide sat on the edge of the bed, and the doctor went to work. He cleaned the ear and confirmed that the ear drum was, in fact, ruptured.

"We have to fly back to France tonight," Sebastian told the doctor. "Will he be all right at high altitude?"

The doctor thought a moment. "It's going to hurt like hell up there," he sighed, "but he should make it. I'll numb the ear and give him some antibiotics. Have it looked at as soon as you can when you get where you're going."

The doctor carefully worked on Davide's ear, preparing it for travel as best he could. He gave Davide two bottles of pills; an antibiotic, as promised, and something for pain. He smiled now that his work was done and wished the men well. They thanked him and continued to the airport. They needed to get back to France. Sebastian and Davide wanted the full story on this girl who nearly cost them their lives.

Chapter 132

Stephanie's mind felt like it was wrapped in lead. She could hear muffled sounds around her, but couldn't make out any images. When she tried to open her eyes, she saw only brightness with blobs of distorted darkness. Her mouth felt like it was full of sticky cotton. She closed her half-open eyes and allowed herself to fall back into the warm embrace of unconsciousness.

Slavo had to call on every ounce of his emotional reserve to handle the tedious hand-over at the airport. The flight nurse meticulously processed the paperwork for Stephanie's transfer. Slavo took small consolation in the fact that she was fussing over paperwork that was entirely fictitious. They finally loaded her into their spurious ambulance with dramatic care as the flight nurse observed. They pulled out of the airport, carefully maintaining the charade until they were a safe distance away.

There was still the second half of this transportation operation, and Slavo knew they couldn't get sloppy. Slavo was cheap, so now that she was in his care, it would be no frills for the remainder of the journey. They transferred from the ambulance to a car in an abandoned building on the outskirts of Paris. They drove to the nearest town that had a train stop for Vienna. Slavo loved the efficient European train system.

They pulled into the station and Slavo yanked a rickety wheelchair from the trunk. He pulled Stephanie roughly from the backseat and dumped her in the wheelchair. Stephanie's head flopped around and she had a stream of saliva drooling from her mouth. Slavo grabbed the sleeve of his nearest man and wiped her mouth. The man's face wrinkled in disgust.

They wheeled her into the station, bought tickets, and made their way to the handicapped section of the train. People ask few questions when someone is pushing a person in a wheelchair. They just give a quick sympathetic glance and carry on about their business. Slavo knew this.

The ride to Vienna was smooth, but Stephanie was beginning to show signs of coming around toward the end of the trip. Slavo clenched his teeth in anger when Stephanie began to mumble loudly as the train slowed to a stop in the station. She wasn't supposed to come around until the journey was over, according to the Canadian Connection. *'Why can't anything just go according to plan?'* Slavo thought.

What to do next was the big question. They disembarked from the train, and Slavo quickly wheeled Stephanie away from the public venue. They couldn't risk her coming to and running her mouth, so she needed to be silenced for the final leg to Kosovo. Once there, it wouldn't matter. Running out of options, Slavo had to make a command decision.

He turned to one of his men and shoved 100 Euro in his hand. "You're going to have to head to Gurtel Road and score some junk." The Serb minion shrugged as if it was no big deal and turned to the street to hail a cab. *'She's going to get hooked on it sooner or later,'* Slavo thought. He just hated to have to pay for her first hit.

Heroin was one of the most popular control methods for human traffickers. Easy to come by and incredibly addictive, heroin kept the girls nearly comatose while they were repeatedly violated day after day.

Slavo's man returned in less than an hour. He produced a half-gram of heroin and to Slavo's surprise, a syringe still in its sterile wrapper. *'Always first class in Vienna,'* he thought. They ducked into an alleyway and one of the men kept guard while the other cooked the heroin into liquid form. The process was quick to the skilled, and these men had experience to spare.

Slavo sucked the liquid from the spoon through the needle and searched for a prominent vein under Stephanie's skin. She was beginning to get movement back in her extremities and her words were forming more clearly. Slavo didn't have time for this searching around crap; he took the needle and stuck it straight into the carotid artery in her neck. The reaction was nearly instantaneous. Stephanie was now back under control. They threw the remaining heroin and used syringe in a dumpster, emerged from the alley, and hailed a cab to the airport.

Their flight to Pristina, Kosovo, would leave in just over two hours.

Chapter 133

Sebastian and Davide landed back in Paris where a military vehicle and driver were waiting for them. Sebastian had seven voicemails on his cell phone. He started listening to each of them as they walked to their transport. He learned that the black van had been found abandoned in the woods, but there were no further leads. The house had been entered by forensics; currently processing the scene. Each voicemail walked him chronologically through the investigation, as it had progressed, while they were airborne. He forwarded to the next message; initial forensic reports indicate three bodies found in the remains of the house; two males, one female. Sebastian's heart sank. He played the last message; elderly male and female homeowners were identified as two of the victims. Last male was a RCMP Captain identified as de Armand. No other bodies were found.

"The girl may still be alive," Sebastian told Davide who nodded his acknowledgement but remained silent, eyes forward, planning.

Arval dropped his cell phone to the floor when he heard the news. His dear friends killed, along with the police captain, and Stephanie…missing. When he had regained his composure, Arval called the Legion Brigadier General.

"We've got nothing further, I'm afraid," the General told Arval solemnly. Arval hung up, racking his brain on how to help, how to find this poor young nurse who had stumbled into a nightmare that continued to get worse. He stared at his cell phone…who did he know? Who could he call?

Out of desperation, Arval called an old friend at INTERPOL. After two rings, she picked up. "Hello?" the female voice, deepened by years of cigarette smoking, answered.

"Kaila?" Arval asked.

"Arval?" Kaila replied, her surprise evident. "Are you ok? I haven't heard from you in ages."

Kaila Shalev was an Israeli police commander now working with

INTERPOL. Arval had known her parents very well. He and his wife had, in fact, stayed at their place in Tel Aviv many times when he wore a younger man's shoes.

"Kaila, do you have a minute?" Arval asked.

"Yes, of course. What can I do for you?"

Arval told her the whole story up to the minute. When he was finished, there was a pause on the line. "We do not have any information on the girl, Arval. We just got a briefing on her possible abduction about forty minutes ago. We're working it, but so far…nothing. I am so sorry."

Arval closed his eyes at the thought of another dead end. "Ok, Kaila. Thank you anyway. Would you please keep…"

"Wait a minute," she interrupted. Arval felt his heart jump. "This may be nothing, but we did receive a call from a man in Croatian intelligence who gave us information about a war criminal that he said was in Paris right now."

Arval knew immediately this *had* to be connected. She told him about Slavo Petrovic and his father. They were bad news. "Is there any way I can talk to your contact in Croatia?" Arval asked.

"I don't know about that, Arval," she answered cautiously. "You know how this game works; trust is a fragile platform. If one too many step on it, it all comes crashing down."

"Believe me, I understand." Arval clenched his fist, willing Kaila to bend the rules just once and help him. "Kaila, you know I would not ask this unless I felt it to be of the utmost importance." Another pause.

"Remember the training exercise in Cairo?" Kaila asked, referring to a class Arval taught several years ago to analysts with stratospheric security clearance from their respective countries.

"Of course," Arval answered without hesitation.

"Same rules. Watch your text. Destroy your phone."

"Thank…" Arval began, but the line went dead.

Kaila sent Arval information in a text message that looked like gibberish. It was indecipherable even to sophisticated code breakers, unless you knew the baseline information from which to start. The code was based on Elliptical Curve Cryptography. Arval's tradecraft had evolved to incredible levels of sophistication since his time of dodging the enemy through the French countryside. The Elliptic Curve Discrete Logarithm Problem, or ECDLP, was complicated and required concentration and quiet.

It took some time, but Arval got his information: Damir Tadic, Croatian Intelligence, and an international phone number. Arval took the elevator to the basement of his apartment building where he promptly threw the phone in the incinerator.

Arval called the Brigadier General from the house phone in his flat. "I may have something," Arval said. "I am coming to your office; can you get me an encrypted phone?"

"It will be waiting for you when you get here," the General replied. Arval hung up without saying goodbye and moved as fast as his legs would carry him to his BMW.

Chapter 134

Sebastian and Davide lounged around the intelligence center waiting for updates. Davide paced restlessly, and Sebastian saw him working his jaw in response to the pain in his ear. Davide's ear must have been in excruciating agony while they cruised at 30,000 feet, but he showed no signs of it. Now, they both just wanted to locate this girl and get green-lighted to go get her.

Sebastian glanced out the windows that made up one wall of the conference room they were in. He saw an old man hustling down the hallway, and then saw General Rion rush up to him, handing him a phone. The General tapped on the glass and motioned for Sebastian and Davide to come with them.

The two soldiers quickly followed the General and the old man back to Rion's office. Once inside, the General made quick introductions, "Arval, these are the two commandos that went to retrieve Stephanie." He turned to Sebastian and Davide. "Men, this is Arval Tristam; recipient of the Legion d' Honneur and my close personal friend and mentor."

Sebastian and Davide snapped to attention, showing their respect for a winner of France's highest Medal of Honor. "Thank you, gentlemen," Arval said in acknowledgement. "I am very grateful you have returned alive. I am responsible for this missing woman, and I would very much like to get her back safely and unharmed." Sebastian and Davide nodded and relaxed their positions. Arval continued addressing the General, "I have the number of someone who may be able to point us in the right direction." He held the phone in one hand, paper with the information in the other, and began pressing numbers.

Arval put the cell phone on speaker so everyone could hear as it rang. On the forth ring an accented voice answered, "Yes?"

"Damir Tadic?" Arval asked in a strong voice. The line was silent.

"Who is this?" Damir asked in Croatian.

"May we speak French, please?" Arval asked politely. No answer.

"My name is Arval Tristam, I know that you were in Paris recently and went eyes on with Slavo Petrovic. I know about the document, the professor, the girl, everything." Silence.

"What do you want?" Damir finally responded in French.

"Mr. Tadic, I understand the gravity of what the document represents to your people and all peaceful peoples of the Balkans. I want to help you recover it however I can, but my concern right now is the girl. Does Slavo Petrovic have her?" All the men in the office listened intently.

"Probably," Damir replied.

Arval lowered his head, concentrating, "Why did he take her, why didn't he kill her with the others in Canada?"

"Why should I help you, Mr. Tristam? Who are you? Why are you interested in this woman; in my country's affairs?"

"Young man," Arval said with a clarity that defied his years, "I have had my country taken from me; I have risked everything to get it back. I have seen death, destruction, and cruelty on a level that crosses the line between human and beast. I know your plight; I understand in a way that few others can. You should help me because you know you must. You cannot allow yourself to sacrifice any more of your humanity to those devoted to taking all you have left. The girl is innocent, you know this, help me find her." Again the line fell silent.

"Slavo took the girl for two reasons," Damir finally said. "First, she inconvenienced him; second, she represents property now; you can sell property. Slavo never turns down a chance for profit. Never. He acts like a noble nationalist, but he is nothing more than a world-class criminal."

Arval nodded as Damir spoke. "Can you find her?" Arval asked plainly.

Damir sighed on the other end. "Give me ten minutes." The other end of the line disconnected.

Chapter 135

The flight from Vienna to Kosovo was without incident. Slavo and the invalid he was assisting were allowed to deplane first. As they walked to the terminal, Slavo felt a pang of anxiety as he hoped his own fake documents would hold up under scrutiny one more time. He knew he was running on borrowed time.

Stephanie's condition helped him whisk through customs uncontested. There was a taxi with a Serb driver waiting on them. When they were finally loaded into the car, Slavo began to relax. The men chattered in relief, the driver handing out cigarettes and talking of the "Rakia" that awaited them all. Rakia, the Serb national drink like vodka to Russians, was made from distilling fermented fruit, and it packed a tremendous alcoholic punch.

They drove straight to a safe house in Gracanica where the final negotiations with the Albanians would be made for the girl. It was a strange set up: sworn enemies working together for illegal profit; but this was Kosovo, all the rules were blurry here.

Once inside the house, the celebration began in earnest. Bottles of Rakia were passed out liberally, along with food and other drinks. Slavo constantly checked the package that would secure his country's future and his status as savior of his people.

Stephanie finally stirred, coming down from her heroin high. She blinked slowly, trying to get her eyes to focus. She was lying on a couch, and there were people all around, they looked to be all men from what she could tell. She felt nauseous, and very thirsty.

Slavo had been watching her like a hawk, staying separate from his men as they continued their revelry. He saw her wake and walked to her, sitting on the coffee table near her head. He handed her a bottled water.

Stephanie sat up, a wave of nausea crashed over her, and her eyes watered as she tried to keep from retching. Bile rose in her throat and she fumbled with the water, too weak to remove the cap. Slavo grabbed it from her, loosened the lid and handed it back. "Welcome back, Stephanie Boulanger," Slavo said in French. The men quieted around the room as they heard Slavo talk to the woman.

Stephanie gulped the water desperately. It ran down the corners of her mouth and onto her shirt as she struggled to regain simple motor function. She lowered the now half-empty bottle from her lips. "Who are you?" she asked, barely above a whisper.

"My name is Slavo Petrovic. I am the rightful owner of the document you helped Dr. Fournier steal." Stephanie tried to protest, but Slavo held up a hand. "No matter now. The document has returned home and tomorrow, on the Field of Blackbirds, it will be our declaration of war." He waved the package that Stephanie had tried so hard to deliver in the air like a trophy.

"Where am I?" Stephanie asked, panic now seeping into her aching bones.

"Kosovo," Slavo answered. "But only for tonight. By this time tomorrow only God knows where you'll be. But one thing is for sure, the life you knew is over. You have entered the devil's den. Soon you will know limitless suffering and will be praying for death. Of that, I feel very sure." Slavo's eyes flashed something inhuman, and Stephanie felt her body convulse, craving the new drug introduced into her system in Vienna.

Slavo stood abruptly. "Tie her up. Let's get her to the Albanians. I want my money." Stephanie was grabbed roughly by several sets of hands and restrained. Her mind was screaming. Her mouth would be, too, if she could just get her body to respond correctly.

Damir slowly closed his cell phone after his interesting conversation with Mr. Tristam. He turned to look at his two Albanian team members. "Can you locate the girl?" he asked simply.

The older of the two Albanians looked insulted for a minute. Damir was implying that his people were criminals, and worse yet, all connected. Sad to say, it was pretty much true. "Yes," was all the man said in reply. He turned, flipping open a cell phone and began conversing with someone on the other end in the difficult Albanian tongue.

After exactly ten minutes, Arval called Damir back on the secure line.

"She is in Kosovo," Damir told Arval flatly. "But only for tonight. By tomorrow she will be in the vacuum of human trafficking. Do you have something to write with?"

Arval grabbed a pen from the General's desk. "Yes, go ahead."

Damir gave GPS coordinates, and Arval carefully wrote them down.

"You have less than 24 hours. It's the best I can do."

"Thank you," Arval said sincerely. Damir hung up his phone and threw it as hard as he could into the Adriatic Sea.

The General turned to Sebastian and Davide. "Go get her," was all he said. The two commandos bolted from the office.

Chapter 136

Sebastian and Davide were driven at high speed to a military airstrip near Legion Headquarters. The two soldiers were taken to a completely off-limits side of the military airfield. Sebastian was impressed and amazed at the layers of sophisticated security, including closed circuit cameras, electric fencing, and heavily armed guards.

He felt like he was entering back into a prison yard. Once inside, the vehicle sped to an enormous hangar, tucked in a far back corner, with no exterior lighting. They got out and were escorted to a side door. They entered and the artificial illumination nearly blinded them. It was like daylight inside, and the hangar was polished to a high shine. They felt like they had just entered a gigantic sterile operating room; and then Sebastian saw why.

"You've got to be shittin' me," Davide said in awe, his first words for many hours. Before them was the new Airbus A400M Military Transport Aircraft. "The Grizzly," as the plane was nicknamed, was the newest, most technologically advanced and militarily flexible transport airship in the world.

The enormous hangar door, leading to the runway, began to slowly open and Sebastian and Davide heard the unmistakable whine of the aircraft's four turboprop engines yawning awake. This plane could hold somewhere in the neighborhood of 350 combat soldiers; and it was rolling out for just two.

There was no time to gawk as the chocks holding the giant bird in place were already being removed from the wheels. Sebastian and Davide ran to jump on board. In the cargo hold, was operational gear, including weapons, parachutes, oxygen tanks, communications, etc. They immediately began to dress in the tactical uniform of operational commandos. The flight to their destination would not take long in this behemoth cruising in the thin air. Once on station, there would be no need to regroup, debrief, or wait for others to tell them what to do when they hit the ground.

Sebastian took a deep breath. No civilian clothes, no making do with what they could find, no more training, no running, no turning back. It was as simple as their line of work got. Two elite soldiers, sent in to rescue an innocent hostage…by any means necessary.

They checked their silenced H&K MP-5s, silenced Beretta 9mms, communications, and NVGs. They had an aerial photo of the target house and surrounding topography. The very latest intelligence reported 11 subversives on scene and possibly seven or eight female detainees.

Sebastian and Davide checked their parachute rigs in silence; they had to because of the roar of the engines. Although their ride still had that 'new car smell,' it still wasn't much quieter than the old C-160 Transtalls they were so used to jumping out of.

The soldiers were efficient and methodical, going over every inch of their rigging, packing, and primary and reserve chute integrity as they had done a hundred times before. They would conduct a HALO or High Altitude Low Opening jump on this mission. Stealth and surprise will always be the cornerstone of Special Operations.

They helped each other into their parachute packs, strapped on oxygen tanks and checked all their gages. When they finally settled in for the final 30 minutes of the flight, Sebastian laughed out loud at just the two of them in the cavernous belly of this airborne whale.

Well, they weren't the *only* two. Two airmen stood near the ramp that would be lowered for Sebastian and Davide's departure. They were low ranking guys with extremely high-pressure jobs. It was their responsibility to make sure the commandos left the aircraft safely, on target, and did so without being sucked out into the night themselves. It was not as easy as people thought.

The signal was given for five minutes to target. The ramp was in the process of being lowered as Sebastian and Davide hooked on their oxygen masks and waddled to the door like a couple of heavily armed penguins. They stood at the break of the ramp, where it began its descent into the unknown, and waited.

One of the airmen pointed at the commandos, and gave them the signal. In two steps the Legionnaires leapt into the thin, cold night air.

Chapter 137

Stephanie's hands were bound behind her back. She was blindfolded and gagged and thrown into the back of a vehicle. She thought it was a van or SUV because she was lying on a floor that was flat and square. The vehicle sped toward its destination, and Stephanie bounced around uncomfortably until they finally slowed to a stop.

The door opened, and Stephanie was yanked from the floor. These were cruel, unfeeling men that now controlled her fate, and she was virtually paralyzed with fear. She was shoved inside another structure. She imagined it was a house, but she couldn't see anything. It was warm inside, and there were a lot of voices; men's voices.

She was dragged up a set of stairs and jerked to a stop in front of a door. One of her handlers reached up, pulled her blindfold off, cut the ties on her wrists, and pushed her into the room. Inside were seven other women. Not women, girls; the oldest one couldn't have been 18. They all stared at her, too scared to cry, too scared to move. Stephanie rubbed her wrists as she slowly walked among them. The room had no windows; the door was made out of some kind of reinforced metal. There was no escaping here.

Deputy Prime Minister Dragan Bradic couldn't sleep. He paced the floor of his cosmopolitan apartment in downtown Belgrade, Serbia. He practiced his speech over and over, trying to perfect the sections he needed to emphasize and remember when to get emotional. Everything had actually come together, against all odds. The document, an ancient and Papal-ordained survey of Serbia's boundaries, had returned home. It would be the crescendo of his speech. Once he had stirred his people's Nationalistic fervor at the celebration at the Field of Blackbirds, he would raise the document and demand Serbia reclaim what was rightfully hers!

With the country re-focused and firmly justified, the attack would begin, and he would insist that he be sworn in as President at the monastery in Gracanica, Kosovo. Bradic could taste his legend, see his great-great grandchildren read his name in their history books, and most importantly, stand as the first leader of Greater Serbia since 1389. The title was President, but the position was King.

Chapter 138

Sebastian and Davide jumped from 27,000 feet. There was nothing to do for the moment but fall. They each monitored their own descent, making sure to stay on course with the Thommen Nightwing Altimeter and digital compass on their wrists. The HALO rigs had automatic deployment systems built into their designs. When the soldiers reached a certain altitude, the chutes would automatically deploy. This action was much better at night because you couldn't see the ground approaching at alarming speed. Automatic release, thereby, removed the temptation to pull your chute prematurely out of fear.

Unlike the low altitude static line jumps, HALO jumps gave one time to think. Sebastian closed his eyes and breathed evenly into his oxygen mask. He used the wind whipping by him at terminal velocity to act as the figurative device to push everything from his mind, except the mission at hand. In a short time they would be taking lives, and even for a professional and elite soldier, this was never a small task. Fighting is about mindset, and freefalling from the troposphere had a way of focusing one's attention.

Sebastian felt his parachute release and braced for the snap of inflation and the dramatic slowing of descent. With the grace of a practiced hand, Sebastian flipped down his Night Vision Goggles and used his steering straps to bring him gently to the ground. He landed softly, and saw Davide touch down about 200 meters away in the same field. A spike of pride hit Sebastian with the landing; *we own the night,* he thought.

They rolled up their chutes and met each other in the middle. No words were spoken as the men found a culvert nearby where they stashed the parachute rigs and oxygen tanks. They covered it with camouflage netting and placed a GPS beacon on the stack. French soldiers from the military base in Mitrovica, Kosovo, would pick up the equipment at daybreak.

Sebastian and Davide were two-and-a-half kilometers from their target. They broke into a light jog. The soldiers could cover this distance without even breathing hard. Their equipment was deftly secured on their bodies, so they moved across the countryside without a jingle, squeak, or rattle. They were silent shadows gliding across the plain, bringing death with them.

They came within range of the target and began the final approach using maximum stealth. They watched three men outside talking loudly, smoking and looking generally unaware. The hunters moved in; when they were about 25 meters away, both soldiers raised their silenced MP-5s, choosing targets automatically through years of training together.

Sebastian peered through his EOTech XPS3 Holographic Night Vision sights, leveling the red dot on the side of his target's head. He raised a finger indicating a silent countdown had begun. The two commandos began their own private countdown cadence that they had practiced hundreds of times. Sebastian focused on the sound of his own voice in his head. *Three, two, one...*

Both triggers depressed simultaneously and a puff of red spray exited the far side of the heads of their marks. The men collapsed, and Sebastian dropped the remaining man before the other bodies hit the ground. Davide was up and running before Sebastian had even killed the last man. Sebastian rolled and popped up smoothly, now running full speed to the house. The commandos stood on either side of the door. Davide opened it, and they both entered like a drifting fog. Their skill and efficiency were terrifying; eight men remained.

Chapter 139

They entered a small foyer inside the doorway. A room to their left was dark and unoccupied. To the right, about two meters away, was a large room, well lit, with lots of voices. Davide looked at a framed picture in the hall, mounted directly across from the open room. In the reflection he could see five men sitting around a table counting money.

Sebastian saw Davide's eyes narrow. '*Oh shit*,' Sebastian thought to himself. He'd seen that look before. Davide was one of the best sub-machine gun operators he had ever witnessed. Shooting a gun accurately on full automatic was not easy. The weapon would rise off target with each discharge, and holding it on the mark required strength and skill that few possessed.

Davide gave quick hand-signals confirming what Sebastian already knew. Davide would take this room, while Sebastian charged past and took the stairs at the end of the hall. Sebastian would clear the upstairs and then they could search for the girls. Davide gave a snap nod and turned to the open room.

With silenced weapons, all that can be heard is the chambering of new rounds. The metallic slide offers the only noise as it works forward and backward. Davide caught everyone's attention as soon as he stepped into the open. In motion that could be described as nearly poetic if it were not completely lethal, Davide acquired one target after the next. He worked around the table clockwise, and the men fell from their seats, faces frozen in horror.

Sebastian flew past Davide as soon as he turned. He swung his sub-machine gun behind his back, smoothly replacing it with his silenced pistol. Hearing the commotion of falling bodies, two young thugs with the low job of guarding the girls, stood from their chairs. Sebastian crested the stairs and double tapped each of them. They had no time to react.

Davide hit the bottom of the stairs to come up. In his mind, Sebastian counted the men as they dropped. '*That only makes ten,*' he thought. He turned to let Davide know there should be one target left when, to his alarm, the last man emerged from the back of the house behind Davide. Davide was about five steps up the staircase when the man appeared. A shot rang out, striking Davide through the left shoulder. Davide was blocking Sebastian's ability to shoot.

In an act that Sebastian could scarcely believe, Davide turned with the momentum of the impact with his shoulder. He jumped from the stairs toward the shooter like a lion on its prey. He slammed the Albanian into the back wall, bouncing the man's head off the surface. From somewhere that Sebastian couldn't see, Davide pulled a knife, and moved like vapor behind the criminal as the impact with the wall now carried him forward. Davide grabbed the man's hair, jerking his head back and cut his throat just as they had been taught in Commando School.

Davide shoved the man forward to the ground and looked up at Sebastian.

"Through and through?" Sebastian asked in reference to the gunshot wound.

"Feels like it," Davide answered.

"Take your shirt off. We'll quick clot it so we can move." Davide began peeling off his top layers.

Sebastian went to the heavy door that the two dead Albanians lay before. He dragged them out of the way and worked the door's heavy locking bolt. He opened it and looked inside. Eight pairs of eyes looked back at him from within.

Chapter 140

As the first hint of daylight began to chase away the night, Nikolin knelt in prayer and meditation inside the ancient monastery in Gracanica, Kosovo. He didn't need to look at the date, the village was alive and crowded with friends and family who had risked the trip for the celebration. It was June 28. The day would begin with a ceremony at the ancestral battlefield known as 'The Field of Blackbirds.' It was a wide open plain near the town of Obelic. Deputy Prime Minister Dragan Bradic, a real crowd favorite, was scheduled to give a speech, and possibly announce his bid for presidency. Nikolin knew the crowd would ignite in delight at the news.

After the ceremony, many Serbs would return here for a day of celebration and festivities. Nikolin wondered what the future held. He wondered about the future of his beloved Kosovo, the future of his church, and of course, he wondered what would happen to him. The one thing he knew for sure, his father would kill him if he knew that he had talked with Damir Tadic.

The day dawned; Deputy Prime Minister Bradic made his way, with his protection detail, toward the border of Kosovo. Soon he would need no protection to walk on the land Serbia rightly owned. Things would be a little touch and go in the wake of his speech, but if he delivered, they may invade tonight.

Chapter 141

"Stephanie Boulanger?" Sebastian stepped into the dingy room and called out in French. A woman rose slowly to her feet from the back of the quarters.

"I am Stephanie Boulanger," she answered hesitantly.

"My name is Sebastian Bishop. I am French Foreign Legion. We're here to get you out." The woman just stood for a moment in disbelief. He extended his hand toward her and beckoned reassuringly.

Stephanie broke into a run, wrapping her arms around his neck, nearly knocking him off balance. She wept in relief, praying that the man she held would not evaporate like a mirage.

The other girls in the room rose to their feet, hope beginning to rise with them. Sebastian looked beyond Stephanie's embrace at the haggard girls, all petrified with fear.

"Ok, it's alright now," Sebastian said, gently prying Stephanie away from him. "We still have work to do." He motioned for the girls to come out into the light of the hallway. They filed out one by one and stood looking at him with wide eyes, some shaking with trepidation.

"You are a nurse, yes?" Sebastian asked Stephanie.

"Yes. Yes I am," she said through sniffles.

"Please, I need you to examine the girls quickly for injuries, or anything else that may affect their mobility. We are going to take you all to safety from here, but if we have to move on foot for some reason, I need to know they can all keep up." Sebastian really just needed to give Stephanie a task to keep her busy so she wouldn't go into shock. Severe trauma often results in shock, whether the trauma is mental or physical. Stephanie went to work immediately, reassuring the girls and calming them through her practiced bedside manner. The chaotic situation was beginning to level out.

Sebastian ran down the stairs to find a shirtless Davide sitting on the bottom step. "Lean back," Sebastian said. Davide did so without protest. Sebastian pulled from his pack a packaged powder substance commonly referred to as Quick Clot. It was a chemical concoction that rapidly accelerated the body's ability to clot a wound that was bleeding severely. It was readily available to many combat soldiers.

The powder can chemically burn undamaged skin, so it must be administered carefully, if possible. This is easier said than done when a combat medic is trying to treat a serious wound while bullets are flying around his head. Sebastian was in a controlled environment, however, which allowed him to concentrate. He used the powder sparingly, and tapped it slowly and accurately into the wound. They just needed to patch Davide enough to move.

Davide yelled as the powder went to work, but in no time he was out of danger from significant blood loss and ready to go. Sebastian helped him put his uniform shirt back on and then went back upstairs.

"Ok, there are two vans beside the house that your abductors were going to transport you all in." Sebastian saw Stephanie react to the image of being taken away and he instantly regretted the insensitivity of his statement. "Stephanie," he said softly, looking straight into her eyes, "You are safe now. We've got you. Arval is waiting on you." The thought of seeing Arval again seemed to help resettle her resolve.

They all hurried out of the house and loaded evenly into the vans. Out of necessity more so than to keep Stephanie's mind occupied, Sebastian situated her behind the wheel of one van with Davide in the passenger seat. Accepting the responsibility, she started the engine and followed Sebastian as he led the way into the night.

As she drove, she started processing everything she had overheard from Slavo and his men while fading in and out of consciousness before they turned her over to the traffickers. She began talking rapidly about a package, declaring war, and other things that Davide couldn't make sense of. He was too focused on the pain he was in now that the adrenaline had worn off.

They drove to an International Police compound on the outskirts of Pristina. They pulled in and Sebastian identified himself to the gate security. "I need to talk to the base commander immediately," Sebastian demanded with authority. It was coming up on 7:00 a.m. and the base was just starting to show signs of life.

Chapter 142

The gate security would not let the vehicles inside because of the possibility that this may all be a diversion and the vans were actually packed with explosives. A marked police Toyota 4 Runner pulled in behind the vans, and a uniformed police officer from Germany stepped out. "What is happening here?" the officer asked in English.

Sebastian identified himself as French Foreign Legion and gave a quick explanation of their situation. The officer was the Police Compound Commander. He looked at the vans full of young girls, contemplating what to do.

"Leave your weapons here, and we will go inside to discuss the situation, he ordered."

Sebastian would not relinquish his weapon to this guy or anyone else. He walked back to the van to talk with Davide. "Ok," he said. "Let's get these girls out. We're going to have to take Stephanie and make a run for it." At Sebastian's instruction, Stephanie coolly backed the van onto the street to unload the girls.

With the vans moved from in front of the gates, the German moved his SUV forward to be let inside. As the last girl exited the vans, Sebastian jumped in and moved the empty van directly behind the German's police vehicle, effectively trapping him at the gate. Sebastian took the keys with him and jumped into the other van with Stephanie and Davide. They sped off leaving the German, mouth agape, with seven girls and nowhere to go.

As soon as they hit the open road, Stephanie began telling Sebastian that this situation was bigger than just getting her back home. She spoke very fast, trying to explain the package and the intent of the Serbians to declare war again on Kosovo. Sebastian told her that they were ordered to rescue her and get out, nothing further. Stephanie could not explain this as well as Arval, and obviously her rescuers were uninterested in pushing their luck any further.

"We need to get Davide medical attention," Sebastian said, dismissing Stephanie's ramblings.

"I'm fine," Davide said. "Let's stop and have a leisurely breakfast." Sebastian smiled at his friend.

Stephanie was getting angry and frustrated. "We need to get to this 'Field of Blackbirds!!' Where is Arval?!" She yelled at Sebastian. He jumped a little at her ferocity.

"Listen lady, we are going to go straight to the French military base in Mitrovica. Davide is going to have a doc stitch him up, and you are going to get a first class flight back to France."

Stephanie took a deep breath, regaining her composure. "Please," she said politely. "Just call your commander, give him an update, see what he says."

Sebastian did need to call the General and give him a situation report. "Ok, ok, I'll call him." Sebastian hoped this would shut her up.

He pulled the satellite phone from his BDU pants. "Mr. Tristam?" Sebastian said, surprised the old man answered the General's phone. "Yes sir, we have Steph…"

With speed that took Sebastian totally off guard, Stephanie snatched the phone from his grip. "Arval, the Serbs have the package; they are using it for a declaration of war…today!!" Sebastian grabbed the phone back from the crazy girl.

"Sorry about that, Mr. Tristam," Sebastian said into the phone. "Oh, General, I'm sorry. I was just talking with…"

Sebastian was abruptly silenced and spent the next several minutes listening, interjecting the occasional, "Yes, Sir." After a lengthy one-sided conversation, Sebastian hung up the phone with a final acknowledgement of his orders. He looked at Stephanie angrily as he pulled a topographic map of Kosovo out of the other pocket of his cargo pants.

"Looks like we're headed to the Field of Blackbirds," he said, not even trying to mask his displeasure.

Chapter 143

Nikolin was on his knees, head bowed, when a figure stepped in the doorway of the church. The morning sun silhouetted the man perfectly, casting a long shadow on the worn stone floor. Nikolin's father, Plamen Petrovic, crossed himself and kissed the door's frame before entering, as was customary. He walked up behind his youngest son slowly, and Nikolin could feel his presence even though his eyes remained closed.

"Good morning, Father," Nikolin said, breaking the stillness of the air.

"Nikolin," his father replied. The young Bishop rose and turned; his father grabbed him in a firm embrace. "It has been such a long time. It does my heart wonders to set eyes on my prodigal son." He smiled while Nikolin's face remained emotionless.

They stood in the small sanctuary. There was no furniture, no central air system to cool or heat the air, just the intimacy of a meeting place of man and God. Nikolin knew his father did not belong here.

"Are you not happy to be home, my son?" Plamen asked.

"Slavo has brought me here against my will; you know this. My love for this Monastery will never fade, but you taint that love with your radiating hate." Nikolin saw his father's face contort with anger as he pushed back from him. "You think you *own* this place," Nikolin pressed, "these people, Kosovo itself? This is God's house, God's people, *He* owns everything; not you." Nikolin could see his father struggle to control his rage.

"Just tell me this, you ungrateful knave," Plamen began in a menacing tone. "What was your role in betraying your country? Were you going to take the document from the professor and give it to our enemies? Tell me the truth, and I may let you live to cower within the walls of this rotting place and worship a god who turned his back on us long ago." Plamen stepped toward his youngest son, lowering his head, delirious with his own warped indignation.

"God has never turned His back on us. We used our own self-righteous greed to justify acts of abomination. I will not let it happen again." Nikolin stared at his father, no longer fearing this legendary leader of the Black Tigers. "We turned our backs on Him, and we pay for our sins, Father. Mark my words, we *pay* for our sins."

Plamen saw movement from the corner shadows within the church. From behind him, from hidden depressions in front of him, from the doorway he had entered through; men and women pointed weapons at him. "INTERPOL!" he heard shouted over and over. "Hands on your head, NOW!" The orders were barked at him in his native Serbian.

He blinked his eyes slowly, realizing his son had betrayed him for the last time. The ring of authority closed in around him. He complied with their orders, placing his hands on his head, never taking his eyes off his son.

"Remember the Kosovo Curse, my traitorous son," Plamen hissed at Nikolin. "You are dead to me today. And everyone will know that you are an enemy of Serbia."

Plamen was handcuffed roughly and dragged from the monastery. It was strictly forbidden to have weapons inside the walls of the church, but Nikolin felt this was a sin for which he would gladly repent.

Chapter 144

It was 8:25 a.m. Sebastian, Davide, and Stephanie pulled to the side of the road behind a long line of cars already parked. On the hill in the distance, they could see the monument marking the battleground where Serb forces took on the mighty Ottoman Empire on June 28, 1389. The crowd was swelling into the thousands. Sebastian estimated at least four to six thousand people were already there.

The military and police presence was as heavy as it could be. Military personnel searched people and their belongings before entering the large expanse where the ceremony itself would occur, near the base of the monument. Dogs and armed personnel were inconspicuous, but seemed highly inadequate for the amount of people pouring through the gates.

With no other option, they hid their gear in the cavity reserved for the spare tire, under a hard plastic shell, in the back of the van. They set off for the entrance with no weapons, Sebastian wearing only a T-shirt with his BDU pants, and Davide sticking with his thicker uniform shirt. Davide's arm was out of the short sleeve, in a sling against his chest, leaving the empty sleeve to flop about. The three newly acquainted compatriots followed the crowd toward the narrow admission area at the end of a long stretch of gravel road. No vehicles, other than military or police, were allowed within a kilometer of the ceremony grounds.

Davide saw an Italian Carabinieri police jeep with two Italian International Police Officers, parked near the fence. They walked to them, and Davide began to converse with them in Italian.

"They said there hasn't been a crowd like this here for over ten years," Davide informed Sebastian and Stephanie. He spoke with them some more. "Are you sure you remember what this Slavo guy looks like Stephanie?" Davide asked.

"I will never forget his face," she answered.

Davide spoke some more, motioning to the top of their jeep. The two police officers looked at each other and shrugged. They nodded back to Davide.

"Get up on top of their jeep and survey the crowd," Davide instructed Stephanie. "See if you can spot this Slavo character. It's a long shot, but it's the best we can do under the circumstances." The Italian police officers boosted Stephanie onto the hood where she then stepped up to the roof.

She studied the crowd that stretched out before her. The ceremony started, and the people began to settle down as the first speaker took the podium. It was now easier to examine faces, but this was definitely like looking for a needle in a haystack. All the men had similar features, roughly the same height, hair color, build, etc. *'This is impossible,'* she thought to herself.

Stephanie remembered the package and Slavo's taunting remark about how it would be used to declare war. Then it dawned on her that one of the speakers would likely use the document as a visual aid. Of course, he could probably hold up a roll of toilet paper and the people would go nuts believing it was the sacred claim of ownership. But the Serbs wouldn't make a promise they couldn't back up. They had learned from their mistakes in the past. The country needed to be unified, demonstrating solidarity of purpose, following a true call to arms. They would show them the real item. That meant Slavo would have to be near the stage.

As Stephanie strained to see, the announcement was made for the next speaker: Deputy Prime Minister Dragan Bradic. The crowd roared. Stephanie put her hands up over her ears to shield them from the noise.

"Hey!" Sebastian yelled up at her. "Try these!" He tossed up a pair of binoculars the Italians had with them. The noise dissipated, and Stephanie began to search around the stage area, peering now through the binoculars. She scanned back and forth, squinting into the eyepieces. She suddenly stopped; eyes fixed on Slavo.

Chapter 145

"I got him!" Stephanie said to herself in disbelief, "I got him!!" she yelled down excitedly, drawing curious looks from those in the crowd closest to them.

Davide turned back to the Italian Policemen, "Do you have a talk-around channel on your radios? Something that is used for close distance communication?" he asked them urgently.

"Ah, si, si," one answered, pulling his radio from his belt. He turned the dial to the appropriate channel and handed it to Davide. His partner followed suit and handed his to Sebastian. Sebastian took it, looking quizzically at Davide.

"Take this. I'll walk you to him. Once you get to him, take him down." Davide turned and said a couple quick words in Italian to the officers. One of them obligingly took a pair of handcuffs off his belt and handed them to Sebastian. "These guys aren't too keen on getting involved in anything, but they will be more than happy to transport a war-criminal and take credit for the arrest." Davide winked at Sebastian.

"Thanks a lot, pal," Sebastian said. Snatching the cuffs, he waded into the massive crowd.

Under Stephanie's guidance, Davide directed Sebastian right up to Slavo. He was standing in the wings on the side of the stage waiting for the cue to march up and hand the great Dragan Bradic the call to arms.

Sebastian walked up to the Serb and tapped him lightly on the shoulder. "Excuse me? Do you speak English or French or Russian?" Sebastian asked in French, feeling like an idiot. He wasn't a cop; he didn't know how to *arrest* someone. What was he supposed to say?

"I speak all three, now fuck off," Slavo replied venomously.

"Well, you're under arrest, and I need your little envelope, too." Sebastian was tired and in no mood to play around with Mr. Tough Guy.

Slavo turned ominously toward Sebastian. "I do not know who you are, but you have picked a good day to die." Sebastian saw Slavo reach for a gun in his waistband.

Time stood still. The Deputy Prime Minister suddenly stopped talking. Sebastian and Slavo looked up at the podium simultaneously. They both saw the same thing. A perfect, red round hole had appeared in the middle of Bradic's forehead. His knees went limp and he crumbled to the stage floor. A bullet had come from who knows where and penetrated the Deputy Prime Minister's head, killing him instantly.

Chapter 146

Realization of the assassination swept through the crowd. Pandemonium ensued, bodies flung in every direction. Screaming and wailing amplified the panic, fueling the chaos. Slavo turned his attention back to Sebastian, gun in hand. Sebastian reacted by grabbing Slavo's hand with both of his and squeezing the pressure points of his wrist, trying to force him to let go. The struggle was fierce, but brief, as Sebastian slammed Slavo's hand on the corner of the stage, sending the pistol flying out of reach.

Slavo retaliated with a swift punch to Sebastian's kidneys and shoved him roughly, causing separation of the two warriors. They squared off like gladiators, and Sebastian quickly realized there was no *arresting* this man; it would be a fight to the death.

People ran frantically all around them, bumping and shoving, but their focus was never broken. The sound and commotion was tuned out, they were in the eye of the storm. It was the moment before battle when every sense heightens, when one can actually feel the blood flow through their veins, when life is experienced in a richness that can barely be described. But it was only for a fraction of an instant.

The two combatants set upon each other with truculent intensity. Blows, strikes, and holds were delivered, received, and countered in a blurring fury. Sebastian knew this was no amateur. Seconds felt like hours as Sebastian locked grips with the ferocious Serbian.

Slavo pulled Sebastian to him and delivered a fierce head-butt. It split the middle of Sebastian's right eyebrow and blood instantly flowed liberally into his eye. There was no mistake, Sebastian Bishop was in the fight of his life.

Chapter 147

Svetozar Dimitrijevic watched in horror and disbelief as all his work fell apart before his eyes. He was in a VIP section near the rear of the stage when everything went terribly wrong. His highly trained bodyguards lifted him from his seat and now practically carried him to the waiting car. Dimitrijevic couldn't think, he couldn't speak, he was numb, and his old body began to shake. *'This cannot be! This cannot be!'* His mind screamed.

As they rushed to the car, two dark-skinned men of apparent Middle-Eastern descent stepped from behind the vehicle. They fired twice, dropping the two bodyguards mid-step. They then grabbed Dimitrijevic, one under each arm, and ushered him into another car idling nearby. There was a partition separating backseat from front that now lowered automatically. A distinguished looking Arab gentleman in the front seat turned to face Dimitrijevic. "It is somewhat ironic, isn't it?" the man asked, speaking Serbian. "Your ancestors lost to my ancestors on this battlefield over 600 years ago, and today…" the Arab lit a cigarette, "doesn't look too good for you, either."

A man named Juergen Marten slid behind the wheel of his rental car parked on the main road a short distance from the monument. He dialed a number from memory on his cell phone. The commotion of the crowd was reaching a fevered pitch and people ran by his car like wild horses let loose from their pen. He had watched his colleagues grab the old man and speed out of the area.

"It's done," was all he said into the phone, hanging up immediately.

"The Black Hand," he scoffed. "Minnows among sharks."

Shiekh Abdullah Al Mutlaq closed his cell phone, turning his attention back to the cricket match.

Chapter 148

Slavo and Sebastian grappled while people continued to run and shout all around them. Sebastian couldn't see out of his right eye, and Slavo took full advantage, working that side of his body and head. Slavo finally broke his arm free after Sebastian had locked him up in a Jiu Jitsu grasp. He swung his elbow forward savagely impacting with the side of Sebastian's head, knocking him to the ground, nearly unconscious.

Slavo stepped quickly behind Sebastian who was lying on the ground facing away from his attacker. "You are only the first of many I will kill today," Slavo spat, his bloodlust building the mucus in his mouth.

Sebastian recognized this moment. His energy reserves expended, his mind swimming through pain and exhaustion, no help, no more options; he had to make this right. He had to stop this monster; it was his *purpose*. Blood dripped to the earth from his open wound. He would have one chance to end this.

He gathered his waning strength and sprang from the ground as Slavo closed in for the kill. With timing, force, and accuracy innate within him, Sebastian punched the charging Slavo in the throat. He stopped in his tracks, head snapping forward, hands trying to somehow fix his crushed windpipe.

"Hell awaits," Sebastian whispered.

Slavo fell back on the ground and looked up at a blue cloudless sky. He could no longer draw breath. It would be just a few seconds before he suffocated. He blinked slowly, and across his realm of vision, a flock of blackbirds flew. He could think of no more fitting place to die.

Epilogue

Stephanie's first day back to work was shaky, but she made it through. With each day that passed, her life got a tiny bit easier. She still welcomed the prescribed sedative to help her sleep, but the nightmares continued to find a way to surface. Not a day passed when her stomach didn't tighten in fear as some normal task reminded her of running for her life.

Twice a week she had breakfast with Arval. It was the only time she felt truly, completely at ease. He was her port of safe harbor from the tempest that raged in her mind. She knew that she would heal over time and eventually reclaim her life completely. One thing was undeniable, she had tapped reserves of strength and courage within herself that she didn't know existed. That was the starting point for facing a future beyond her ordeal. Arval helped her to concentrate on these traits and to use them as the cornerstone for a new life foundation on which to build. He always made her feel better.

Sebastian leaned back in his big comfortable chair in the business class section of the aircraft. He never imagined that you could be this comfortable on a commercial flight. His U.S. Airways flight was halfway over the Atlantic en route to Charlotte, North Carolina. It had taken over eight months for Sebastian to be cleared for the vacation that had been due him for quite some time. He was finally on his way home to his family and Camden's relaxed lifestyle for some down time. He smiled as he thought about his comrade, his friend, Davide who was on his way home, too.

He snapped open his complimentary newspaper and read an interesting article on page 3C about a Russian General by the name of Chernov who was arrested for acting independent of the Russian Federation. Another rogue General; Sebastian imagined it wouldn't be the last time he would see a story like this. Power is an all-consuming intoxicant.

The businessman in the seat beside him stood and walked to the bathroom. Another gentleman took his seat, offering his hand. It took

Sebastian a little by surprise.

"Nice work in Kosovo," the man said as Sebastian shook his hand. He immediately recoiled. "Easy, Mr. Bishop. Your secret is safe with us." He handed Sebastian a business card. "We're in the business of secrets," he said, pointing to the card. "That's me, Jeff Kendle, Central Intelligence." Sebastian stared at the man blankly. Jeff stood up. "We would love to talk to you when you can spare the time." He was smiling again. "Enjoy your vacation." And just like that, Sebastian was alone again in his comfy, business class seat.

He turned and looked out the window. The world lay in darkness 32,000 feet below. Sebastian closed his eyes, took a deep breath, and tried to relax. It didn't work; after four years of the highest caliber of military training and experience, he had been re-wired to never truly relax. He wasn't sure how he felt about that. '*Time will tell, I guess,*' Sebastian mused.

His mind searched for a silver lining, but he could find no consolation in the fact that no matter where he went, who he tried to become, or how far and fast he tried to run, he would never be alone. '*Comforting or maddening?*' He wondered. That would be for a time when he was feeling more Socratic. In this instant, he made the decision that he would not look to a future he couldn't control, but rather heed the words of Martin Luther King, Jr. and focus on '*the fierce urgency of now.*'

Dan McCallister thumbed through the mail for the Berman Museum of Ancient History in Anniston, Alabama. His attention was drawn to a large envelope with international postage. He opened it carefully and found inside a strange, flat, plastic package that seemed to be vacu-sealed. It looked as though it may contain a document of some sort. There was a note attached that read:

Dear Dan,
A piece of history has presented itself to me under the most unlikely of circumstance. I know that people fight and fuss over such a thing and their possessive zeal can

often be most unpleasant. I relinquish this into your capable hands with one caveat — this document must be preserved for the sake of history alone; and not for public display. The time will come when the world will be ready for its unveiling, but in the interim, it should remain in your safekeeping. Your discretion is unquestioned, and my thanks unending.

My entire life's perspective was changed by your words that I now see as so very true: 'Everyday is an adventure.'

Warm Regards,

Steve Holland

Coming Soon: the second installment in the Sebastian Bishop Series…

Turn the page for a sneak peak…

Sebastian returned to the tiny apartment to find it exactly as he left it. Davide sat on the couch, the prisoner sat firmly secured to his chair, and the unidentified soldier dead on the floor. Sebastian looked at Davide who was fiddling with his knife. "Hmm," Sebastian mused, "I thought you might have tuned this guy up some. I have to admit, I was a little worried."

Davide shrugged. "I thought about it, but what is that saying? Sometimes the anticipation of death is far worse than death itself?" Davide stood up. "Besides, I have no doubt this guy has a list of charges on about five different continents that should be addressed. Death is too good for him. I'm sure the authorities will have some creative ideas regarding his future."

Sebastian nodded, impressed with his friend's rationale and restraint. "Ok. Well the gears are turning on finding out who this guy is." He thumbed toward the soldier on the floor. "We should know something by morning, so why don't we take shifts, try to get some rest and see what we get. I'll take first watch and keep trying to reach Kasimir." Davide nodded and stretched out on the couch.

"Oh hey, look what I found," Davide added as an afterthought. He handed Sebastian a matchbook from the Best Western Museum Hotel in downtown Athens.

"Where was this?" Sebastian asked.

"Under the back corner of the couch. It may be nothing, but it looks fresh." With that he lay back and closed his eyes. Sebastian flipped the hotel matchbook in his fingers noticing a subtle physical reaction from Heb the Rat in his peripheral vision. The hotel meant something, of that he was certain.

Sebastian woke Davide up at 2:00am and took his turn on the couch. At 6:30am Sebastian's phone vibrated. He had just started to settle into a decent sleep and jerked awake. The tingle of disorientation peppering his mind, he grabbed his phone. "Bishop," he answered.

"Ok, I have a high-probability identification on your man," Arval said plainly on the other end.

Sebastian sat up. "Go with it."

"His name is Cirio Barbas, he's a Greek. He was with the 1st Raider/Paratrooper Brigade, 13th Special Operations Command, Alpha Amphibious Raider Squadron. He was set to face a Court

Martial and civilian charges for a brutal rape in Donggala, Indonesia. He fell off the radar four months ago."

"What was his military specialty?" Sebastian asked.

"Explosives," Arval replied solemnly.

Sebastian's eyes widened, he looked at the matchbook still in his hand. "Call you back," Sebastian said hanging up. He snatched their prisoner, who was dozing uncomfortably in the chair, by the hair and snapped his head back. Heb yelped involuntarily; Sebastian held the matchbook in front of his face. "Was he going to blow this place up?!" Sebastian hissed at Heb. "Ask him!" Sebastian yelled at Davide.

Davide barked at him in Italian; Heb's bloodshot and terrified eyes darted back and forth at the two Legionnaires. "Damnit!" Sebastian yelled, letting go of the man's hair. "Do you think this is the next target?" he asked Davide. The two soldiers began to consider the scenario. American hotel, filled with tourists, centrally located; it would be catastrophic.

"I don't know," Davide said, rubbing his forehead. They stood in silence, thinking. "We have to err on the side of caution," he said looking into his friend's face.

They both knew what had to be done. "You're right," Sebastian said, nodding. "I'm going to the hotel." He tucked the pistol they found in his waistband. "Try to get some answers from this piece of shit. Call me if you get something." Sebastian ran out of the apartment, and Davide looked at the prisoner with malice.

"I'm afraid I'm going to need those answers now," Davide said, unsheathing his knife.

Sebastian jumped from the cab before it had even come to a complete stop in front of the hotel. It was situated on the corner of the block with other buildings receding adjacently down the street. The hotel was seven stories high with distinctly American amenities, and it was located close to many of the tourist areas that made Athens famous.

It was now nearly 7:30am and the hotel was just beginning to show signs of life. Sebastian glanced around the hotel lobby looking for anything out of the ordinary. Everything looked calm and normal. Sebastian ran to the reception counter. "You need to evacuate this hotel immediately," he said in English to the pretty morning receptionist.

"Pardon me?" she replied politely.

"You need to get everyone out of this hotel right now!" Sebastian said loudly.

The receptionist jumped at his voice, and looked over to the security officer on duty. The guard began moving toward Sebastian. "Get everyone out of here..." Sebastian began again, but didn't finish as the security guard now began to run toward the unruly patron. Sebastian turned, effortlessly grabbing the guard and flipping him over his hip. The guard slammed to the floor hard on his back, and Sebastian reflexively had his pistol in the man's face. He snapped his gun to the ceiling and fired three shots. People in the lobby screamed and ran for the exit. Sebastian brought the gun down toward the receptionist and raised his eyebrows expectantly. She, and the other desk staff, ran from behind the counter toward the exit.

Sebastian grabbed the fire alarm and pulled it. A piercing alarm began blaring throughout the hotel. Sebastian ran down the hall shouting 'FIRE!' and yelling for everyone to get out. He went up floor-by-floor, running the length of each hallway, directing people toward the stairs.

He grabbed a distinguished gentleman passing by. "When you get outside, get everyone as far away from the building as possible. Tell the police there is a bomb in the building." The man stared at Sebastian with alarm. "Do it!" he yelled at the man who nodded his understanding and ran for the stairs.

Sebastian finally made it to the rooftop where there was a pool and veranda for people to relax and enjoy a poolside meal or drink. Sitting at a table were two older couples waiting apparently for their breakfast. Sebastian ran to them. "Can't you hear the fire alarm?" Sebastian asked, irritated at their cavalier attitude.

"This kind of thing happens all the time, young man. They will reset the alarm and we will hopefully be able to enjoy our breakfast in peace and quiet." The American looked arrogantly around the table at his companions as they politely chuckled.

Sebastian glanced at his watch as he took a few steps toward them; it was exactly 8:00am. He was about to physically remove the guests from their breakfast table when it happened. Sebastian felt more than heard the detonation, and he saw the arrogance on the hotel guest's face replaced with speechless terror. Instinctively, Sebastian began to sprint toward the edge of the roof. He could feel the roof beneath his feet move as the hotel was beginning to collapse. Sebastian used his last moment of sure footing to leap into thin air.